Forty minu[...] three shots ap[...] the fifty dollars charged to his room card. Only once in a million years is a guy lucky enough to attract two beautiful, voluptuous and drunken women. Dwayne didn't know if it was the boat, his cologne or the drinks, but he did know that the woman called Mona was inexplicably attracted to him, and this was turning into the best night of his life.

Dwayne had a raging boner, which was usually cause for embarrassment in a setting like this, but Mona didn't mind at all. In fact, she had put her hand in his lap a dozen times already. Dwayne felt that he was just one pick-up line away from sealing the deal, but he didn't even have to do that.

The bartender came to take orders for a fourth set of shots, and Mona waved him off. She said something to her friend, and they laughed, and then she turned and fixed her inebriated eyes on Dwayne.

"So, are we going to screw or what?"

Dwayne's heart shot up into his throat and he could barely articulate his response.

"Yes."

He tried to sound like Barry White, but his voice cracked and Dwayne sounded more like Mickey Mouse. But even that wasn't a deterrent. Mona's smile didn't' falter at all. She slipped off her stool and leaned on the bar to steady herself. Her skirt was so short.

"You ready to go?" Mona asked her friend. Rene laughed and said she was.

❧

The Finley Sisters' Oath of Romance

Keith Thomas Walker

Genesis Press, Inc.

INDIGO LOVE STORIES

An imprint of Genesis Press, Inc.
Publishing Company

Genesis Press, Inc.
P.O. Box 101
Columbus, MS 39703

ISBN-13: 978-1-58571-441-4
ISBN-10: 1-58571-441-0
Manufactured in the United States of America

First Edition

Visit us at www.genesis-press.com
or call at 1-888-Indigo-1-4-0

Dedication

This book is for Brandy. Lol

Acknowledgements

I would like to thank God, first and foremost, for guiding me through this crazy life of mine. I would like to thank my mother for encouraging my interest in books and my wife for putting up with all the time I spend on the computer, composing these stories. It takes a real special lady. I would also like to thank, in no particular order: Janae Hampton, Denise Bolds, Sabrina Scott, Dianne Guinn, Brandy Rees, Erika Caez, Vicki Williams-Lookingbill, Trey Williams, Jody Wayne Thomas, Shonya Carter, Keisha Mennefee, Kierra Pease, Trina Wright, Vollie Walker, Anna Garza, Judd Pemberton, Anthony Douglas, and Uncle Steven Thomas, one love. I'd like to thank everyone who purchased and enjoyed one of my books. Everything I do has always been to please you. I know there are folks who mean the world to me that I'm failing to mention. I apologize ahead of time. Rest assured I'm grateful for everything you've done for me.

CHAPTER 1
FINLEY HIGH

"It's over! It's all done. I, I spent so much time on this, and I don't get nothing!"

Theresa clasped her hands in her lap, and Mona was shocked to see tears in the older woman's eyes.

"What do you mean, '*It's over*'?"

Theresa sniffled. "I, I can't do anymore." She sighed and looked towards the heavens. "I've been talking to him for the last forty-five minutes. He, he won't listen to me. I told him the buyers were backing out, and, and, and he still won't listen. He said he don't care. He wants me to find somebody else."

Mona took a deep breath and shook her head, a tiny knot of tension forming in her belly. She didn't know what was worse; the ineptitude of her employee, or the pretentiousness of their client. Mona leaned forward in a sleek leather chair and rested her elbows on her mahogany desk. She narrowed her eyes and pursed her lips, and Theresa squirmed like someone dropped a hot coal down the back of her shirt.

Mona's office was the most spacious in the building, and Theresa looked very small right then. The older woman brought a hand to her mouth and subconsciously nibbled her thumbnail. Theresa was brown-skinned with short hair and full lips. She wore a white blouse with burgundy slacks and a good deal of make-up. Theresa was in her late forties, but age and wisdom do not always come hand-in-hand.

Theresa had many careers throughout her lifetime, but so far she hadn't mastered any of them. She never considered the tricky business of real estate until she saw an infomercial on television three years ago. Mona knew giving her the Pennington property was a risk, but that was the best way to determine her resolve: through trial and error. This setback was disappointing, but hopefully it wasn't too late to salvage the deal.

"So you informed him of the buyer's concerns?" Mona asked.

Theresa nodded. "Yes…yes ma'am."

The irony of being referred to as *ma'am* by someone twenty years her senior was not lost on Mona, but she started this agency from the ground up, and she would expect nothing less.

"He wouldn't come down on the price *at all*?" Mona asked.

Theresa nodded and then shook her head. "I got him down to one-five, but that's it."

Mona frowned. "You spoke with him in person? You called him down here?"

Theresa nodded. "Yes. He's in my office right now. I've been in there with him for almost an hour."

"You told him we only found *one* buyer?" Mona asked. "That if he loses this one, that's it—there's nothing else we can do for him?"

"I did," Theresa assured. "I told him everything."

"The penalties?"

"I told him."

"The lost deposits?"

"Everything," Theresa said.

Mona grinned. It appeared her protégé had done a thorough job. The only thing missing was the fine art of finesse.

"He's still in your office?"

Theresa nodded. "Yeah. He still in there."

Mona stood and made her way around the desk with the air of a divine healer. She paused long enough to retrieve Mr. Pennington's papers from her employee.

"Gimme that file."

Theresa handed it over graciously, and Mona walked out of the office, her expression barely giving away how upset she would be if they lost out on the seventy-thousand-dollar commission due at closing.

∾

Mona's office employed over a dozen agents, clerks, and consultants, and most of them made an effort to greet her as she passed their cramped cubicles. Today their boss wore a gray skirt suit with a tweed jacket that had a stylish Peter Pan collar. There were no rings on Mona's fingers, but her right wrist twinkled with a slew of pearl bracelets that ranged from gray to gold to white in color.

Mona's skin tone was smooth and rich like Georgia red clay. She had long hair that was mostly all hers and a slim figure that hadn't changed much since her teenage years. She never needed a lot of makeup, but today she wore eyeliner that made her small orbs appear a bit larger. Mona's breasts were always an attention-grabber. Her knee-length skirt hugged her other assets enticingly. She walked into Theresa's office and immediately had the full attention of their dubious client.

Mr. Pennington wore a gray Armani suit with a white shirt and a dark blue tie. He was a handsome man with short hair and steely eyes. His skin was dark and smooth like Coca Cola. At first glance Mr. Pennington was a powerful man one should respect and possibly even fear, but Mona was hardly impressed.

She knew that their client had accumulated the majority of his wealth from the inheritances of dead relatives, and most of his personal business deals hurt his vast family fortune. If left to his own devices, Mr. Pennington would have become indigent long ago, but for each trust fund he depleted, there was always another one available.

Mona dropped his folder on the desk and gave him a good once-over. Rich black folk were definitely the most peculiar breed of people she had the pleasure of working with.

"Hello, Mr. Pennington. I'm Mona Pratt."

He stood hesitantly and offered a hand to shake. "Pratt?"

"The one and only," she said. Mona's name was on the building's marquee, as well as eight billboards scattered throughout Austin. Mr. Pennington was a man who appreciated authority, and he smiled broadly.

"So I finally get to talk to the bigwig."

The client's hand was soft, almost as delicate as Mona's. She liked a cultured black man, but not one with tender hands like Mr. Pennington's. She doubted if this guy ever performed manual labor more strenuous than washing the dinner dishes when he was a child.

"It's nice to meet you," Mona said. She released his hand and took a seat across from him. "Unfortunately, most clients only make my acquaintance if there's a problem."

Mr. Pennington nodded and took his seat as well. "Yeah, there is a problem."

"Tell me about it," Mona offered.

"The problem is your agent doesn't follow instructions," the client replied gruffly. "I gave that woman very specific instructions. There was no need for her to call me back so many times, and there was certainly no need for me to come down to your office this afternoon. I'm a busy man. If she can't handle this sale, she should've passed my property off to someone else."

"First of all, I apologize for your inconvenience," Mona said. "And Theresa did pass your property off to someone else. I'll be handling your sale personally from this point on."

"Good."

"Well, it's not all *that* good," Mona said with a smile. "You're still going to have to drop another five hundred thousand off your asking price."

Mr. Pennington's smile evaporated. "What? I already told that other lady I'm not going any lower!"

"That other lady is Theresa," Mona informed him. "And I'm sorry, but everything she told you is correct. You're not going to get more than one million-two for that property. One-point-seven is out of the question."

"I told her I'd go one-point-five."

"Yeah, we need you at one-point-two."

"I'll, I'll keep it then." Mr. Pennington put his foot down, but his poker face had many tells.

"And do what with it?" Mona asked with a smirk. "The property value in that neighborhood is looking worse every quarter. There are already four houses on that street with signs in the yard, and your grandmother's estate has been vacant for two years. I think you should cut your losses now before things get even more out of hand."

"That house is worth *three million dollars*," Mr. Pennington fumed. He was in his mid-forties, and his jowls hung like a bulldog's. "I'm not going all the way down to one-point-two! That's ridiculous!"

"No, what's ridiculous is you're still holding on to quotes from ten years ago," Mona countered. "A lot has changed since that property was worth three million, and you need to get with the times. That area is not what it used to be, and that house isn't, either."

"There's nothing at all wrong with my grandmother's house!"

Mona saw a vein bulging in his neck, but she wasn't fazed. "What about the plumbing problems?" she asked. "The toilets won't drain in any of the upstairs bathrooms."

"That's nothing."

"The hardwood floors need to be refinished."

"That's not bad."

"Nobody likes that ugly wallpaper."

"Again—not a big deal."

"The roof needs work, that big crack in the drive-way means you have a foundation problem, and ter-mites are devouring the place as we speak. If you want to fix all of that, then maybe we can get you back up to two, maybe a little more. But as it stands, you should consider yourself lucky to have a million-dollar offer still on the table."

The color drained from his face, but Mr. Penning-ton still had a little fight left in him. "I, I don't believe you," he muttered. "Even with all of that, I still think it's worth one-eight. *At least one-five*. I'm not going less than one and a half—absolutely not."

Mona sighed and shook her head ever so slightly. "Mr. Pennington, this is a decision you will no doubt regret. Your grandmother's estate is nice, but to be hon-est, there are better properties in that neighborhood with better price tags. I'm not exaggerating when I say we were *lucky* to find you a buyer. I promise no other realtor will be as helpful as we've been, and when you finally do find another sucker willing to take that place off your hands, it will be for a lot less than the one-point-two you could've made today."

Mona stood and smiled down at him smugly. "I'll send Theresa back in, and if you have your checkbook, we can settle our account before you leave."

"Our, our account?"

7

Mona narrowed her eyes. "Mr. Pennington, we've done a lot of work for you in the last couple of months. The inspection and appraisal aside, we also had to furnish the home, hire a crew to clean it, and maintain the lawn. There were minor repairs here and there… It shouldn't be that much. I'm sure Theresa has the exact numbers."

Mr. Pennington's eyes bugged, and Mona had to stifle a chuckle. She smiled even more radiantly and continued towards the doorway. She knew she wouldn't make it too far, and her squirrelly client didn't disappoint.

"Wha-wait," he said.

Mona turned back to face him. "Yes?"

"You, you said one-point-two, right? I can still get that today?"

"Actually that was Monday's offer. You've given the buyer such a hassle, I wouldn't be surprised if he's down to one-point-one by now…"

Mr. Pennington swallowed roughly. "All right. I'll, I'll take it. You can call him and tell him I'll take it."

"Great," Mona said. "I'll get Theresa back in here so you can sign the papers."

She turned, but he stopped her again.

"Wait, Miss Pratt. It is *Miss*, isn't it?"

She nodded. "Yes, Mr. Pennington?"

"I was, I was wondering if you might like to go out for drinks later on, tonight maybe. We could, uh, we could celebrate the closing, if you'd like…" He looked her up and down, his smile like a peeping Tom's.

"I'm sorry," Mona said without a pause. "I never date our clients." *Especially a fool who can't even maintain a ready-made fortune.* "I'll get Theresa back in here so you can sign the papers."

 birds

It wasn't unusual to bring in a seventy-thousand-dollar commission at Pratt Realtors, but this particular client put them through so much hell, Mona offered to take her closing agent out to lunch as a reward for her hard work.

"Cool," Theresa said, her face bright like a firefly. "Let me file these papers and grab my purse. I'll be right back!"

While she waited, Mona popped open her brief-case and went through a few letters that arrived at her home yesterday. Most of the correspondences were bills, but one envelope had a return address that quickly grabbed her attention. It was from her home-town: Overbrook Meadows, Texas.

Mona hadn't thought about Overbrook Meadows very much since she left the metropolis in her rear-view mirror almost a decade ago. She thought about her old high school even less than that, but the mys-terious letter brought both of these places to the fore-front of her attention. Mona read the letter twice, her heart growing light in her chest.

When Theresa returned with her purse, Mona was fully enthralled in a daydream that featured packed auditoriums, noisy hallways, and cute adolescent boys as far as the eye could see.

"What's on your mind?" Theresa asked with a grin. "You already got plans for that money?"

Mona snapped out of her reverie. "No," she said. "I was, uh, I was thinking about home. Looks like I'm going on vacation in a couple of weeks."

"Really? What's the occasion?"

"My high school reunion," Mona said. "It's been ten years since I graduated." She shook her head wistfully. "God, I can't believe it's been that long."

Theresa frowned. "Girl, you don't want to do that," she advised. "Everybody who goes to class reunions are just as fake as you remember them. They only want to show each other up: *Look what I did with my life. Look how good I still look.* It's all a bunch of crap."

Mona chuckled, surprised by how little Theresa knew about her.

"Woman, that's *exactly* why I'm going. Ain't no way nobody from Finley High did it bigger than me. And I *know* nobody looks as good!"

❧

Approximately one hundred and fifty miles away, in an upscale Houston high rise, Rene Packard girded herself for what was sure to be her most stressful meeting of the day. She sat behind a large desk made of mocha cherry wood and leaned back on leather cushions that were very similar to the executive chair Mona had in her office.

"Who's supposed to fire her?" Rene asked her secretary.

Mrs. Gentry was a large woman with rosy red cheeks and bright eyes that couldn't conceal the amusement bubbling within her. "Um, Mr. Peters, I believe."

"It's not funny," Rene told her.

"I'm not laughing," Mrs. Gentry replied.

"I see it in your eyes," Rene said. "You want to laugh. You're just trying to hold it in."

With that, Mrs. Gentry could hold it in no longer. She grinned, put a hand over her mouth, and then a chuckle escaped her lips. She tried to swallow it back down, and her belly jiggled like Santa Claus'.

"Ooh, excuse me."

"I told you it's not funny," Rene griped. "That's my cousin."

"I know," Mrs. Gentry said. She tried to regain composure, and her eyes watered.

Rene stood and walked to one of her windows overlooking the city's hectic downtown area. For work that day, Rene wore a black tweed skirt with a turquoise cardigan over a white camisole. Her stockings were black, highlighting what Rene always thought was her best feature: long, smooth legs that stretched from the floor like a ballerina's.

Rene didn't have one of those coveted corner offices, but her digs were still spacious and well-decorated. All of her furniture had rich, earthy colors, and she had plenty of fresh greenery, from angel ivies, to cactuses, to the tropical bonsai tree she kept on her desk.

Rene never let her jet black hair get longer than shoulder-length, and today she wore it in a loose bob. She had dark skin like polished mahogany, and she had always been a slim girl—even though the girth of her hips eclipsed her chest size way back in high school. Rene didn't like to wear makeup, and today was no exception. She knew she was pretty, striking actually, but she didn't let it go to her head like some of the girls she grew up with.

"They couldn't just write her up again?" she asked her secretary.

"No." Mrs. Gentry shook her head. "I'm sorry, but they're going to let her go. It's a definite. I don't think even you could stop it at this point."

Rene crossed her arms over her stomach, still looking out of the window. "I'm not going to try to stop it," she said after a while. "I can't keep sticking my neck out for people. One day I'm gonna come across someone who *really* wants to work, but I won't be able to get them on because of messes like this. Human resources will put my referrals at the bottom of the pile."

"It's not that bad," Mrs. Gentry offered.

"Please, this is three in a row," Rene reminded her. "They fired my other cousin Angela for smoking *weed*—and don't forget about my nephew. You remember I got Scooter a job in the mailroom…"

"Oh, well, he doesn't count. He was here for almost a year," Mrs. Gentry said.

"Yeah, but he still got fired," Rene insisted, "for *stealing*. You don't think HR's keeping track of all of that?"

"I doubt it," Mrs. Gentry said. "Really. Scooter got fired three years ago, and no one even remembers Angela. She didn't make it past her probation period, did she?"

"No, she didn't," Rene said. She turned from the window and faced her secretary. "And Chameka's only been here two months. She didn't make it past probation, either."

Again Mrs. Gentry had to stifle a giggle.

"How come you don't like her?" Rene asked.

"Well, I wouldn't want to offend…"

"Just spit it out."

"Um…" Mrs. Gentry cleared her throat. "I don't like to be negative, but I'd have to say Chameka is the absolute *worst* secretary I've ever met. She may be a good person, but–"

"*You* trained her," Rene reminded her.

"Yes, and let me tell you those were three weeks of sheer *horror*. She's insolent. She thinks she knows everything. I can't tell you how many times I asked her to spit her gum out before she answered the phone. Let's see, um…" Mrs. Gentry began to count on her fingers. "She doesn't dress appropriately for the workplace. She called in twice during her first two weeks. It takes her *forever* to do the simplest things, but she won't ask any questions. If you offer to help her, she'll snap at you: '*I got it. Did I say I needed any help?*' "

Rene had to chuckle because her secretary matched Chameka's mannerisms perfectly.

"All right, maybe she does need to get fired," Rene said. "But I'm done after this. This nepotism crap hasn't done nothing but make me look like a fool."

"It's really not that bad," Mrs. Gentry said consolingly.

"It is for me," Rene said. She went back to her desk and plopped down in the seat. "I worked too hard to get where I'm at. I don't need Chameka and Ray Ray and Scooter coming in here making me look bad."

"Who's Ray Ray?"

"That's my *other* nephew. I was thinking about getting him a job up here. But not now. He's going to have to figure something out on his own. What's Mr. Peters' extension?"

"Uh, twenty-four forty-five," the secretary said.

Rene picked up her phone and punched the digits. A gruff-sounding gentleman answered after a couple of rings.

"Advertising. This is Mark."

"Hey. This is Rene from sales."

"Oh, how are you doing, Ms. Packard?"

"I'm fine. I, uh, I hear you're going to fire my cousin Chameka…"

"Oh, uh, yeah. I'm sorry, Rene, but she's highly incompetent. I didn't know she was your cousin."

"It's okay. I'm starting to wish I didn't recommend her. Do you, could you do me a favor?"

"Sure, Rene. What's up?"

"Could you let me fire her—if you haven't done it already?"

"Actually no, I haven't," Mr. Peters said. "I was looking for her ten minutes ago."

"Looking for her?"

"It's not break time, but she's not at her desk," the advertising manager informed Rene with a sigh. "This is one of many issues we've been having with her."

"I'm sorry for that," Rene said. "I really am. Could you send the termination papers to me and send Chameka to my office—if she ever comes back. I'll sign them and forward them to human resources."

Mr. Peters laughed. "Okay, Rene. Will do."

∞⨯∾

Chameka didn't return to her department for a full twenty minutes, and she looked excited rather than concerned when she walked into Rene's office five minutes after that.

"What's up, girl? We going out to lunch?"

Rene looked at her watch. "It's eleven-thirty."

"I thought we was gon' take a early lunch," Chameka ventured. "Since you a *manager*, I know you can do that if you want."

"I heard you've been taking early lunches already," Rene said. "Early breaks and unauthorized breaks, too."

Chameka took a seat across from her cousin and looked down at her nails with a frown. "Huh?"

Today Chameka wore a short, denim skirt with a shiny pink blouse. Her skirt ran out of material at least three inches above her knees, and her blouse was unbuttoned all the way down to the top of her bra. Rene knew her secretary was right about Chameka's ongoing inappropriate attire, but she also knew there was a good deal of jealously mixed in with Mrs. Gentry's accusations. Chameka looked absolutely voluptuous with her bulging breasts and enticing thighs. If Mrs. Gentry could get away with wearing an outfit like that, she'd sport one every other day.

But then again, Chameka *was* popping chewing gum at that very moment, and even Mr. Peters complained about her ineptness…

"Where were you earlier?" Rene asked, "at eleven?"

"What you mean?" Chameka had fair skin, the color of a sugar cookie. She had long hair that was braided and twisted like curly fries. Her pink lips glistened with shiny gloss. She was twenty years old, but she could easily pass for sixteen or seventeen.

"I mean you weren't at your desk at eleven o'clock," Rene said. "Where were you?"

"I don't know. In the restroom…"

"For twenty minutes?"

"Oh, I was down there talking to *Quincy*," Chameka suddenly recalled. "He's the security guard on the ground floor."

"I know who he is."

"Girl, he fine, ain't he?"

"He's all right," Rene said. "Don't you know we can't wear jeans to work here?"

Chameka looked down at her ensemble and stated the obvious. "I'm not wearing jeans."

"Blue jean skirts are the same as jeans," Rene informed her. "Actually they're worse because those are so short I can see your panties when you sit down."

Chameka furrowed her brow and crossed her legs. "What's up, girl? You starting to sound like them people up on *my* floor."

"Them people? You mean your *superiors?*"

"They ain't superior to me," Chameka said with plenty of *umph*. "I don't even like that word."

Rene shook her head in exasperation. "Chameka, you're fired."

The girl's jaw dropped. "What?"

"You heard me," Rene said with a frown. "You're a terrible secretary, and I need you to give me your ID badge and go clear out your desk."

"Uhn-uhn!" Chameka rolled her neck. "They can't fire me!"

Rene was incredulous. "First of all, *they're* not firing you. I am. And second, they can fire you any time they want to. Girl, who the hell do you think you are? You should be ashamed of yourself."

"Why? They just mad 'cause they know they can't talk to me any old kind of way."

"They're not talking to you *any kind of way*," Rene said. "All they asked was for you to *do your job*—you know, the one they hired you for? You think they're going to pay you twelve dollars an hour so you can go downstairs and flirt with the security guard?"

"That ain't no kinda money anyway," Chameka complained. She folded her arms under her chest and switched to severe pout mode.

"Some people would *love* to have twelve dollars an hour," Rene said. "As a matter of fact, three months ago you were begging me to get you a job for *ten* dollars an hour."

Chameka lowered her gaze.

"And look how you repay me," Rene went on. "Don't you know how stupid you made me look?"

Chameka sighed, and the anger subsided. "I'm sorry."

"Yeah. You should be."

"I'm, I'm fired, for real?"

"It's done," Rene confirmed.

"You can't make them let me stay?" Chameka wondered.

"Even if I could, I wouldn't," Rene said honestly. "You're the third relative I brought up here who showed their ass the first chance they got. You couldn't even make it past probation."

"But you don't see how they be hating on black people up here," Chameka whined.

"Don't even go there," Rene said. "Your manager was black, nearly all of the supervisors are black, and one of our vice presidents is black. And if you haven't noticed, I'm black, too."

"It's hard to tell, the way you be acting up here," Chameka muttered.

"Excuse me?"

"Nothing."

"No, go ahead and say what you got to say. And look me in the eyes while you're at it."

"I didn't say nothing."

"Yeah, I didn't think so," Rene said. "You keep thinking your attitude doesn't matter at work, and you're going to keep on getting fired. I don't change who I am at work; I just follow the rules and decorum expected of me in this building. If you think all there is to being black is popping chewing gum and dressing like you're going to the club, then you need to grow up and read some books. People died so you can get a job in a place like this. Show some respect."

"All right, Harriet Tubman."

"What?" Rene felt her blood starting to boil, but Chameka laughed, and after a while Rene did, too. "Girl, you need your butt whooped."

"So I'm fired for real?" Chameka asked.

"I wouldn't play about something like that," Rene assured her.

"Dang," Chameka said. "Mama gon' be mad."

"I'll talk to her," Rene offered. "I'll tell her you sucked, but I won't tell her how bad."

"Thanks. Oh, and while you calling relatives, Memaw wants to know why you don't never call her no more. She say she haven't seen you in like, four years."

That warmed Rene's heart even more. Memaw was what everyone in the family called her grandmother, the matriarch of the clan.

"I'm going to see her when I go home in a couple of weeks."

"Really? You going on vacation?"

"Yeah. I'm going to a ten-year reunion for Finley High."

"*Ten years*? Dang, you old!"

"No, I'm not!"

"Naw. I'm just kidding," Chameka said. "I can't wait till we have a class reunion for my school. I can see all my old homegirls and boyfriends. I know some of them dead by now. Did you have a lot of friends when you was in school? Was you popular?"

"I was homecoming queen," Rene said with a big smile. "I was real popular. Me and my friends used to have that school *locked down*. People called us the Finley Sisters." She chuckled. "We were bad, girl. Cute and sassy. Couldn't nobody tell us nothing."

Chameka grinned, too. "The *Finley Sisters*? Ha ha! That's wack!"

"Forget you. It wasn't wack back then."

"Naw, I'm just kidding. Do you still keep up with your homegirls?"

"No, we kinda fell apart," Rene admitted. "I miss 'em, though. I've been thinking about them ever since I heard about the reunion. I'm gonna try to find their numbers and call them when I get off today."

"That's cool," Chameka said, then, "You think you could let me stay in your office until five? That's when my ride's picking me up."

"They can't pick you up early?"

"He don't get off till four-thirty."

"Why are you down there flirting with the security guard if you already have a boyfriend?" Rene wanted to know.

"I'm too much woman for just *one man*," Chameka said.

Rene rolled her eyes.

"Don't look at me like that," Chameka said. "I know you got more than one boyfriend."

"No, I don't."

"Well, what about when you was with your *Finley Sisters*?" Chameka laughed. "I know you had some freaky-deaky going on back then!"

Rene shook her head but couldn't stop from grinning. "Girl, I'll give you a ride home when I take my lunch at twelve-thirty. You think you can be quiet and try to maintain some professionalism until then?"

"Yeah, whatever," Chameka said and dug through her purse for a nail file. "I should take me a couple of laptops with me when I go. These fools got the nerve to fire me. They must not know who I is."

"Naw, that's why you got fired," Rene said. "Trust me, they know *exactly* who you is."

CHAPTER 2
THE GRUMPY GROUCH

Far removed from the glitz and glamour of Austin and Houston high-rises, Dawn Wright slid her time card into a mechanical clock and exhaled pleasantly when the device stamped four digits on it with an audible **CHUNK**; indicating she was finally free to leave for the day.

"You out?"

Dawn turned to find her friend Rosalie watching her from the counter.

"Yeah, finally," Dawn said. "I was supposed to be gone at five."

Both girls could see clearly through the store's front windows, and the lack of sunlight in the parking lot was a clear indication that 5 p.m. had come and gone a couple of hours ago.

"I'm sorry you had to stay late," Rosalie said. "We're supposed to be getting another girl in here pretty soon."

"Yeah, right," Dawn said. She went to the counter and removed her purse from the shelf under the cash register. "Ain't nobody gon' take a job here for what Mr. Le is offering—especially when they find out how shady he is with the overtime."

Rosalie's eyes widened, and she looked around in mock fret. "Girl, you'd better watch it. You know he's still here, right?"

"You know I'se just kidding," Dawn said in her best southern Negro voice. "I wouldn't *never* talk bad about Massah Le. Nuh-uhn. Not me. You know I gots better sense than that!"

The girls laughed even though the subject matter was rather serious, and Dawn had come to understand that some of the things that went on at the cleaners were downright *illegal*. Their boss, Mr. Jin Le, was a hardworking man who had migrated to the United States four years ago after fleeing his oppressive Chinese homeland.

Given the newfound liberties and freedom he enjoyed in the great US of A, one would think Mr. Le would shy away from the brutal customs he learned as a child, but this was not the case. Mr. Le owned four dry cleaning businesses in Overbrook Meadows, and he ran all of them with an iron fist. Not only did he not pay overtime when his employees worked more than forty hours, but Mr. Le would fire anyone who complained about it too often.

"You're crazy," Rosalie said. She yawned and swiveled her head from side to side. Dawn heard her neck pop from six feet away.

"Damn, you all right?" she asked. "Sound like you broke something."

"I'm just tired," Rosalie said, rubbing the back of her collar. She gave her friend a robust smile, but Dawn saw the stress and fatigue in her eyes.

Rosalie was a young girl, just twenty-three years old, but she was already burdened with four young children, no education past the eighth grade, and an absentee husband currently serving twelve years for drug trafficking. Rosalie was petite and attractive. Most people wouldn't know how bad life treated her unless they looked deeply into her eyes. Rosalie's bright smile and rosy cheeks could lie to the outside world, but her gloomy orbs always told the truth.

"You gonna get some sleep tomorrow?" Dawn asked her. "You off?"

Rosalie got a chuckle out of that. "Course not. I'm closing tonight and opening up tomorrow. What about you?"

"I'll be here bright and early, too," Dawn said. "But I'm gon' get some sleep tonight."

"You and Henry ain't doing nothing?"

Now it was Dawn's turn to laugh. Friday night stopped being special for her a long time ago. "Yeah, right," she said. "I can tell you what Henry's plans are right now, and they got something to do with the TV, the remote control, and a six pack of Colt 45s—the tall cans. And if I don't get home in time to put some food on the table, his plans prolly gon' have something to do with going upside my head!"

Dawn snickered, but Rosalie didn't laugh at that. In fact, her already dismal eyes became even more sullen.

"You need to hurry up and leave that asshole," she advised. "Drop that Ike Turner like Tina did."

"*Okay…*" Dawn said. "I'ma do that as soon as you see me walking around here looking like Tina."

"Your looks don't have nothing to do with it."

"I'll probably need me some of that Tina money, too," Dawn went on.

"I make just as much as you," Rosalie said. "And I been doing fine since Lupe got locked up. You don't need that man."

"Girl, you been working two jobs, ten days a week," Dawn countered.

"It ain't that bad."

"Anyway, I was just kidding," Dawn said. "You think I would stay with some man who be beating on me like that? I'm a big girl, but I ain't *desperate*."

"You not that big," Rosalie said, but that didn't help at all.

Anytime someone used a clarifier like "You're not *that* big" or "You're not *that* ugly," it usually meant you were indeed big and ugly as hell. Besides, Dawn had perfectly good mirrors and a man who spoke his mind at home. She didn't need anyone else to point out how overweight she was.

Always a chubby girl, Dawn's weight issues came to the forefront in high school, where she struggled to maintain a size nine until graduation. That was ten years and two babies ago. Since then, her dress size blossomed to a meaty 18W.

Her only saving grace was that even with the added pounds, Dawn still considered herself pretty. Her skin was dark like molasses. She wore her shoulder-length hair in a ponytail on most days. Dawn thought her chubby cheeks made her look like a cherub. And she liked her full lips that could easily suck the meat off a chicken bone—or any other bone she was inclined to put into her mouth.

Plus her breasts were so big, she could really use a reduction surgery. And her ass and thighs were still desirable to the many brothers out there who liked a gal with a good deal of junk in her trunk. Dawn's current boyfriend was apparently not one of those guys, but such is life. If everything fell in place perfectly for her, Dawn would be suspicious rather than grateful for the change.

She threw her purse over her shoulder and bid her friend adieu as she headed for the front door. "See you tomorrow, girl."

"All right, you take it easy," Rosalie said, but Dawn stopped short after a couple of steps.

"Oh, crap. I almost forgot those uniforms." She went back behind the counter and scanned the garment bags on the clean rack.

"What uniforms?" Rosalie asked.

"I brought Henry's work uniforms with me today," Dawn explained. "I put them on the counter right here…" She pointed to an empty space to the right of the register.

"Oh, those gray uniforms?" Rosalie said. "I saw Irma take them back before she left."

"Well, where are they?" Dawn asked. She pushed a button to make the hangers on the clean rack circulate slowly. The machine had a mechanical growl that sounded too much like work. Dawn couldn't wait to get out of that place.

"I don't know," Rosalie said. She began to look around as well. "Didn't you wash them?"

"I never did see them," Dawn said, her eyes still on the plastic bags. "I thought one of y'all got them."

"*I* didn't do them," Rosalie said definitively. "But I know I saw Irma take them back."

Dawn frowned, and the two ladies watched the circulating hangers together. The clean rack was over forty feet long, and it took a while for every garment to pass before their eyes. When they started seeing duplicates, Dawn let go of the button and shook her head.

"I saw Irma take them," Rosalie said again. Unfortunately Irma had been gone since three, so there was no way to ask her about it.

"I wonder what she did with them," Dawn mused. She headed towards the back of the store with Rosalie on her heels. The farther into the maze of machinery and laundry they went, the stronger the smell of the dry cleaning chemicals became. The ladies found Henry's uniforms on a table next to one of the pressing machines.

"Aw, hell."

Dawn hoped against hope that they were clean, just not bagged yet, but she could tell from a few feet away they were still as dirty as when she brought them in.

"That's them?" Rosalie asked.

"Yeah." Dawn held one of the uniforms up and studied the dark stains on the chest and knee areas, her heart and posture sinking by degrees.

"I'm sorry," Rosalie said. "I thought she–"

"It's not your fault," Dawn said. "You were working the register. I should've checked on them way before now."

"*I* told her not to clean."

Both girls turned and were startled to see their boss standing behind them. Mr. Le was a short man with thick, black hair and a pencil-thin moustache. He wore gray slacks with a white button-down and black sneakers.

"What are you talking about?" Dawn asked him.

"You bring your clothes from home *too much*," Mr. Le explained. His accent was thick, but totally understandable. "You never make receipt," he went on. "I know you don't pay."

Dawn's mouth fell open. This man's greed never ceased to amaze her.

"Everybody brings clothes from home," she said.

"From now on, *everybody pay*!" Mr. Le snapped. "Uniforms seven dollar each. You pay thirty-five dollar, *then* you can clean." The little man had the nerve to look her dead in the eyes.

Dawn's blood went from lukewarm to boiling in 0.2 seconds, and the whole building exploded in a flash of bright red. Her nostrils flared like a bull's, and she advanced on her boss before better sense could stop her.

"*How you gon' charge me for these uniforms after all the crap I put up with around here?*"

Mr. Le stood his ground, even though Dawn was nearly twice his size. "Everybody pay!" he repeated.

"*Well how come you not paying for all this damned overtime we working?*"

"Dawn!" Rosalie stepped between them and tried to push her friend away.

"You don't like it, you quit!" Mr. Le shouted. "Nobody make you stay!"

"Man, I'ma–" Dawn grabbed hold of Rosalie's shoulders. She was half a second from tossing her friend to the side and giving Mr. Le a letter of resignation he would never forget, but Rosalie said something that took all of the fight out of her in the blink of an eye.

"Stop, Dawn! You need this job. Think about your kids!"

Her words cut like a knife, and the fire behind Dawn's pupils was replaced with snapshots of her two young boys. How could she forget about Tim and Luther when they were the only reason she came to this hellhole day after day?

Dawn looked around the shop, seeing things with her physical eyes rather than her emotional ones, and embarrassment washed over her like a cold shower. She unhanded her friend and lowered her gaze.

"I'm, I'm sorry, Mr. Le."

The shop owner expressed no fear throughout the whole episode, and he didn't look angry now that it was all over. "You quit, or you still work here?"

Dawn almost choked on a throat full of humble pie, but she managed to say, "I'll be back tomorrow morning. I don't quit. I'm sorry I yelled at you." She reached for her boyfriend's uniforms, and Mr. Le turned to go back to his office.

"You can leave them there," he called over his shoulder. "I give you discount. Three dollars each."

Dawn knew that was the closest he would ever come to apologizing. Plus three dollars to dry-clean a work uniform wasn't a bad deal at all, but still tears began to stream down her face. She left the uniforms where they were and hurried to leave the cramped shop.

"I can give you fifteen dollars," Rosalie called after her, but Dawn didn't stop or acknowledge the gesture. Money was always a problem, but finances weren't Dawn's main concern at that moment.

The fact was Henry had to work tomorrow morning, and he needed his uniforms back *tonight*. There would be hell to pay if he didn't have them. Dawn said her relationship with Henry was nothing like Ike and Tina Turner's, but it was a lot more similar than Rosalie would ever know. It was a lot more similar than anyone in Dawn's life ever dared to imagine.

Fifteen minutes later Dawn parked her two-toned Ford Festiva in front of her mother's house on the east side of town. Her boys were usually glued to the television or out back playing with their grandmother's chow/poodle mix, but both Tim and Luther emerged from the front door before Dawn made it out of her car. She continued up the walkway so she could give her mama a big hug and kiss for the day, which was usually the only payment she could offer for the baby-sitting services.

"What's going on?" Dawn asked her sons. "Why y'all in such a hurry to get home?"

"I don't like it here," Tim said.

"Tim got in a fight," Luther said, offering a better version of the truth.

Dawn's boys were born within a year and a half of each other. Eight-year-old Tim was smart and skinny. He had almond brown skin, like his daddy, and long arms and legs that grew out of his school clothes like clockwork, always three months before the school year ended. Seven-year-old Luther was short and silly. He had chestnut-colored skin, like *his* daddy, and Dawn never had to worry about him wearing out his clothes in the middle of the school year. Most of Luther's clothes were hand-me-downs from his big brother, and they were already pretty worn to begin with.

Dawn had enough stress in her life, but she always tried to be attentive to her children's needs.

"A fight with who?" she asked.

"It's these boys down the street," Luther reported. "They was throwing rocks at us."

"Throwing rocks? For what?"

"They always—"

"No," Dawn cut her younger child off. "I want to hear it from *you*," she said to Tim.

Tim looked away, and Dawn saw that he had a slight bruise in the corner of his mouth. She reached for it, her heart melting like butter.

"They always talking about us," Tim said. He kept his hands to his sides and allowed his mother to inspect the wound. "They make fun of us 'cause we can't get a haircut, and our shoes come from Wayless."

The bruise wasn't that bad, but Dawn saw that her son's hair was noticeably kinky. Luther's was, too. If she could afford ten dollars apiece, Dawn would take them to the barber every Saturday, but it was hard enough to pull that off during the school year. Haircuts became even less of a priority during the summertime.

"They hit you with a rock?" Dawn asked.

Tim shook his head.

"They was throwing them for a long time," Luther offered.

"I told them to stop, but they wouldn't," Tim said.

"Why didn't you just go in the house?" Dawn asked.

Tim couldn't answer that, but his expression told the whole story: It's a lot easier to talk about turning the other cheek than actually doing it in the heat of the moment.

"They woulda still been there when went outside later," Luther deduced.

"That's still no excuse for fighting," Dawn said, but she rubbed Tim's shoulder and ran comforting fingers through his nappy hair. She knew this nurturing was giving him conflicting signals, but that's the way Dawn was raised, and she still didn't know any better. Contrary to popular belief, sometimes it's okay for a boy to raise his fists in anger. Defending yourself from a shower of rocks sounded like as good a reason as any.

"Hey, Dawn. I thought I heard you pull up."

Dawn looked up and saw her mother standing in the doorway. Virginia was the strongest woman Dawn knew even though she was struggling with a debilitating illness that left her physically weak most of the time.

"Hey, Mama. You doing all right?"

"Yeah, I'm fine, child. We had a little mess up the street earlier," the older woman said, "but everything's okay now."

"They was just telling me about it," Dawn said. She continued up the steps and gave her mom a soft kiss on the jaw. "Do you know those boys who was throwing rocks?"

"I know their mama," Virginia said. "She work at the post office; she ain't there most of the time. She buy them boys whatever they want, and they ain't got enough sense to be happy with the blessing. They'd rather run around making fun of everybody who ain't got a lot."

"I told Tim not to be fighting over here," Dawn said. "Is everything all right now, or do I need to go down there and talk to their mama?"

"It's all right, child," Virginia said. "Just boys being boys."

"I'ma buy some hair clippers," Dawn said, "so I can cut their hair at home from now on." She rubbed the top of Luther's head, and he looked up at her with a smile.

"You don't know how to cut hair," he guessed.

"I can learn," Dawn said with a grin.

"Why don't you see if Henry can cut it?" Virginia suggested.

Her comment changed the mood on the porch immediately. Dawn's smile slipped away, and the boys looked down at their Wayless sneakers.

Dawn knew Henry wouldn't be comfortable with the closeness required for the haircuts, but it was her sons' reactions that really hurt her. She used to think the boys were apprehensive about Henry because he didn't father either of them, but deep inside she knew it was something more than that.

"Well, I'm sure you could learn to do it," Virginia backtracked, and then she wisely changed the subject. "Baby, I made some chicken for dinner tonight. Do you want to take some home so you don't have to cook? It's already dark; I know you're tired and don't feel like fooling around in that kitchen. I got some corn and green beans, too…"

Dawn's smile came back. "Thanks, Mama. That sounds real good."

"Come on in here and fix you a couple of plates." Virginia held the door open for her, and Dawn followed her inside, loving the homey feel of the place.

Twenty minutes later Dawn arrived at her home in a relatively quiet neighborhood known as Berry Hill. It was after eight by then, and her back and feet were killing her. Dawn wanted nothing more than to crawl into bed and close her mind to everything until daybreak, but Henry's truck squatted like a gargoyle in the driveway, and she knew her day of servitude was not yet over.

Dawn never had the greatest luck with men, but sometimes she thought she hit the absolute *bottom* of the barrel with her current boyfriend. Henry Turpin currently worked as a mechanic, but he was a jack of all trades. When Dawn first met him, Henry was a self-employed house painter. He dabbled in landscaping during the summertime, and last year he worked as a handyman for a struggling apartment complex.

His hard work ethic was one of the main things that attracted Dawn to him, but Henry wasn't a bad-looking fellow. He had a thick goatee and bushy eyebrows that blended well with his coal black skin. Henry kept a full head of hair. It was usually styled somewhere between a shag and an afro.

Dawn's boyfriend had a large nose and large hands. He was of average size and build—except for his big belly. Dawn used to tease him, telling him he looked about five months pregnant, but she stopped when she realized how much he didn't like it and how important it was to show respect to the head of the house.

Henry didn't have a sense of humor *at all*, but that wasn't what made Dawn think about leaving him on almost a daily basis. It wasn't his short temper, and it wasn't his controlling nature, either.

The thing that gave Dawn the most grief was how Henry responded to her kids—but then again, Dawn knew she couldn't really fault him for that. There weren't too many men out there who were willing to raise two boys that weren't his, and contrary to whatever child-rearing books got published, Dawn believed her sons needed to grow up with a father figure in the house. That was almost non-negotiable.

Inside, Dawn found her man in his usual spot: Henry had an old, green recliner that was officially *his chair*. The soft cushions had molded to the contours of his body over the years, and even if someone dared to take a seat on his throne, they wouldn't be comfortable on it.

Henry was watching his favorite program, *The First 48*, on their twenty-nine-inch television. Dawn entered her home quietly, and the boys didn't make a sound, either.

"Why you just now getting home?" Henry asked without looking away from the television.

Dawn paused in the living room, but Tim and Luther hurried to their room.

"I had to work late," she said. "I already have dinner, though. My mama made fried chicken. I got some green beans and corn, too…"

Henry wore a dingy wife beater with faded Dickey pants. His hair was soiled and packed down in the back from lying under cars all day.

"I don't want no greasy-ass chicken," he said. "Yo mama can't cook. That shit gon' give me the runs."

Dawn's face burned. She was cool with him complaining about her, but she couldn't stand it when he said mean things about her mother. "I can, I can make you something else if you want."

Henry looked up at her with a long stare that spoke volumes: *You failed me, woman. Every day I give you another chance, and every day you let me down again.*

"Just hurry up and fix me a plate," he growled. "I ain't got time for you to make nothing else. It's too damned late. I wanna go to bed."

"Okay, baby."

"Hurry up!"

Dawn rushed to the kitchen thinking that wasn't so bad. It definitely could have been worse. Sometimes you have to count your victories one incident at a time.

❧

Henry didn't remember his work uniforms until halfway through dinner. Dawn could tell he was very upset about it, but he never let his anger get the best of him in front of the boys. He only asked a few questions, and Dawn tried to placate him as best she could.

"Why you didn't pay for 'em when he said he was charging you?"

"He didn't tell me until I was on my way out. It was too late by then; they were already closing up. Plus I don't have no money."

"Why you didn't check on them before that? Better yet, why you ain't wash 'em yourself?"

"I wasn't running the washers today," Dawn explained. "Another girl was doing it, and I thought she had done your uniforms."

"What the hell am I supposed to wear to work tomorrow?" Henry wanted to know. "The same dirty-ass shit I had on today?"

"You still have another uniform in the closet," Dawn reminded him. "I saw it this morning."

"I can't fit that uniform," Henry said calmly. "That's why it's been sitting in the closet this long. Have you ever seen me wearing it?"

"I, I don't know," Dawn said. "They all look the same to me."

"You can't do *nothing* right," Henry decided. "Gon' have me at work tomorrow looking like a goddamned fool… Got me eating this nasty-ass chicken…" He looked down at his plate in disgust. "You worthless. I don't know why I put up with this shit."

That wasn't a question, so Dawn felt no need to reply. Plus Tim and Luther were watching the argument like a tennis match, and there was no need to put them through any more of that.

They ate the rest of their meal in silence, and the boys retreated to their room when they were done. Henry cleaned his plate and let out a huge belch on his way back to his favorite recliner. Dawn cleared the table by herself and got started on the dishes, still wearing the jeans and tee shirt she put on for work fifteen hours ago.

Henry's remarks swirled around her head like the swirling soap bubbles in the sink, and once again Dawn decided things didn't go too badly. At least Henry didn't raise his voice during the berating, and he didn't put his hands on her, either. The boys didn't look too happy about what they saw, but Dawn blamed herself for that. If she did better, Henry wouldn't get upset so much.

That was simple cause and effect.

❧

When the phone rang at eight fifty-nine, Dawn had no idea who it could be. She didn't have any friends who might want to chit-chat at that hour, and it was the middle of summer, so it couldn't have been any pissed off teachers either. Dawn took the call in the kitchen. She leaned against the counter just as Henry appeared in the doorway.

"Hello?"

"Hello? May I speak to Dawn?"

It was a woman's voice she didn't recognize. Henry's eyes asked *Who the hell is that?* Dawn's expression told him she had no idea.

"This, this is me," she said.

"This is Dawn?" the caller asked. *"Dawn Wright?"*

"Uh, yeah," Dawn said, now wondering if she'd unwittingly revealed herself to a bill collector.

"Well *goddamn!*" another voice on the line said. This one was a female also. "Yo ass ain't never left the city, but you were the hardest one to find."

Dawn did recognize the second voice, vaguely, but she still wore a mask of confusion.

"Who is this?" she asked.

"Don't tell me you don't remember me," the second voice said. "This is *Mona Pratt*. I got Rene on the line, too…"

"Hey, Dawn! What's going on?" Rene said.

Dawn's mouth fell open, and her heart nearly climbed up her throat. The hairs stood on her arms, and she felt like she was thrust into a time warp. She heard school bells and clanging lockers. She saw glimpses of beautiful teenagers that used to be her best friends. "Oh, my God," was all she could manage.

"Ha ha!" Mona laughed. "I bet you never thought you'd hear from us again!"

"It took *forever* to find you!" Rene added. "Where you been, girl? It's like you fell off the face of the earth!"

"I, I been here," Dawn said. "Y'all the ones who left. I, I been right here…"

Dawn's smile was laced with wonder, and Henry's frown grew steadily. Dawn put a hand over the receiver and whispered, "*It's my friends from high school!*"

But that assertion only made Henry narrow his eyes in addition to his bulldog scowl. He continued to eavesdrop in the doorway, but not even his insecurities could spoil Dawn's joy at that moment.

"Where y'all been?" she asked.

"I'm in Austin," Mona said.

"*H-Town, baby*," Rene replied.

"But we coming back to the 'Brook in a couple of weeks!" Mona announced.

"Really?" Dawn could hardly contain her elation. "What for?"

"You didn't hear about the reunion?" Rene asked.

"No," Dawn said. She looked up at Henry because he brought the mail in most of the time, but she had no intention of asking him about it.

"How you not gon' know about it when you still live in the same damned city?" Mona wondered.

"I, I don't know," Dawn said. "What reunion?"

"Finley High's having a *ten year reunion*," Rene explained. "Me and Mona are coming home!"

"The Finley Sisters are gonna be back in effect!" Mona confirmed.

"*Oh, my God…*" Dawn's whole body was engulfed in a calming warmth. Her head felt so light, she thought it would float away from the rest of her body.

"I *know* you didn't forget about the *Finley Sisters*," Rene said.

"No," Dawn said quickly. How could she forget about the best years and the best friends she had ever known? "I could never forget about y'all. Not in a million years…"

CHAPTER 3
DENNIS AND BLAKE

"So, what's been up with you, girl?" Rene asked.

"Nothing really," Dawn said. She took a seat at the kitchen table, and Henry leaned against the doorframe. Dawn didn't pay him any mind. If his plan was to wait there until she got off the phone, then he was going to be there for a while. Maybe she should offer him a sandwich.

"I know *something* must be going on," Rene said. "It's been *ten years*."

"I didn't do nothing important like y'all," Dawn admitted. "As you can see, I'm still in this same city. Y'all the ones who moved away and did it big."

"Are you married?" Rene asked.

"No," Dawn said. "But I got two kids. What about y'all?"

"You got kids?" Mona asked.

"Tim and Luther," Dawn confirmed.

"That's awesome," Rene said. "I didn't know you were a mama."

"I haven't talked to y'all in at least nine years," Dawn said. "Do you two stay in touch?"

"No," Rene said. "I looked Mona up today, and then we called you. I talked to Mona a little bit before I started college, but we were in two different cities doing totally different things. We kinda lost touch. You know how it goes…"

"That's sad," Dawn said, but she was actually kind of happy she wasn't the odd man out. "So do y'all have kids or what? Are y'all married?"

"Never that," Mona said right away. "No husband and no babies. I don't need some dumb nigga thinking he can control me. And I don't need a bunch of crumb-snatchers tearing up my house, either. I got too much going on to get married."

"I'm not married, either," Rene said. "But I do think about having kids one day."

"I thought you and Terrence were going to get married," Dawn said.

"Aw, hell. I don't even want to think about that fool," Rene said.

"Hold up, I remember Terrence," Mona said. "You were homecoming queen, and he was homecoming king."

"You were the best cheerleader," Dawn added, "and Terrence was like, the MVP of the football team. Y'all was a match made in heaven. Everybody *knew* y'all was gon' be together forever…"

"Yeah, well, somebody forgot to tell his dick that," Rene said, and Mona laughed.

"Girl, what happened?" Dawn asked.

"I don't even like talking about him," Rene said. "I'll tell y'all, 'cause you my girls, but I'm not finna be telling this story over and over at the reunion."

"That's cool," Mona said.

"Yeah, just tell us," Dawn agreed.

"Well, y'all know I was head over heels for that boy," Rene said. "He was my man since we were sophomores, and when we won homecoming king and queen, I just knew that was it: He was gonna be mine forever. We went to the prom, and that was like... I mean, to this day that was the most romantic night of my life."

"He took your virginity," Dawn remembered.

"In the back of his Cutlass Supreme," Rene mused. "My mama paid three hundred dollars for my dress, and I hiked it up like it was some T Mart shit."

"You was so happy," Dawn recalled. "I remember when y'all showed up at that party later. You was glowing. You looked so beautiful."

"Me and Terrence were like a fairy tale," Rene said. "My mama wanted me to go to college, but I didn't because of him."

"I thought you did go to college," Mona said.

"Not right off," Rene explained. "I missed a whole year messing around with Terrence. He got a scholarship to Texas Tech, and he moved me down to Lubbock with him."

"Didn't y'all get married?" Dawn asked.

"Yeah, we did," Rene said.

"You didn't invite nobody," Mona recalled.

"It was a real small ceremony," Rene said, "just our parents and a few aunts and uncles. It was in Lubbock, and we didn't want to make our friends from Overbrook Meadows come way over there."

"I woulda came," Dawn said.

"Me, too," Mona said.

"Well, y'all didn't miss nothing," Rene said. "We were married a total of *seven months*."

"What?" Dawn gasped.

"Let me finish," Rene said with a chuckle. "See, Terrence wanted me to be his stay-at-home wife. I never wanted to do nothing like that–"

"Naw, that ain't even you, girl," Mona agreed.

"But I thought Terrence was going places," Rene said. "He had a high-profile football scholarship, and he was the hottest thing on campus, y'all. He was always telling me how he was gonna go to the NFL and get rich, and I didn't have to do nothing but stay at home and look after the babies.

"He said he was gonna buy me a big house, and I could decorate it however I wanted, and we'd have all kinds of fancy cars. He said I'd have diamonds bigger than Kobe's wife. You know, blah, blah, blah."

"You didn't believe that shit, did you?" Mona asked.

"I did," Rene said. "I was only eighteen, so you know I was naive as hell. Plus Terrence was already kinda famous. Y'all know he could play some ball, and everybody said he was going to be big one day. All I had to do was stay pretty and push a stroller around. We didn't even sign a pre-nup. I was down for that."

"That don't sound like you," Dawn said.

"It doesn't," Mona agreed. "How come you never had any babies, then?"

"I didn't even get a chance to," Rene said. "Before I got pregnant, I started getting real suspicious about what was going on at his school. Me and Terrence had an apartment off campus, but he would spend the night in the dorms sometimes."

"Oh, hell no," Dawn said.

"He would say he was studying for a test or he got drunk after a party," Rene said, "but you know I'm not stupid. I started going up to his school more often, and he would be tripping like, '*Why you following me around?*' and '*Why you don't trust me?*' But pretty soon I found out he was one of the biggest hos on campus. We had only been married for four months, and he knocked off two bitches already."

"Damn!" Dawn's eyes widened. "He didn't seem like that type in high school."

"College is a different story," Rene said. "It's so big, and you're not dealing with little girls no more. It's some grown women there with grown bodies; fake titties and all that. They were offering him some stuff I didn't even know *existed*, and he couldn't get his pants off fast enough."

"That's messed up," Dawn said.

"I hope he comes to the reunion, so we can clown his ass," Mona said.

"That would be sweet," Rene agreed.

"Did he ever get to the NFL?" Mona asked.

"Nope," Rene said. "He had two knee surgeries in college, and last I heard he went to play for a Canadian league."

"So you went to school after y'all broke up?" Dawn asked.

"Yeah," Rene said. "I was on my own, and I was a year behind, but I wasn't helpless *at all*. I got me a student loan and went to Baylor."

"What'd you major in?" Dawn asked.

"Marketing," Rene said.

"What kind of work do you do?" Dawn asked.

"I'm a sales manager for BNP Solutions," Rene said. "It's a software company in Houston."

"I went to *Spelman*," Mona said with undisguised hubris. "I shoulda stayed my ass in Atlanta, but I got too much family in Texas. I own a real estate agency in Austin."

"You *own* it?" Dawn shook her head subconsciously.

"Oh, yes, honey," Mona said. "I started it from the ground up. You should come to Austin sometimes. I got billboards all over the place with my face on them."

"That's nice," Dawn said, but her cheeks started to burn, and she dreaded what was coming next.

"What about you?" Mona asked. "What's life been like for Miss Dawn Wright?"

Dawn closed her eyes and sighed in embarrassment. "I ain't done nothing like y'all; I can tell you that right now. I don't make a lot of money."

"We don't care about all that," Rene said.

"Yeah, you our girl," Mona said.

"Our *sister*," Rene clarified.

"Yeah, but y'all done been all around the world," Dawn said. "Got your own businesses and stuff."

"We haven't been *all around the world*," Mona said.

"And I don't own my company," Rene said, "nowhere near it."

"Yeah, but—"

"Girl, we not gon' judge you," Mona assured. "We might judge those other heifers at the reunion, but you our girl."

"We love you," Rene agreed.

Dawn sighed again. "All right. I work at a dry cleaners. I almost make ten dollars an hour. I got two kids by two different men, and I live in Berry Hill with my boyfriend Henry. He's a mechanic, and we're barely making ends meet. My car needs new tires right now, and my boys need haircuts that I can't afford. That's my life."

There was a long pause, during which Dawn thought she might start crying.

"I thought you went to college," Rene finally said.

"I took some classes at the junior college," Dawn said, "but I didn't make it through my first year."

"Why not?" Mona asked.

"It was different," Dawn said, "different than high school. I didn't have classes with nobody I knew, and I couldn't find nothing I was good at. Nobody cared when I stopped going, so I just didn't go back."

"Why didn't you—"

"*And* I'm fat now." Dawn figured she might as well get that out of the way, too. "I was a size nine in high school, and now I'm a 18."

There was another awkward silence, and Dawn wished the earth would crack open and swallow her up.

"You, you're not *depressed*, are you?" Mona asked.

Dawn frowned. "No, I'm not depressed. Why should I be depressed?"

"I'm just saying," Mona said. "If you're not depressed about none of that, what makes you think we would have something to say?"

"Yeah," Rene said. "I don't care how much you weigh."

"But I know both of y'all are still skinny," Dawn said. She hoped she was mistaken, even though she knew it was wrong to wish for cellulite.

"Yeah, I still look good," Mona said right away.

"I ain't that much bigger than I was in high school," Rene said.

Dawn shook her head. "See! Man, I don't think I'm going to the reunion. People gon' be talking about me—especially if I'm with y'all."

"What? You *gotta* go," Rene said.

"And ain't nobody gon' say *nothing* about you while I'm standing there," Mona said. "You must not remember how we used to run that school."

Dawn did remember. Back then she was a little chubby, and Rene and Mona stuck up for her whenever someone tried to put her down. "That was a long time ago," Dawn pouted.

"We're still the Finley Sisters," Rene assured. "If somebody messes with one of us, we'll *all* take 'em out. Ain't nothing changed."

Dawn smiled.

"Do you remember when we chased the Perkins twins out of the pep rally?" Rene asked, and everyone laughed.

"Ooh, ooh, what about that bitch *Viola*?" Mona said.

Dawn hadn't heard that name in ages. "Viola?"

"*Viola Smalls*," Mona said. "I know you remember her. She stole the class presidency from me!"

Rene laughed. "Damn. You still tripping on that?"

"I never forgot her," Mona said, and she sounded pissed all over again. "I hope she's there *for real*. I would love to see how that bougie bitch's life turned out."

The girls laughed again, and after a while Dawn felt like she really was a part of her old clique again.

She didn't get off the phone until well after 10 p.m. Henry was in bed by then, but he wasn't asleep yet. He rolled over and watched Dawn while she undressed for her shower.

"What?" she said.

"Who was you talking to?" he asked.

"Those are my girlfriends from high school," Dawn said. "One lives in Austin, and the other one is in Houston. They're coming back in a couple of weeks for our high school reunion. I can go, can't I?"

Henry wrinkled up his nose. "What for? So you can see some of them niggas you used to go with?"

Dawn chuckled. "No, boy. I want to see my homegirls. I don't care about nobody but them."

"You don't even sound like yourself when you was talking to them," Henry noticed.

Dawn thought about that for a second and decided he was right. "I may not sound like the Dawn you know, but that was still me. I guess everybody acts different when they get around their old friends."

Henry didn't like the idea of a new Dawn, but he said she could go to the reunion, as long as she took him with her. Dawn was so happy she didn't care if he tagged along or not. Seeing Rene and Mona again was going to be like reclaiming a piece of her childhood. Not even a grumpy grouch like Henry could spoil that for her.

❧

Time slowed to a crawl for the next couple of weeks while the Finley Sisters made preparations for the class reunion. Dawn never moved out of Overbrook Meadows, so there wasn't much planning needed on her end, but Mona and Rene had a lot of responsibilities at their workplaces. Rene had a crucial sales meeting she would have to miss, and the weekends were always the busiest days for Mona's real estate agency.

But both ladies were okay with letting go of the reins for a little bit. The class reunion was scheduled for just three days, Friday night through Sunday night. Mona purchased round-trip plane tickets to her hometown, rather than subject herself to hours on the freeway, so she could make it back to work on Monday morning if she wanted.

Anticipation made the days drag by, but finally Friday June the fourth was upon them. The sun was bright in the sky that afternoon with hardly any clouds to block the summer heat. Mona left the office at twelve with a noticeable pep in her step and a sinful smile parting her lips. Her expectations for the reunion varied, but with Mona there was always something sadistic flitting around her cerebrum.

Mona was genuinely interested in reuniting with her homegirls and seeing her old teachers and some of the boys she thought she was in love with back in the day. But Mona also wanted to see people she *never* liked. She wanted to see who got fat and who couldn't afford real diamonds on their rings and necklaces. She wanted everyone to see how good she still looked and how successful she became while they wasted their lives away in dead-end jobs with no benefits or 401Ks. She wanted to point out and ridicule anyone foolish enough to show up with a fake Dooney & Bourke or a bootleg Coach bag.

But most of all Mona hoped Viola Smalls would be there. There were few things Mona regretted in life, but she still felt pangs of grief and embarrassment when she thought about losing her bid for senior class president. Next to deceased relatives, that was biggest loss Mona ever experienced, and it didn't jibe with the woman she was today or the girl she was back then.

And the fact that she *still* believed the presidency was stolen from her by means of deceit made her defeat that much more frustrating. Mona could never get to the bottom of the trickery in high school, but her search for the truth was ongoing. She would solve the caper at the class reunion—of that she was certain.

In her condo Mona packed the last few essentials in her carry-on bag, and then she went to the living room to wait for her boyfriend to show up. The term *boyfriend* was actually not what Mona liked to refer to Dennis as, but he put up with her crap for eight months so far, and she figured she owed him at least that much.

Dennis appeared on her doorstep at one o'clock wearing khaki pants with a white button-down and brown loafers. He was a fair-skinned gentleman with reddish brown hair and hazel eyes he inherited from his Caucasian grandmother. Dennis had a wide nose and full lips he got from his father's side of the family, and he had a nice bulge behind his zipper that Mona assumed came from his daddy as well.

Dennis was handsome, and he was educated. He worked as the head pharmacist at one of the Walgreens on San Gabriel. When he first approached Mona at a downtown café, she saw his white lab coat and thought he was a full-fledged doctor. She went out with him anyway when she learned he was a *mere* pharmacist.

"Hey, baby," Dennis said. He stepped inside and gave Mona a hug and a kiss on the corner of her mouth. "You got everything packed up? You ready to go?"

"Yes I am," she said. Mona wore a green, knee-length skirt with a loose-fitting white blouse. She didn't have on any makeup now, but she planned to get dolled up a little when she got to her hotel in Overbrook Meadows. "Thanks for giving me a ride to the airport," she told Dennis. "I only have a couple of bags, but they're kinda heavy…" She smiled demurely.

Dennis looked down at the three luggage items and shook his head with a chuckle. He hefted one of the larger suitcases, and his eyes bugged. "Dang, woman. What do you have in here?"

"Just some clothes, baby. A big guy like you, I know you can handle it."

Dennis was only six feet, one hundred and eighty pounds, but he grinned and poked out his chest a little. "Sometimes I think you only want me around so I can move heavy things for you."

Mona grinned, too. That wasn't the *only* thing she wanted from him, but it was the only reason Dennis was there today. The pharmacist was a little naive, but still insightful.

"Don't act like you don't like to show off your muscles," Mona said.

She gave his little arm a squeeze, and ignored the way it trembled as Dennis hefted the bulky suitcase into the hallway.

"It's, it's got wheels, right?" he panted.

"Of course, baby," Mona said. "You should definitely use the wheels."

❧

Dennis didn't ask where she was going until they were halfway to the airport. Mona was sending text messages to her staff at work, and she really didn't care for the distraction.

"To my hometown," she said without looking up. "To a high school reunion."

"Really?" Dennis was only twenty-five. His graduating class hadn't had any such rituals yet. "You're going by yourself?"

"Yeah," Mona said. "What's wrong with that?"

"How come you didn't ask me to go with you?" Dennis asked.

"Why would I do that?"

"I don't know." He shrugged. "You might not want to travel that far by yourself."

"It's only a thirty-minute flight," Mona informed him. "And I'm not going to some strange place I've never been. I grew up in Overbrook Meadows."

"What about the people at your school?" Dennis went on. "I know you like to do a little boasting and bragging. You don't want your old friends to think you're single, do you?"

That was an odd question on a couple of levels. Firstly, Mona didn't like to do a little boasting and bragging; she liked to do that *a lot*. And secondly, Dennis was just *barely* her boyfriend. Whenever the occasion suited her, Mona considered herself *very* single. She looked away from her iPhone and met her chauffeur's eyes.

"I don't need to show off a man like I'm some desperate skeezer."

"I didn't say all that."

"Well I don't know what you're saying," Mona quipped.

"I'm saying you didn't even tell me where you were going," Dennis said. "I'm starting to wonder if you're embarrassed of me or something. Don't you plan on seeing some of your family while you're there? You don't want me to meet any of them, either?"

"Dennis, it's not like we're getting married or something."

"I didn't say that."

"Well, what—"

"I'm just saying you make me feel left out sometimes. You don't want me to meet your friends, and you don't want me to meet your family. I wouldn't even know where you were going if I didn't ask you just then. You make me feel like I'm not really a part of your life."

"Okay, I'm sorry," Mona conceded. "I didn't know it was that big of a deal to you. If I had known, I would've invited you."

"Why can't I still go?" Dennis pondered.

Mona frowned. "I bought my tickets already."

"I doubt if the flight's sold out."

"Well, you don't seem to have any luggage with you," Mona said.

"I can buy a couple of outfits when we get there," Dennis said. "You're only gonna be there till when, Monday?"

Mona shook her head. "You tripping?"

"I'm serious." Dennis stared intently into her eyes. "Can I go with you?"

Mona returned his gaze and shook her head. "No, Dennis."

His face fell for a second, and he returned his eyes to the road, where they should've been all along.

Mona went back to her text message with hardly a care about his poor little feelings.

Jeez, she thought, *some people will wear your nerves, if you let them…*

༺༻

One hundred and fifty miles away in Houston, Rene was having an entirely opposite problem with her boyfriend. Blake had known about the trip to Overbrook Meadows for two weeks already, but he'd waited until the last minute to start complaining about it.

"They're just some *lowlife niggas*," he said. "I don't see why you care about what they think."

The couple was at Rene's home in the River Oaks neighborhood, and she was already a little perturbed because they were running late. Rene had all of her bags packed hours ago, but Blake was still searching the closet for shirts and ties he might need.

"I didn't get an attitude when we went to your family reunion last month," Rene reminded him. She sat on the corner of her bed wearing jeans and a tee shirt. Unlike Mona, she and Blake were driving rather than flying, and Rene was eager to get started on the four-hour trip.

"That was different," Blake said.

"I don't see how," Rene said. "We're going to see my family when we get there."

"Yeah, but the whole point of this trip is to go to a *class* reunion," Blake countered. "You can't compare that to a family reunion. You'll probably never see those people again in your life."

Blake emerged from the closet wearing black slacks with a white tank top. He slid his arms into a gray dress shirt and fixed a frown on his girlfriend. Even with the grimace, Blake was an extremely handsome man. He was brown-skinned with a head full of thick black hair that was a little curly on top. Blake had thin eyebrows and serious eyes. He had a strong jaw line like a drill sergeant.

Blake Dunham wore no beard or moustache. He had a nice chest and strong arms, despite the fact that he was allergic to manual labor. Blake worked as a PR rep for one of the larger investment firms in Houston. He and Rene had been romantically involved for the better part of two years. Blake was an attentive lover, and he never disappointed with a birthday or Valentine's gift, but he and Rene both knew that it was the business side of their relationship that made them so compatible.

Rene wasn't looking for a husband, and Blake never considered popping the question, but they were always there for each other whenever it was appropriate to bring a date—no matter the occasion. Rene had been to all of Blake's company picnics, and Blake came to Rene's Christmas parties every year. Whenever Rene needed an escort for a luncheon, Blake was always the best-looking guy there, and when Blake needed companionship at a funeral, Rene dazzled, even in her mourning garb.

They had been there for each other for so long, everyone in Rene's and Blake's lives assumed the couple was a match made in heaven. All of Blake's family thought Rene was the best girl he ever had. They couldn't wait for her to become an official Dunham and start pumping out babies. Likewise, the folks at Rene's office thought Blake was absolutely *dreamy*. The girls said Rene was lucky to have such a beautiful beau, and the guys wanted to hang out with Blake and go fishing or play poker or whatever he was interested in.

Whether it was a real relationship or just an *arrangement*, Rene thought what she and Blake had was perfect. It irked her that he would bitch about her class reunion.

"You only see your family once in a blue moon," she said. "They're no different than the people I went to school with."

"That's ridiculous," Blake said. "My mother loves you."

"If you liked me half as much as she does, we wouldn't be having this conversation," Rene muttered.

Blake knitted his eyebrows and then smiled. He came and stood before Rene and placed a soft hand on her cheek. "How could you say something like that?"

Rene sighed. "I'm just pissed 'cause you don't have any enthusiasm. What if I went to your company parties all mad and rolling my eyes at everybody?"

"I'm not going to roll my eyes at anyone," Blake said with a chuckle. "When we get there, I'll look just as excited as you. You know how I get down."

"Yeah, you're the best actor I know," Rene replied.

"I'm not acting when I say I love you," Blake said. He cradled her face with both hands and bent to deliver a soft kiss. Rene smiled when he backed away.

Blake turned and went back into the closet to find a tie, and Rene got up and followed him inside. She turned off the light and backed him against one of the walls. She pressed her body close to his and they kissed again, with real passion this time. Blake clutched her ass with both hands, and Rene reached between his legs to see if his soldier was standing at attention. It was. Rene caressed him through his slacks, and Blake cleared his throat.

"Um, in the closet, baby?"

Rather than respond, Rene unbuttoned her jeans and slid them down her frame with the panties still entangled. With her bare butt in his hands, Blake was nearly bursting from his trousers. Rene unbuckled his belt and set his manhood free.

"So, I guess we're not in that big of a ruuhhh…"

Blake couldn't finish his sentence because Rene dropped to her knees, and the words got tangled in his mouth.

CHAPTER 4
THE REUNION

Dawn changed clothes five times that evening, growing more frustrated by the second. Henry came to check on her, but he was never any help during a crisis.

"I thought you was wearing that red dress."

"It don't fit," Dawn said, pealing off an equally undersized green skirt.

"It looked fine to me," Henry said. For the reunion he wore the only suit he owned. It was black and drab, but it worked well on any occasion, from a funeral to Easter Sunday.

"You must not have seen how tight it was on my stomach," Dawn said about the red dress.

"You can't blame the dress for that," Henry replied. "It probably got something to do with—"

"Don't even say it."

"Say what?"

"Whatever it is you got on your mind," Dawn said. She was near tears, but her boyfriend was oblivious. "I know it's something *ugly*."

Henry chuckled. "I wasn't gon' say nothing ugly."

"Well, if it don't got nothing to do with helping me find something to wear, then I don't need to hear it."

Dawn disappeared back inside the closet wearing only a bra and panties. Rather than return to the living room, Henry gave his two cents anyway.

"You wouldn't have so much trouble finding clothes that fit, if you leave them Little Debbie's alone."

Dawn shook her head in exasperation, and tears squirted from her eyes. She exhaled hot fumes and stepped out of the closet with more pain than anger marring her features.

"You just had to say it anyway, huh? You had to get it out."

Henry grinned. "Either that, or you could buy you some new clothes. You can go down to the fat girl store and get something that fits."

"Where's that at?" Dawn asked, "next to the *fat boy*'s store? You probably need to come with me, 'cause you ain't no Tyson Beckford yourself."

It was unusual for Dawn to defend herself in that manner, and Henry's grin slipped away immediately. He opened his mouth for an even more brutal jab, but he saw the tears on his woman's cheeks and changed his mind.

"If you hate me so much, why don't you leave me?" Dawn wondered. "You ain't gotta come in here talking noise. I know I'm fat! I don't need you to throw it in my face all the time!" She tossed the green skirt to the floor and stomped back into the closet. She pulled the door closed so hard, the whole room shook.

Henry stood there for a second, and Dawn regretted her tantrum right away. Her man was not one to put up with such outbursts. The last time Dawn pulled a move like that, Henry chased her down and grabbed hold of her shoulders; shaking her hard enough to cause death if she was an infant.

But this time Henry stuffed his hands into his pockets and left the room without another word. Dawn wondered if it was her Tyson Beckford comment that caught him off guard, or if he was still on edge because of the reunion. For the last couple of weeks, Henry behaved oddly whenever Dawn talked about Finley High or whenever one of her friends called the house.

Dawn knew he was worried that an old fling might sweep her off her feet and move her far, far away from the hell she called life. There was no chance of that happening, but Dawn was okay with letting Henry have his suspicions. At least he cared about the possibility of losing her, and anything that made him a little less mean was a plus.

❧

Dawn finally found an outfit she didn't hate (green capris with a billowy white blouse), and they left the house a few minutes after eight. That wasn't good timing, considering the reunion started at 8 p.m. sharp, but Dawn figured they'd be okay. She had to drop the boys off at her mother's house on the way to the school, but thankfully her mom lived within ten blocks of Finley High.

Her sons usually didn't talk much when Henry was in the car with them, but Dawn didn't go out very often, and the idea of a high school reunion was strange to them.

"Are you going to take a test?" Luther asked.

"What kind of test?" Dawn asked. She sat in the passenger seat applying the last touches to her make-up.

"Like a SAT," Luther said.

"She already graduated, stupid," Tim replied. "They grown. Why they gon' take a test?"

"Don't call him stupid," Dawn warned. "You don't like it when people call you names."

"So are you gonna take a test?" Luther asked again.

"No," Dawn said. "At least I don't think we are." She frowned. "We better not. I haven't studied for nothing…"

"What *are* you gonna do?" Luther pressed.

"Just a bunch of silly stuff," Dawn said with a chuckle. "We're going to tour the school a little. Most of us haven't been there in ten years. We'll get to see some of our old teachers and friends. We're having dinner in the cafeteria, and they'll have some more fun things. I think there'll be some music and dancing." Dawn was beaming. Henry rolled his eyes, but she didn't pay him any mind.

"And that's just for *today*," Dawn added. "They got stuff planned for tomorrow and Sunday, too."

"You got work tomorrow," Henry said.

"Not all day," Dawn said. "And I don't work at all this Sunday."

"You'll probably be tired of them people by then," Henry predicted. "They didn't give a shit about you for this long. I don't see why they all in your face now."

Dawn knew he was talking about Mona and Rene in particular, but she didn't respond. Henry was getting upset again, and she didn't want him to go into another one of his rants.

Henry pulled into Virginia's driveway six minutes later, and Dawn got out to walk her boys to the front door. Her mom said she looked really pretty, but Dawn didn't feel very attractive. She didn't feel like being with Henry for the rest of the night, either.

"Can you bring me a piece of cake, if they have some?" Luther asked, hanging on his grandmother's arm.

"I don't think they're going to have cake," Dawn said. "But even if they do, I don't want to take some home with me, like I'm poor or something." Dawn was actually more concerned with everyone seeing the big girl smuggling sweets, but her mom still had something to say.

"Girl, you can't be worried about what people think about you. You may not have a lot of money or a fancy car or a good job like some of them, but that don't mean they're better than you."

"You give the worst motivational speeches," Dawn said.

"Don't get sassy with me," her mom said.

"So you'll bring me some cake then?" Luther asked.

65

"No," Dawn told him. "Absolutely not."

Finley High was an average size school with a sprawling green lawn out front and ten portable classrooms scattered out back. A huge banner over the main entrance welcomed back the class of 2000. Both the student and faculty parking lots were packed with vehicles, both luxury cars and hoopties. Dawn never felt self-conscious about Henry's old truck before, but she hoped he'd park close to the back so no one she knew would see her climbing out of the rust bucket.

Possibly out of malice, Henry circled the entire parking lot slowly before finding a spot somewhere in the middle. Most of the guests were in the auditorium already, but there were still a few people exiting their vehicles. Dawn did her best to avoid eye contact with them.

"You couldn't have parked in the back?" she asked her boyfriend.

"Naw. And don't start acting bougie," Henry warned. "You need to let these people see you for who you are."

That was good advice. Dawn gave her sons the same lecture all the time, but she wasn't feeling it tonight. She rolled her eyes and didn't feel comfortable until they put a respectable distance between themselves and Henry's old–timey F-150.

The auditorium was packed. Dawn felt like a freshman again as she sought a seat for Henry and herself. A lot of the faces she encountered were immediately familiar, while others were barely recognizable. Nearly everyone was chubbier than she recalled, and that took a lot of the pressure off right away.

Dawn still remembered the names of most of her old friends, but a lot more of them remembered her. On the way to her seat, she was constantly being poked and waved at by people who were only marginal acquaintances ten years ago.

"Dawn!"

She turned and saw a pretty girl with a sharp nose like a bird's beak.

"Do you remember me?" The woman grinned anxiously.

Dawn smiled and nodded, and someone called her in a different direction before she had to lie.

"Dawn Wright!"

This time it was a man who looked like one of Mona's ex-boyfriends.

"Oh, my God," he said, "you still look exactly the same!"

"Darryl, right?" she asked.

"Yeah. It's me. Have you talked to Mona? Is she coming?"

"She's coming," Dawn called. "I talked to her yesterday."

"Hey, Dawn!" Yet another stranger grabbed her wrist. "It's me, Stacy!"

"Everyone, take your seats!" someone announced on the overhead speakers.

Dawn looked towards the stage and saw her old principal standing with a team of vice principals she didn't recognize.

"We'll have plenty of time to meet-and-greet later…" Mr. Miller wore a patient smile. He was still as handsome as Dawn remembered. "But right now we have a few announcements to make," he said. "So please, everyone take your seats or we'll be here all night."

The stage was decorated with another large banner, and there were red and silver streamers hanging from the walls. Dawn and Henry passed more old friends before they found empty seats near the back row.

Dawn couldn't get over how genuinely happy everyone was to see her. No one said anything about her being fat, and no one paid attention to the man hanging desperately onto her arm. Dawn felt like all of her popularity had instantly returned. She felt like she was *somebody* again. It was heart-warming. It was better than any drug or alcohol high.

❦

It took more than ten minutes, but the principal was finally able to quiet the crowd long enough to give his speech. He thanked everyone for coming, saying he wasn't surprised by the huge turnout because 2000 had one of the best graduating classes Finley High had ever known. He mentioned a few peers whose success made national news, and he took a couple of minutes to give a somber list of the classmates who were no longer with them.

Mr. Miller ended his speech on an up note, giving the itinerary for the night as well as plans the alumni association made for the rest of the weekend. When he was done talking, everyone was anxious to meet up with their closest friends. Dawn didn't have to wait much longer, because the first thing on the agenda was for the graduates to report to their old homeroom classes.

Ten years ago Dawn shared homeroom with both of her best friends. She shot to her feet and grabbed Henry's hand when the principal dismissed them.

"Come on!" Dawn's eyes were bright like new pennies.

"Where we going?"

"Mr. Lamb's class, third floor!"

Henry got up lethargically, but he couldn't steal Dawn's joy. She didn't even need him at that point. If he didn't get a little pep in his step, Dawn would leave him behind without a second thought.

"You is really tripping," Henry noticed.

"I wanna see my sisters!" Dawn squealed, only then realizing how much she truly missed them.

∽⚬∽

Mr. Lamb taught French and history, and his classroom was still decorated as Dawn remembered it. He had a red, white, and blue French flag hanging on one side of the chalkboard with the equally appropriate stars and stripes unfurled on the opposite side. Mr. Lamb stood behind the same aged desk he had a decade ago, and Dawn saw that the years had not been kind to him.

"Hey, Mr. Lamb." She gave him a quick hug. "How's it going?"

Before he could answer, someone yelled at her from the back of the classroom.

"Dawn! *Girl, get over here!*"

Dawn turned and saw a beautiful woman standing next to an equally beautiful man. Rene Packard wore a silk leopard-print dress with black stockings and a three-tiered gold necklace. Her hair was styled in a short bob. Her skin was dark like a moonlit beach. Rene's waist was small enough to fit her necklace around it, but there was no animosity when the two ladies locked eyes. Dawn rushed to her friend and wrapped her up in the biggest hug she could muster.

"Rene! Oh, my God, I missed you so much!"

"I missed you, too, Dawn!"

"You look beautiful!"

"You do, too!"

The women backed away, still holding hands. Dawn shook her head, a tear glinting in her eye.

"It's been *so long*. I thought I wouldn't *never* see you again."

"I know," Rene said. Her smile was ear-to-ear. "I can't believe we waited so long. Have you seen Mona?"

"No," Dawn said. She looked back and saw her boyfriend fidgeting with uncertainty. "This is Henry," she said. "Henry, this is Rene. She was one of my best friends in school!"

"Hey." Henry stepped forward and shook her hand.

Rene looked him up and down, and her smile didn't falter.

"This is my boyfriend, Blake," she said.

Blake gave Dawn and Henry hearty handshakes. He smelled great, and he exuded confidence. "Good evening. Nice to meet you."

"Oh, snap!"

Everyone looked up and saw the most boisterous and popular Finley graduate standing in the doorway. Mona Pratt stepped into the room and all eyes were immediately fixed on her. It was an involuntary response that would've happened even if she hadn't announced her arrival with the lively shout.

Mona was the type of girl men had naughty dreams about and women cursed under their breath. She was tall and slender with long, flowing hair and fiery red skin. Tonight she wore a solid black dress that was sleeveless and form fitting. Her bare legs were smooth and awe-inspiring. Her hips and breasts made even gay men's hearts skip a beat.

"I know y'all not getting reacquainted without *me!*" Mona said.

"Never," Rene said. She and Dawn ran to her and took turns hugging the final member of their clique.

"You know it ain't no party unless Mona's here," Dawn said.

"Y'all better recognize!" Mona said and threw an arm around both of her friends' shoulders. "Man, I missed y'all so much!"

By then the classroom was filled with more acquaintances from those carefree days of yore, but at that moment none of the other alumni mattered. Dawn felt like she was reunited with her very own flesh and blood, and she prayed they would never spend so much time apart again.

With the Finley Sisters officially a trio again, the world was theirs for the taking, and the school was the kingdom they presided over. The ladies talked amongst themselves for the rest of the night and paid little attention to the instructions from their former principal and teachers. No one was surprised to see the threesome as thick as thieves again, and everyone commented on what beautiful women they had become.

They took a brief tour of the school, and then the former students were ushered to the cafeteria where an elegant meal of pork tenderloin or roast beef was waiting for them. The Finley Sisters did more chatting than eating, and Dawn noticed Henry was starting to show signs of stress.

After dinner the crowd headed for the final event of the night in the school's gymnasium. Upon entering Dawn was surprised to see strobe lights, a DJ booth, and a projector splashing random pictures from the yearbook against one of the walls. The alumni were free to dance and mingle. The Finley Sisters split up for the first time, and Henry didn't follow Dawn when she went to hug the rest of her forgotten girlfriends and some of her long-lost boyfriends, too.

∽❧∾

At a quarter till ten Dawn finally had a spare minute to spend with her man, but it didn't last long. Mona burst through the crowd and grabbed hold of her hand.

"Dawn! Come on, girl! I finally got her!"

"Got? Got who?"

Dawn's face was a mask of confusion, but Mona was already pulling her away from Henry.

"Got who?" Dawn asked again.

"*Viola Smalls,*" Mona growled. "I *knew* I'd get her."

"What are you, what are you talking about?" Dawn didn't know whether to get angry like her friend or laugh.

"Where's Rene?" Mona asked, dragging Dawn through a thick crowd of dancers.

"I don't know." Dawn's legs were much shorter, and she was starting to trip over her heels. "Girl, slow down! What's the problem?"

Mona continued to look around frantically. "*RENE!*" she shouted over the music. "*GIRL, WHERE YOU AT?*"

Dawn's mouth fell open, and she knew this was something serious indeed.

"Mona what are you–"

"*RENE!*"

This time they spotted their third head next to the drink table. Rene was trying to spend a little quality time with her boyfriend, too, but it was not to be. She ran to her friends with her eyes wide.

"Mona! What's wrong?"

Mona turned again, looking around wildly. "Now, where that *bitch* at?"

"Who?" Rene asked.

"*Viola Smalls!*" Mona shouted.

"*Right over there!*" Rene shouted back. "What the hell's going–"

Mona streaked past them and stomped up to a high-yellow woman with her back turned. Mona grabbed her by the shoulder and spun her around violently. Dawn still didn't know what the deal was, but she immediately began to slip out of her shoes. If it was going down, she had her friend's back. She could figure out the who's and why's once the hair stopped flying.

"What the hell?" Viola Smalls was a bit shorter than Mona, but she was a lot more stacked. She wore acrylic nails and a long weave that went past her shoulders. She was still as pretty as she was back in the day, but she looked a little worn now, a little *used* in Dawn's opinion. Viola wore a white party dress that clung nicely to her curves.

Mona got in her face like Viola was her child.

"Bitch, I *knew* you fixed that vote! *I was supposed to be class president, you ugly ho!*"

Dawn's jaw dropped even more, and Rene stared in shock as well.

Viola frowned and then cocked her head to the side.

"Bitch, you better get out of my face with that mess! It's been *ten damned years*, Mona! Shit, get over it!"

Inwardly, Rene was thinking the same thing, but she fixed mean eyes on Viola anyway. Right or wrong, she had to side with Mona.

"I'm not getting over it, because I know you cheated!" Mona said, her finger in the other woman's face now. "And now I can prove it!" She scanned the gymnasium and then began to yell again. "*Quinton*! Quinton, get yo ass over here!"

There was a large crowd gathering, and Rene started to feel embarrassed. This was something Mona would have pulled back in 1999. She couldn't believe her friend was still so hotheaded.

But sure enough a nicely dressed gentleman sheepishly emerged from the multitude. Dawn remembered him as Quinton Marshall. He was a member of the student council their senior year.

"Quinton!" Mona pulled him into the fray. "Tell this *bitch* who was supposed to win class president in 1999!"

Quinton lowered his head and spoke softly. No one would've heard him if not for the fact that the DJ stopped spinning records so he could see what the commotion was.

"You was," Quinton said, and there was a collective gasp from the onlookers.

"Mmm-hmm," Mona said. "And why did this slut win?" She shot a thumb back at her adversary.

Viola fixed her face with a *Well, I never!* expression, but it didn't stop the truth from coming forth.

" 'Cause she gave me some head," Quinton said.

Most of the alums' eyes grew wider, and a few people started to snicker.

"What?"

"What he say?"

"He say Viola gave him some *head*!" Mona yelled.

By then their old principal had made his way to the epicenter. Rene had never seen anyone so bewildered.

"What the hell is going on here?" Mr. Miller demanded.

"I won senior class president back in '99," Mona said with a twist of her neck. "And *this* hussy stole it from me!"

"What?" Mr. Miller looked around angrily. "That was *eleven years ago*!"

"I told her!" Viola said.

"It don't matter!" Mona spat. "I finally found out the truth, and I want it *exposed*! Viola only won 'cause she gave Quinton some–" Mona caught herself. "She gave him some *fellatio*!"

The crowd burst into laughter, and Viola's face turned as red as a fresh tomato.

"Who the hell is *Quinton*?" Mr. Miller wanted to know.

"Um, it's, it's me, sir…" Quinton took another step forward. "I was in the student council, and I manipulated the votes so, um, so Viola would win. It was close, but Mona was supposed to win by twenty votes."

Mr. Miller put a hand on his hip and shook his head. "Why in the world would you do that, son?"

Viola gave Quinton the most evil look Dawn had ever seen, but whatever power Mona had over him held firm.

" 'Cause she, she gave me some, some fellatio, sir…"

The crowd erupted again, and Viola turned her fury on Mona.

"I can't stand yo ass! Why you always starting shit?"

Mona was smaller, but she advanced on her anyway. "You better get out my face! It ain't my fault you was a ho! And you *still* a ho! I heard you got *three baby-daddies*!"

Dawn was at Mona's right side by then. "And yo weave look *tired*!" she added.

Rene took her usual spot on Mona's left. "*And* you got herpes in the mouth! Mmm-hmm. Don't think nobody don't see them bumps."

Viola's eyes grew very large. She looked like she soiled her panties, but Rene didn't feel any guilt. This is what happened when you tangled with the Finley Sisters. These hos had better recognize.

There was no way to explain her fellatio, her three babies' daddies *or* her herpes, so Viola turned tail and stormed out of the gym. Everyone she passed was laughing, and a few people laughed *and* pointed. Kids can be so cruel, even grown-up kids.

When the dust settled, Mr. Miller gave Mona a stern look of disapproval.

"Are you done now?" he asked. "Did you get what you wanted?"

"Nope," Mona said. "I want a certificate that says *I* won class president back in '99. No, better yet, I want a *plaque*."

"Fine," Mr. Miller said.

"For real," Mona said. "I want to hang it on my wall."

"I said I will get it for you," Mr. Miller promised. "Now, can we get on with our party, or do you have some more *old dirt* to sling around?"

"Yeah, you can get back to your party," Mona said, her mood suddenly subdued. "What you looking at me for?"

Before Mr. Miller could blow a gasket, Mona turned from him and threw her fists in the air. "I'm president, y'all!" she screamed.

And the populace exploded in cheers and applause.

Rene snickered and shook her head, but she had to give her friend some props.

"You a bad bitch."

"No doubt," Mona agreed. "No doubt!"

❧

Thirty minutes later the party was winding down, and Henry was ready to leave. Everyone had had a good time, and no one cared that the Perkins twins and Rene's ex-husband never showed. Dawn found her friends and told them she was taking off.

"You're coming to the other events this weekend, right?" Rene asked her.

"I work tomorrow," Dawn said. "But I'ma try to get to the ones on Sunday."

"We gotta see each other again," Mona said, still glowing from her victory.

"Yeah, for real," Rene said. "We need to spend more time together. I didn't know how much I missed y'all!" She hugged both of her sisters, and they returned the love.

"Let's go on vacation!" Mona suggested. "I know y'all can take some time off. Let's go somewhere together."

"Ooh!" Rene's eyes lit up. "We can go on a cruise. My cousin works for Carnival, and she can get us tickets. They always have a few openings."

Dawn immediately knew she couldn't afford time off work or a cruise ticket, but her friends looked so happy. "I don't know, y'all…"

"Come on, Dawn," Mona said. "If we can get the tickets, you *gotta* go. I wanna kick it like we used to. Didn't you have fun tonight?"

"I had fun," Dawn said. "I haven't had this much fun in years. But, man…" She lowered her eyes. "I can't afford no–"

"Uhn-uhn." Mona cut her off. "If it's about money, *I'll* buy your ticket."

"I will, too," Rene offered.

"We can split it," Mona said.

"What?" Dawn had never felt so loved and so bad at the same time. "Naw, I can't have y'all doing that for me."

"Girl, please," Rene said. "It's no big deal. I can probably get the tickets for four hundred apiece."

"That ain't nothing," Mona said.

But that was a whole lot of something to Dawn. "I don't know…"

"Just think about it," Mona said.

"I'll call my cousin tomorrow and find out when the next boat's taking off," Rene said.

Dawn sighed and said, "All right."

"Good!" Mona gave her another hug.

"I'll give you a call tomorrow." Rene gave Dawn a hug and a kiss on the cheek.

"All right," Dawn said, her beautiful smile back in place. "See y'all later."

But when she turned away from them, her grin quickly evaporated. The money aside, Dawn knew Henry would *never* let her board a cruise ship without him. She would have to be crazy to even ask him.

But then again Dawn had been with Henry for almost two years, and he never made her feel *wanted* like Rene and Mona did. He never made her feel like family. Surely that had to count for something…

CHAPTER 5
ALL EXPENSES PAID

The next morning Rene got dressed for one of three events the alumni association planned for the second day of the reunion. At nine o'clock she had to return to Finley High for a pancake breakfast followed by a fundraising event for the renovation of the school's library.

At noon Rene was to meet with her old classmates at the Colonial Country Club near TCU for an expensive lunch followed by a relaxing round of golf. Rene was an absolutely terrible golfer, but the Colonial was beautiful and historic. She couldn't wait to swing her clubs on the same greens Tiger Woods played on a few years ago.

After the Colonial Rene planned to visit with her family before attending the final reunion event of the day, dinner at Don Pablo's. The dinner would no doubt pale in comparison to the luxury of their lunch, but Rene was happy to be back in her hometown. She couldn't wait to see her grandmother, and Mona's antics at the party last night made her laugh every time she thought about it.

Rene bathed and dressed conservatively in denim capris with a grapefruit-colored halter top. When Blake stepped out of the shower wearing only a towel around his waist, Rene lusted for him openly. She wanted to lick the remaining droplets of water from his chest and stomach. But Blake wore a sour expression that made all thoughts of intimacy flutter away.

"What's wrong?" Rene asked him. "You didn't sleep well."

"I slept all right," Blake said. He dropped his towel and went to fetch a pair of boxers from his suitcase. He avoided eye contact with his woman. He was nervous about something, and Rene knew it wasn't his nudity.

"You feeling all right?" she asked. She pressed mute on the television and watched her man step into a pair of Calvin Klein boxer briefs. He scratched the back of his head and looked up at her reluctantly.

"I think, um… I think I'm going to check out a little early."

Rene frowned. "Check out? From where?"

Blake shrugged. "You know, from here, this city. I need to go back to Houston." He walked to the closet nonchalantly and came out a few seconds later with a pair of pressed slacks. Rene still had the same frown on her face.

"What do you mean? You're going home?"

Blake sighed and slipped his legs into the pants. "Listen, Rene. I came to the reunion, like I said I would. But I can't stay all weekend. That's too much of a commitment. I don't have that much time to spare."

Blake tried to back out before they left Houston, so Rene wasn't *totally* surprised, but she hoped he wasn't serious.

"I told you about this *two weeks ago*."

"Yeah, and I said I might–"

"You didn't say *might*."

"I told you I didn't think I would be able to stay the whole weekend."

"Yeah, and then you said you would."

"No, *you* said I would."

"I didn't make you do anything. Don't try to–"

"Rene, I've been trying to tell you all week. You didn't want to listen."

"I didn't back out when your director had that dumb-ass tea party," she reminded him. "That was the stupidest thing I've ever been part of. *And* those people were racists."

Blake chuckled. "No, they weren't."

"Yes, they were. You know they were."

"Well, anyway–"

"And I didn't back out when you–"

"Exactly," Blake said.

"Exactly *what*?"

"This is exactly what I'm talking about. Every time I tried to get out of this reunion bullshit, you–"

"*Bullshit?*"

"You know it's bullshit. And every time I tried to tell you I didn't want to go, you kept throwing shit in my face, all the places you went for me."

"I did do it for you."

"Yes. I know you did, Rene."

"I'm always there for you."

"And I'm always there for you, too," Blake said. "But three days is too much of a commitment for me

83

right now. Bottom line. I've never asked you to do anything that took more than a few hours."

Rene chuckled. "Is that all it's about? You only do for me because I do for you? It's all about favors?"

Blake laughed at that. "*You're* the one who guilt-tripped me into coming here, Rene. You're the one who kept throwing your *favors* in my face. But it's only okay to look at it like that when it's convenient for you?"

She knew he was right, and the truth hurt. "So why are we sleeping together?" Rene asked. "Why don't I just send you an email when I need you to go somewhere with me, and we can call it what it is: an escort service?"

Blake shook his head and he looked genuinely hurt by that. "Rene, I know you're upset, but I think you're going overboard. You're my woman, and you know that. You know I love you, and I know you love me, too. Just because I don't want to stay in Overbrook Meadows for another two days doesn't mean I don't want to be with you."

That was good to know, but Rene still didn't want him to leave. Her face burned, and her eyes glossed over, but she wouldn't allow any man to make her cry. No way, no how.

"What about my memaw?" she asked. "You said you wanted to meet her."

"I would love to meet her," Blake confirmed. "But it's going to have to be another time. I've got to be back in Houston by one. I already told the guys to meet me at the office." He went back to his suitcase and removed a pristine white tank top.

Rene frowned again. "You already scheduled a meeting *before* you told me you were leaving?"

Blake pulled the shirt over his head and headed for the restroom to style his hair.

"I'm sorry, baby. We've got a lot of stuff to go over."

Anger replaced Rene's grief, but she didn't rise from the bed. "And how are you getting home?" she pondered. "We only have one rental car."

"You can keep it," Blake said. "I'll get another one."

"I don't want to drive home by myself," Rene said. "Have you ever thought of that?"

"It's just this *one time*," Blake said. "I'm sorry." He had his back to her, and Rene couldn't tell if he was really sorry or not.

"What about this hotel?" she asked. "I coulda stayed at my mama's house if you weren't going to be here."

"I'm still splitting it with you," Blake said, but that only reminded Rene how business-oriented their so-called relationship was.

"You're an asshole," she decided.

"No, your friend Mona is an asshole," Blake said. "I don't know how you could enjoy being around that boorish woman. She's disrespectful and ghetto as *hell*. I'm glad you're not like that."

Rene's jaw dropped, but before she could come up with a suitable response, Blake kicked the bathroom door closed. Rene knew he was ending the conversation rather than seeking privacy, and his arrogance made her blood boil.

But Blake was right about one thing: Rene wasn't like Mona. Even though every one of her molecules wanted to kick and scream, she maintained her cool. Only a foolish girl would let a man know how much he hurt her; that would only give him the power to hurt her again whenever he felt like it.

Instead Rene grabbed her purse and left the hotel before Blake came out of the bathroom. Rene still had forty-five minutes to kill, so she headed to her mother's house to see how her *real* loved ones were doing.

When she got on the freeway, Rene gave her girl-friend a call because Mona always had the best advice when it came to bone-headed men.

"Man, *forget that nigga*," Mona said halfway through Rene's story. "He fine, but he ain't *that* damned fine."

Rene laughed, and she felt better right away. "You sho' right, girl."

"Of course I'm right," Mona said. "I'm the freaking *president!*"

∽

Dawn had to work on Saturday, but she made sure she left the cleaners before 5 p.m. so she could attend the reunion dinner at Don Pablo's. Her boss gave her a hard time about clocking out while the lobby was filled with customers, but that was nothing compared to the opposition Dawn faced when she got home.

Henry didn't get off until six, so with the one hour head start, Dawn thought she could make his dinner and get ready to leave without having to argue about where she was going. But once again Dawn couldn't find a nice outfit that still fit her. Henry pulled into the driveway while she was squeezing into a third pair of pants.

Fresh off work, Henry was always tired and filthy. His hair was matted in the back, and he had smudges on his face from where he wiped away sweat with his greasy paws. When he walked into the closet, he effectively filled the whole doorway with his presence, and Dawn knew she was in deep, deep trouble.

"What you doing in here?"

"I was, uh…" There were clothes strewn everywhere, so there was no need to lie. "I was looking for something to wear."

"For what?" Henry spoke softly, but this was his routine. He hardly ever raised his voice, even when he was mad enough to spit fire.

"I already made your dinner," Dawn said, her eyes big like poker chips. "It's spag-spaghetti. It's in the oven."

Henry half shook his head. "I didn't ask you all that. I wanna know where the hell you think you're going—and I'd better not hear no bullshit about that damned reunion, either."

Dawn knew his threat was real, but Henry always knew when she was dishonest. He could smell it like a dog sniffing a blood trail.

"It's, it's just a little get together at Don Pablo's," Dawn said. "My friends Rene and Mona gon' be there. They, they the only ones I want to see."

Henry's face changed into something very scary, but in the blink of an eye, it went back to normal. He shook his head, his nostrils flaring.

"You ain't going to no *Don Pablo's*. I already told you; that shit's *over*. You ain't got no Don Pablo's money, and you ain't got time for them loud-mouth heifers who ain't give a shit about you for the last ten years. I don't want to hear nothing else about that goddamned reunion, Dawn. You hear me?"

"But what about—"

Henry advanced on her in a quick blur and Dawn's words got caught in her throat. She threw her arms up to protect her face, but Henry didn't throw one of his patented slap-punches. Instead he shoved her in the chest with both hands—hard enough to force all of the wind from Dawn's lungs.

"*Oof!*"

She flew backwards with enough force to leave a dent in the sheetrock when she impacted the wall, but one of her pumps caught under her foot and Dawn fell hard on her butt instead. She landed on another discarded shoe, and it dug painfully into her coccyx. But Dawn couldn't cry out this time because she still hadn't caught her breath. Plus her boys were in the other room, and she never screamed while they were at home if she could help it.

"Now get in there and fix my plate," Henry ordered. He hovered over her like Satan himself. "I work too damned hard. I ain't got time for this."

Dawn nodded, more out of reflex than anything else, and Henry turned and left her to think about the problems she caused.

Dawn's eyes welled, and the tears spilled like blood down her cheeks, but she would look like her old self in a few short minutes. Henry wouldn't ask what was wrong with her at the dinner table, and Dawn was pretty sure her sons would be none the wiser.

～✺～

Rene called at nine o'clock, and Dawn told her she couldn't make it out that night.

"Why not, girl? We're going to Club Tron after we leave here. You should come with us."

"I'm sorry," Dawn said. She was washing dishes by then. She heard Henry come into the kitchen so he could listen in on her conversation. Dawn didn't turn to see what kind of look he had on his face. "It's too late," she said. "I'm getting ready for bed in a minute."

"*Bed*? It's Saturday night!" Rene said.

Dawn heard rustling over the phone, and Mona came to the line.

"Dawn? You said you're going to bed?"

"Yeah. I'm tired."

"Girl, it's only *nine o'clock*! You're sounding like some *old maid* or something."

"It's different when you have kids," Dawn said. It's also different when your man is an occasionally violent control freak, but Dawn didn't tell them that part.

89

"Well, you're coming to church with us tomorrow, right?" Mona asked. "We're having lunch afterwards, and then me and Rene gotta head home."

"I'm going to church tomorrow," Dawn said.

"That's what I just said," Mona said. "All of the re-union folks are meeting at Ebenezer for morning services, and then we're going to the Golden Corral for lunch. And then that's it; the reunion's over."

"I always go to church on Sunday," Dawn said. Her heart was pounding, but Mona didn't get the hint.

"What? Girl, you tripping." She handed the phone back to Rene. "Here. I can't understand what she's saying."

Rene returned to the line laughing. "Dawn? What's wrong?"

"Nothing," Dawn said, but she could feel Henry's eyes burning the back of her head. "Hey, I gotta go."

"All right," Rene said. "You're going to be at Eb-enezer tomorrow morning, right?"

"Yes," Dawn said, glad one of her friends had sense enough to ask a *yes* or *no* question.

"And you're going out to lunch with us afterwards?"

"Yes," Dawn said again. The trip to Golden Corral was against Henry's wishes, but Dawn knew she could pull it off. Henry never went to church with her and the boys, and Dawn usually stopped by her mother's house afterwards for lunch.

"Cool," Rene said. "I'll let you get back to your *family life* now." She laughed. "I always knew it would be you, though. Out of the three of us, I knew you'd be the first one to settle down and start a family. You got so much love to give. I know your boyfriend loves you to death."

That statement caught her so off guard, Dawn couldn't come up with a response.

"I'll talk to you later," Rene said.

"Okay, bye," Dawn said and hung up the phone. She waited a few seconds and then turned to see if Henry was still watching her. He was.

"What them hos want now?"

"They're not hos," Dawn said. She returned her attention to the sink because she couldn't stand Henry's face sometimes.

"I said *what they want*?"

"Nothing," Dawn said. "They asked if I was going out tonight, and I said no."

Henry watched her for a little while longer and then returned to his favorite seat in the living room. Dawn wiped the sweat from her brow when he was gone, wondering if tomorrow's get-together was worth the trouble.

∽♡∾

But on Sunday morning, Dawn decided that she did need to see her friends—no matter the cost. It was worth the lies she would have to tell on her way out of the door, and it was worth the whooping she would receive if Henry saw through her deceit. Dawn wasn't worried about her boys because they wouldn't tell Henry anything she asked them not to.

Rather than spend an hour in the closet looking for a nice outfit, Dawn grabbed one of the old Sunday dresses she normally wore to church. She never realized how dreary her clothing was before. She knew Rene and Mona would look *spectacular* in whatever they had on.

But Dawn had to play it cool, so she even wore white sneakers with her dress because this is what Henry was used to seeing. And it worked. He didn't question her at all as she got ready to leave. Dawn let out a huge sigh of relief when she got in the car, and she decided to tell her boys the truth when they turned at the first intersection.

"Hey, I'm, uh, we're going to a different church today. But I don't want you to tell Henry about it."

"Why not?" Luther asked.

"He doesn't want me to see my old friends," Dawn confided. "But today's the last day they're going to be in town, so I'm going anyway."

Luther's eyes grew big with fright, but Tim looked angry.

"You should see your friends whenever you want to," Tim said. "You grown, Mama."

"I know I'm grown," Dawn said. "But I don't feel like arguing with him."

"He always mad," Tim said, and Dawn was surprised by his attitude. She thought he might express these feelings when he got bigger, but Tim was only eight years old.

"That don't have nothing to do with it," Dawn said. "All that matters is we're going to a different church today so I can see some of my friends. I want y'all to be good, and don't tell Henry where we went when we get home. Deal?"

They both nodded. Luther was excited about the venture, but Tim still looked upset.

"Pinky swear?" Dawn asked.

The boys reached and locked pinkies with her one at a time.

∾

Ebenezer was a huge church with a cluster of adjacent buildings that housed the pastor's office, the cafeteria, and over a dozen classrooms for the children's chapel. Dawn was a little on edge when they first arrived, but midway through praise and worship she felt the Holy Spirit settle upon her, and she was at peace.

The pastor's sermon was appropriately titled "The Importance of Friends." By the end of his lecture, Dawn knew Henry could never sever the bond she shared with Rene and Mona. And as long as she remained faithful to God, the devil could not prosper in her home or in her heart.

Dawn didn't meet up with her sisters until the service was over, and she felt a brief pang of jealousy when she found out Rene and Mona arrived at the church together and sat next to each other the whole time. They looked totally content as a twosome, but their eyes lit up when they spotted Dawn in the crowd.

"Dawn!"

They rushed forward and grabbed onto her as if they hadn't seen her just two days ago.

"Girl, why didn't you come with us last night?" Mona asked.

"Mona got drunk as a skunk," Rene informed Dawn.

"I wanted to," Dawn said. "I really did."

"Come on," Rene said. She threw an arm around Dawn's shoulder and led her towards the parking lot. "Let's hurry up and get to the restaurant. I know it's gonna be packed, and I don't feel like waiting in a long-ass line."

"Wait." Dawn pulled back. "I gotta get my boys from the children's chapel."

"It's *definitely* gonna be a long line," Mona said with a sigh.

"We don't have to go to Golden Corral," Rene said. "Y'all the only two I really care about seeing. We can go to another restaurant."

"That's fine with me," Dawn said.

"Cool," Rene said. "Go ahead and get your kids. We'll wait for you right here."

"What about Henry?" Mona asked before Dawn took off. "You didn't bring him?"

"Oh, uh, he never comes to church with me."

"Good," Mona said. "It's something about him I just don't like…"

She waited for her friend to fill in the missing pieces, but Dawn declined.

"Okay, I'll, uh, be right back."

✦

Dawn knew this would be her last bit of quality time with her friends before everyone returned to their regular lives, so she dropped the boys off at her mother's house. The Finley Sisters piled into Rene's rental car and headed for the southwest side of town. Mona picked Red Lobster for their dining pleasure, and before Dawn could open her mouth to complain about the prices, Mona said it was all on her.

The ladies had a good time together and enjoyed succulent seafood, but towards the end of the meal, their conversation drifted into waters that made Dawn uncomfortable. Her friends still wanted to go on vacation, and Dawn was still sure it could never happen.

"I talked to my cousin," Rene said. "She said she can get us three tickets for the next ship taking off on June 21. The cabins won't be that close together, but we'll all have a room to ourselves."

"That's what I'm talking about!" Mona said. "We can get some *thangs* going on, if we want to…"

From the look in her eyes, it was clear Mona wanted to.

"The boat's going to Mexico," Rene went on. "It's a five-day cruise, and it's going to make two stops. It's not supposed to rain the *whole time*."

"Gotta bring some bikinis," Mona said.

Rene was beaming, but she noticed Dawn didn't look excited at all.

"Girl, you ain't gotta bring no bikini," Mona said.

"Yeah, don't trip about that," Rene added.

"No, it's not that," Dawn said.

"Well, what's wrong then?" Rene asked. "You still want to go, right?"

Dawn sighed and shrugged. "I keep telling y'all I don't have no money for that."

"The tickets are only four-fifty," Rene said. "And me and Mona already told you we'd pay for yours."

"Yeah," Mona said. "We got your back."

"But I can't afford to take that much time off work," Dawn explained.

"It's only a week," Mona said. "You don't have no kind of savings?"

Dawn closed her eyes and shook her head. She bounced her knee nervously, more embarrassed than she'd ever been. Her friends looked so stylish in their church outfits, and here she was, wearing a grand-mamma dress with sneakers. Financially, Dawn was *leagues* behind her cronies. It was hard to believe she failed so miserably in this big game of life.

But Rene wasn't giving up. She calculated quickly in her head. "Dawn, you said you make ten dollars an hour."

"*Almost*," Dawn clarified.

"That's four hundred before taxes," Rene went on. "What if I loan you five hundred dollars?"

Dawn's eyes bugged. "What?"

"I can loan you some money, too," Mona said, "so you can get some new outfits before we go."

Dawn first thought Mona was making fun of her wardrobe, but Mona's expression wasn't malicious at all. She looked compassionate. Dawn still shook her head.

"I can't," she said. "If I owe y'all money, we might as well not be friends no more. I could *never* pay nothing like that back. Y'all should just go together. Y'all two would have more fun anyway."

"You can keep it," Rene said right away. "You won't owe me anything back. I'll *give* you the money."

"Me, too," Mona said after a noticeable pause.

Without warning Dawn began to cry again. "Why y'all wanna do that? This ain't right."

Rene frowned. "Dawn, I don't know what's not right about us wanting to spend time with you."

"Yeah," Mona agreed. "That's more right than anything I ever heard of."

"But y'all don't even know me," Dawn moaned.

"Yes, we do," Rene said with a comforting smile. "We lost touch for a minute, but it's not too late to get it all back. I'm willing to give you this money. That's how bad I want us to be like we were. All you have to do is take it."

Dawn thought about it for a few moments. Deep down she knew it was best to leave the Finley Sisters in the past, but the future only offered the same dreary days she muddled through for the last ten years. She wanted her friends back in her life. She *needed* them, in fact.

"All right," she said, and wiped her face with the back of her hand. "But can't we go somewhere that's not so expensive?"

"Like where?" Mona asked.

"I don't know. Six Flags?"

Rene chuckled. "We're going on a cruise," she said. "Me and Mona will take care of everything. All you have to do is get on the boat."

Dawn nodded and forced a smile, even though that was the scariest thing she ever heard in her life.

CHAPTER 6
EXODUS

The next fourteen days flew by as the Finley Sisters made arrangements for what was sure to be the baddest, livest, and crunkest vacation the world had ever known.

June was one of the hottest months in Texas, and the girls couldn't wait to strip down to the barest essentials and tour their cruise ship with a piña colada in hand, sporting rubber flip-flops that smacked the bottom of their newly manicured feet. They couldn't wait to see Mexico and dive into the pristine blue waters along the foreign coastline.

Mona planned to get things as steamy as possible on the boat, but she already had things pretty steamy in her condo in Austin. The day before their ship was to set sail, Mona had a ravenous pharmacist between her legs, and he was munching so expertly, she would've sworn he took classes on the fine art of cunnilingus.

Dennis wasn't the best guy to call if she needed her brakes changed or wanted a stout fellow to accompany her to the beach, but when it came go licking the kitty, Mona couldn't think of too many men who did it better.

It was 9:37 p.m., and the stars were shining brightly through her bedroom window on the eighteenth floor.

Mona's condo smelled liked buttery vanilla from scented candles still smoldering in the bathroom. Her bed sheets smelled of passion fruit with the underlying fragrance of Burberry cologne. From a stereo in the living room, the Isley brothers crooned about love lost and a mystical place called Atlantis.

Mona's night was perfect, from their dinner at Finn & Potter on East Fourth Street to her sensual sponge bath ten minutes ago. But none of that compared to the magic Dennis worked with his tongue when he was really in the mood to please her. He sucked her labia like taffy, inserting a stiff tongue every now and then. He licked her hard enough to make Mona squirm, but he never lingered in the same spot long enough for her to hump his face out of sheer desperation.

She held onto his ears like handle bars, loving every sensation he brought her. She didn't have to guide the action because (unlike every other aspect of their relationship) Dennis was in full control when he had her juice box in his face. He knew that when he flattened his tongue and licked slowly, he could make Mona gnaw on her bottom lip in anticipation. He flicked his tongue like a serpent to make Mona's left leg tremble. The faster he licked, the more she spasmed.

The feel of his hot exhalations on her pubic hair made Mona squeal. She climaxed within a couple of minutes. She stared between her legs, and Dennis watched her eyes until she closed them and let her head fall slowly to the pillow. Even as her vaginal walls contracted around his tongue, Dennis never slowed up.

"I love the way your cum tastes," he whispered, and this must have been true because he slurped her sweet juices like a kitten lapping the last traces of milk from a dinner bowl.

Dennis didn't make his way to her clitoris until Mona was on the verge of tears. He licked it until she arched her back and cried out in pleasure. He wrapped his lips around the hardening organ and sucked with increasing pressure when her ass started to slide across the mattress.

Mona thought she might pass out from an overdose of bliss, but Dennis slipped two perfect fingers inside her while he sucked, and she was wide awake again. She stared between her legs, wanting to express her gratitude in some way, but she couldn't get the words out. So instead of offering a compliment, Mona squeezed his ears tighter and rode his face and hand for what felt like a heavenly half hour.

When Dennis finally backed away and pulled his boxers off for the *real* sex, Mona was positive she could take no more. Her bare chest, slick with sweat, rose and fell erratically. Her head swam. She didn't smoke, but she wanted a cigarette. She wanted to go to sleep. What she *didn't* want was some five-inch dick that would pale in comparison to the marvels of Dennis' tongue, but he mounted anyway, and Mona realized she was wrong on all accounts.

She still had another level of ecstasy heretofore unexplored. And what Dennis lacked in length and width, he easily made up for with technique and dedication.

The stereo in the living room went through another three songs before Dennis finally had an eruption of his own. He was so exhausted by then, he barely had the strength to roll to his side of the bed. He lay flat on his back, staring vacantly up at the ceiling with his mouth slack. His cheeks glistened in the moonlight. Mona knew his jaws would be sore in the morning.

"Wow," she panted. "That was awesome. What, what's the occasion? Is it my birthday or something?"

"No," Dennis said. "It's *my* birthday, remember?"

"Oh, yeah," Mona said. "Happy birthday, baby…"

Two hours later Dennis stepped out of the shower in the wee hours of the morning. He dressed quietly while Mona lay motionless, wrapped like a baby in the sheets. She was still grinning, relishing the afterglow of their lovemaking.

Mona knew Dennis had to open his pharmacy at 7 a.m., so she wasn't concerned with him leaving. He had a key to her condo, and she didn't have to get out of bed and walk him out.

When he was fully dressed, Dennis came to the side of the bed to kiss her goodbye, but then he crossed the room and, much to Mona's dismay, he turned on the lights. She immediately rolled away from the brightness, burying her face in the pillows.

"What are you doing?" she moaned.

"Check it out," Dennis said. He was on her side of the bed again. "I wanna show you something."

Mona didn't have to do anything but roll over and open her eyes, but that was too much of a hassle. "I'm tired," she whined. "Show me later."

"No, you need to see this now," Dennis informed. "It's important. It's the most important thing *ever*."

Mona sighed and rolled over reluctantly. She pulled the covers from her face and stared at him groggily. Her eyes widened a little when she saw what he had, but it wasn't the sudden excitement Dennis was hoping for.

The pharmacist was kneeling on one knee. He held a small jewelry box like an offering. The ring inside was nice, but Mona needed a rock *twice as big* if she was going to take herself off the market. But the thing about that was, Mona wasn't ready to take herself off the market—not for a guy like Dennis.

She hoped this was just some silly anniversary she forgot and Dennis wasn't stupid enough to do what it looked like he was about to do, but his dopey grin told her he was, in fact, that stupid.

"Mona, I want to get married. I want us to… Will you marry me?"

He was so pathetic Mona almost started laughing—literally. She had to put a hand over her mouth and clear her throat.

"Um, no, Dennis. I don't think we, I mean, no. That's not a good idea."

She thought he would've been prepared for such a response, but Dennis' smile fell like he stepped barefoot into a warm pile of dog shit.

"Wh-what?"

Mona sat up on one elbow. "Come on, Dennis. You're not serious, are you?"

He frowned. "What do you mean?"

"We've only known each other for eight months," Mona said. "We never talked about marriage before. What gave you the idea I wanted to settle down?"

"I, I wanted to surprise you," Dennis explained. "It wouldn't be a surprise if I asked you about it beforehand."

"But usually a girl will give you some kind of *hint* that she wants to get married," Mona reasoned.

"Like what?" Dennis closed his jewelry box and returned it to his pocket.

"Like they'll see a baby and say, '*I can't wait to have a family,*' " Mona offered. "Or they'll take you to a wedding and say, '*I can't wait till it's my turn.*' I never said anything like that, Dennis."

Mona normally wasn't this kind when she rejected a man, but this wasn't some random guy hitting on her. This was a proposal for marriage. And after the tongue work Dennis put in a few hours ago, Mona felt she owed him at least a soft rejection. Plus it really was his birthday.

"So, is that it?" he asked. "You don't want to think about it or anything? Your answer is just *no*?"

Mona still didn't believe he was serious. She knew she was the most awesome woman on the planet, but she never treated Dennis like he was the man of her dreams.

"Okay, let me think about it," she said, only because it was obvious that was what he wanted to hear. "I'll give you an answer when I get back from Mexico."

Dennis narrowed his eyes. "You're going to *Mexico?*"

Oops. "Uh, yeah. Me and my friends are going on a cruise tomorrow."

"*Tomorrow?*"

"I thought I told you."

Dennis shook his head. "No. You never said anything about that."

And that's not a clear enough sign that I don't want to marry you? Mona wondered. "I'm sorry."

Dennis shook his head and made it to his feet. He lumbered across the room and turned the light off. A few seconds later Mona heard her front door open and close. Dennis even had the decency to lock the deadbolt.

Mona waited a few seconds more and then rolled back onto her side and tried to recapture some of that good sleep she was enjoying before Dennis' awkward interruption. She thought he ruined a great night of pleasure with that proposal, but all Mona had to do was imagine his head between her legs and she felt a mighty aftershock.

"Ooh…" she cooed and squirmed, a delicious smile parting her lips. That was almost good enough to make her want to get married. She chuckled and sighed dreamily.

Yeah, right.

❧

The following afternoon in Overbrook Meadows, Dawn was ready for the final phase of a plan so monumental she was calling it *Operation Exodus*.

When her friends left town two weeks ago, a small part of Dawn hoped their vacation plans would fizzle once everyone reconsidered the financial aspects. No way was Rene going to give her five hundred dollars *and* pay for half of her cruise ticket. And Mona was by no means a philanthropist. She wasn't going to give Dawn that kind of money, either.

But the following Monday, Rene called to announce that the deal was already underway: Rene secured three cruise tickets from her cousin, and she was ready to mail Dawn a check for the five hundred she promised. Dawn almost backed out, but Rene was so happy and Henry was such an asshole. And the idea of getting on a real, live cruise ship was starting to tantalize, just a little. In all twenty-eight of her years, Dawn had never traveled past the Texas border. This was a once-in-a-lifetime opportunity to leave the *entire country*.

Dawn asked Rene to mail the check to her mother's house so Henry wouldn't see it—and God forbid find some way to cash it himself—and a few days later the funds arrived. Dawn's mouth went dry when she opened the envelope, and her fingers trembled when she filled out the deposit slip at the bank. At that point

Dawn knew she was *obligated* to go, and she began to strategize a stealthy escape.

Mona only sent four hundred dollars for Dawn's new outfits, but that was a huge blessing. In fact, it was more than Dawn spent on her wardrobe over the last three years.

Shopping and packing proved to be a bit of a hassle, but it wasn't as taxing as Dawn feared. Henry was always interested in her comings and goings, but he only became suspicious when Dawn was *out of bounds*. So she made every effort to stick to her normal routine.

There was a Super Target across the street from her dry cleaners, and Dawn did most of her shopping there. She left work early as often as possible so she could run over and pick up a new pair of tennis shoes, new shorts, towels, tee shirts, and pretty underwear. Over the next two weeks she bought new capris, fancy blouses, and she even found a beautiful evening gown for sixty dollars. She left the shopping bags at her mother's house each day when she went to pick up the boys.

The hardest part was getting suitcases and other things she needed from her house. Dawn found time to do this whenever she got home before Henry, or whenever he'd leave to visit a friend or relative. Even if she only had a thirty-minute window, Dawn rushed to grab a suitcase or an armful of clothing. She'd store the luggage in the trunk of her car and unload it at her mother's house the next day. It was risky, but after a week and a half of this, she was almost done. Henry never noticed the dozens of hangers missing from their closet.

ॐ✦

On the day before the cruise, Dawn had two suitcases and a smaller travel bag fully packed at her mother's house. The boys still hadn't spilled the beans, and Henry was totally oblivious. The last thing on Dawn's to-do-list was to grab a few necessities from the bathroom that would draw serious attention as soon as she took them. Plus she still had to tell Henry she was leaving.

Dawn never felt so rebellious, but she wasn't coldhearted at all. She couldn't leave the country without saying a word to her boyfriend of two years. Henry's love for her was warped, and it was even dangerous, but it was still love.

On Sunday morning Dawn woke up early and got ready for church like she normally did. After breakfast Henry went to the living room and posted up in his usual spot in front of the television. Dawn took the boys to worship the Lord, and she dropped them off at their grandmother's house afterwards. This was nothing new except for the fact that Tim and Luther would be there for a whole week this time.

Dawn didn't spend too much time with her sister Denisha, but she asked her to tag along when she went to pick up her last few necessities from home. Dawn knew Henry would still be there, watching sports most likely, and he would have a lot to say when she told him about the cruise.

Henry might try to prevent her from taking her things. He might raise his voice in anger, but Dawn knew he wouldn't throw a punch if there was a witness present. Henry was big and bad in the privacy of his own home, but he had a serious fear of prison. He never jeopardized his freedom in any blatant ways Dawn could remember.

When Dawn and Denisha arrived at her home, Henry's truck was parked right where it should be, and the sight of it made a hard, slimy knot form in the pit of Dawn's stomach. Her knuckles grew white on the steering wheel, and her chest tightened. Denisha noticed her apprehension, but she didn't know Henry like Dawn did.

"You all right?" she asked. "What's the problem? You're only going to get a couple of things out the bathroom, right?"

"Yeah," Dawn said. "But Henry don't know I'm leaving."

Denisha frowned. "Why not?"

" 'Cause I know he don't want me to go," Dawn said. "He might try to stop me."

Denisha's eyes widened. "Stop you? Stop you how?"

"I don't know," Dawn said. "That's why I got you with me."

Denisha nodded slowly, not sure she liked the position Dawn put her in. Denisha had had a couple of abusive relationships in the past, and they never ended well.

"I didn't know Henry was like that," she said. "Why didn't you tell me?"

"I'm telling you now," Dawn said. "Now come on. I wanna hurry up and get away from here."

Inside the house, Henry barely looked away from the television when Dawn passed him on the way to the kitchen.

"My sister's here," she called. "She in the living room."

Henry didn't get up, but he leaned to the side and turned his head in that direction. Denisha stood stoically in the doorway.

"Hey, Henry," she said.

He nodded at her. "What's up."

Dawn emerged from the kitchen with two plastic grocery bags in hand. She walked past Henry again, heading for their bedroom this time.

"I got to get something out of here," she told him.

Henry nodded and narrowed his eyes, but he didn't say anything. He was only wearing boxer shorts with a dingy tee shirt. Dawn knew he was upset because she brought company in the house without giving him time to throw on a pair of pants. She also knew he wouldn't get up and follow her with Denisha standing there.

In the bedroom Dawn's hands were shaking so badly she could barely pick up her hoop earrings from the dresser. Frustrated, she swept all of the sparking trinkets into her grocery bag, figuring she could sort it out later. In the bathroom she grabbed her curling iron, her blow dryer, and a few other toiletries.

She tried to take a couple of things from the medicine cabinet, but her fingers trembled, and she ended up dropping them in the sink. She kept looking back, expecting Henry to come and see what the commotion was, but he remained seated.

Finally Dawn decided she had everything she needed. She sighed loudly and wiped the sweat from her forehead. She planned to spend the night at her mother's house today, and if she forgot something, she could make another trip to Target later on. She took a deep breath and returned to the living room with her heart thumping. Henry looked up at her expectantly. Denisha was still standing in the doorway.

Dawn thought maybe she should just keep walking. She could call Henry from her mother's house and let him deal with his anger all by himself. But on second thought, she figured it was best to get it over with now. She was sure he wouldn't do anything but yell at her, and she didn't want him to bring his bad attitude to her mother's doorstep. Tim and Luther were having a good time over there, and Dawn wanted to keep it that way.

"I'm, um…" Dawn paused next to the television. "I'm going out of town for a little while," she said. "I won't be back until next Saturday."

Henry's eyes widened. His face turned into something dark and ugly. Usually when he got mad, his face transformed for only a second or two, but this time it stayed that way. Dawn's knees trembled, and she had a terrible feeling that she would be with Jesus soon. She took another step in her sister's direction.

"What'd you say?" Henry asked.

"I'm going on vacation with my fr-friends," Dawn said. "Rene and Mona, from the reunion."

That bit of news pushed Henry the rest of the way from angry to pure evil. He bared his teeth and took a deep inhalation through his nose.

"Naw, you ain't," he said. "You need to go put that shit back. We gon' talk."

"It's too late," Dawn said. She took another step, but she was still within punching distance. "We already made plans. It's too late to talk."

Henry dropped the remote and put his hands on the arms of the sofa so he could push himself up. His fingers were long and strong, like talons. His thumbnail was almost completely black from an injury at work. Dawn took another step, but she saw all of this very clearly.

"Sit yo ass down right there," Henry said and pointed to the couch.

"She ain't gotta sit down," Denisha said. "You can't talk to her like she yo child."

Dawn never had backup before, and it was a thrilling yet chilling experience. She knew she had upped the ante by bringing Denisha. Henry had no choice but to fold or add more chips himself.

"You shut yo ugly ass up!" Henry told Denisha. "This ain't got shit to do with you."

Denisha's jaw dropped. "Uh-uhn!" She reached for her sister. "Come on, Dawn. You need to get the hell away from–"

Before Denisha could finish her sentence, Henry leapt from his chair and grabbed hold of Dawn with both hands. His left hand caught a huge lock of hair in the back of her head. His right hand locked onto her triceps, and Dawn's forward progress came to a painful halt.

"*OWW! LET ME GO!*"

She dropped her bags and reached for the back of her head because that's where it hurt the most. Henry pulled her hair so hard, it felt like her skull was being ripped in two.

"*OUCH! HENRY, LET ME GO!*"

Denisha was stunned stiff for a second, but her sister's screams snapped her out of the daze. She rushed forward and grabbed both of Dawn's arms.

"*Let her go!*" Denisha screamed. "*You dumb-ass nigga! Let her go!*"

Dawn was caught in a vicious game of tug-of-war. Henry's grip on her arm was vice-like, and her hair wasn't slipping through his fingers at all.

"*STOP!*" she wailed, at both of them this time. "*STOP! PLEASE! LET ME GO!*"

Denisha did let go because she learned a long time ago that a woman could never fight a grown-ass man. "All right," she said, nodding her head frantically. "I bet you ain't so bad when the police get here."

Tears burst from Denisha's eyes. She clawed through her purse and produced a cellphone. Before she flipped it open, Henry growled and shoved Dawn forward, hard enough to bowl both of the women over.

Dawn scrambled to her feet first, panting and crying, her hair wild like a lost child. She helped Denisha to her feet and pulled her towards the door. But Denisha yanked her arm away. She saw this scene too many times, in reality and in her nightmares, and she was sick of tucking her tail between her legs.

"FORGET YOU, YOU UGLY BASTARD!" she yelled at Henry. *"You're going to jail, nigga! Don't nobody put his hands on my sister! I'ma kill yo ass!"*

She actually tried to go after him, but Dawn grabbed her by the waist and nearly lifted her feet off the ground.

"Come on!" she pleaded. *"Forget him! Just, come on!"*

"Naw, Dawn! Forget this nigga! I can't stand this punk!"

"Please," Dawn begged. "Please, just come on!"

White flames burned behind Denisha's pupils, but she conceded and allowed Dawn to pull her out of the house. They jumped into the car, and Dawn backed out of the driveway going way too fast. By the grace of God she didn't plow into her neighbor's car parked on the curb or mow down a crowd of school-age children playing touch football in the middle of the street.

The following afternoon in Houston, Rene was poised to be the only Finley Sister to leave town without any man problems, but fate would not allow such a thing. Blake drove her down to the boating dock in Galveston, and he couldn't wait until Rene walked away from his car before he messed everything up.

In the past two weeks, Rene gradually forgave him for leaving her in Overbrook Meadows. In retrospect she knew Blake was right about everything: Just because he couldn't attend reunion events all weekend didn't mean he wasn't in love with her. And just because they always made themselves available when it was proper to bring a date didn't mean that was the nexus of their relationship.

The truth was Blake was an all-around great catch. He was smart and devoted and successful. He was black and proud. He was fine and handsome. He was passionate. He was a good listener and a great lover.

Blake drove a sleek, black Navigator, and he jammed a Lil' Wayne CD on the way to the boat dock. Rene didn't care for rap music, but she liked the way Blake got in the zone when he listened to it.

Blake's parents were rich and so were his grandparents. He was a private school, Ivy League brat his whole life. The only time Blake went to the ghetto is when he took the wrong freeway exit, but he nodded his head and tapped his fingers on the steering wheel like he understood every problem Lil' Wayne was singing about.

"You sure are in a good mood," Rene noticed.

"Huh?" He looked over at her casually.

"I said you seem to be in a good mood."

"Aw, it ain't nothing." That was another thing Blake did when he listened to rap music; he tried to act *blacker*.

"Are you gonna miss me?" Rene asked.

"Fuh sho," Blake said. He put his free hand on her thigh and squeezed it comfortingly.

Rene put her hand over his and smiled warmly.

❦

Rene saw her ship in the distance when they got close to the shoreline, and the sight of it made her heart swell in her chest. This wasn't her first cruise, but it was the first one she would take with her sisters. She couldn't wait to get on board.

Blake pulled into the dock with thirty minutes to spare. He hopped out of his truck and started unloading Rene's baggage with what looked like enthusiasm. Rene barely had time to stretch her legs before he had all of her suitcases out of the trunk and a porter was rolling up to help get her things on the boat.

"Wow," Rene commented. "You got somewhere to be?"

"Nah," Blake said. He walked to her and gave her a big hug. "Why do you say that?"

"We're a little early," Rene said. "We could've sat in the car and talked for a minute if you wanted to."

"What's that?"

"We could've…"

Blake's phone started to ring.

"Hold on a sec." Blake pulled his cellular from his pocket and looked at the display. He looked at Rene, and then he turned away from her slightly. "Hello? Oh, hey. Uh… Okay, um, let me call you back, okay? All right. Bye." He disconnected and turned back to his woman. "What was that?"

Rene's eyes narrowed. She wasn't the jealous or confrontational type, but sometimes shit is so obvious…

"Never mind," she said.

Blake dropped his phone back into his pocket and went to help the porter load Rene's luggage onto a cart. He gave the man a ten-dollar bill and tried to give his woman a kiss goodbye. Rene turned her head at the last moment, and Blake's smooch landed on her cheek. He looked into her eyes and frowned.

"Is something wrong?"

"Is that why you're in such a rush to get rid of me?" Rene asked.

"What's that?"

Rene rolled her eyes. She hated doing this. It made her feel weak and insecure, even though she knew she was right. "Was that your girlfriend calling?" she asked. "Is that why you're so happy I'm leaving?"

Blake knitted his eyebrows and then he smiled, as if finally understanding a complex riddle. "Oh, you think…" He reached for his phone. "That was my, did you say girlfriend?" He chuckled. "That was Mark," he said. "We're supposed to go over some numbers later on today." He removed his hand from his pocket but didn't come out with the phone. Instead he put two empty fists on his hips. "Are you, are you serious?"

Rene knew Mark was one of his business partners, but she was still convinced it wasn't Mark who had just called. Blake wouldn't have to turn his back to speak with Mark. And if he really wanted to prove her wrong, all he had to do was show her the last call on his phone.

But then again, Rene wasn't the jealous type, and she never asked to look at his phone before. She never confronted him about *any* phone call that she could remember.

"Never mind," she said and turned to follow the porter into the terminal.

"Wait, Rene," Blake called. "Are you serious? You really don't believe me?"

"I believe you," Rene said, but she didn't stop walking. She did turn and smile at him though. "Have a nice vacation."

Blake's frown intensified. "I'm not going on vacation. You are."

"You get a vacation from me," Rene said and turned her back on him for the last time. Inwardly she hoped Blake would run after her and grab her arm and refuse to let her get on the boat until she saw that it really was Mark on his phone display. She hoped he would chase her down and profess his love once again and *make* her give him a proper hug and a real kiss.

But he never did.

CHAPTER 7
THE OATH OF ROMANCE

Unlike Rene's leisurely boarding at 2:45, Dawn's first experience with a cruise ship was an enormous headache. Their ship, curiously named the *Ecstasy*, was scheduled to cast off from Galveston at exactly 3:30 p.m. Yet Dawn was still on the freeway at 3:45, and she was so frantic, she felt like her head might explode.

Her sister Denisha volunteered to drive her from their mother's house. The ladies took off a full five hours ago, but that was still not enough time. Traffic got bad when they arrived in Galveston, and no amount of nail-biting, head-shaking or foot-stomping would make the endless lines of commuters disperse or speed up for them.

"Come on, come on," Dawn mumbled from the passenger seat. She leaned forward with her hands on the dashboard, her eyes wide and almost tearful.

"I'm going as fast as I can," Denisha said for the umpteenth time.

"Not you," Dawn cried. "I'm talking about *them*! We not gon' make it. *Oh, Lord, we not gon' make it*. All this stuff I bought… All this crap I've been through. Jesus. I can't believe it."

Dawn's right knee bounced uncontrollably. She stared at the freeway exits one at a time, praying their off ramp would be next, but it never was.

"Calm down," Denisha said.

"The boat's supposed to leave at three-thirty!" Dawn reminded her. "It's three-forty-five!"

"Well, I can't go no faster," Denisha said. "Do you want me to take you back home, or what?"

"No." Dawn scooped her cellphone from her lap and checked the display. She didn't have any missed calls. She talked to Rene ten minutes ago, and Rene said she would find whoever was in charge and make sure the boat didn't leave without Dawn. But Dawn knew her friend could only do so much. The Carnival people had deadlines and an obligation to everyone who got there on time.

Dawn felt she'd get a call at any moment, and it would be Rene informing her that the ship was leaving the dock. That phone call would break Dawn's heart more than anything ever had, and she would cry all the way back to Overbrook Meadows.

But the call hadn't come yet, so there was still hope.

At 3:52 Dawn and Denisha saw police lights flashing up ahead, and the traffic slowed even more. A few minutes later Denisha pulled alongside the cause of the traffic jam. A van full of travelers, possibly headed for the same ship, didn't have their load tied down properly, and they lost nearly all of their suitcases in the middle of the freeway. The police shut down two lanes so the embarrassed father could collect his belongings and tie them down again with better care.

"Thanks a lot!" Dawn yelled out of the window as they passed the troublemaker.

"Calm down," Denisha said.

"He made me miss my boat," Dawn whined.

"You said your friend wouldn't let them leave without you."

"She said she would *try*."

"Them Carnival people want all the money they can get," Denisha predicted. "They won't leave you. And the freeway cleared up now. Check it out."

Dawn looked and saw that traffic was back to a normal pace. Denisha pushed her Corsica to seventy miles per hour and, at 3:56, Dawn finally saw their exit.

"That's it!" she screamed. "That's it right there!"

"All right," Denisha said. "Girl, calm yourself. You need to pray some more."

Dawn didn't feel like praying, but that usually meant it was a good time to pray, so she lowered her head and asked the Lord to give her peace and tranquility. She asked for mercy and compassion. And even though she knew it wasn't right, she prayed that the captain of their ship would get diarrhea or some other minor ailment that would delay him from taking his seat in the *Ecstasy's* control room.

She closed the prayer by stating the obvious: *Lord, you know I need this. I need it bad…*

At 4:01 Denisha finally made the last turn onto Carrier Parkway, and Dawn nearly jumped out of the car when she saw a huge cruise ship idling in the distance. She stared starry-eyed out of the window, like a child seeing snow for the first time.

"Is that it?" Denisha asked.

"I don't know," Dawn said. "I hope so."

"It says *Ecstasy*," Denisha informed.

Dawn looked closer, and she saw it, too. "Yeah," she said, smiling for the first time in three hours. "That's it. That's my boat…"

Denisha pulled in next to a huge building that housed the terminal, and Dawn saw that she wasn't the only late arrival. There were dozens of travelers and Carnival employees running—all in the same direction. Before Dawn had to wonder how she would tote her luggage, a homely fellow with long, scraggily hair ran up to the car.

"You need help with your bags, ma'am?"

"Yes!" Dawn jumped out and yanked the trunk open. "I still have time? The boat ain't leaving yet?"

"We're pushing it," the porter informed. "But they're not leaving without you. Do you have your baggage slips?"

Dawn ran back around the car and grabbed a large envelope she kept her Carnival paperwork in. She handed over the tags and threw her head back in relief.

"Thank you, *thank you*, Jesus!"

"You already filled these out?" the porter asked.

"Yes," Dawn said confidently. "Everything's ready."

The porter loaded her things onto his cart and instructed Dawn to go on without him.

"What about my bags?"

"We're going to take them to your room for you," he said. "It's a courtesy."

"Wow. Thanks!" Dawn had never experienced anything like that, but this was just the beginning of her pampering. She turned to give her sister a hug. "Thanks, Denisha. I love you so much!"

"I guess you want me to pick you up, too," Denisha kidded.

"I don't know," Dawn said. "It might be so pretty over there, I won't never come back."

"I'm sure it will be better than that mess you got going on with Henry," Denisha said. "You need to make some decisions while you gone."

"I will," Dawn promised. "Thanks for bringing me."

"Girl, I'd do anything for you," Denisha said, and then she held out her hand, palm up.

Dawn laughed and pulled her billfold from her purse. "I'm so glad you'd do anything for *me*," she said, flipping through crisp twenty dollar bills. "I'd sure hate to think it was all about the money…"

❦

The terminal was packed with confused guests and frustrated employees who instructed people to go here and there. They had areas cordoned off with felt ropes that snaked all the way across the building. But the lines were all gone by now, and Dawn rushed from room to room with few hindrances.

Just when she was starting to wonder where she was in relation to the boat she saw outside, Dawn was ushered into a long corridor that was constructed from different material than the rest of the terminal. When she emerged on the other side, the color scheme was completely different, and Dawn knew she had finally arrived.

"Oh, my God…" She put a hand over her chest and looked around in wonder.

Dawn's first impression was that her cruise ship was *huge*. She was standing in the middle of a lobby that was twice as big as her home. As far as she could see, there was beauty and entertainment, shiny chandeliers, bars, and stores and even a grand piano.

The second thing Dawn noticed was how *packed* the ship was. There were people walking all around her. Everyone was dressed casually in shorts and tee shirts, and they all looked as excited as Dawn felt. The Carnival crew stood out in their black slacks with white shirts, and they were all smiling brightly, directing folks to their cabins so they could grab their lifejackets and head for orientation in the Starlight Lounge.

Dawn checked her paperwork and saw that her cabin was on the L (Lido) Deck, and she headed in that direction with the biggest grin imaginable. Everything still had the ethereal quality of a dream, but she knew it really was happening. She was so giddy she felt like running, or at least skipping, but there was enough of that going on already; a lot of vacationers brought their children with them.

The hallways narrowed considerably when she got to the sleeping quarters. Dawn found room L17 with no assistance. Her key card opened the door with a buzz and a flashing green light. Dawn took a deep breath when she turned the doorknob, and she squealed uncontrollably when she walked into her very own room.

There wasn't anything special about Dawn's cabin; just one bed, a small dresser, a closet, and a rest room, but still this was a very special place. There were two port holes on one of the walls where she could watch the sun disappear into the ocean after they set sail. Her bed was a queen-size, and she wouldn't have to share it with *anyone*. She wouldn't have to share her bathroom or the television remote, either.

But most of all Dawn's room filled her with a sense of *freedom* that most people wouldn't understand. For the next five days she was free from work, free from her raggedy car, free from cooking and cleaning and laundry and toilet-scrubbing. She wished Tim and Luther could see this place, but she was free from her boys, too. And best of all she was free from the grumpy old grouch.

Dawn's eyes filled with tears, but it wasn't a sad cry. If it was possible to *die* from happiness, Dawn felt she was on her last leg.

"*Hey, girl!*"

Dawn turned and saw Rene standing in the doorway. Rene wore beige canvas shorts with a pink tee-shirt. She had a loud orange life preserver draped over her shoulder.

"Hey!" Dawn ran to give her a hug.

"What's wrong?" Rene asked, noticing her tears. "You don't like your room?"

"No," Dawn said with a sniffle. "I mean, *yes*. It's perfect. Everything's so, it's so perfect. I don't think I can ever thank you enough."

"Just have a good time," Rene said. "That's all the thanks I need. Grab your lifejacket so we can go find Mona. Orientation's about to start."

"You haven't seen Mona yet?"

"No, but knowing her she probably has a man in her room by now."

Dawn laughed and found her very own lifejacket hanging in the closet. There was even a safe in there so she didn't have to carry anything but her room key. The Carnival people thought of everything!

❧

Mona did not have a man in her room, but she was checking for potential bedmates already. And so far she was largely disappointed. The majority of people they saw on their way to orientation were Caucasian, and most of the brothers appeared to be with their wives.

"It's gonna be slim pickings up in here," Mona told her cohorts. "I might have to lower my standards a little."

"Or maybe you could *not* have sex with anybody," Rene suggested, but Mona rolled her eyes at that.

After orientation, which mostly included instructions on how to use their lifejackets, the crowd was

lead outside where they had to listen to another lecture about the many lifeboats mounted on the side of the ship.

"If it ever comes down to it," Mona whispered to her friends, "none of this is going to matter. How are they going to *assign* me a boat? Shit, I'm jumping on the first one I can, and I'll be damned if some snotty-nosed *baby* is going before me!"

Dawn and Rene got a laugh out of that, but they knew Mona was dead serious.

With the safety lectures out of the way, the vacationers were set lose to unpack, explore the ship, or do whatever else they pleased for the rest of the day. The first thing Dawn wanted to do was look at the water. She didn't get to see the boat pull away from Galveston because of orientation, but it was never too late to watch the ocean.

Dawn took her friends to the ship's bow, and her mouth fell open when she saw the awesome view. The sun was still bright in the sky, but the temperature was a mild seventy-seven degrees. The winds were strong at the front of the boat, and the water was perfectly blue. There was nothing in their path but ocean and clouds.

"This is so nice…."

"It's beautiful, isn't it?" Rene said.

"It's like a dream," Dawn said. "I've never seen anything like it."

"Wait till it's nighttime," Rene said.

"What's it like then?"

"It's like, it's like sitting on top of a mountain in the middle of the desert," Rene said. "Have you ever looked out and as far as you could see there are no street lights, just darkness and stars?"

Dawn shook her head. "I can't even imagine."

"Then that's what we're doing," Rene said. "Tonight we're going to come right here to check out the view."

"And we'll bring some drinks," Mona said. "Everything's better with alcohol."

Dawn didn't know if that was true, and she wasn't a big drinker, but for the next five days, she was down with whatever her friends were down with.

"Cool," Rene said. "Now I got to get unpacked."

❧

On the way back to her room, Dawn saw that there was luggage piled outside of everyone's door rather than taken inside like she expected. Always a child of the ghetto, Dawn's first thought was that someone could easily steal her belongings. But when she got to her cabin everything was as it should be. The only problem was Dawn's suitcases were a lot older than everyone else's. She quickly dragged them inside so no one would know there was a poor person on board.

Dawn tried to unpack, but she was so giddy it was hard to keep her mind on the task. She plopped down on her bed and rolled around like a child. She flipped through all of the channels on her television until she found one that played hip-hop and R&B videos. Dawn

pulled a few things from her suitcase while singing with Melanie Fiona, and then she ran to Rene's room when she could hold her excitement no longer.

Rene wasn't done packing, and she was a lot less cheery than her old friend.

"What's wrong?" Dawn asked.

"I can't find my camcorder," Rene said. Her suitcases were open on the bed, and she had clothes strewn everywhere.

"Someone stole it?" Dawn asked. "They went through your bags?"

"I didn't have it in my bag," Rene said with a sigh. "I had it tied to the side of that suitcase." She pointed, and there was clearly no camera affixed there.

"Somebody who works here stole it?" Dawn guessed.

"It could've been anybody," Rene said. "Our bags have been sitting outside the door for God knows how long. Anybody could've snatched it up and kept going. Or maybe I left it in the car… Our cellphones don't work now, so I can't call Blake to ask him."

"Did you report it?" Dawn asked.

"Not yet," Rene said. "I was about to."

"Come on," Dawn said. "I'll go with you. Do you want to go get Mona?"

"No," Rene said with a chuckle. "I don't need her causing a big scene. You know she'll go from filling out a report to cursing somebody out in ten seconds flat…"

❧

The ladies went down to the guest services desk in the grand atrium and watched a professional musician play the piano while they waited in line. The attendant apologized for Rene's loss and promised to initiate an investigation for the missing camcorder.

Rene didn't put too much stock into that. If a Carnival employee took it, they would never risk their job by admitting to it. And it wasn't possible to search every cabin on the ship to find out if a guest lifted it.

"Oh, well," Rene said with a weak smile. "I'm not going to let it ruin my vacation."

"It would probably ruin mine," Dawn admitted. "Those things cost, like, three hundred dollars."

"At least I didn't lose it *after* I had a bunch of stuff on it." Rene was always looking for the bright side.

"Are you sure you didn't have any old videos on it?" Dawn asked. "You know, some *nasty* stuff?"

"Definitely not," Rene said with a grin. "I erased those on the way down here."

Dawn was glad her friend wasn't too upset because she wouldn't be able to enjoy herself if her girls didn't have a good time. She and Rene went to fetch Mona from her cabin on the Verandah level, and the threesome embarked on a full tour of the ship. Dawn knew this was a *luxury cruise*, but that term didn't fully register until she saw it with her own eyes.

Among other sights, there was a swimming pool, a spa, a jogging track, and a tennis court on the boat. There were bars everywhere, a fitness center, and lounges for late-night comedy shows, karaoke, and even Vegas-style musicals.

"They got everything you could ever want," Dawn said.

"Even some *men*," Mona said. "I saw a few who just might be worth my time."

"I wasn't paying attention to no men," Dawn admitted.

"You better keep your eyes open," Mona recommended. "You never know what you can find on this cruise. Don't forget: *Whatever happens on the boat, stays on the boat.*"

Dawn hadn't forgotten that because she heard it three times since their lifejacket training. But Dawn had no intentions of losing her morals on this vacation, so for now, that motto meant nothing to her.

❧

The girls had pizza and hotdogs for dinner. They got three bahama mamas and sipped them at the poolside while watching kids and adults splash around without a care in the world.

At sunset the Finley Sisters ordered margaritas and took them to the upper deck so they could sit and watch the stars together. As Rene promised, it was truly a sight to behold. The sheer blackness was something you could never see on land.

Dawn sipped her drink pleasantly. This was the best time she had ever spent with her friends. She was already getting tipsy, and after all of the stress she experienced earlier that day, Dawn knew she'd be sleepy soon.

"This was a *long* day," she mused. "I can't wait to curl up in my blankets."

"It's only eight-thirty," Mona said. "People are gonna be partying until two, three in the morning."

"Not me," Dawn said with a satisfied smile. "I doubt if I'll make it past eleven. It's good to sit out here with you guys, though. Back when we was in school, I never thought we'd be on a cruise together one day."

"I didn't know it would be a cruise," Rene said, "but I always knew we would still be together. Do you remember when we met in Mrs. McIntosh's class?"

Dawn did remember. That was in the fifth grade. Rene was the prettiest back then, and Mona was always the loudest and most confident. Dawn was as skinny as Rene in those days, but that didn't last long.

"I loved Mrs. McIntosh," Dawn said. "Do you remember when we had that sleepover at your house?" she asked Mona.

"Mmm-hmm," Mona said. "That was in the eighth grade. Everybody went to sleep before us, and we put Rosalyn's hand in a bowl of warm water, but she didn't do nothing."

"Yes, she did," Rene remembered. "She woke up and wanted to fight when she saw what we were doing."

"She didn't want to fight," Mona recalled. "She was crying."

"She was crying because you yelled at her and told her to go back to sleep!" Dawn said, and they all laughed.

"Do y'all remember graduation?" Rene asked. "We went to that party at Chris' house."

"He bought those nasty *Coors*," Dawn recalled. "I still can't drink beer today because of that fool!"

"Do y'all remember how we got stuck over there?" Rene asked.

"You locked your keys in the car," Mona said.

"I had to call my mama," Rene agreed, "and I knew she was gon' be mad because we were out so late and we smelled like beer."

"But she wasn't mad," Dawn remembered. "She was just happy we stuck together."

"We always stuck together," Mona said, and Dawn's eyes lit up.

"Hey, do y'all remember what we were talking about while we was waiting for Rene's mama to show up?"

The girls thought for a second, but no one could come up with anything.

"We was sitting on the front porch," Dawn prompted. "We was watching the stars. It was a pretty night, something like this…"

The girls looked out onto the waters, and something clicked in Rene's head.

"We made a vow," she said. "We promised to always be friends forever."

"I remember that," Mona said, her smile big and toothy. "We said that no matter what happened, we would always be there for each other."

Rene chuckled and then looked away uneasily. "Guess we kinda forgot about that."

"It's not too late," Mona said. "We're here for each other now. We can still keep that promise, if we want."

"I want to," Dawn said right away.

"Me, too," Rene said.

Mona laughed. "Man, look at us! We sound like a Toni Morrison book."

"The *Ya-Ya Sisterhood*!" Rene said, and she laughed, too.

"Wait," Dawn said with a finger in the air. "I got something else…" She giggled.

"What?" Mona asked.

"We made *another* promise that night," Dawn said. "Actually, it was more like an *oath*…"

"Aw, shit," Mona said.

"What?" Rene said.

"You don't remember?" Dawn asked.

"No," Rene said. "Tell me."

"*The Oath of Romance*," Mona recalled, and Rene's eyes widened.

"Whoa," Rene said. The breeze stirred softly through her hair. "I hadn't thought about that in *years*."

"Me neither," Dawn said.

"So who fulfilled that one?" Mona asked. "Which one of y'all lived love to the fullest?"

"Don't look at me," Rene said and lowered her gaze. "What about you?"

"I'm asking *y'all*," Mona said.

"You took the oath, too," Rene said.

"What about you?" Mona asked Dawn. "Are you and Henry living love to the fullest?"

Dawn almost choked on her drink. "Uck, um, no."

"For real?" Mona pressed.

"No," Dawn said, her smile completely gone now. "Not at all."

"What about you and Blake?" Mona asked Rene. "I know y'all in love."

"Uh-uhn." Rene shook her head. "Me and Blake were never really *in love* like that. And earlier today, I found out he's cheating on me."

Dawn's jaw dropped. "Nuh-uhn."

"For real," Rene said, and after a few moments, she and Dawn looked at Mona expectantly.

"What?"

"What about you?" Dawn asked. "Do you live love to the fullest, or what?"

Mona grinned and shook her head. "Well, I hate to break it to y'all, but yeah, I do. My man pleases me anytime I want it. I mean, just yesterday he went down on me for so long, I thought he had a snorkel or something." She laughed.

"So you love him?" Dawn asked.

Mona frowned. "Naw, I don't *love* him. I mean, he cool. He asked me to marry him, but we ain't got it like that."

"Then you haven't fulfilled the oath, either," Rene stated. "It wasn't about someone pleasing you *sexually*. We swore that we would find true love and live happily ever after and never settle. We said we would find the man of our dreams."

"That shit doesn't happen," Mona said. "I get what I can get and then move around when I'm done. I'm not finna fall in love with some dumb nigga."

"That's like me," Rene said. "After Terrence, I wouldn't never give my heart to nobody. Blake was the closest I came to it, but I never really gave my heart to him, either. I knew he would try to break it, and I was right."

"Dang, we all a mess," Dawn said. "None of us did what we said we was gon' do."

"We was just kids," Mona said. "That stuff doesn't matter."

"Yes, it does," Rene said. "Just like we said we would be there for each other, and we didn't do that. Those promises do matter. All of it matters because what we wished for back then was *real*. We were innocent, and our dreams were pure."

"Damn, you're talking like a Hallmark card *for real*," Mona said. She tried to sound indifferent, but Dawn saw her chin quiver a little.

"Let's renew our promises," Dawn suggested. "*Both of them.*"

The girls looked around doubtfully. Rene was the first to stick out her hand.

"Okay. I'm in."

Dawn put her hand on top of Rene's, and after awhile Mona followed suit.

"This is stupid," Mona said.

"No, it's not," Rene said. "It wasn't stupid then, and it's not stupid now."

A few more seconds passed and Mona sighed. "All right," she told Dawn. "This was your idea, so you lead us through it."

"Okay," Dawn said, her lovely smile back in place. "Do y'all swear that we will always be friends, and we will always be there for each other?"

"I do," Rene said.

"Me, too," Mona said, and she shivered. "Damn, I got goose bumps."

"Me, too," Rene said, and she shuddered as well.

"All right, I promise, too," Dawn said. "Now, do both of y'all promise to live love to the fullest and never settle for somebody who ain't making you happy? Do you promise to find the man of your dreams?"

"I promise," Rene said, her large eyes glistening.

Mona gave this one some serious thought before saying, "I got a better chance of finding a leprechaun, but I promise... I guess."

"I promise, too," Dawn said, and the mood was so solemn, she felt they all had a good chance of pulling it off this time.

CHAPTER 8
PICK ONE

True to her word, Dawn's eyelids started to get heavy at ten-thirty, and she was ready to retreat to her cabin twenty minutes later. Rene and Mona went with her, but they planned to change into something sexy and explore the ship's nightlife for a few more hours.

"I still can't believe how big this boat is," Dawn said, heading down a third flight of stairs.

"We can take the elevator next time," Mona replied.

"No, I'm cool going *down*," Dawn said. "I'll probably take the elevators if I'm going up, though. Thank y'all again for paying for my ticket. I know I never would've gone somewhere like this if it wasn't for y'all."

"You and Henry don't go anywhere nice?" Rene asked.

Dawn shook her head. "Not even."

"What's your relationship with him like?" Rene wondered. "You got a little sensitive up there when we were talking about that oath."

"I didn't get sensitive."

"You did have a pretty strong opinion," Rene said.

"For real," Mona agreed. "You was like, '*Hell, naw, we ain't in love!*'"

Dawn forced a smile. "I didn't say that."

"Not those exact words," Mona said. "But you didn't sound like you like him at all."

"It's fine," Dawn insisted.

"We're your girls," Rene pressed. "You can talk to us about it if you want."

"Ain't nothing to talk about," Dawn said. "Henry, he just a man. Ain't nothing bad about him, but ain't nothing special about him, either. He not the romantic type, I can tell you that. He's not gonna bring me flowers and chocolates–"

"Not even on your birthday?" Rene asked.

"No," Dawn admitted. "Not even on my birthday. But that don't mean he's a bad person. That's just who he is."

"But he does treat you right?" Rene went on.

"He treats me just fine," Dawn said, happy they had arrived at her cabin. "Now I'm going to bed. You two have a good time tonight."

"You sure you don't want to come?" Mona asked.

"No, I'm good. I'm gonna sleep like a baby," Dawn said. She yawned lazily, her eyes half closed. "I just wish I could feel the boat rocking. We riding so smooth, it feels like we're on land."

"I'm going to have my bed rocking pretty soon," Mona predicted and continued down the hallway. Rene and Dawn looked after her and laughed.

"Thanks again, for real," Dawn said when Mona was out of sight.

"Girl, you don't have to keep thanking me," Rene told her.

"But this is the nicest thing that anyone's ever done for me." Dawn giggled and then sang merrily: *"It isn't every day—good fortune comes my way…"*

"Damn," Rene said. "You must be happy if you're singing Ebenezer Scrooge! Or you're drunk!"

Dawn inserted her keycard and the door opened up for her. *"…And if I had a bugle I would blow it…"*

"Goodnight, Dawn!" Rene pushed her into the room playfully. She headed for her own cabin giggling and shaking her head.

For her first night on the boat, Mona put on a sleek red dress that exposed a lot of yummy flesh around the chest and back areas. The dress ran out of fabric just a few inches past her butt, and Mona's bare legs looked good enough to eat a full-course meal off of.

Rene wore a black cocktail dress that was form-fitting and a little longer than Mona's. Rene complimented her outfit with a pearl necklace and matching bracelets. Her look was a bit classier than her friend's, but Rene was also fine enough to cause a stampede at a penitentiary.

Together these women were a force to be reckoned with, and Rene liked how all of the married women cut their eyes at them and all of the married men tried their best to sneak a peek without alerting their spouses.

"Look at them hating," Mona said about no one in particular. "If their man comes up missing, you already know they're coming straight to *my* door."

Rene laughed.

The girls headed for the casino, but they had no particular destination in mind. Rene wanted to get a picture next to the blackjack table. Mona spotted a fully operational Rolls Royce parked on the Lido Deck, and she thought that would make an even better backdrop.

"Ooh, take a picture of me in front of this car."

Rene had her digital camera strap looped around her wrist, and she eagerly obliged. "Now get one of me," she said and passed the camera to Mona.

Rene struck a low-rider model pose and laughed when Mona snapped the shot.

"Let's get one together," Mona said, and she looked around for a bystander to help them out. Luckily there was a crowd of mostly men who had slowed to watch them. A chunky Hispanic fellow threw up his hand.

"I'll do it."

"Thanks." Mona flashed him an awesome smile and gave him the camera. "Just push that button on top," she said and positioned his finger accordingly.

"Oh, okay…" The good Samaritan began to sweat visibly, and Mona teased him a little more when she turned and headed for the antique car. Her booty bounced sensually with each step, and the cameraman swallowed hard. His Adam's apple bobbed like a fishing float.

"All right," Mona said. She threw an arm over Rene's shoulder and they both smiled.

The stranger snapped the shot while his friends grinned wolfishly in the background. All of his buddies were Hispanic, except for one Caucasian guy. Rene thought a couple of them were cute, but she wouldn't date them. She knew Mona wouldn't, either, but you couldn't tell by the way she performed.

"Thanks a lot!" Mona retrieved the camera and gave her helper a quick hug. "You're such a sweetie!"

His friends looked on with envy, and the cameraman's cheeks turned red.

"Any, anytime," he managed.

The best friends continued on their way, and Rene burst into laughter after a few steps.

"Girl, why'd you do that?"

"Do what?" Mona asked innocently.

"Play with that boy's head like that."

"I didn't play with his head," Mona replied. "He wanted to take our picture. Didn't you see how happy he was?"

"Yeah. As happy as a dog with a bone."

Mona laughed. "I probably made his day. Hell, I might have made his whole *cruise*."

"Probably so," Rene agreed, still chuckling. "But what's in it for you?"

"I don't know. What's in it for *you*?" Mona countered.

"What do you mean, *me*?"

"I mean you didn't go throw on a pair of overalls, either," Mona pointed out. "You know you like attention. You got your little booty poking out."

"My booty's not little," Rene said with a roll of her neck.

"Mine looks better than yours," Mona said confidently.

"Yeah, you wish."

"Um, excuse me," Mona grabbed the arm of the closest guy and pulled him over. "Who's booty do you think is bigger, mine or hers?"

She turned to show off her assets and Rene almost fell out laughing. But she was starting to get used to her friend's antics. Back in high school, Mona was the same way. It felt good to be around such a free spirit again.

The gentleman Mona chose to be the judge was dark-skinned and in his mid-sixties. And he looked plenty interested in the competition.

"Uh, I don't know," he said. "I can't see hers." He nodded at Rene and she shook her head.

"Uh-uhn!" she told Mona. "I'm not showing him my ass."

"He's gonna see it as soon as you walk away," Mona informed her.

"Him looking at it and me showing it are two different things."

"Sounds like you're conceding," Mona said, her bum still exposed for the judge. "I win."

"Never that," Rene said and half-turned to expose her rump.

"*Damn!*" the judge called. He rubbed his eyes comically. "My, my, my…"

"Which one?" Mona asked.

"Well, I got to say they're both *real* nice," the judge said. "But I'll have to give it to her." He pointed to Rene and she snapped her fingers in Mona's face.

"Ha! Told you!"

"Whatever," Mona said with a sassy roll of her eyes. "He don't know what he's talking about."

"I can, I can probably get a better idea if I can, uh, touch 'em," the old fogey said.

"Man, get out of here!" Mona waved him off and she and Rene continued towards the casino.

"Don't get mad at him because my ass looks better than yours," Rene said.

"Yeah, well, I bet I'll get laid before you," Mona replied.

"I'm not getting in that competition," Rene said. "Dang, I can't believe you still got such a big problem with losing."

"I hate to lose," Mona admitted.

"Even against me?"

"Yes."

"Even over some stupid booty contest?"

"I. Hate. To. Lose," Mona said, and she was starting to look pissed for real.

"Girl, get over here." Rene grabbed her arm and led her to the Society Bar. "Let's get some drinks in you before steam starts to shoot out of your ears."

After a couple of cosmopolitans Mona was feeling better about her loss, and Rene was feeling some uncomfortable nostalgia. Whenever she got tipsy, Rene thought about Blake because of all the laced punch bowls at the office parties she attended with him over the last two years.

But Blake was nowhere around. Rene wondered if he was in the arms of his other woman—and that was the absolute *last* thing she wanted to think about during her vacation.

"So, are you really planning to sleep with one of these dudes?" she asked her friend.

"Yep," Mona said. She downed the rest of her drink and gingerly made it to a standing position. Her dress took a hiking trip northwards when she took a seat at the bar, and a handful of guys watched in awe as she pulled it back down.

Rene got off of her barstool as well. "Where you going?"

"These drinks are expensive," Mona said. "I need to find somebody to treat me for the rest of the night."

"You don't have to look too far," Rene said. "Everybody in here is looking at you."

"How you know they're not looking at you?" Mona asked. "You the one with the better ass."

"Yeah, you're right about that," Rene said with a grin. "But I already know that if a man buys me drinks, he'll want to follow me to my room later."

"What's wrong with that?"

"I don't see how you can do it."

"Do what?" Mona asked. The ladies were walking now, and Rene could definitely feel the ocean beneath them.

"Is the boat rocking?"

"That's the alcohol," Mona said.

"Oh. Well, I was saying I don't know how you can sleep with somebody you don't even know," Rene said.

"It's easy," Mona replied. "As long as they got a dick, and they're clean, and their breath doesn't stink, the rest is just biology. We ain't no different than squirrels and rabbits."

Rene frowned. "Yeah, we are. We're a lot different."

"Well, we're on a boat in the middle of the ocean," Mona reminded. "It's not like we're going to see these people again. Don't you ever get a wild hair up your ass?"

"Sometimes," Rene admitted.

"You'll have a lot more fun in life if you just run with it," Mona advised. "So as far as this vacation is concerned, anything goes."

"Anything?"

"Well, not if they're *disgusting*," Mona clarified.

"But you'll sleep with any of these regular-looking dudes?"

"Yep."

"I don't believe you."

"Pick one," Mona said.

Rene laughed. "What?"

"Go ahead. Pick one," Mona said. "I'll show you how The Seductress gets down."

"*The Seductress?*"

"I got a tattoo and everything."

"You got a 'seductress' tattoo? Uh-uhn. Let me see it."

"Naw, I'm just kidding," Mona said. "But I'ma get one, though."

"Yeah, right," Rene said, chuckling.

"Are you going to pick one or not?"

"All right," Rene said. "What about that guy?" she nodded towards and average Joe headed in their direction.

"Uhn-uhn," Mona said. "I can't do the beard."

"What's wrong with beards?"

"I just don't like 'em. They itchy and dirty. *Ugh!*" She shuddered.

"Okay," Rene said. "What about him?" She nodded at another gentleman.

"Hell, no!" Mona said. "I'm not gonna sleep with some nasty *fat man.*"

"You said *anybody.*"

"Anybody *within reason,*" Mona clarified. "Don't try to hook me up with somebody you wouldn't sleep with yourself."

With that guideline in mind, Rene looked around a while longer until she spotted a handsome gentleman sitting alone at the Metro bar. "Okay. What about him?"

Mona scrutinized the prospect and narrowed her eyes. "He look all right, but I don't like them shoes."

"What?" Rene shook her head. "Now you're just being picky."

"All right, all right," Mona said. "Come on."

Mona led the way to the bar, and they took a seat right next to her sponsor for the evening. He was a fair-skinned man of medium height and build. He had short, cropped hair and a thin moustache and goatee. He wore white Dockers with a red golf shirt. His loafers were imitation leather, but overall Rene thought he looked nice—a little square, though. He reminded her of a school teacher.

Mona's victim couldn't help but notice when she took a seat next to him, but he looked away nervously, lest she accuse him of ogling.

"Don't be shy," Mona told him.

The stranger looked up with a start. "Um, excuse me?"

"I said *don't be shy*," Mona repeated. "My name is Mona. What's yours?"

"I'm, uh, I'm Dwayne."

"Are you sure?" Mona teased.

"Uh…" He looked down at his beer and then met her eyes reluctantly. "Yes, my name is Dwayne."

His lack of confidence was an immediate turn-off. Under normal circumstances Mona would've gone about her business, but this interaction was for instructional purposes, so she pushed forward.

"Who you here with, Dwayne?"

"My family; my uncle and my cousins."

"Is it a family reunion?"

"No."

"You didn't bring your girlfriend with you?"

He shook his head. "Uh-uhn."

Could you be any more boring? Mona wondered. She waited a couple of beats, but he didn't say anything. That was fine with Mona. Taking charge was something she absolutely *loved* to do.

"I want a drink," she said. "Will you buy me a shot?"

Dwayne's eyes widened, and he reached for his pocket. "Sure. What do you, what kind do you want?"

"I don't know." Mona turned to Rene. "What do you want to drink?"

"I don't know," Rene said with a chuckle. She sat on Mona's right. She no longer had a clear view of the mark, but she knew he was trying to figure out what the hell was going on.

"Tequila?" Mona asked.

"Okay," Rene said.

Mona turned back to her new friend. "We want tequila shots. Can you get one for my girl, too?"

"Um, okay," Dwayne said. He produced his key card, which doubled as a credit card anywhere on the ship, and the bartender appeared with a big smile on his face.

"What can I get you guys?"

"Two tequila shots," Dwayne said. "For the, for the lovely ladies."

"Aww, you think I'm lovely?" Mona said with a well-choreographed batting of her eyes.

"Sure I do," Dwayne said. "You're very beautiful."

"Ooh, I'd better watch you," Mona said and placed a hand on his thigh. "You'll probably charm the panties right off me."

149

Dwayne's mouth fell open. He cleared his throat and swallowed roughly.

"Could you make mine a double?" Mona asked the bartender, her eyes locked on Dwayne's the whole time. "Is it all right if I get a double?" she asked him.

Dwayne nodded absently. "Yea, yes. Anything you want…"

∽⚬∾

Forty minutes later Rene and Mona had consumed three shots apiece, but Dwayne couldn't care less about the fifty dollars charged to his room card. Only once in a million years is a guy lucky enough to attract two beautiful, voluptuous, and drunken women. Dwayne didn't know if it was the boat, his cologne, or the drinks, but he did know that the woman called *Mona* was inexplicably attracted to him, and this was turning into the best night of his life.

Dwayne had a raging boner, which was usually cause for embarrassment in a setting like this, but Mona didn't mind at all. In fact she had put her hand in his lap a dozen times already and sought out his erection with no shame. Dwayne felt he was just one pick-up line away from sealing the deal, but he didn't even have to do that.

The bartender came to take orders for a fourth set of shots, and Mona waved him off. She said something to her friend, and they laughed, and then she turned and fixed her inebriated eyes on Dwayne.

"So, are we going to screw, or what?"

Dwayne's heart shot up in his throat, and he could barely articulate his response.

"Yes." He tried to sound like Barry White, but his voice cracked, and Dwayne sounded more like Mickey Mouse. But even that wasn't a deterrent. Mona's smile didn't falter at all. She slipped off of her stool and leaned on the bar to steady herself. Her skirt was so short, Dwayne caught a brief glimpse of what was either a naked bottom or G-string clad booty cheeks, and he nearly shot his load right then.

"You ready to go?" Mona asked her friend. She laughed and said she was.

❧

Dwayne thought he was on the verge of one of those fabled *three-ways*, but the ladies walked (mostly stumbled) to the quiet girl's cabin, and she said she was going to bed.

"See you tomorrow," Mona said.

"Bye," her friend replied. "Y'all have fun!" And then she closed the door and Dwayne was left standing there with just Mona. She threw her arm around his neck for support.

"Where's your cabin?" she asked with a hiccup.

"On the Atlantic Deck."

"Is that up or down?" Mona asked. "I can't do the stairs."

"It's down," Dwayne said.

"Well, let's go, cowboy."

Dwayne's smile was as bright as a jack-o-lantern's, but he toned it down because there were other people in the hallway, and he didn't want to look like a pervert or a date-rapist. He knew he was only moderately handsome, and no one would believe this *goddess* initiated their contact and was the true aggressor.

With all of the laughter and stumbling into walls, Dwayne didn't think they would ever make it to his cabin, but they did, and Mona's demeanor changed drastically once they got inside. Dwayne expected to deposit her on the bed and ravage her thoroughly until breakfast time, but Mona was nowhere near as tipsy as he thought she was.

She wouldn't let him turn off the lights. She wouldn't let him undress her. She wouldn't even let him fondle her breasts until he produced a three-pack of condoms from his suitcase. And even then, things didn't go as Dwayne envisioned. Mona stripped him down and applied the condom herself, but she wouldn't yield an inch when Dwayne tried to guide her face towards his erection.

"Uh, what are you doing?"

"Oh, I thought, maybe, you know…"

"Uh-uhn." She shook her head. "Never that."

Mona backed towards the bed and took a seat. Dwayne was disappointed, but this was still a dream come true. He followed her with a dopey grin pasted on his face, and she allowed him to slide her panties off. Dwayne saw that her pubic hair was shaved low and neatly. Her labia was glistening and inviting. It was like a magnet to his mouth. He dropped to his knees and went in for a taste, but she stopped him again.

"Uh-uhn."

"Huh?"

"You got a dental dam?" Mona asked.

Dwayne shook his head in confusion. "What's that?"

"Plastic wrap?" Mona offered.

"No. But I'm clean. I don't have anything."

"Sorry," Mona said. "I don't get down like that."

By then Dwayne sensed his date wasn't drunk at all, and he tried to wrap his mind around everything that happened in the last couple of hours. But oral or no oral, Mona was still as hot as a habañero, and he couldn't wait to dive in. He mounted her like a gorilla, and damned if she didn't stop him *again*.

"Roll over," she said.

"Huh?"

"On your back," Mona instructed. She pushed him in the direction she wanted, and Dwayne yielded to her will, more out of surprise than anything else.

When she got him in the desired position, Mona climbed on top and pulled her dress above her waist. She eased down onto his manhood, and Dwayne temporarily forgot how strange this encounter was. Mona's juice box was warm and moist, and Dwayne quickly determined she was the best he ever had. He reached for her bare ass (Mona did allow this), and he held on for dear life as she began to pound and buck, her torso whipping like a belly dancer.

Dwayne's penis was more wide than it was long, and Mona took him in fully, her ass slapping his thighs audibly with each pump. Her fingernails gripped his chest like handle bars.

"Oh!" she moaned. "Goddamn, nigga! Hit that shit! *Move your hips, man!*"

Dwayne already knew there was something *not right* about this woman, but now he knew this was a dream. Not only was Mona terrifyingly aggressive, but she was on top telling *him* to hit it harder. This was ludicrous. It was fantastic. She wasn't a woman at all. She was a tigress. She had to be a succubus.

But by then Dwayne was under her spell, and he was powerless to refuse her in anyway. He timed the locomotion of her hips and slammed in as hard as he could at the apex of her thrust. He thought she would cry out in pain, but Mona threw her head back and growled angrily.

"Yeah, nigga! Come on! Come on! *Do that shit!*"

Jesus Christ! Dwayne was in over his head, but he kept pumping because this was still the best lay he had had in the last decade. He thought that if he could somehow wear Mona out, he could take control of the situation. He would make her take that dress *completely* off, and he would play with her melons and slap her ass and hit it from the back too. And she'd be so whipped, she'd let him suck her clit all night.

But unfortunately for Dwayne, none of this would come to pass.

After a couple of minutes Mona's lovemaking became harder and faster. Dwayne felt she was going to cum, so he plunged harder and deeper, and her explosion felt like a wolverine clamped onto his dick. Dwayne screamed just as loudly as Mona did—hers a shriek of pleasure (his a wail of pain)—and after a while her hips slowed and then graciously stopped altogether.

She looked down at him with her hair hanging in his face. Her smile was maniacal like the Joker. Sweat glistened on her neck and chest. The room was filled with the scents of their sex.

"Damn, Dwayne, you got a short, *fat* dick!"

Dwayne didn't know if that was a compliment or an insult, so he forced a smile and tried to sound as cocky as her. "It gets the job done."

"No, *I* get the job done," Mona said with a cackle, and she gingerly climbed off of him one leg at a time.

Dwayne sensed he'd been had, but he tried to roll her onto her back anyway. As expected, Mona resisted with the strength of a very sober woman, and she easily made it to her feet.

"Sorry, Dwayne. I gotta go."

"But, but I didn't even cum," he whined.

"That ain't my fault," Mona said. She pulled her dress down and combed her hair straight with her fingers. "I was there, and you were there," she said, just barely out of breath. "We both had the same opportunity."

"What are…are you serious?"

"Yes, I'm serious. I'm going to bed."

"Wait!" Dwayne almost got up to stop her, but Mona—if that was even her real name—stepped into her shoes and made it to the door in a couple of seconds. She pulled it open, and Dwayne yanked the sheets over his lap so no one would see him sitting there wearing only a sticky condom.

"I can't believe this shit," he muttered.

"G'night, Dwayne." Mona disappeared through the doorway and closed it behind herself.

"*Sonofabitch!*" Dwayne muttered. He was pissed, but this wasn't the first time he was left in a lonely room with a hard dick and no woman in sight. Dwayne was resourceful, and he would not go to sleep with blue balls. He still had his memories. Plus, in her haste, Mona left behind something even more valuable. Dwayne stared in disbelief for a few seconds, and then he scrambled to the floor and retrieved the lacy, G-string panties.

Hello!

Dwayne brought the underwear to his face and inhaled the wonderful scents. And, because she wouldn't let him have a taste earlier, he ran his tongue along the crotch of the panties and shuddered in ecstasy. His penis was still hard and pulsating.

With a delightful smile, Dwayne took the panties to the bed and snatched his Jergen's lotion from the nightstand. This still had the potential to be a great night after all.

CHAPTER 9
PURPLE SPOTS

Dawn woke up early on the second day of the cruise feeling totally refreshed and well-rested, and that was remarkable. She usually found it hard to sleep in a new environment, but that was not the case on the *Ecstasy*. Dawn wondered how long her friends continued their partying without her last night. Mona said she wanted to get laid, and Dawn couldn't wait to hear if she accomplished that X-rated goal.

Dawn dressed quickly in a new pair of denim shorts with a bright yellow tee shirt. It was still before 7 a.m. when she got done with her hair and makeup, so Dawn took a solo trip to the upper deck so she could get a few pictures of the sunrise. When she got there, she saw that a handful of other vacationers had the same idea. Dawn leaned on the railing with them and snapped a dozen shots that were beautiful enough to make into a postcard.

It was a pleasant 63 degrees that morning. The soft saltwater breeze was absolutely delightful. One of the guests pointed out a school of flying fish skimming across the ocean's surface, and Dawn watched them until they were completely out of sight. She knew she was blessed to lay eyes upon such wonders.

Back inside the ship, Dawn stopped by Mona's room first because it was closest to the entrance she used. After a couple of knocks, Mona answered the door, and Dawn was surprised to see she was already out of bed and bathed. Mona wore one of the fluffy, white bath robes provided by the cruise line.

"Morning," Dawn said. "I didn't think you'd be awake."

"I always wake up early," Mona said. "No matter what goes on the night before, I'll have my butt up by seven—at the latest. You can't be the best if your ass is in bed all day."

Mona held the door open for Dawn, but she didn't want to intrude.

"I can come back when you get dressed," she offered. "I'm going to check on Rene anyway."

"Did you eat breakfast yet?" Mona asked.

Dawn shook her head. "No. I was waiting for y'all."

"All right, well give me about fifteen minutes," Mona said. "I'll meet you in the atrium or in the cafeteria."

"Cool." Dawn continued merrily on her way.

Rene's cabin was on the U Deck. Dawn made the mistake of taking the stairs up rather than wait on the elevators. By the time she got to Rene's hallway, Dawn was out of breath, and she reminded herself to start a workout regimen pretty soon before things got totally out of hand.

To make matters worse, no one answered Rene's door after several knocks. Dawn left to check the atrium and two of the ship's cafeterias. Rene was nowhere in sight. Dawn went back to Mona's room after ten minutes of searching.

Mona was dressed by then in a grapefruit-colored sundress with floral prints and was on her way out of the door.

"Oh, you came back for me?"

"I didn't have nothing else to do," Dawn said. "I can't find Rene."

"She wasn't in her room?"

"Um, yeah, that's like the first place I looked," Dawn said sarcastically.

"Don't get smart," Mona replied. She pulled her door closed and headed back in the direction Dawn had just come. "Well, let's go look again."

"I went to both cafeterias, too," Dawn said. "This boat is so big, I'll probably lose twenty pounds before Friday, just looking for y'all every day."

"Don't worry about your weight while you're on vacation," Mona advised. "They're going to be throwing so much good food in your face, you'll go crazy trying to count calories."

Her comment was flippant, but it made Dawn feel good just the same. Other people in Dawn's life, a certain grumpy grouch in particular, would've jumped at an opportunity to criticize her portliness.

"So, how'd it go with your quest last night?" Dawn asked. "Did you catch a man in your black widow's web?"

Mona laughed at that. "Yeah, but I'm only telling that story *once*, so let's find Rene first…"

❧

Mona insisted they start their search at Rene's cabin, and Dawn followed her up there even though she knew no one would answer. Not surprisingly, Rene was still not in her room. Next Mona and Dawn searched the atrium and both of the cafeterias that were serving breakfast. Still no sign of Rene.

They were headed to the upper deck to see if Rene was catching some early morning rays when they happened upon the Internet Café. This was the only place on the ship where you could gain access to the World Wide Web (for a fee), so you could check your emails, your work emails, or whatever else people felt they couldn't live without for five full days.

Dawn was surprised to see Rene sitting at one of the computer desks, but Mona was downright offended.

"Girl, what the hell are you doing over here? We' been looking all over for you!"

"Oh, sorry," Rene said and quickly exited out of her program.

"Don't tell me you're doing *work* on your vacation," Dawn said.

"No," Rene said, but she didn't offer a better explanation.

"You'd better not be doing work," Mona threatened. "All of that shit can wait. If I can forget about *my* office, you can, too."

"No, it's not work," Rene said and stepped away from the computer. "Are y'all ready to get breakfast?"

"You still haven't said what you were doing," Mona said.

"I just wanted to get in touch with Blake," Rene said. "I wanted to ask him if I left my camcorder in his car."

That sounded reasonable to Dawn, but Mona was like a private eye.

"It took you thirty minutes to send an email? Dawn said she went to your room at seven o'clock, and you weren't there. Plus I saw you was on Facebook when we walked up."

"Damn," Rene said. "Why you all up in mines?" She chuckled. "All right. I did want to ask Blake about my camera, but I also wanted to check on some other stuff. I'm trying not to think about it, but I *know* he's cheating on me. I can't get it out of my head."

"What are you gonna find on Facebook?" Mona wondered.

"I don't know," Rene said. "I wanted to see what people posted on his wall. Maybe one of them is his other girlfriend."

The women were walking now, which was good because Dawn's stomach was starting to growl.

"If he's cheating on you," Mona said, "he's not going to be stupid enough to leave her posts out in the open. You're not going to find anything on Facebook."

"I know," Rene said with a sigh. "But I don't know what else to do. I'm stuck on this boat, and I can't call him or nothing. He could be–"

"Hold up," Mona said. "You're not *stuck* on this boat. You're supposed to be relaxing. You won't have a good time if you're too busy worrying about that dumb boy. You need to tell us what's going on and then forget about him completely. You gotta get him out of your system—at least 'til we get back to Galveston."

"All right," Rene said. She was glad her friends were willing to listen, because she was eager to purge.

For breakfast the ship offered a buffet that included sausage, bacon, oatmeal, grits, fruit, dry cereal, and hash browns. They also had a plethora of sweets from raspberry Danishes to cinnamon rolls. The Finley Sisters packed their plates with a little bit of everything, but they didn't eat much while listening to Rene's worries, which included more than just a suspicious telephone call two days ago.

Rene said she had doubts about Blake going back as far as a year. Blake was always a busy man, and Rene was never one to question the many hours he spent working late or the large amounts of time he devoted to his career on the weekends. Rene said there were two of Blake's coworkers who seemed to give her the evil eye whenever she accompanied him to one of his company functions, but she never thought much of them, either.

Rene assumed these women were haters, or maybe they had a crush on Blake. But now she wondered if it was something more sinister. Like when Blake left her in Overbrook Meadows so he could "get back to work." Maybe there was something more to that, too.

Come to think of it, Rene realized that every time Blake had to leave her unexpectedly, his job was the excuse he'd use. Once Blake left her in the middle of a movie so he could take a call from "work." He stayed in the theatre's lobby for so long, Rene eventually went looking for him. When she found him, he hung up quickly and they returned to the show. Another time, Blake got a call at 6 a.m., and he left Rene's bed right afterwards, saying he had to be at "the office" early that day.

"I used to think that was cool," Rene said. "That was something I liked about him, how he was doing so well with his job. But if he's cheating on me with somebody he works with, that's the perfect excuse. I ironed his clothes *many times* so he could go be with his other bitch."

"You talking like you know for sure," Dawn noticed. "I think you should give him the benefit of the doubt—at least until you talk to him."

"Talking to him won't do no good," Mona stated. "It's not like he's gonna admit it. You don't have proof of *anything*. It'll be easy for him to squirm his way out of that stuff you mentioned."

"I know," Rene said. "I'm not going to ask him. I feel like I need to bug his phone or something."

Dawn chuckled. "That's impossible."

"No, it's not," Rene said. "There's this company that will set up a link between my cellphone and Blake's phone. All I have to do is get the number off his SIM card and give it to them. I can set it up so that every time he gets a call, my phone will beep, and I can listen in on his conversation. Plus, if I get within five hundred feet of him, I can punch a code into my cell that will let me listen to any conversation going on around his phone. He doesn't even have to be using it; it just has to be turned on."

Mona's eyes widened, and Dawn's mouth fell open.

"Damn," Dawn said. "They got a company like that?"

"Mmm-hmm." Rene nodded. "I looked them up a few months ago."

"A *few months ago?*" Mona frowned. "You're really thinking about doing something like that?"

"I know it's wrong," Rene said. "I don't want to invade his privacy. But I don't think there's any other way to find out the truth."

"It's not wrong because of his funky-ass privacy," Mona said. "It's wrong because you feel like you need to go through that. You shouldn't let no man stress you out that bad. The moment you felt like you needed to do some surveillance should've been the same moment you told his ass to get to packing. Ain't no man worth all that."

"Maybe not to you," Rene said, "because you already have it in your mind that men are objects. Whatever they can do to please Mona is great, but when they're no longer useful, you drop them without a care in the world."

"What's wrong with that?" Mona wondered.

"It's bad because you don't ever fall in love," Rene said. "You probably can't remember the last time you actually loved one of them."

"I guess now you're talking about that dumb oath," Mona said with a roll of her eyes.

"It's not even about the oath," Rene said. "But now that you mentioned it, yeah, I did make a promise, and I think it's a good promise. There's nothing wrong with falling in love with the man of your dreams. That's like, that's the best feeling in the world."

"Are you in love with Blake?" Dawn asked.

Rene looked away, and Dawn saw that her eyes were misty.

"I know I said I wasn't," Rene said, "but I've been with Blake for two years. I didn't want to fall in love with anyone else after what happened with Terrence, but I can't stop my heart from feeling what it wants to. I can convince my brain, but my heart has a mind of its own."

"I can fix my brain *and* my heart," Mona said.

"So what happened with that guy you left with last night?" Rene asked, mostly to change the subject.

"*Hmph!*" Mona chuckled. "I don't know what to say about that boy. He's nice and all, but I won't be hitting that again—that's for sure."

"You, you slept with him?" Dawn asked. She didn't know why that surprised her. It was the very thing Mona foretold.

"I gave him a little something-something," Mona confided. "But he wasn't working with nothing. I had to do all the work. Plus he was too quiet, like a little boy."

"Yeah, he was quiet," Rene agreed.

"You met him?" Dawn asked.

"He bought us some shots," Rene said. "I knew he wasn't Mona's type as soon as she got to talking to him."

"What did he look like?" Dawn asked.

"He looked good," Rene said.

"He was *all right*," Mona corrected.

"He bought y'all drinks?" Dawn asked.

"He was good for that," Mona said. "We could've got more shots out of him, but I was sick of talking to his silly ass."

"Why'd you let him buy you drinks if you didn't like him?" Dawn wondered.

"Thank you," Rene said.

"*Please*," Mona said. "Don't y'all start getting all preachy on me. You don't have to like a man to let him buy you drinks. I know y'all been to the club and some fool with a Jheri curl wanted to buy you something. You can take his drink and go on about your business."

Dawn shook her head because she'd never done that, but Rene shrugged like maybe she had.

"Plus I went to that fool's room afterwards," Mona continued, "and he got *way* more than his money's worth. I mean, just to see me naked; that's worth over a thousand dollars. And me and Dwayne went all the way—for six stanky tequila shots. If you want to know the truth, he owes me *way more* than I could ever owe him."

Dawn laughed at that. "*Dwayne*," she said. "I want to see what he looks like. Y'all point him out if you see him again."

"Be careful what you wish for…" Rene said and lowered her gaze.

"Aw, ain't this a bitch," Mona said and she lowered her eyes, too.

"What?" Dawn asked.

"Here hc comes now," Rene said.

"*Don't look*!" Mona instructed, but that didn't help. If Dwayne lived to be one hundred, he would never forget Mona, and he had his sights set firmly on their table. He approached with a lot more confidence than he had the night before.

"Good morning! How are you ladies doing?"

"Fine," Dawn and Rene said. Mona just sat there and sulked.

"And how are *you* today?" Dwayne asked Mona directly. He wore baggy canvas shorts with a white tee shirt and brown sandals. Dawn thought he had nice legs and a fit upper body. Overall he was nice-looking. She didn't understand why Mona looked so embarrassed.

"I'm fine," Mona snapped. "What do you want? What are you doing over here?"

"*Damn*," Rene said under her breath.

Dwayne's eyes flashed wide for a second, and he lost half of his confidence right before the girls' eyes. It was one of the strangest things Dawn had ever seen. His shoulders began to droop and his chest caved in like he got punched.

"I was, I just wanted to say 'hi,' " he stammered.

"Don't you have some other people you could say '*hi*' to?" Mona wondered. "I thought you said you were here with your family." Her lips were curled back, exposing fierce fangs, and her venom was clearly poisonous. Dawn thought Dwayne would take that as his cue to skedaddle, but this was one confused, determined, and thick-headed chap.

"My family's over, over there," Dwayne said. He shot a thumb back to a group of men sitting at a table together. All of them were watching Mona with much interest, and she wondered what kind of sick stories Dwayne had been telling them. Rather than find fault in her own behavior, Mona focused her anger on Dwayne.

"Man, I'm trying to have breakfast with my friends," she growled. "You need to get back over there with your peeps. Leave me alone. Damn. Why you sweating me?"

"Wow," Rene said.

"Oh," Dwayne said. "I was, I was just…" He shifted his weight from one foot to the other and scratched the back of his head. He looked like he might cry. Dawn's heart went out to him. "I was wondering if you wanted to go to the pool after breakfast," Dwayne asked.

Rene shook her head and lowered her eyes again.

Mona cocked her head slowly, until it became a stiff 45-degree angle. "No," she said. "I don't want to go swimming."

"You, you wanna play volleyball later?" Dwayne asked.

"Wow," Rene said with a chuckle.

"No. I don't want to play no damned volleyball," Mona said.

"You wanna—"

"I'll tell you what I want." Mona looked him dead in the eyes. "I want you to go back over there with your family and leave me over here with my friends. If I want something from you, I will find you. Do you understand?"

Dwayne nodded slowly.

"Don't come talking to me again," Mona went on. "This is a big-ass boat. I know you can find somebody else to mess with."

"Oh, okay," Dwayne said. He gave Mona the saddest puppy dog eyes *ever*, and then he turned and commenced the death march back to his kinfolks.

"Oh my God," Rene said when he was gone. "I can't believe you talked to him like that."

"It's his own fault," Mona said and took a mean bite out of her toast. "Didn't nobody tell him to come over here messing with me. I don't know what he was thinking."

"Maybe he's thinking that since you slept with him, you must like him," Dawn offered.

"Well, now he knows better," Mona said. "You gotta be firm with these niggas, or they'll turn into bugaboos."

Rene laughed, and after a few seconds Dawn chuckled, too.

"You wrong," Dawn said.

"And I hope you learned your lesson," Rene said.

"What lesson?" Mona asked.

"That you can't be sleeping with strange men on a cruise ship," Rene said, a little exasperated. "There's a lot of people here, but this boat's not that damned big. You're bound to run into them again sooner or later."

"What? I'm not gonna change my life for that fool," Mona said. "I'm at my sexual peak, and–"

"No, you're not," Rene said.

"Not what?"

"You're not at your sexual peak. You're only twenty-eight."

"Who said I can't be at my sexual peak at twenty-eight?"

"It's not supposed to happen until you're in your thirties," Dawn said.

"Well, my sexual peak is gonna last a couple of decades then," Mona said. "I love men, and that punk's not gonna stop me from having fun on this boat."

"So, you're gonna sleep with someone else?" Rene dared to ask.

"I'm not a *whore*," Mona said, "but yes, I may get romantically involved if I see some... *Mmmm.*" Her eyes lit up, and she smiled devilishly. "Check *that* out."

Dawn and Rene followed her gaze to a frozen yogurt machine. Standing next to it were two exceptionally handsome men. They were both young, in their early twenties, and they both had athletic, well-toned bodies. The one on the right was black with a completely shaved head and no moustache or goatee. He had a strong jaw line and nice, suckable lips. The man on the left was a very dark-skinned Hispanic, possibly from Puerto Rico or maybe Spain. He had a head full of luscious, curly locks and the most beautiful gray eyes.

"Damn," Rene said. "That is nice."

"Which one?" Dawn asked, her smile big and curious.

"It don't even matter," Mona said dreamily. "I'll lick peanut butter off either one of 'em."

"Ooh, you nasty," Rene said.

The two men started to walk away, and Mona quickly made it to her feet. "Come with me," she told her friends.

"With you *where*?" Rene asked.

"To catch them," Mona said, "find out who they're here with."

"Uh-uhn," Dawn said. "I can't go up to no strangers like that."

"I'm with Dawn," Rene said. "You don't want to have more people following you around tomorrow, do you?"

"Whatever," Mona said and continued by herself. "I'll catch up with y'all later."

Rene and Dawn watched her go, and they couldn't do anything but shake their heads and laugh.

"I don't know what you're laughing at," Rene said. "That's *your* friend."

"You spend more time with her," Dawn countered.

"That's only because you went to bed early," Rene said. "And you'd better not do that again tonight."

"You didn't have fun yesterday?" Dawn asked.

"I did," Rene admitted, "to a certain extent. But Mona can be *too* wild sometimes. She had me in a booty contest and everything!"

"Nuh-uhn!"

"For real," Rene said. "I won, of course…" She gathered her napkins and plate and cleaned up Mona's side of the table as much as possible. "Are you done eating?"

"Yeah," Dawn said and took one last bite of her apple turnover. "Where you going now?"

"I'm going to see if they found out anything about my camera," Rene said. "After that, we can do whatever you want."

"I want to check out the spa," Dawn said. She rose with her tray and Rene followed close behind.

"We can do that," Rene said, and then she frowned and stared curiously at the back of her friend's arm. "Hey, what's that?"

Dawn strained her neck but couldn't see what she was talking about. "What?"

"On the back of your arm," Rene said. "You got two purple bruises. Did you, how'd you get those?"

Dawn knew exactly what Rene was talking about, and her heart froze into a block of ice. The bruises had been there for three days now. Dawn thought they were fading away, but apparently not quickly enough. The purple spots were towards the bottom of her triceps, spaced two inches apart. One was the exact shape of Henry's thumb. The other was a perfect match for his index finger.

Thinking about the marks took Dawn's mind back to that fateful day when Henry roughed her up in front of her sister.

OWW! LET ME GO!

Let her go! You dumb-ass nigga! Let her go!

You shut yo ugly ass up! This ain't got shit to do with you.

"I bumped my arm when I was unpacking," Dawn told Rene.

"You bumped it *twice*?" Rene asked. "That hard? In the same spot?"

"Yeah, I guess so," Dawn said, and she didn't turn to see if her friend believed her or not. Dawn knew she wasn't the best liar. Her eyes would surely betray her if Rene stared deeply enough.

CHAPTER 10
INTERVENTION

The first full day on the ship started off great.

After breakfast Rene and Dawn went to the guest services desk to see if any kind soul found her camcorder overnight and turned it in. As expected, no one had. Rene wondered if she should stop worrying about it altogether.

"It's only the second day," Dawn said. "You know it's on this boat somewhere. I think you should pay more attention to some of these people walking around. One of them could be using your camera right in front of your face."

Rene thought about that. She looked around and saw that nearly everyone had a camcorder in hand.

"There's no way I can tell theirs from mine."

"What color was yours?" Dawn asked.

"Gray with a black screen that flipped open."

"Okay, so you can rule out all of the blue ones and anything with red on it," Dawn deduced. "That's gotta take away at least half of them."

"There's still too many to look at."

"That's 'cause you're looking at it from a *money* point of view," Dawn guessed.

"What do you mean?"

"You're only thinking about how much it cost. Three hundred dollars ain't that much to you. But it's the principle of the matter. Back in high school you wouldn't let nobody steal from you. You remember when one of those Perkins twins took your compact?"

"That was Clarissa," Rene said with a frown. "I wanted to yank her weave out."

"That's what I'm talking about," Dawn said. "Somebody on this boat disrespected you just like that, and you need to find them."

Rene nodded. "You're right. I'm going to start looking more."

"Just don't start no mess unless me or Mona is around," Dawn advised.

"All right," Rene said. "I won't make a move unless I got some back-up."

Dawn nodded gruffly, and the girls headed for the spa in the aerobics room. They were told they had to come back at eleven, so the twosome had to find something to occupy the next three hours.

"What do you want to do?" Dawn asked.

Rene pulled an itinerary form from her back pocket and unfolded it. "There's so much. We could stay here *two* weeks and never fit it all in."

"Do you want to look for Mona?"

"Nope," Rene said. "She's on her own mission. It's just you and me."

Dawn grinned. "I need to take some more pictures."

❧

The girls went to the Sun Deck and snapped a few shots, and they stood in line to "Meet a Golf Pro" while they were up there. Rene hoped it would be somebody famous like Jack Nicklaus or Phil Mickelson, but it was a relative nobody named PJ Mitchell.

PJ never played on a course with Jack or Phil, but he was a very talented. He taught Rene how to perfect her stance, and she sank a nine foot putt for the first time in her life. Dawn couldn't match that success, but she still had a good time.

After their golf lesson, the ladies went to the Lido Deck to check out some temporary body art. The artists at that event were serious professionals. Rene and Dawn watched a woman get a full dragon painted on her back.

"Dang," Dawn mused. "They're good."

"Are you going to get one?" Rene asked.

"I want to," Dawn said. "But I'd have to go change into a swimsuit or something…"

"Let's go change."

"I don't know." Dawn frowned and looked down at her shoes.

Rene narrowed her eyes and took Dawn's hand. "Girl, come over here."

She led her to the main pool and pointed out a few unnatural wonders of the world.

"Look at that," Rene said.

"She's big," Dawn noticed.

"Look at those two," Rene said. She gestured towards two women in their mid-sixties. They were tanned to the max, and their wrinkly skin looked like burnt leather. Their age-appropriate figures sagged unattractively, but both of them still wore bikinis.

"All right. I get your point," Dawn said.

"So you're ready to change?"

"Yeah." Dawn grinned. "I'll meet you back here in fifteen minutes…"

❧

Dawn's swimsuit was solid black (because she heard that color makes you appear thinner), and it had a skirt attached to hide some of the cellulite in her booty. Even still, Dawn felt self-conscious about the pounds she had stacked on since high school.

When she met up with Rene, Dawn's self-esteem plunged even further. Rene wore a fiery red bikini, and her figure was perfect in every way. She didn't have big, chunky arms like Dawn, and her stomach was as flat as a clipboard. Rene's facial beauty was the icing on the cake, and her Versace shades were to die for. Dawn shook her head and folded her arms over her stomach.

"What's wrong?" Rene asked.

"I can't be walking around with *you*," Dawn said. "I look like your ugly stepsister."

Rene laughed. "Girl, no you don't. Why would you say something like that?"

"I'm so *fat*," Dawn pouted. "I hate it. I hate my body!"

Rene saw that she was serious, and her smile faded. "Dawn, don't talk like that. You're beautiful, you know that. If you want to lose weight, you can. I can help you, if you want. But don't worry about it while you're on this cruise. You're here to have fun. And you look better than half of the women here."

"Whatever."

"I'm serious," Rene said. "I think you–"

"Hey, y'all headed for the pool?"

Rene looked back and saw a familiar group of men. She recognized one of them as the nice guy who took her and Mona's picture in front of the Rolls Royce last night.

"Maybe," Rene said.

"Can we go with y'all?" the cameraman asked. "We just gotta go throw on some shorts."

"You can go anytime you want to," Rene said. "We might not even get in the water."

"That's cool. We just want to hang out with some pretty girls."

Rene grinned. "What's your name?"

"Hector," the cameraman said. "This is my brother Lupe, and those are my cousins Abel and Mike." The whole crew smiled brightly.

"All right," Rene said. "Go put on your shorts, and we'll meet you out there."

"Awesome," Hector said, and they took off.

"See," Rene said when they were gone. "He said they wanted to hang out with some *pretty girls*."

"I know," Dawn said, and she was clearly excited. "Did you see the way the tall one was looking at me?"

"Doesn't Henry look at you like that?" Rene queried.

"Come on," Dawn said, heading for the pool. "If you want me to have a good time, stop asking about him."

"All right," Rene said with a chuckle, but her eyes returned to the purple marks on the back of Dawn's arm as she followed her friend outside.

⌒⌘⌒

Hector and his crew were a joy to be around. They were carefree and fun-loving. Nearly everything cracked them up. Rene learned they were all from San Antonio, and they loved to meet new people and have a good time.

After a ridiculous game of pool volleyball, Rene and Dawn had lunch with Hector's family on the Sun Deck. Mike bought a round of Coronas after the meal, and Rene downed hers graciously even though she wasn't into drinking that early in the day. Rene and Dawn bid them adieu at two-thirty. Hector promised to find them for more fun in the sun on a later date.

"Did you have a good time?" Rene asked on the way back to their cabins.

"Yeah," Dawn said, her smile big and blissful. "That tall one grabbed my booty while we was in the pool."

Rene's laughed. "Nuh-uhn."

"For real," Dawn said. "I thought it was an accident, but when I saw the look in his eyes, I knew it was on purpose."

Rene shook her head. "What'd you do?"

"I told him, '*You better watch it*,' and he was like, '*I am watching it*,' you know, trying to look all sexy and stuff. I couldn't do nothing but laugh."

"Hmph," Rene said with one eyebrow raised. "Dawn, Dawn, Dawn…"

"What? I didn't do nothing."

"I'll say…"

"Whatever." Dawn pushed her friend's shoulder. "You didn't see Mona out there, did you?"

"Uh-uhn," Rene said.

"You think she's still with those two guys?" Dawn asked. "Do you want to look for her now?"

"She'll pop up when she's ready to," Rene predicted. "I'm sure she's having the time of her life."

❧

Rene and Dawn changed into sexy dresses and met on the Empress Deck for a dance contest. They thought they'd be shoe-ins because only a handful of blacks chose to participate. But much to Dawn's dismay, a German couple in their late forties walked off with the shiny trophy.

"That's not fair," she told Rene. "They look like dance teachers or something. This is supposed to be for amateurs."

"Just because they made *you* look like an amateur doesn't make them professionals," Rene quipped.

"You lost, too," Dawn pointed out.

"I blame that on my amateur partner," Rene said with a grin.

"Whatever," Dawn said. "I bet if they have a rump-shaker contest, I'd win that."

"I'm sure you would," Rene said. She checked her itinerary again. "Have you ever been to a wine tasting?"

Dawn shook her head. "No. But I want to."

"Come on," Rene said. "It'll be over in thirty minutes."

The girls went to the Atlantic Deck and tried to play the part of true connoisseurs. They sniffed expensive liquors and swished them around their mouths like they really knew what they were doing.

"This one is *quite exquisite*," Rene said about their third selection. "An excellent concoction, indeed."

Dawn sniffed the same chardonnay and wrinkled her nose. "I dare say it smells like the sweat from a baboon's balls," she countered, in her snootiest voice. "No, I'm afraid I shall not be making *this* purchase!"

Rene laughed, along with a few nearby patrons.

At six o'clock the friends headed for the Windstar Dining Room for the first of what was to become the most memorable meals on the cruise. The Windstar was gracefully decorated like the dining rooms on the *Titanic*, and all of the wait staff wore crisp tuxedos. The tables were set expertly with more forks and spoons than Dawn could ever figure out how to use. The menus had real leather cases with the most beautiful calligraphy written inside.

For dinner that night, the guests could choose from sugar glazed pork loin with apples and prunes, fettuccine with sautéed shrimp and salmon, or fresh scampi Provencal sautéed in virgin olive oil.

Mona had been gone for so long, her friends didn't wait to order, but she showed up midway through the meal with much a huff and puff. She took a seat next to Dawn and looked around for a menu.

"Am I too late? Did I miss dinner?"

"Where the hell have you been?" Dawn asked. "We haven't seen you since breakfast."

"I been with Bart and them," Mona said, looking around furtively. "You haven't seen Dwayne, have you?"

"Who's Dwayne?"

"That boy I slept with last night," Mona groaned. "He's been following me around *everywhere*. Every time I look up, he's in my face."

"Who's Bart?" Rene asked.

"*Bartolo Romero*," Mona said with her best Spanish accent. "That's the guy I met this morning. His friend's name is Xavier."

"Dwayne's been following you around?" Dawn asked.

"Oh, my God." Mona sighed. "He's a stalker for real. He saw me with Bart, but he still won't leave me alone. He followed us to, like, two different places. I swear he's starting to creep me out."

"Who's Bart?" Rene asked again.

"I told you," Mona said. "That's *Bartolo*."

"I know, but which one was he?"

"Oh, he's the taller one," Mona said. "The one with the curly hair. He's from Brazil. His friend is, too."

"That black guy?" Rene asked.

"Yeah, they play soccer for some university," Mona explained. "Except they don't call it soccer. They call it *fútbol*. They're so funny—and fine. Bart took off his shirt and I wanted to rape him right then. He got some–"

"Y'all had sex already?" Dawn asked.

"Not yet," Mona said. "*But we're gonna*! Girl, I'm hungry. Where can I get a men–"

Before she could finish her sentence, their waitress approached the table. "Good evening, ma'am. Would you like a menu?"

"Naw, just gimme…" She looked from Rene's plate to Dawn's. "Gimme what she's having," she said, pointing at Dawn's meal.

"Very good," the waitress said and disappeared.

"How come we haven't seen you?" Rene asked Mona. "Were you in their room or something?"

"For a little bit," Mona said. "But we were walking around mostly. I saw y'all at lunchtime. You were in the pool with those Mexicans."

"Why didn't you say something?" Rene asked.

"I was headed the other way," Mona said. "Plus y'all were having fun on your own. I saw you hugged up with one of them," she told Dawn.

"I wasn't *hugged up*," Dawn said.

"Girl, he was close enough to kiss the back of your neck," Mona recalled. "I thought that's what he was doing at first."

"No, he was grabbing her booty," Rene informed Mona.

"No, he wasn't!" Dawn said with a giggle.

"Don't be shy," Mona said. "Just 'cause you got a man don't mean you can't get something popping on this boat."

"I'm not like that," Dawn said.

"And that's fine," Rene said. "But I do want to talk about your boyfriend. You cut me off every–"

"I don't want to talk about him," Dawn said. Her smile vanished, and Mona raised a curious eyebrow.

"That's, um, that's what I'm talking about," Rene said. "Whenever I bring him up, your whole mood changes."

Dawn sighed loudly and looked down at her plate. The food was delicious, but her appetite was completely gone.

"I don't, I don't want to accuse him of anything," Rene said, "but does Henry have anything to do with those bruises on your arm?"

Dawn turned slowly and gave her friend a terrible look that was stuck somewhere between anger and shock. It was such an ugly expression, Rene flinched and subconsciously inched away from her.

"Your boyfriend's beating on you?" Mona asked. In a split second she was on the verge of a hissy fit, and this was why Rene waited until the three of them were together before she posed the question. Dawn could put off Rene's curiosity with no problem, but Mona's personality would not allow such a thing. If there was a mystery afoot, Mona would get to the bottom of it.

"Why you tripping?" Dawn asked Rene. "I told you I don't want to talk about him."

"I don't want to talk about him, either," Mona said. "I just wanna know if he's hitting you. Let me see your arm." She reached for it, and Dawn jerked away roughly. Mona was shocked, and she backed away, too. "What the hell?"

"He don't be hitting on me," Dawn said, looking down at her plate again. "He just grabbed my arm."

"Why'd he grab your arm?" Rene asked.

"It don't matter," Dawn said.

"He *never* hit you?" Mona asked.

Dawn hesitated two seconds too long, and Mona's mouth fell open.

"Girl, he be hitting on you?"

"It's, it's not that bad," Dawn said. Her eyes filled with moisture and the room faded in a saltwater blur.

"What do you mean it's not that bad?" Mona said. "One time is *that bad*, Dawn. How long he been beating on you?"

Dawn gave Rene another hard stare, as if to say, *Do you see what you did?*, but Rene was on the same page as Mona.

"It's not right," Rene said. "You shouldn't stay with somebody who hits you."

"It's not—"

"Or pushes you or grabs your arm like that," Rene said. "A man should *never* put his hands on a woman. You can do better than that."

Dawn felt like she was being cornered. This was embarrassing and hurtful, and if her so-called friends really cared about her, they wouldn't assail her like this.

185

"You don't know what I can do better than!" she spat. "You don't even know me, so get out my business."

Rene's jaw dropped. "What?"

"Who you talking to?" Mona asked.

"I'm talking to *you*!" Dawn said. "To both of y'all."

"Why are you getting an attitude?" Rene asked. "We're only trying to help."

"I already told you I don't want to talk about it."

"I know," Rene said, "but if you got problems like that at home, I think you do need to get it out in the open. You can't let some man hit on you, Dawn. That's, that's–"

"That's stupid," Mona offered.

"So, what, I'm stupid now?" Dawn said.

"I didn't say you were stupid," Mona said. "I said *that* was stupid. If you stay with a man who's beating on you, *that's* stupid. You can do better than that."

"How do you know?" Dawn's voice quivered. "How do you know what I can do better than? I didn't go to college like you did. And I got *two kids*. You don't have any. You don't know what it's like."

Rene shook her head. "None of that–"

"And I'm *fat*!" Dawn reminded them. "If I looked like you, maybe I could pick and choose. But I don't. You don't know what my life is like. You don't know what it's like to be me!"

By then people from other tables were starting to notice the commotion, and Dawn felt like the biggest loser ever. Who was she trying to fool? This cruise ship, expensive dinners, margaritas under the moonlight; this wasn't her life.

Dawn was a poor, hardworking, uneducated mother from the hood. That's all she ever was, and that's all she would ever be. She was crazy to let Rene and Mona talk her into this ridiculous trip in the first place.

Tears streamed down her cheeks, and Dawn covered her face in shame. Rene reached for her, but Dawn pulled away and made it to her feet.

"I'm going to my room."

"Wait," Rene said.

"No! *Leave me alone!*" She stormed away with her hands hiding her eyes.

Rene started to go after her, but Mona grabbed hold of her arm.

"Let her go."

"No, I'm not going to let her go! That's wrong. I don't want her crying all night. We need to talk to her."

"She'll be all right," Mona said reassuringly. "She probably never talked to anyone about what's been going on, and it's hard for her. Give her some time to calm down and think about it. She knows we're trying to help."

"Yeah, but–"

"*And*," Mona went on, "we're on a boat in the middle of the ocean. She doesn't have anywhere to run to. She has to talk to us sooner or later."

Rene stopped and eyed her friend queerly, surprised by Mona's insight. Reluctantly, she returned to her seat.

"I know what you're thinking," Mona said. "How could someone as beautiful and talented as myself *also* be good at psychology?"

Rene wasn't in the mood for jokes. She shook her head and rubbed between her eyes. "Actually I was wondering how someone so understanding could still be such an *asshole*."

"I must've learned that from yo mama," Mona said.

"Don't be talking about my mama," Rene warned.

"Don't be talking about my mama," Mona mocked.

Rene glared at her and then rolled her eyes. "Girl, you stupid."

❧

Rene and Mona remained in the Windstar for the next thirty minutes while Mona devoured her gourmet dinner. They talked about Dawn mostly. Part of Rene still wanted to run to her friend's cabin and force Dawn to talk to them, but Rene always had a good deal of patience. She knew Mona was right about giving Dawn time to think things through on her own. Surely their friend would be more approachable tomorrow, after a good night's sleep.

"So what are you going to do tonight?" Rene asked Mona. "Or do I even have to ask…?"

"I'm kicking it with Bart and them," Mona said. "And you're coming, too. I'm telling you, his friend is fine as hell."

"He doesn't mind you calling him *Bart*?" Rene wondered.

"That's what everybody calls him," Mona said.

"I assume he knows about The Simpsons…"

"Everybody knows… Oh, my God." Mona stared over Rene's shoulder, and her eyes grew very large.

"What's wrong?" Rene asked, and then she looked back and saw for herself. "Damn. Is he serious?"

Dwayne approached their table wearing blue slacks and a heavily starched white button-down. He toted a bouquet of roses acquired from God knows where.

"I gotta get away from him," Mona said under her breath. "Can you give me a head start?"

"What do you mean?" Rene whispered.

"Just thirty seconds," Mona hissed.

"What?"

But the stalker was at their table by then.

"Hi, Mona," Dwayne said. "I, I bought these flowers for you. I was, I was–"

"I'll be *right* back," Mona said. She threw her napkin onto her plate and promptly left the table. Rene finally understood what she meant by *give me a head start*, and she didn't like it at all. Dwayne was Mona's problem. She shouldn't be pawning him off.

The stalker stood quietly and watched her go. And then his eyes settled on Rene.

"Hey," he said.

"Hi."

"She, um, she went to the bathroom?"

"Yeah, I think so," Rene said.

They watched each other for a few seconds, and an uncomfortable silence ensued.

"You wanna, you wanna sit down?" Rene offered.

"Okay." Dwayne took a seat across from her, and Rene looked around for the relatives he was supposed to be on vacation with. She didn't see them anywhere. Rene took a deep breath and sighed. She didn't like to hurt people's feelings, but this was getting out of hand.

"Listen, man, I don't think Mona likes you."

Dwayne didn't look totally shocked by this. "She told you that?"

"Not in so many words," Rene said, and then she caught herself. No, she shouldn't let one morsel of hope linger. She had to nip this in the bud. "Yeah, she did say that. It's kinda obvious, isn't it?"

He shook his head. "We, we spent time together last night. We had—"

"Yeah, I heard about that," Rene said. "And Mona hasn't spoken to you since. That doesn't tell you anything? I mean, has she been nice to you at all today?"

Dwayne knotted his eyebrows in confusion. "I brought her these flowers…"

Rene stared compassionately for a second and then shook her head. "Yeah, I ain't gon' be able to do it." She stood and walked deliberately away from the table.

"Where are you going?" Dwayne called.

"To get Mona for you." Rene hated to treat him like that, but she was starting to understand why Mona would rather flee the scene than have a rational conversation with him. Dwayne had to be at least a *little* mentally defective.

When she stepped out of the dining room, Rene almost got run over by a rowdy group of teenagers who didn't bother to stop to say excuse me. One of the boys was tall with long hair, and in his left hand he carried a camcorder that looked *exactly* like the one Rene was missing.

She started to go after him, but Rene didn't have the backup or the courage to approach a complete stranger and accuse him of stealing. She did make a mental note of him, though, before she continued on her way to find out where the hell Mona had gone.

After a few steps she looked back at the Windstar to see if Dwayne was following her. He wasn't, but the thought gave Rene a fresh crop of goose bumps.

CHAPTER 11
BOYS FROM SÃO PAULO

When she was confident Dwayne wasn't following her, Rene went to the Promenade Deck and found Mona at the bar with her two new friends. Mona called Rene over as soon as they made eye contact.

"Damn, girl! Where you been?"

"You're the one who left me," Rene said.

"Oh," Mona said. And then she turned to the men sitting on her left. "Hey, y'all, this is my friend, Rene. Rene, this is Bart, and that's Xavier."

"How y'all doing?" Rene said.

"Great," Bart said.

"Nice to meet you," Xavier said.

The men offered their hands, and Rene shook them gingerly. Bartolo was the dark-skinned Brazilian. He wore a short-sleeved, tan button-down with white Dockers. He was no older than twenty-two, and he was strikingly handsome. His dark hair was long and curly. Rene could get lost in his gray eyes.

His friend Xavier was good-looking, too, even though Rene didn't generally like men with shaved heads. Xavier's skin was dark like molasses, and it looked tasty enough to lick every crevice of his body. Xavier had full lips and serious eyes. He wore blue jeans with a white button-down. And, much to Rene's surprise, Xavier spoke with an accent almost as thick as Bart's.

"You guys are from Brazil?" she asked.

"We attend the University of São Paulo," Bart said. "We are in our third year."

"I hear you're athletes," Rene said.

"We are on the *fútbol* team," Xavier confirmed. "It's one of the best teams in the country."

Rene giggled. "You talk so proper. I like your accent. Were you born in Brazil?"

"Yes," Xavier said, "but my father's from Texas. He was in the Air Force, and he traveled all around the world. He was stationed in São Paulo for a while, and he fell in love with a beautiful Brazilian woman. This was my mother, and I am their love child."

Rene's grin broadened. "That's so *romantic*. How'd you guys end up on this cruise?"

"My father lives in Dallas," Xavier explained. "He sends me money and plane tickets every summer so that I can come and visit with him. Bartolo, he is my friend, and he accompanies me sometimes. This year my father purchased cruise tickets for me and Bartolo. It was a surprise. I did not expect to be here."

"That was nice of him," Rene replied.

"Eh." Xavier shrugged. "My father does nice things for me; this is true. But I did not meet this man until I was eighteen years. My mother says he uses his wallet to fight his guilt."

Rene smiled. "That's probably true." She turned to Bartolo. "So what about you? You got an interesting story?"

He laughed. "No. I'm afraid not. I was born in São Paulo, and I lived there for all of my life. I come from a poor family. I would never made it to the *universidade* if I could not kick that *fútbol*. And I would have never see such a beautiful boat if it wasn't for *meu amigo* Xavier."

"What language do you speak?" Rene asked. "That's not Spanish, is it?"

"No," Bartolo said. "The most language in São Paulo is Portuguese."

Bart was just as charming as his friend, and Rene couldn't say who was cuter—or sexier. She thought Bart was more exotic, and his hair was downright *luscious*. But she was more intrigued by Xavier because at first glance he looked like a black American. You wouldn't know any different unless he spoke to you. Rene wanted to know more about the culture shock when he traveled from Brazil to Dallas each summer.

In any event, Mona already had her hooks in Bartolo, so Xavier was Rene's date by default.

"So, what do you think of my friend?" Rene asked Bart.

He looked Mona in the eyes and smiled warmly. "I like Mona. She is fun, a lot. She is, eh, *muito belo e muito quente*."

Mona smiled brightly, but Rene needed a little help with the translation.

"What was that?"

"He said she's very beautiful and…" Xavier grinned in embarrassment. "He thinks she's *very hot*."

"Yeah, that's Mona," Rene agreed.

"In my country," Bart went on, "she would be, eh, *rich man's wife*. She would have many cars and servants, and, eh, dresses made from finest fabrics."

"Aww, ain't he sweet?" Mona said. She gave Bart a big hug, and he smiled at her with a look that was unlike anything Rene had ever seen directed towards her friend. There was no lust in Bartolo's eyes. What Rene saw was respect, and (dare she say) *honor*.

"So, what are we doing tonight?" she asked her new international buddies.

"We would like whatever you ladies would like," Xavier said.

"I wanna dance," Mona said. "Let's go to one of the clubs." She jumped off her barstool and pulled Bart to his feet.

"That's sounds good," Rene said. She looked back to Xavier, and he followed hesitantly.

"I am not a very good dancer," he admitted.

"That's all right," Rene said. "We're just having fun. There's no pressure."

"That is good."

After a few steps Rene asked, "So, do you have a girlfriend in Brazil—or Dallas?"

Xavier shook his head. "No. My girlfriend was not true to me. She became, uh, *with child*, while I was attending school this year."

"That's sad," Rene said. "I'm sorry to hear that."

"And you?" Xavier asked. "Are you married or promised to a man?"

"I have a boyfriend," Rene said, "but I don't think he's true to me, either. I think he has another girlfriend."

"He would be foolish to do something like that," Xavier said. "I hope you're wrong about him, and I will be respectful of your relationship."

"Thanks," Rene said, but a part of her wondered if she should've mentioned Blake at all.

❧

The couples went to the Stripes Disco Lounge, but they left after only thirty minutes because Mona didn't like the records the DJ was spinning. They picked up more drinks and went to check out some karaoke instead. Everyone had a good time there, mainly because a lot of the poor saps who got behind the mic couldn't sing worth a lick. Rene felt like she was watching amateur night at the Apollo. Mona must have felt the same way because she actually booed a couple of people.

After karaoke, the group went to another lounge to see an adult comedy show. The comedian was amusing, but Mona didn't catch half of the jokes because she was flirting with Bartolo relentlessly. Rene and Xavier didn't have anything explicitly romantic going on, but there was chemistry between them, and she had a good time, too.

❧

The next morning Mona was up bright and early. She dressed and made it to her friend's cabin just as Rene was getting out of the shower.

"Dang. Do you ever sleep late?" Rene wondered.

"You can't be the best if your ass is in bed all day," Mona quipped. She stepped past her friend and plopped down on the bed. "We're finally gonna see land today." Mona pulled an itinerary from her purse and looked over the excursion list.

Rene stepped into the bathroom to style her hair. "Is today—oh, yeah, you're right. It's Wednesday, isn't it?"

"Look at you," Mona said. "You've got your head wrapped around that boy already; you don't even know what day it is."

"Please," Rene said, staring at the mirror. "I know you didn't. How was Bart, by the way?"

"I have no idea," Mona said.

Rene stuck her head out of the bathroom and frowned. "Don't tell me you didn't hit that."

"I tried," Mona said. She threw her head back. "Oh, how I tried!"

Rene laughed. "You said you were taking him to your room when we split up. What happened—is he gay?"

"Hell, no!" Mona said. "I think he's just a gentleman. He wouldn't go in my room."

Rene couldn't believe it. "Nuh-uhn."

"For real."

"And you gave him the green light?"

"Girl, I damned near gave him my *panties*," Mona replied. "But he just kissed me goodnight and said he'd see me tomorrow."

"That's hard to believe," Rene said.

"I know." Mona shook her head with a sigh.

"So, I guess you got something to look forward to."

"What about you?" Mona asked. "You and Xavier hit it off?"

"He's a nice guy," Rene said. She stepped back into the bathroom before Mona could decipher her expression.

"Did *you* hit that?" Mona asked.

"Of course not!"

"You ain't gotta say it like that."

"He's just a kid," Rene said.

"You're only *twenty-seven*," Mona said. "What is he, twenty-one, twenty-two?"

"Twenty-one."

"Girl, you need to quit tripping. You and Xavier look good together. Did you at least *try* to hit it?"

"No," Rene said. "I told him I had a boyfriend."

"You stupid," Mona stated.

Rene had a really good comeback for that, but she bit her tongue. Calling Mona a hussy was probably not the best way to maintain their friendship.

∽×∾

Rene dressed quickly, and she and Mona went to get Dawn so they could have breakfast together. But after four knocks, no one answered Dawn's door.

"You think she's at breakfast already?" Mona asked.

"I don't know," Rene said. "She was upset, but I don't think she'd eat without us."

"Well, she's not here," Mona said, stating the obvious. "Let's go check."

The ladies went to both cafeterias, and they didn't see Dawn in the chow lines or sitting down already.

"Let's check her room again," Rene suggested. "Maybe she was in the shower."

"Let's go up top first," Mona said. "I think we're anchoring."

Up on the Sun Deck, the girls saw that they had indeed arrived in Progresso, Mexico. The weather was warm, already over 80 degrees, and the view was not as picturesque as Rene envisioned. As a matter of fact, it looked like they were landing in a poor Vietnamese village.

"I can't believe they picked *this* dock," she told Mona. "This place looks like crap."

"I'm sure it's pretty once you get off the boat," Mona predicted.

They went back to Dawn's cabin, and there was still no answer at the door. By then Mona was getting frustrated.

"Girl, I'm fixin' to go get me something to eat. I can't be doing all of this running around on an empty stomach."

"What about Dawn?" Rene asked.

"Nobody's got off the boat yet, so she's on here somewhere," Mona reasoned. "Maybe she doesn't want to eat with us."

Rene thought about it and figured that might very well be the case. "All right. Let's go."

❦

It felt weird to dine without their third head, and again Rene wondered if she should've mentioned those purple bruises at all. But that wasn't right. Domestic violence is like a drug addiction; it must be exposed before someone ended up seriously hurt, or worse. Dawn had to go through this or things would never get better.

"So why'd you tell Xavier you got a boyfriend?" Mona asked around a cream-cheese-slathered bagel.

"I don't know," Rene said. She had a more manly meal of bacon and grits and fried potato chunks. "Maybe because *I do* have a boyfriend…"

"He never would've known," Mona said.

"I don't get down like that," Rene said.

"You *never* cheated on your man?"

"Blake? No. I probably did some stuff like that when I was a kid, but Blake's the only man I've slept with in the last two years."

"Damn," Mona said. "You're like, Mother Teresa in this bitch."

"No, I'm not," Rene said. "I'm just a regular person. One day you'll find a man you want to be committed to."

Mona nearly choked on her bagel. "*Uck*! Girl, please. Two years with the same old dick? That nigga would have to be Bill Gates rich or something."

"Or you'll have to be really in love," Rene offered. "Don't think it can't happen."

"It can't."

"One day you'll–"

"It can't," Mona repeated. "I'ma be a playa for life."

Rene laughed. "God should've made you a man."

"Then I'd be a *gay* playa," Mona said. " 'Cause I love me some penis!"

Rene cracked up again. "Girl, you stupid." But her smile slipped away just as easily. "Oh, shit. You're not gonna believe this."

"What?" Mona said. She looked over her shoulder and her eyes widened. "Are you kidding me?"

Both women stared in awe as Dwayne approached their table *yet again*. Rene used to think Mona was misleading him. Or maybe the sex was so good he just had to give it another shot. But this was their third day on the ship, and Rene knew she'd been direct with him last night. It was now clear Dwayne was a psycho. Rene wondered if it was possible to get a restraining order on the boat—or maybe they should buy some mace in Mexico.

"Hell-hello," Dwayne said when he reached their table. He wore a gray tee shirt with white soccer shorts. When she first met him, Rene thought Dwayne was handsome, but he wasn't cute at all anymore. He was weak and desperate and as ugly as they come.

"What. The. Hell. Do. You. Want?" Mona asked. She spoke slowly and deliberately, and there was plenty of acid in her tone.

"I, I just, I just, I just–"

"Just *what*, fool?" Mona was at her meanest, and Dwayne looked like he might cry.

"I, I just, I just, I just wanted to know why you mad at me…" he managed.

" 'Cause I don't like you," Mona spat, without missing a beat. "You dumb, and you *worrisome*. You get on my goddamned nerves! I don't want nothing to do with you, and I want you to leave me the hell alone!"

A few people turned to see who was getting told off, which was, of course, exactly what Mona wanted. Dwayne swallowed roughly, but he didn't turn tail like Rene expected.

"I, I, I just…" He shifted his weight from one leg to the other. "I'm sorry," Dwayne said. "I didn't mean no harm."

"Where your people at?" Mona asked.

"Huh?"

"The people you got on this boat with, where are they?"

Dwayne turned slowly and pointed at a nearby table. "Over, over there…"

"Come on," Mona said. She got up and grabbed hold of Dwayne's wrist and marched him to his family members. Rene got up, too, and she had to jog to keep up.

"Do you know this man?" Mona asked the four men Dwayne claimed to be related to. She had one hand on her hip and the other still locked on Dwayne's arm, like he was a naughty child and she was looking for his mother.

A couple of the gentlemen looked down in embarrassment. The oldest man at the table cleared his throat and nodded. "Yeah. That's my nephew. Is he bothering you, ma'am?"

"Yes, he is," Mona said. She pushed Dwayne forward and proceeded to read him the riot act. "I do not like this man. I don't want him following me around, and I don't want him talking to me. If he doesn't leave me alone, I'm going to call the police—or whatever law enforcement they got on this boat. I know they have *somewhere* to lock people up."

Dwayne took a seat and sank so low he looked like a turtle trying to disappear into its shell.

The older gentleman gave Dwayne a stern look of disapproval. "I told you to leave that lady alone! Didn't I tell you?"

Dwayne nodded, but he wouldn't look up at anyone.

"I'm sorry," the uncle told Mona. "I don't know what got into him. But I'll make sure he don't cause you no more trouble. You can just go on about your day and have fun. We'll take care of Dwayne."

Mona stared him down for a second and then nodded. "Fine." She turned and looked surprised to see Rene standing there. "Come on, girl."

Rene followed Mona out of the cafeteria, and after a while everyone's eyes returned to their breakfast plates. Rene *almost* told Mona that she brought the whole episode upon herself, but it didn't seem like an appropriate time for an *I told you so*. Besides, if this wasn't enough to teach Mona a lesson, nothing Rene could say would help anyway.

❧

Back at Dawn's cabin, their friend finally answered the door. And Rene was shocked to see that Dawn had a breakfast tray with dirty dishes sitting on the nightstand.

"You ate already?"

"Uh, yeah," Dawn said. She wore shorts with a white tee shirt, but she didn't look ready to take on the world. Her hair wasn't done, and she didn't have on a lick of makeup.

"Why'd you eat in here by yourself?" Mona asked. She and Rene stepped into the room even though Dawn didn't look like she wanted them there.

"I got up early," Dawn said. "I didn't think y'all was up yet." Dawn went and stood next to the portholes that were her windows. She crossed her arms over her chest, and Rene could tell she was still in a defensive state of mind.

"How you feeling?" Mona asked. "You still mad at us?"

"I'm fine."

"Are you, are you going to go out with us today?" Rene asked. "You know we're in Mexico, right?"

"Yeah," Dawn said. "I saw when we docked."

"Me and Mona were thinking about going scuba diving," Rene said. "You coming with us?"

Dawn started shaking her head before Rene finished the sentence. "Naw. I looked at those excursions already. They cost too much. I can't afford it."

"I'll pay for yo—"

"Naw, that's all right," Dawn said. "I already owe you too much money. I don't want to owe you another hundred dollars just so I can look at some stupid fish."

"Hey, you really need to snap out of this funk," Mona advised. "We're on a cruise, trying to have fun."

"Then go have fun," Dawn said.

"We want you to have fun, too," Rene pleaded.

"I'm not getting in any more debt," Dawn said firmly. "If you want to do something free on this boat, I'll do that with you. But I'm not going scuba diving or kayaking or any of that other mess."

"So you're just going to stay on the boat?" Rene asked. "We're going to be docked for six hours. Don't you at least want to get off so you can say you went to Mexico?"

"No, I'm all right."

Rene wanted to push harder, but Dawn appeared close to tears, and Rene didn't want to see her friend cry two days in a row. This was supposed to be a vacation.

"All right," Rene said. "If that's what you want. We'll, uh, we'll come check on you again when we get back…"

Dawn nodded, and she turned away from them and stared out of her portholes. Rather than ocean, Dawn saw land and trees now, and she really did want to get out—just so she could say she'd been to Mexico.

But her depression was like a warm, fuzzy hole, and it takes a lot of strength to climb out once you get good and settled in. Dawn waited until her friends left the room before she grabbed the remote to see what was on television.

CHAPTER 12
THE EXCURSION

Progresso didn't look any better once the girls got off the ship. Mona expected palm trees and bright sunny beaches, but the first thing they encountered was a downtown area that looked as bad as some of the poorest neighborhoods in Overbrook Meadows. It was actually worse because the health and safety laws are a lot less strict in Mexico.

Mona saw vendors selling smelly fruits and vegetables on almost every corner. She saw a butcher shop with no front wall to protect the counters from the environment. From the ceiling hung cuts of fly-infested meats. Mona already had it in her mind that she wouldn't eat or drink anything that wasn't individually wrapped, but now she wondered if she should even risk that.

The cruise ship docked next to a huge flea market, and the vacationers were inclined to walk through it on their way to whatever excursion they had planned for the day. And the Mexicans were out in droves waiting for the Carnival ships to come in. You could hardly take a step without being accosted to buy this shirt or that necklace or this cross or these puppets.

The worst part about it—aside from the smells—was the sheer desperation in the eyes of many of the street vendors. They gave you the impression that their children may not eat a good supper tonight if you didn't spend your five-dollar bill on something you could get at any Wal-Mart for a mere ninety-nine cents.

The most heart-wrenching thing Mona saw was a poor, old nun with a link of rosary beads in one hand and a large pickle jar half-filled with coins in the other. Her English was not the best, but it only took a few words to get her message across:

"Give money? Please? For the orphanage…"

The nun was small and frail, and she had a mighty hump on her back. Mona's heart melted like butter, and she produced a ten-dollar bill with no hesitation.

"This is terrible," she told Rene as they sought an exit from the marketplace. She knew Mexico was a third-world country, but she didn't expect such blatant poverty.

"Hey! Check that out," Rene said. She pointed her camera and got a few shots of two uniformed men who hoisted a drunken vagrant from the curb and tossed him into the back of a pickup truck.

"What are they doing to him?" Mona asked, her eyes wide and disbelieving.

"That's the *police*," Rene said. "They don't allow hobos to get drunk near the beach, especially when the tourists are coming in."

"Are they taking him to jail?" Mona wondered.

"They'll probably take him deeper into the city and drop him off," Rene guessed. "They don't really care about him getting drunk. They just don't want *us* to see it."

Mona looked around at the rest of the unsightliness and shook her head. "They need to throw a tarp over this whole damned city—if they're worried about our opinion."

Rene chuckled. "Do you want to take a tour?"

"Might as well," Mona said. "Those aren't the tour buses, are they?" She pointed to a line of trashy school buses that had been altered to add another row of seats on the roof—as if anyone would risk their life to sit up there.

"Yeah, that's them."

"This is some *bullshit*," Mona said. "Why would they bring us here?"

"It can't be *all* bad," Rene said, and she was right, sort of…

❧

The bus tour got the girls off of their feet for a while, but it wasn't what Mona would describe as a comfortable experience. It was hot as hell that day, already 92 degrees by 9 a.m., and the bus didn't have any air conditioning. Everyone had their windows down, but it wasn't windy. Stray breezes were sparse at best.

But the girls did get a nice history lesson from their tour guide. He was a dark-skinned man who wore dingy jeans with a tee shirt and a straw hat. He stood at the front of the bus with a microphone, informing everyone of what they could see if they looked to the left or the right.

Nearly every building they saw was rundown, but there were a lot less street vendors about as they ventured further away from the docks. Mona thought the beach was the best attraction the city had to offer. The water was pristine blue, and everyone there looked like they were having a good time. Mona couldn't wait to take her shorts and tee shirt off and strut around in the bikini she had on underneath.

Other than the beach, there wasn't much to look at until the bus returned them to the flea market. Out of her window, Rene saw a fresh crowd of vacationers who had just got off the ship. Among them, Rene spotted the same long-haired teenager who almost ran her over outside of the Windstar the night before.

"Ooh, ooh! That's him!" She pushed Mona's shoulder and pointed. "That's him!"

"Who?" Mona asked, a little perturbed by Rene's roughness.

"I think that boy stole my camera!"

Mona squinted at the group. "Which one?"

"The tallest boy," Rene said, her eyes glued on the perp. "The one with long, blond hair, blue shorts, yellow shirt. He got my camera right now!"

"How do you know it's yours?"

"It looks just like it. Nobody else has a Samsung like that. I got a little nail polish on the screen a couple of months ago. If I could get close enough to look at it, I would know for sure."

"So, are you going to take it from him?" Mona asked.

"I can't do that."

"Are you going to ask him to let you see it?"

The youngster in question was flanked by a man and a woman who were presumably his parents. There were also half a dozen teenagers and four smaller kids in their group.

"I can't do that, either," Rene said. "What if I'm wrong? I'll look like a fool."

"Then forget about it," Mona suggested.

That made sense, but Rene remembered what Dawn told her.

"It's a matter of *respect*. He's not even hiding it or nothing."

"If you're not going to take it from him, shut up about it," Mona said. She wiped the sweat from her neck with a hankie.

"You shut up," Rene told her.

"Where are we supposed to meet up with the scuba diving people?" Mona wondered.

"Somewhere around here."

"We need to get the hell off this bus," Mona said. "It's hotter than a Mexican lunch plate up in here."

"How utterly inappropriate," Rene said.

Mona laughed.

❧

The girls found their scuba diving contact, and they were ushered onto a much prettier bus that would take them further down the beach. The new bus was small, and it had excellent air conditioning.

Mona took a seat on the soft cushions and sighed contently. "This is *nice*. I wish Dawn came with us. I understand she's upset and all, but you gotta put that shit behind you and get on with your life."

"Has some man ever knocked you upside the head?" Rene wondered.

"Hell, naw!" Mona replied with a sneer.

"Then you can't say how easy it is to get on with life."

Mona thought about that and nodded. "We should go back to Overbrook Meadows with her so we can cut Henry's dick off."

"And pickle it," Rene said.

"And make him watch while we serve his pickled dick to a dog," Mona went on.

Rene laughed. "You're taking it a little far, ain't you?"

"No. You have to get rid of the evidence, or they'll just sew it back on," Mona explained.

"They can't sew it back on if we pickle it," Rene countered. "The veins would be all messed up. And dogs don't like pickled dicks."

"How do you know?"

"Because dogs don't eat *pickles*!"

"That's because they don't like *vegetables*," Mona said. "But a pickled dick would be *all meat*."

Rene giggled, but she knew this was no laughing matter. "No, but for real, we need to get his ass."

"We can't do nothing until Dawn wants to change," Mona said, and that was the long and short of it.

"She'll make the right decision," Rene predicted.

Mona wasn't so sure, but she hoped that was the case.

✌✍

The scuba diving adventure was great, and Mona took back all of the bad things she said about the poor city of Progresso. Their instructor was pretty and well-toned and very knowledgeable. She taught them how to put on their gear, how to submerge, how to return to the ocean's surface, and, most importantly, what to do if their tanks malfunctioned and stopped delivering that all important oxygen to their masks.

Rene was a little nervous at first, but once she descended and saw that she really could breathe underwater, the experience took on the surreal quality of a dream. She followed their guide and watched the bubbles drizzling from everyone's masks, and she felt like Aquaman or Jacques Cousteau exploring deep and dangerous aquatic worlds never before seen by man.

Afterwards, Rene and Mona had lunch together on the beach. They played in the water and spent another hour sipping Coronas.

"This is what life's all about," Mona said. She lounged on a beach chair, soaking up as many rays as possible before they had to return to the ship.

"It is nice," Rene said, "but I can't be out here tanning, like I'm white or something." She looked from her dark skin to Mona's much lighter complexion. "I want to go shopping before we leave."

"I'm not going anywhere," Mona said. She had her shades on and her eyes were closed.

"There are some stores by the flea market," Rene said. "You don't want to get any souvenirs?"

"Not here. Maybe in Cozumel."

"You don't want to get anything for Dawn?"

"Go ahead," Mona said. "I'll meet you back on the boat."

"Do you know what time—"

"Two-thirty. I read my itinerary."

Rene checked her watch. They had a little less than an hour.

"You want me to leave you here?"

"I'm grown," Mona said. "I know how to get back to the boat."

Rene had a bad feeling, but she couldn't think of any reason not to leave Mona to her own devices. The dock was only a half mile down the beach, and there were buses returning Carnival guests to the ship every ten minutes or so.

"All right," Rene said. "I'll see you later." She got up and put her shorts and tee shirt back on.

"Get me a souvenir, too," Mona called, but Rene rolled her eyes at that.

"Get it yourself, lazy bones!"

∾

Things didn't go badly until 2:22 p.m. After checking back onto the boat, Rene went to Mona's room to show off the goodies in her shopping bag. When she didn't get a response, Rene went to Dawn's cabin to see if her friends were chilling in there. Dawn answered the door wearing the same thing she had on that morning.

"Hey," Rene said. "You doing all right?"

"Yeah," Dawn said, and she did look better.

"You been in here all day?" Rene asked. She saw another tray on Dawn's nightstand. This one was filled with a new set of dirty dishes, presumably from her lunchtime meal.

"I got out for a little bit," Dawn said. "I'm sorry I was tripping this morning."

"That's cool," Rene said. "Have you seen Mona?"

Dawn shook her head. "I thought she was with you."

"She was. But we split up after lunch. She didn't get back on the ship yet?"

"If she did, she didn't come by here."

Rene thought that was odd, but then again Bartolo was Mona's main attraction these days. Maybe she was with him.

"Do you want to help me look for her?" Rene asked. "We're supposed to be back on the boat by two-thirty. I won't feel good about taking off unless I know she made it."

Dawn forgot all about her depression and stepped into a pair of flip-flops. "Okay, let's go."

Rene and Dawn checked Mona's room again, and they went to both of the pools and cafeterias. That turned up nothing, so they raced through the whole ship, starting at the sun deck and ending back at Mona's cabin. Rene didn't know where Bartolo's room was, so she held out hope that Mona was with him until she spotted Xavier and Bart on the Verandah Deck.

"Hey," Xavier said. He wore shorts today with a black tank top. Rene was surprised by the muscle tone in his arms, but it was 2:42 by then, and she didn't have time to fully admire him.

"Have y'all seen Mona?"

The Brazilians shook their heads.

"Not since last night," Xavier said. "With you…"

"Oh, my God…" Rene threw a hand over her mouth and took off in the opposite direction.

"Is something the matter?" Xavier called, but Rene didn't stop. She and Dawn made a quick right at the next corridor and disappeared from sight.

❧

Getting back on the ship after the excursion in Progresso was a bit of a hassle, but getting *off* the ship fifteen minutes before they were due to set sail was mission impossible. Rene and Dawn argued with the woman who was checking the passports of people still boarding the boat.

And then they had to argue with two porters who sufficiently blocked the exit with their brawny physique. After Dawn threatened to get past these two fellows, *one way or the other*, she and Dawn argued with one of the ship's lieutenants who came all the way from the control room to defuse what was turning into a full-blown crisis.

"Ma'am…" The lieutenant wore a naval uniform that looked militaristic. "No one is getting off the boat right now. We are going to pull up the anchors in exactly *eight minutes*. If you get off the boat, we will have to leave you in Progresso."

"I don't care!" Rene bawled. Sweat glistened on her face, and she was close to tears. "My friend's not on the boat, and I'm not leaving without her!"

Dawn had never seen Rene so upset, and her heart raced, too. Terrible thoughts filled her mind. Dawn had visions of Mona drowning in the ocean. Or maybe a group of thugs kidnapped her and were ravishing Mona at that very moment. It was sickening, but Dawn couldn't help it. There was no rational explanation for Mona's tardiness.

"Ma'am," the lieutenant pleaded. "I'm afraid I cannot allow–"

"Move!" Dawn was never good with reasoning, so she pushed through the crowd like a linebacker. Rene followed close behind, and after a few traumatic seconds the girls found themselves on Mexican soil. There were a lot of people screaming behind them, but that only made Rene run faster.

She took the lead on the familiar streets, and Dawn didn't fall very far behind. Her flip-flops couldn't keep up with the frantic pace, so Dawn kicked her shoes off and sprinted full out, without a care in the world for the curious stares she was accumulating from Mexican street peddlers and tour guides and sweet little nuns who were shuffling about with coin-filled pickle jars.

Rene had no idea where Mona was, but common sense dictated she should start with the last place she saw her friend. So she and Dawn headed for the sandy beach. They had to travel nearly half a mile, but Rene ate up the yards, feet, and meters like an Olympian. Her long legs flexed, and her arms cut through the air. She hoped all of this stress was for naught, but she saw trouble before she was even halfway there.

There were police officers and lifeguards and a horde of bystanders gathered on the beach. They were all looking towards the water, and a few of them were pointing at the deadly waves.

Rene's heart grew hard and heavy. Thick tears squirted from her eyes as she ran. She knew her worst thoughts had come to fruition, but just as she cried out in despair, Rene saw Mona standing among the group of police officers. Mona was looking at the waters, too, and she looked worried, but she was *alive*—and in all of her twenty-seven years on earth, Rene had never seen a more beautiful sight.

She ran straight through the crowd, almost knocking over a policeman on the way, and wrapped Mona up in the biggest hug imaginable. Mona looked startled at first, but she hugged Rene back.

"Oh, my God! *What are you doing here?*" Rene cried.

"I'm sorry," Mona said. "I didn't, I didn't know what time it was."

Rene backed away and held her friend at arm's length. She was about to migrate from worried to angry, but she saw a look of terror in Mona's eyes.

"What, what happened?" The stress from her two-hundred-yard dash caught up with her in an instant, and Rene doubled over. She braced her hands on her knees and sucked air like a vacuum. "What, what are you…"

"It's not me," Mona explained. "It's–"

Dawn burst through the crowd at that moment, and she also wrapped Mona up in a ferocious bear hug. "What are you doing! I thought you was dead!"

"It's not me!" Mona cried. Tears streamed down her face, and this was the first time Rene had *ever* seen her cry. "It's not me," Mona said with a shudder. "It's not me…"

∽◦∾

When the Finley Sisters calmed down enough to have a rational conversation, Mona explained that Dwayne was the cause of all of this commotion. Her stalker got away from his family somehow, and he accosted Mona at the beach after Rene left for her shopping trip. Mona assumed Dwayne wouldn't get the message until she *totally* emasculated him, so she cursed him out thoroughly, calling him everything from *weirdo* to *pencil-dick*.

What Mona didn't know was Dwayne was not so much of a weirdo as he was clinically depressed and suicidal. Rather than listen to her tirade, Dwayne started to scream, and he made a dash to the ocean. Mona didn't hear everything he shouted, but from what she did understand, Dwayne intended to drown himself. He said that since Mona hated him so much, she could watch.

Rene thought Mona was a cold-hearted bitch who would walk away from such a scene with little more than a *good riddance*, but she couldn't have been more wrong. Not only did Mona not turn her back, but she jumped into the water to try to save her crazy stalker. She almost reached him, but Dwayne swam out much farther than Mona dared to venture. She returned to the shore and summoned the lifeguards and policemen who were currently scouring the waters for the lovesick loony.

And Mona wasn't the only Carnival guest who was late in getting back to the ship. Dwayne's uncle and cousins showed up when Mona was frantically looking for rescue personnel, and all four of them were currently in the water looking for their relative.

The only question Rene had after Mona's elaborate explanation was, "Why didn't you come get me and Dawn? We thought something happened to you when we saw all of these people over here."

"I, I couldn't leave," Mona said. "I knew it was time to go, but I couldn't—not 'til I knew if he was okay."

By then it was 3:23, well after the *Ecstasy's* three o'clock departure time, but thankfully Rene saw their ship still anchored in the distance. Before she had to ask the uncomfortable question of whether it was okay to leave *now*, the police made a startling discovery:

Two lifeguards in a motorboat found Dwayne clinging to a metal bridge support nearly a mile away from where Mona reported seeing him last.

"He, uh, he say he try to *scare* you," an exasperated police sergeant explained. "He say, uh, he want you think he dead, so you will, eh, *hurt your heart*. But he is okay. He was just hiding; play trick. We find him, okay…"

The officer's statement pissed Mona off to the highest point of pissticity, but when she looked down the beach and saw Dwayne in handcuffs, surrounded by a gang of policemen, shivering with a pink blanket draped over his shoulders, all of the anger wafted from her.

"I'm just glad he's okay," she told the sergeant.

"Would you and your friends like a ride to your boat?" the policeman asked. "Everyone is waiting for you."

"Yes," Mona said. "Thank you. But, what about him?" She nodded in Dwayne's direction.

"He, uh, I'm afraid he cannot go back to the boat," the sergeant reported. "The boat, they no want him back. He stay here, in Progresso, for a little time. We put him in hospital, for, eh…" He couldn't come up with the word, so he twirled a finger around his ear, the universal sign for *cuckoo*. "We treat him good. He no trouble you no more…"

CHAPTER 13
PROMISES, PROMISES

The Finley Sisters returned to the boat together, and they were inseparable for the rest of the day.

Mona expected the Carnival employees to drag her to a barely lit dungeon deep in the belly of the cruise ship and thrash her soundly until they were satisfied with the explanation for her tardiness. But all of the staff on the boat knew about the incident with Dwayne already, and they were the ones who were apologetic. Even the lieutenant who gave Rene and Dawn a hard time said he was sorry for not being more understanding, and he hoped the ladies could get past the commotion and enjoy the rest of their cruise.

The friends retreated to their individual cabins to shower and change into casual dresses for dinner. They met up again in Mona's room and tried to wrap their minds around the freakish incident.

"So, did Dwayne have to stay in Progresso by himself?" Rene wondered.

"I think I heard his uncle say he would stay, too," Mona reported.

"Wasn't there three more people in their group?" Dawn asked.

"Yeah," Mona said. "He said those were his cousins."

"Do you think they're going to be mad at you?" Dawn asked.

Mona balked at that. "It's not my fault Dwayne went crazy. I wish they would say something slick to me. Shit. *I wish they would.*"

"Did you see how scared that lieutenant looked?" Rene asked her friends.

"Which one was he?" Mona asked.

"The one with the blue uniform," Rene said. "He was Polish, or something. When we got back on the boat, he looked like he was the one who did something wrong."

"I saw that, too," Dawn said. "I thought they were going to be mad at us, but they weren't."

"Everybody's acting nice," Rene went on.

"I think I should sue," Mona said.

Rene frowned. "Sue? For what?"

"Think about it," Mona said. All three ladies sat on the bed together. Mona leaned with her back against the headboard, and she was the only one with her feet on the mattress. "Why would everybody be acting so nice unless they know they did something wrong?"

"Like what?" Rene asked. "Trying to stop me and Dawn from getting off the boat?"

"That, too," Mona said. "But I'm talking about them letting Dwayne on the boat in the first place. They're probably liable for that."

"You're not serious," Rene said.

"I don't know," Mona said. "I always get suspicious when people are acting nice…"

"Maybe they feel sorry for you," Dawn offered.

"I can't see how you're thinking about suing anybody," Rene said. "If anything, Carnival could probably sue *you*."

"What for?" Mona asked with a roll of her neck. "I didn't do nothing."

"How can you say that?" Rene asked.

"It's not my fault that boy was crazy," Mona said.

"But you didn't have to sleep with his crazy ass," Dawn said.

"And then you rejected him the very next day," Rene reminded her.

"That don't mean he had to jump in the ocean," Mona said.

"I know that," Rene said. "But you can't run around treating people any way you want without expecting some consequences sooner or later. Maybe ninety-nine out of a hundred men would just go on about their business. But there's always gonna be that one percent who do something stupid."

"He might have tried to hurt you," Dawn agreed.

Mona knew there was some truth to what they were saying, but she wasn't the type of woman who could sit quietly while people lambasted her—especially if one of these people had been crying for the last two days. "You let your man hurt you anytime he feels like it," she told Dawn. "So how are you going to tell me I'm wrong?"

"That's not right," Rene said.

"Naw, it's okay," Dawn said. Mona may have thought she would hurt her feelings, but Dawn was done crying. And she was done being depressed on this ship. "You're right. I do let my boyfriend hurt me."

"That doesn't have anything to do with it," Rene said.

"Yeah, it does," Mona said. "If she's going to tell me that what I'm doing is wrong, then she needs to be doing something right herself. You, too, Rene. You let your boyfriend cheat on you, and you've been faithful to him for two years."

"That's right," Rene said. "I have been *faithful*. I'm surprised you even know what that word means."

"I don't have to be faithful," Mona spat. " 'Cause I'm not some weak bitch who's gonna let a man mess with my head. I got to—"

"So you mess with theirs instead?" Dawn asked.

"I got, what?"

"I said '*So mess with their heads instead?*' "

"I'm not messing with nobody's head," Mona said. "I live my life however I want to. I didn't ask nobody to fall in love with me. I didn't ask nobody to propose to me, and I didn't ask nobody to jump in the god-damned ocean either."

"Of course not," Rene said. "This is *Mona's World*. Whoever gets stepped on or chewed up and spit out—it's their fault for getting trapped in your web."

"I'm sick of y'all talking like I'm some damn black widow," Mona growled. "You must be jealous or something."

"Please," Rene said. "Trust me, I'm not jealous of you. I don't even—"

"Hey, chill!" Dawn interrupted. "We been though a lot today, and we all got a bunch of stuff on our minds. But it ain't no sense in arguing with each other. That's what the devil wants. Why don't we go eat dinner, and we can talk about this some more later?"

Rene rolled her eyes and pushed off the bed. "Fine. Let's go."

Mona cut her eyes, too, but she got up and slipped into her pumps.

❧

The girls weren't in the best of moods during supper, but it's hard to stay mad when you're on a luxurious ship being catered to like a queen.

For dinner that night they had a choice of fried black tiger prawns with a breaded fish fillet, bourbon and honey glazed roasted spring chicken, or grilled filet mignon over Mediterranean couscous. Each of the Finley Sisters ordered a different selection, and they sampled from each other's plates graciously.

After dinner Mona wanted to drink, and after the wild day they had had, even Dawn thought that sounded like a good idea. The ladies went to the Society Bar, and Mona ordered apple martinis for everyone. While sipping the concoction, Rene spotted a group of kids headed for one of the teen lounges on the same deck. She was almost to the point of not caring about her camera, but she said, "There he goes again," as an afterthought.

"Who?" Mona asked.

"That boy with my camera." Rene sighed in resignation.

But Dawn sat up straight and eyed the crowd curiously. "Who has your camera?"

"That boy with the long hair. I think…"

"So why you just sitting there?" Dawn asked with a frown.

"What am I gonna do?" Rene asked. "Go over there and take it from him?"

"Yeah," Dawn said. "Come on."

Rene got a chuckle out of that, but Dawn hopped off her barstool and headed straight for the hooligan.

"Wait. Dawn!"

Rene got up, too, but she didn't make it in time. She watched in horror as Dawn walked right up to the long-haired kid and forcibly snatched the camcorder from his hand.

"Boy, gimme that!" She turned casually and handed it to Rene. "Here. Is it yours?"

"Oh, snap…" Mona left her drink at the bar and stepped cautiously to her friends, shaking her head in disbelief. "I know she didn't…"

The response to Dawn's action was immediate, and it was bad. The long-haired boy just stared in awe, but his hyper friends came to his defense.

"Hey!"

"What'd she do?"

"She took Aaron's camera!"

"*Hey, lady, give it back!*"

And to make matters worse, it wasn't just kids Rene had to contend with. Aaron's parents had been there the whole time. His mother turned around, and her claws extended as she morphed into a protective mama bear.

"What happened?"

"She stole Aaron's camera!" one of the friends yelled.

"He stole it from her *first*!" Dawn corrected.

"He didn't steal it," the friend said. The boy was getting red about the face and ears, and Rene knew shit was about to hit the fan.

"Did you take his camera?" the mother asked.

The father struck a menacing pose next to his wife, and Mona came and stood next to Rene and Dawn.

"Someone stole my camera," Rene explained. "I thought this might be it, bu–"

"You don't take something from a child just because you *think* it might be yours," Mama Bear said. "My son does not steal! Give it back to him! *Now*!"

"She didn't take it!" Dawn barked. "*I did*." She took a bold step forward, and Mona braced herself for war.

"My son does not steal!" Mama Bear yelled again. "Tell her, Aaron!" She pushed her boy into the fray. "Tell her you got that camera from your uncle."

A good number of bystanders had surrounded them by then, and Rene had never been so embarrassed. Her only saving grace was the fact that the main person who should've been asking for the camera back hadn't said a word. Aaron looked worried rather than upset. His guilt was so obvious, you could read it like a roadmap.

"Tell them where you got that camera!" Mama Bear demanded.

"I, uh, it was, um…"

With that, Rene took a moment to inspect the Samsung. She flipped the screen open, and there was a small splotch of red fingernail polish in the upper right corner. It was ruby raspberry, to be exact.

The room suddenly felt ten degrees cooler. Rene looked up slowly and stared Aaron dead in the eyes. The boy knew the gig was up, and he looked down at his grubby sneakers.

"This *is* my camera," Rene announced boldly. "He stole it from my bag the first day we got here. I can prove it."

Mama Bear watched Rene's eyes closely, and her defiance slipped a little. She noticed her son was trying to will himself to disappear, and then she knew for sure.

"Did you, did you steal this woman's camera?"

Still looking at his shoes, Aaron shrugged. "I found it. It was just…"

His friends' mouths fell open, and Mama Bear's nostrils flared.

"You told me your uncle gave that to you."

"It was, I mean…"

KLAT!

The blow came hard and swift. One moment Mama Bear had her hands at her sides. And then there was a blur. And then her open palm impacted the back of Aaron's neck so hard spittle flew from his mouth. It was so unexpected, everyone within earshot flinched.

"OW!" Aaron threw an arm up to ward off any additional blows, and then he looked around at the commotion his one stupid act caused. His eyes filled with tears, and he decided running away was better than crying or getting a whooping in front of his friends.

"Get back here!" Mama Bear yelled. She started to go after him, but she turned back for a second and spoke to Rene.

"I am so sorry. I can't tell you how embarrassed I am. He's going to apologize to you. I'll ge–"

"It's all right," Rene said.

"No, *he's going to apologize*," Mama Bear insisted. "I'm sorry. I got, uh, I'll be right back!" She pushed her husband aside and went after the opportunistic thief. "Aaron! Get your ass back here!"

Rene watched for a few seconds, and then she and her friends returned to the bar.

"I can't believe you did that," she said to Dawn when they took their seats.

"I can't believe she hit him like that," Dawn said. "I thought white people put their kids in time out."

"*I, I got it from my uncle*," Mona mimicked and laughed. "Did you see the way his hair flew up when she smacked him?"

"His eyeballs almost fell out," Rene said.

"I know her hand hurts," Dawn said, and she laughed, too.

Rene pushed a few buttons on her camcorder and didn't immediately find anything out of order. "Thank you," she said to Dawn. "I would've watched that boy

229

for the rest of the cruise and never said anything to him."

"Girl, that's what friends are for," Dawn said. "You know I always got your back."

Rene smiled. She did know that, and it gave her a greater sense of security than any insurance premium she ever purchased.

❦

The girls had another round at the Society Bar, and then they went to the main pool to watch a limbo competition. Xavier and Bart approached the trio while they were out there, but Mona didn't leave to kick it with them as everyone expected.

"I'm chilling with my girls tonight," she told Bartolo, and he smiled.

"That is good. Friendship is greatest treasure. Maybe we spend time tomorrow…"

"That would be nice," Mona said. She smiled with seductive eyes, and Bart gave her a flirty wink.

At sunset the Finley Sisters took margaritas to the upper deck so they could watch the stars appear in the sky. They sat around a small table, and Mona thought this was a good time to get some closure on the issues they were discussing before dinner.

"So, y'all think I'm living my life wrong?" she asked her friends.

"What are you talking about?" Dawn asked.

"I didn't say that," Rene said.

"Yes, you did," Mona said. "Earlier you were talking about how that thing with Dwayne was my fault because I don't care about people's feelings."

"I don't want to argue," Rene said. She reclined in her chair and looked up at the purple sky. It was a pleasant seventy-six degrees now. A soft breeze ruffled her hair and felt good on her face and arms.

"I don't want to argue either," Mona said. "I just want to talk about what you said. Y'all hurt my feelings."

Dawn didn't think that was possible. She looked up and saw that Mona was smiling. "Yeah, right."

"No, for real," Mona said. "Y'all did hurt my feelings. I felt like y'all were coming down on me."

"Well, we weren't." Rene said. "And besides, you were right. How are we supposed to judge you when we can't get our own shit together? I know I'm not in a position to say anything about *anybody*."

"Me neither," Dawn said.

"Somebody's got to be right," Mona insisted. "We can't *all* be messed up."

"Let's take a vote," Rene said. "Which one of us has our shit together when it comes to men?"

The sisters looked around, and no one's hand went up.

"I thought you said you were doing just fine," Dawn said to Mona.

She sighed. "Sometimes I think I am, but, I don't know. I guess y'all are right. I mean, I always get my needs taken care of, but I don't care about a man's needs. That, that's wrong, isn't it?"

"It depends on how you look at it," Rene said.

"Yeah, maybe that's what works for you," Dawn said.

Mona shook her head. "I don't need y'all to tell me it's fine. I want you to tell me what's wrong with me."

Rene was shocked by that request, and it looked like Dawn was, too. "You want us to tell you what's wrong with you?" she asked skeptically.

"I'm not gon' cry," Mona promised. "I want to hear the truth."

Rene looked at Dawn, and Dawn shook her head. Rene figured she had the most insight, so she took a deep breath and let it out slowly. "Okay, well, first let me tell you what's wrong with *me*." She leaned forward in her seat and her friends did the same.

"When I got a divorce from Terrence," Rene said, "I was only nineteen years old. I thought I had my whole future planned out, and when I found out he was cheating on me..." She looked away, and her traitorous eyes filled with tears. "It was the worst feeling I ever felt. I mean, to this day I never felt that bad about anything."

Dawn felt her pain totally. Mona also looked forlorn.

"I made a promise to myself," Rene said. "I promised that I would never let something like that happen again. I wouldn't play the fool anymore. I promised I wouldn't let a man control my future like Terrence did. I wouldn't love anybody that much anymore.

"And I, I really thought that was the answer. I lived the next ten years like that. There were a lot of guys who fell in love with me, but I let them go. They got mad because I wasn't feeling the same thing for them, and instead of opening my heart, I thought it was better to release them, let them go find somebody who wanted to love them back."

Dawn nodded. Mona did, too.

"But I was just cheating myself," Rene said. "A couple of those guys…" She closed her eyes. "A couple of them really could've been the one. I think about it sometimes, what it would've been like to stay with Stephen or Marcus. They wanted to marry me, but I wouldn't accept their ring. I did that because of pain I was still holding onto from Terrence. I cheated myself, and I didn't even know it. I didn't know it until I came on this cruise, and we talked about that oath we made."

Dawn thought that was tragic. "You still have time to fix it," she said. "You can make it right with Blake, can't you?"

Rene chuckled and wiped her eyes with the back of her hand. "It's too late for him, too. Blake has been cheating on me for at least a year. I know it, and he knows I know it. Her name's Rosalyn. I can tell you what she looks like."

Mona was shocked.

"I thought you didn't know for sure," Dawn said.

"No, I told *you* I didn't know for sure," Rene said. "But I do know. I just didn't want y'all to think I was stupid."

Dawn still couldn't believe it.

"But it's my fault," Rene went on.

"No, it's not," Mona said right away.

Rene chuckled and nodded. "Yes, it is. And I'm okay with it now. See, Blake is no different from any other man. And I treated him just like all the others. There was a time when we could've been more. There was like, there was this moment when I made a pivotal decision. I knew he wanted to fall in love with me, and he wanted me to love him back. I couldn't do it. We never really talked about it, but that's when he started looking for someone else.

"We still stayed together because the relationship we had was special, and it was convenient. But every man needs a woman to love him. I couldn't do that for Blake, so he found somebody who could."

Dawn was astonished by the ease with which Rene told her story. She never knew her friend had so much strength and resolve.

"As far as you," Rene said to Mona, "I think your problem is kind of the same, except there was never any incident that made you the way you are. As long as I've known you, you were the one who had to be on top. You always have to win. You need to be in control. And I think the idea of submitting to a man and letting him be dominant in your life—that goes against your personality. I think that's why you treat men the way you do."

Mona inhaled sharply, and she nodded. "That's right. That *is* how I feel."

"But the problem with that," Rene went on, "is you hurt people's feelings right and left, and you couldn't care less. You don't care if you break a man's heart, and you don't care if you make them cry. And anyone who goes through life like that is–"

"Heartless," Mona said. "You think I don't have a heart."

"No, I think you've got a wall up, just like I do," Rene said. "You don't want to feel love because you know that will make you weak. You can't imagine losing control of your feelings, even for a little while, so you keep your heart in a cage. That way no man can ever control you."

"You're right. That's me," Mona said. She shivered and rubbed the goose bumps on her arms. "You're like a psychiatrist."

"Now do me," Dawn said, and they all giggled nervously.

Rene shook her head. "I can't figure you out, Dawn. I know things can get bad sometimes, but I don't understand how a woman can go home to a man who beats on her. I'm sorry, but you're going to have to explain this one yourself."

Dawn nodded and sighed. She knew it would come to this, and she had plenty of time to think about it when she was holed up in her room last night.

"I guess it started right after high school," Dawn said. She looked up at the stars, and her friends were very quiet, hanging on her every wood. "When we was in school, we was popular," Dawn recalled. "Ever since middle school, we was together. Everybody respected us. Some people feared us. We always had each other's back, and nobody messed with us. We promised we would always be there for each other, but we wasn't."

The seriousness of that childhood promise weighed heavily on Mona and Rene's hearts, and they didn't like where this story was going.

"I tried to go to college," Dawn said, "but it was different without y'all. I wasn't good at nothing. I wasn't smart in high school, either, but y'all always helped me. You let me cheat off your chemistry tests sometimes," she said to Rene.

Rene nodded and offered a weak smile.

"But when y'all left town, I found out I wasn't popular," Dawn said. "I was just a dumb, fat girl. I didn't have no friends except for y'all. And when y'all stopped calling after a while, I felt like nobody liked me. I got depressed, and I started getting bigger, and from that point, it was all downhill.

"Tim's daddy, I knew he was gon' leave me. I got pregnant on purpose, but he left me anyway. Luther's daddy was the first man that ever hit me. He got real mad when I got pregnant, and he kicked me in the stomach one time. He took off while Luther was still in diapers."

Mona put a hand to her mouth, and she saw that Rene was crying again.

"I had a couple more boyfriends before I ended up with Henry," Dawn said. "Henry, he calls me fat, and he hit on me sometimes when I don't do right. Sometimes I don't think he likes me at all, but he comes home every night. He don't cheat on me.

"I'll tell you the truth: I stay with him 'cause I don't think I can do no better. I know don't nobody else want me. I got two kids with two different daddies, and I'm not all pretty like y'all are…"

"You are pretty," Mona said.

"And it doesn't matter how big you are," Rene added. "You don't deserve to be treated like that. Nobody does."

"But I don't –" Dawn sniffled. "I don't have nobody else."

"Yes, you do," Rene and Mona said almost in concert.

"You have your family," Rene said. "And you have us. We let you down after high school, but we're back now. We're all going to be there for each other from now on. No matter what."

Mona nodded, and she gave Dawn a tender smile that spoke volumes.

Dawn had no doubt they would keep their promise this time, and her whole body felt warm.

"Whew!" Mona said with a sigh.

Her friends laughed, and that broke up some of the tension.

"So, what now?" Mona asked Rene.

"What do you mean?"

"You're the psychologist," Mona said. "You got us talking about what's wrong with us. What's supposed to happen next?"

Rene grinned. "I don't have to plan a second step because we already did it. We made an oath to live love the fullest. If we all do that, it will solve every problem we just talked about."

The girls mulled that over, and Mona asked, "So are you going to stay with Blake? You gonna tell him you're ready to fall in love?"

Rene shook her head. "I know I said it was my fault he cheated on me, but I can't take *all* the responsibility. If he wanted someone to fall in love with, he should've broke up with me. Even if I opened up to him now, I could never trust him. What about you? Are you going to marry Dennis?"

Mona laughed and she shook her head as well. "I can't marry that boy. If I *do* decide to settle down and fall in love with one man, it can't be Dennis. I like what he does for me, but I don't respect him."

"Maybe you could learn to," Dawn offered.

"It's too late for that," Mona said. "I can't go from bossing him around for the last eight months to bringing him breakfast in bed. Either I have respect for you in the beginning, or I don't. I could probably string Dennis along for another year if I want to, but I'm going to break up with him—just for y'all."

"Don't do me any favors," Rene said.

"All right. I want to do it," Mona decided. "I want to fall in love. I wanna see what it feels like. If I don't like it, I can always go back to the *real me*, but I'm going to fulfill my oath. It's worth a try." She laughed.

"What about Bartolo?" Rene asked with a wily smile. "Are you going to fall in love with him?"

"I doubt it!"

"You're not going to string him along, too, are you?"

"No," Mona said. "But I am going to have sex with him. He'll be my *last fling*. I promise! After him, I'm going to find somebody to fall in love with."

That cracked everyone up.

"What about you?" Rene asked Dawn. "Are you going to leave Henry?"

"Yes," she said. Her smile went away, except from her eyes. "If y'all gon help me through it, I'll do it."

"Me and Rene wanna cut off his dick," Mona informed her.

"What?" Dawn laughed. "Naw, just leaving him will be fine."

"Then it's official," Rene said. "Technically, we're all single again. I know that's not a new feeling for *you*," she teased Mona.

"Not really," Mona confirmed.

"So I guess you're gonna get started on Bartolo tonight," Dawn said.

"No." Mona shook her head and downed the rest of her margarita. "I already told him I'm kicking it with my girls tonight, and that's what I'm gonna do. You down to drink some more?"

Dawn looked up at the starlit sky. It felt like 1999 all over again. "Yep," she said. "I'm down with whatever my sisters are down with."

CHAPTER 14
COZUMEL AND KARAOKE

After their talk Rene checked her camera again and saw that it had four new videos saved in slots that were supposed to be empty. She watched them with her friends, but they were nothing special; typical teenage hijinks. The thief recorded a few sets of boobs he liked, and his friends participated in a God-awful rap battle near the bow of the ship one day.

Rene erased the videos, and for the rest of the evening she played cinematographer while her friends took her on a tour of the ship. They had the most fun in the karaoke lounge. The talent was a little better that night, but the Finley Sisters were all together and they were all tipsy, and ridiculing strangers was the main order of business.

They didn't talk loudly enough for their victims to hear them, but everyone noticed there was a lot of laughter coming from the sisters' table, and this laughter varied in volume, depending on how unsavory the current singer was.

Before they left Rene remembered how Dawn used to be a pretty good singer back in their high school days.

"Why don't you go up there and show 'em how it's done?"

"Why?" Dawn asked with a chuckle. "So y'all can make fun of me?"

"We're not going to make fun of you!" Mona assured her.

"Don't you still sing?" Rene asked.

"Not really," Dawn replied. "I haven't been in a choir since the tenth grade."

"I'ma go get the book," Mona said, referring to a huge binder filled with songs that were available for the karaoke event.

"No!" Dawn grabbed her arm and pulled her back to her seat. "I'm not going up there! I been drinking too much!"

"All right," Mona said. "But tomorrow you're singing before you get all drunk."

"Y'all gotta do something, too," Dawn said with a giggle.

"That's cool," Rene said. "We'll all go up there, give these people a chance to laugh at us for a change."

"Ooh, check this one out," Mona said as their next victim took the stage. This time it was a homely middle-aged woman who said she was singing her favorite Bonnie Raitt song. "She so ugly," Mona quipped, "I bet her husband takes her to work with him so he don't have to kiss her goodbye!"

Rene and Dawn got a big laugh out of that, but by then it was mostly the liquor tickling their funny bone.

The next morning Dawn overslept for the first time in over a year. By the time she jerked her head from the pillow, the sun was shining brightly through her portholes, and someone was banging hard on her cabin door.

Dawn jumped out of bed and rushed to see what the problem was. Mona stood on the other side of the door looking calm and quite beautiful.

"What?" Dawn nearly screamed.

"What do you mean, '*what*'?" Mona said.

"Why you banging on the door like that?"

"It's almost ten o'clock," Mona informed. "This is my second time coming to your room. Just wanted to make sure you were all right."

"Oh." Dawn rubbed her eyes and straightened her hair with her fingers. She looked back and saw land rather than water though her circular windows. The land wasn't moving, and as Dawn shook the cobwebs from her equilibrium, she realized the boat wasn't, either. "We landed again?"

"Yep. You missed it," Mona said. "We're in Cozumel now."

"Where's that?" Dawn asked.

"It's still Mexico. Didn't you read your schedule?"

"Yeah, I did," Dawn said. "Gimme a minute to wake up. Did y'all eat breakfast yet?"

"We're trying to wait on you," Mona said, with just a little impatience. "Come to Rene's room when you get dressed."

"I gotta shower and everything," Dawn said. "Y'all go ahead without me. I'll catch up with you in the cafeteria."

"Cool," Mona said. "Maybe you should order some wakeup calls for the next couple of days. You can't be the best—"

"Yeah, I know," Dawn said. "*... if your ass is in bed all day.* You already told me."

"Oh. Well act like you know." Mona continued down the hallway, her haughty stroll in full force.

❧

Rene and Mona were done eating by the time their friend made it to the cafeteria, but they remained at the table while Dawn wolfed down a simple meal of cereal and toast. Both Mona and Rene had new excursion lists, and they were busy making plans for the fourth day on the boat.

"I wanna go parasailing," Mona said. "I never did that before."

"*Parasailing?*" Rene frowned. "You might as well go bungee jumping if you're going to do something that crazy."

"I did that before," Mona said, "but I can do it again." She scanned the list anxiously. "Where's bungee jumping? I don't see it on here."

"It's *not* on there," Rene said. "I'm just saying, if you want to do something dangerous, you might as well — *never mind.*"

"Parasailing's not dangerous," Mona said with a wave of her hand. "Quit acting like a baby."

"What do you think?" Rene asked Dawn.

She took a sip of orange juice and cleared her throat. "About what?"

"About *parasailing*," Rene said. "Does that sound like something you want to do?"

Dawn shook her head. "I'm not going parasailing. What are you talking about?"

"Today's excursions," Rene said. "Are you even listening to us?"

"Not really," Dawn admitted. "I thought y'all was talking to each other."

"Stop playing," Mona said. "You're coming with us today."

Dawn noticed that was a statement rather than a question, but she still said, "I don't have no money for no excursions. I told you yesterday."

"Mona and I are splitting the price of yours," Rene said. "We already agreed on it, and we're not taking 'no' for an answer. So what do you want to do?"

Dawn sighed. "Man, I–"

"Stop with the whining," Rene said.

"Yeah," Mona agreed. "That shit's getting old. You need–"

"Excuse me."

The ladies looked up and saw that a familiar gentleman had approached their table. It took a second to place him, but Rene remembered he was one of the men who came on the cruise with Dwayne. The uncle was still in Progresso, so this had to be one of Dwayne's cousins.

The stranger was tall and dark-skinned, and he was ten times more handsome than his suicidal relative. And he didn't look one bit crazy. Rene thought he looked like Wesley Snipes in his heyday.

"Yes?" she said.

"My name is Patrick." The cousin spoke to Mona directly. "I don't mean to interrupt, but I wanted to meet you and apologize for what happened with Dwayne yesterday. Actually I want to apologize for everything he put you through since we got on this ship.

"I'm really embarrassed about the whole thing. Dwayne has had problems like this in the past, a couple of restraining orders here and there, but he's never done anything as extreme as that stunt he pulled yesterday."

Mona had a way of flirting with men without making it obvious that she was doing so, and Rene laughed inwardly while she watched her friend in action.

"It's not your fault, Patrick." Mona batted her eyes. "You can't hold yourself responsible for what Dwayne did. Even though you *did* say you would look after him…"

"I know," Patrick said. He flashed an awesome smile that got all of the girls' attention. "That's why I feel like I owe you a formal apology."

"All right," Mona said. "I accept your apology."

Patrick nodded and almost walked away, but something in Mona's eyes made him linger. "I, uh, I never believed anything Dwayne said about you. I mean, he said you liked him, and y'all had some sort of relationship…"

"Oh, not at all," Mona said without a pause. "I had a drink with him on the first night we boarded, but that was it. I'm not sure why he developed this *fixation* on me. It's sad, really…"

Dawn lowered her head and sighed to herself.

Patrick grinned and decided to try his luck. "That's good. It's nice to know that. I, uh, I know this might sound strange, considering what happened with Dwayne, but I've been attracted to you since the first moment I saw you. I would really like to spend some time with you — if my cousin hasn't turned you off our whole family."

He chuckled. Patrick was confident and fine like a ball player.

Here we go again, Rene thought, but to everyone's surprise Mona shook her head.

"I'm sorry, Patrick. You sound like a nice guy, but there's someone else on this boat I like. And we only have two days left… I'm pretty sure I won't have time to spend with you."

Dawn looked up with wide eyes, and she saw that Rene was equally confused.

"Well, maybe we could exchange numbers," Patrick persisted, "and stay in touch afterwards. I live in Midland."

"Um, no," Mona said, her smile still dazzling. "But it was nice to meet you."

That was a huge blow to Patrick's poise, and it showed, but only in his eyes. "Oh, well, it was nice meeting you, too. Good day, ladies."

He nodded and made a hasty retreat. Rene and Dawn stared at their friend when he was gone.

"What?" Mona said.

"What was that about?" Rene asked.

"That's called *rejecting a man*," Mona informed smugly.

"I know what it's called," Rene said. "I want to know why *you* did it. That brother was *fine*. You can't tell me he wasn't."

"He was," Mona agreed.

"I can't believe you'd sleep with Dwayne but not him."

"I already like somebody else on this boat," Mona reiterated.

"That's another thing," Dawn said. "You was actually *honest* with him. Since when do you tell men the truth?"

Mona laughed. "What did I tell you last night?" She answered her own question: "I said I was having *one more* fling on this cruise, and then I'm going to find a man to fall in love with. You didn't believe me?"

"No," Dawn said.

"Me neither," Rene said.

"Well, maybe you believe me now," Mona said. "If I say I'm going to do something, I'm going to do it." She returned her attention to the excursion list. "Now, do you want to go parasailing or not," she asked Dawn.

"I'm definitely not going parasailing," Dawn said, still awed by Mona's supposed transformation. "What else they got?"

❧

Cozumel, Mexico was the exact *opposite* of the poverty Rene witnessed in Progresso. The streets were clean, it was a lot less crowded, and there were virtually no vendors to avoid as the Finley Sisters toured a downtown area that looked brand new.

There were still plenty of markets ready to snatch up the tourists' dollars, but every store the girls visited was neat enough to meet America's standards. There were no butcher shops, no live chickens for sale, no moldy fruit, and no drunks being hoisted into the back of pickup trucks. *And* all of the restaurants were American. Rene saw a Chili's, a Don Pablo's and a very Tex-Mex Three Amigos.

"This is nice," Dawn said.

The girls lounged under a shady bench while they waited their turn to pose with a Three Amigos backdrop. The painting featured three cartoon cowboys with oval-shaped holes cut where their faces should be. There were steps behind the prop, so even the littlest cowpoke could stick his face in and become part of the scene.

"This isn't *nice*," Rene countered. "This is *fake*! It looks like we're in El Paso or something. This isn't Mexico."

Dawn frowned. "Where are we then?"

Rene shook her head. "This may be Mexico, but yesterday we were in the *real* Mexico. This place has been bought out, completely taken over by the white man."

Mona laughed. "The white man."

"You know this ain't right," Rene whined. "You saw what real Mexico looks like."

"Yeah, it was stinky and ugly," Mona said with a frown. "I like this better."

"You would," Rene said.

"I don't really remember Progresso," Dawn said. "I was too busy running. But this is pretty."

"Yes, it is," Mona agreed. "Get off your high horse," she told Rene.

∽•∾

Instead of parasailing the Finley Sisters decided to go on a horseback adventure through what was supposed to be ancient Mayan trails and caves. Rene had fun on her horse because she hadn't ridden one since she was a teenager, but the historical aspect of their excursion proved to be as big a farce as Cozumel's downtown area.

Their tour guide was a real *charro*, and his skill with horses was impressive. Once everyone got saddled up, he led them down an exceptionally long trail that was said to be used by the Mayans before their civilization was destroyed by the Spaniards.

Rene didn't doubt that the Mayans traversed that land once upon a time, but all of the artifacts their guide pointed out were cheap replicas, and they were clearly out of place, scattered strategically along the trail for the purpose of the tour.

They stopped a couple of times to explore caves that probably did provide shelter for the Mayan people, but Rene thought they went overboard with silly cave drawings that looked a few months old rather than thousands of years.

Overall Rene thought the stop in Cozumel was a bust—from an archeological standpoint—but the time spent with her friends made it worthwhile. Dawn had never been on a horse, and Rene got some great footage of her friend struggling to learn the basic riding techniques. And the Mexican landscape was picture perfect, teeming with natural wildlife, like eagles and other birds of prey that fed on a huge population of wild iguanas.

After their outing the ladies had lunch at Three Amigos, and then they hit the beach for a couple of stress-free hours of fun and relaxation. There were no jilted lovers threatening suicide that afternoon and no dissention when Rene wanted to check out a few stores before they left. The best friends did their shopping together, and they made it back to the boat thirty minutes early without a hitch.

ᴖᴗᴖ

From Cozumel, the *Ecstasy* set sail again, heading for Galveston, Texas; the last stop on the cruise. The Finley Sisters knew they only had two days left on the boat, and they wanted to make the most of them.

"I've *got* to sleep with Bart tonight," Mona told her friends at dinnertime. "I haven't spent time with him in almost two days. He's going to think I'm not interested."

"He knows you're interested," Rene said. "I don't think you could've made it any clearer."

"You're right," Mona said. "He was the one playing hard to get." She grinned mischievously. "I like that, though." She licked lobster sauce off a cheddar biscuit. "It makes me want him more."

"Really?" Rene teased. "You want him more because you can't have him? I wonder if that's ever happened to anyone else. That's, that's got to be new concept."

"Whatever," Mona said and then asked, "What about you? What—or should I say *who*—do you want to do before we go home?"

Dawn laughed.

"I'm good," Rene said with a chuckle.

"I know you like Xavier," Mona said. "And you said we're all single. Why don't you take him to your room?"

"I don't know him," Rene reminded her.

"That's why it's called a *fling*," Mona said. "Don't forget: *Whatever happens on the boat, stays on the boat.*"

"That's what they say about Vegas," Rene said. "But a lot of stuff that happens there gets on the plane and follows your ass home."

"Come on!" Mona urged. "*Peer pressure, peer pressure!*"

Rene laughed. "The last time I heard that, you got me to kiss Tremont Story on the last day of school in the eighth grade."

"You liked it, too," Mona recalled.

"I did," Rene admitted, "until he put his tongue in my mouth."

Dawn laughed. "I remember that!"

"You liked that part, too," Mona said.

"Nuh-uhn." Rene shook her head, but her smile said otherwise.

"What about you?" Mona asked Dawn. "What's on your to-do list before we get back home?"

Dawn shrugged. "I don't know. Nothing, I guess. Just kick it with y'all some more."

"You haven't seen any fine men on the boat?" Mona asked. "You're not down with flings, either?"

"No," Dawn said.

"You sure?" Mona asked. "What about that guy you were in the pool with?"

"No," Dawn said again. She wasn't smiling at all, and Mona knew to drop it.

"You're still doing karaoke tonight, though, right?" Rene asked instead.

"Oh, uh, yeah," Dawn said, her bubbly personality back intact. "If y'all do a song, too."

"I can't sing worth a lick," Mona said.

"We'll down a few shots first," Rene suggested. "It'll be fun."

❧

After dinner the girls changed into sexy outfits for their appearance on the karaoke stage. Mona had a strapless cocktail dress that was candy apple red with a slit on one side. It clung to her curves magically, and she couldn't wait to see the look on Bartolo's face when he saw her. Rene's dress was navy blue. It had straps, but it hugged her boobs and hips, and Rene thought she looked better than Mona that night. She already knew her booty was more enticing.

And, not to be outdone, Dawn put on a new dress, too. It was shimmering purple with a sash around the waist. Dawn's dress was looser and less revealing than either of her friends', but she knew she looked good, too. Maybe she wasn't as *fine* as Rene and Mona, but she felt she was just as pretty.

The trio headed for the karaoke club in good cheer, but their confidence began to dwindle when they got there. The singers were surprisingly talented that night, and Mona was no longer keen on the idea of making a fool of herself.

"Uh-uhn." She closed the DJ's big song book and handed it to Rene. "I changed my mind. I can't do it."

"Yes, you can," Dawn urged.

"No. I can't sing."

"I thought you were going to get some drinks to calm your nerves," Dawn said.

"That's not gonna be enough," Mona said. She looked seriously spooked. Dawn laughed at her. "What's so funny?"

"I've never seen you afraid to do *anything*," Dawn said.

"That's because I'm good at *everything*," Mona said. "*Except* singing."

"How about we go up together," Rene suggested. "That way they won't be able to tell which one of us is off key."

Mona thought about that and sighed. "All right. But we need to get some tequila shots first."

Rene and Mona left for the bar, but Dawn stayed to hold their seats and maintain her sobriety. Her friends returned twenty minutes later. By then they were bold enough and tipsy enough to take the stage for an ultra-sexy rendition of No *Scrubs* by TLC. Their singing was as awful as Mona predicted, but they looked so good, every man in the room was hooting and hollering throughout their set.

When they returned to their seats, Mona was once again sure she was the greatest thing since push-up bras, and Dawn didn't say anything to the contrary.

"Y'all did great! I thought you said you couldn't sing."

"I didn't know I could," Mona replied. "Even *I'm* surprised by my awesomeness every now and then."

Dawn laughed. "I wish they would hurry up and call my name so I can be through with it."

"What song are you doing?" Rene asked.

"I'm not telling you," Dawn said with a smirk. "You'll see when I get up there."

The girls had to wait only ten minutes before it was Dawn's time to shine. The DJ called her up after three skinny kids who clowned around with the always popular *Baby got Back* by Sir Mixalot. The crowd was pretty hyper by then, and Dawn wondered if she should've picked a different song.

"Hey, pretty lady, what's your name?" the DJ asked when she got to the stage.

She spoke softly into the microphone. "Dawn."

"Dawn; such a beautiful name. As beautiful as the break of dawn." He laughed, and some in the audience did as well. "What will you be singing for us tonight?" the DJ asked.

"*Loving You*," Dawn said, "by Minnie Riperton."

"Oh, like the Burger King commercial!" the DJ joked. "The Cini-Mini's!"

Everyone laughed, except for Dawn, who had flittering butterflies in her belly.

"All right, let's hear it!" the DJ said. "Give Dawn a hand, y'all!"

The crowd applauded politely, and the music began to play, and Dawn closed her eyes and leaned closer to the mic.

Loving You was a special song for Dawn—had been for a long time. She first heard the piece twenty-six years ago, when Cabbage Patch kids were all the rave, and Dawn was still learning that her mom preferred she used the potty rather than wear diapers. Dawn's grandmother had an old record player she refused to get rid of even though most people had moved on to cassettes by then. Maw Maw had a vast music collection. Her favorite records were Lionel Richie's *Can't Slow Down* and Minnie Riperton's *Perfect Angel*.

Dawn fell in love with *Loving You* before she knew her ABC's, and she started singing along with the record before she could speak well. Her grandmother used to tell her, "Girl, if you can sang *that* song, you *know* you can sang!" and Dawn took pride in that.

Maw Maw died of breast cancer when Dawn was in middle school, and, among other inexpensive yet emotionally priceless items, Dawn found herself in possession of the *Perfect Angel* album. When she later learned that Minnie Riperton died of breast cancer just like her grandma, Dawn cherished the album even more, and she thought about Maw Maw every time she sang Minnie's most memorable ballad.

The people at the karaoke club had no idea how much the song meant to Dawn, but when she sang the first line they knew they were in for a real treat. Not only could this pretty girl in the purple dress sing, but she could *sang*, and that was something none of the amateurs had brought to the table thus far.

Half of the crowd's jaws dropped when Dawn hit the first high note, and the other half scooted to the edge of their seats when she hit it again. People started to cheer before she was halfway through, and by the time Dawn finished the song, everyone in attendance was on their feet. This was the first standing ovation in the karaoke club, and they wouldn't have another one for many cruises to come.

Dawn opened her eyes and thought she was dreaming. People yelled and clapped and some pumped their fist in the air. Mona and Rene screamed the loudest, but Dawn couldn't hear them over the rest of the hoopla. When she stepped off the stage, strangers rushed to congratulate her like she was a real celebrity.

The DJ didn't regain control of his show for a full five minutes.

CHAPTER 15
MISS MINNIE

"Girl, I didn't know you could sing like that!"

The Finley Sisters sat at the Metro Bar, each with a Long Island iced tea in hand. Dawn never drank alcohol on so many consecutive days, but she had no fears that her friends were turning her into an alcoholic. In two days they would be back in Texas, and she planned to go back to only drinking on special occasions.

"I'm really not that good," Dawn said modestly. "I just like that song."

"Stop *lying*!" Mona said. "You *know* you can sing! You tore that shit up!"

"For real," Rene agreed. "I been in there three different times. Nobody on this boat can sing like you. Even in the variety shows, none of them can hold a candle to you. And they're professionals!"

Dawn blushed. "I sing okay."

"How come you're not in your church choir?" Mona wondered.

"I wanted to," Dawn said. "But I couldn't never make it to their practices. I work *a lot*. Y'all just don't know."

"I got it all on camera," Rene said. "I even got the end when everybody swarmed the stage like you were Beyoncé or something." She laughed. "You gotta watch this video, Dawn. They loved you!"

"I'll look at it later," Dawn said.

"Are you embarrassed?" Mona stared into her friend's eyes.

Dawn looked away coyly.

Mona laughed. "Girl, are you embarrassed?"

"A little," Dawn admitted. "It's not that big a deal."

"It *is* a big deal," Rene said. "You got talent, Dawn. You shouldn't take that for granted. You were better than Minnie Rip–"

Dawn cut her off. "Uh-uhn! Don't say that."

"You need to watch the video," Rene said. "Your voice is perfect. And you got more soul than–"

"Minnie is the *best*," Dawn insisted. "I listened to her record a million times. I wanted to be just like her. But I'm not better."

"All right," Rene said. "But will you at least watch the video? I don't think you know how good you are."

"All right," Dawn said.

Rene passed her the camcorder, but it was too noisy at the bar.

"I can't hear it," Dawn said. "Let's go somewhere else."

"We can go to my room," Mona offered. "I need to change anyway."

"Dang, Mona, you *just* changed," Rene said. "Why are you changing again?"

"Tonight's the night for me and Bart," Mona said. "I need to wear something that shows off more of my legs."

Rene looked her up and down and thought her current dress was revealing enough. "Why don't you just strip down to your necklace and call it a day?"

"You think I'm going to take fashion tips from someone with red fingernail polish and *plum* toenails?" Mona shot back. "Nigga please."

Dawn watched her video while Mona changed, and she agreed that she did a good job on stage. She was too nervous to add any arm movements, and she kept her eyes closed the entire time, but her singing was flawless. The crowd was eating out of her hands after the first note.

"I'm going to make you a copy so you can show everybody when you get home," Rene said.

"Thanks," Dawn replied, but she still didn't look half as excited as Rene felt.

"Girl, what's your deal? Why aren't you happy?"

"I am," Dawn said. "I'm just not used to all of that attention."

"You're not shy."

"Yes, I am," Dawn said. "I've always been like that. You and Mona are usually in the front, getting all the attention. I just chill in the background, doing my own thang."

Rene thought for a second and realized Dawn was right. "It shouldn't be that way. We're all equal. You need to step up to the front more often."

Dawn chuckled. "Everybody don't have it in them to be in the front, Rene. That's the way the world works. You got to have your winners, and you got to have your losers. If it wasn't like that, everything would fall apart."

"Hey, I don't ever want to hear you calling yourself a loser," Rene said. "And I didn't invite you on this cruise so you can hang out in the background and be some kind of third leg. I wanted you to come because you're my best friend, just like Mona."

"You and Mona have a lot more in common."

"Maybe so," Rene said. "But we've always been a *three-headed* monster. Each one of us is just as important. I can do some things Mona can't do, and you can do some things I can't do. That's what makes our friendship so special."

"What can I do that you can't do?" Dawn wondered.

"How about when you got my camera back for me?" Rene said. "That's something only *Dawn* could do. Mona told me to leave them people alone."

Dawn grinned. "Yeah. Y'all don't have too much hood rat in you."

"Um, and neither do you," Rene said. "You're more *bold* and *assertive*. I don't want to hear you calling yourself a hood rat either."

"All right," Dawn said. She smiled warmly. "You always helped me be a better person, Rene. Did I ever tell you that?"

"No," Rene said. "But it's nice to hear. So are you ready to stop chilling in the background?"

"Yeah," Dawn said with a chuckle.

But Mona stepped out of the bathroom, and Dawn knew she would have to linger in the shadows for a little while longer. Mona wore a black leather miniskirt with four-inch stilettos and no stockings on her long, luscious legs. Her red lipstick glistened, and this was the first time Dawn saw her with mascara on. Sexuality oozed from every one of Mona's pores.

"Y'all ready to go?"

"Where we going?" Rene asked. "The strip club?"

"Oh, why must you hate?" Mona wondered. "I got this skirt out yo mama's closet. You didn't say nothing when she wore it to those PTA meetings."

"Don't be talking about my mama," Rene warned.

"Don't be talking about my mama," Mona mocked.

"You stupid," Rene said.

❧

Rene also thought Mona's outfit would relocate Dawn to the background, but even Mona's super sexy legs couldn't make the karaoke crowd forget the magic they witnessed that night. When the girls got back to the Lido Deck, people starting pointing and making comments like, "Look, it's her!" and "That's the one I was telling you about!"

Mona assumed this extra attention was directed at her, and she held her head up extra high. But a group of women finally approached and made it clear Mona wasn't the only star in the Finley trio.

"Hey, can we take a picture with you?" they asked Dawn.

She frowned. "What?"

"You were *awesome* tonight," one of the women said. "I never heard *anybody* sing that song as good as you! I took some pictures, but I wanted to get one with you and my friends. Is that all right?"

That seemed like an outrageous request, but how do you turn away admirers?

"Uh, okay," Dawn said.

"Thanks!" The woman looked around and handed her camera to Mona.

"Can you take a picture of us, please?"

Mona chuckled, but she took the camera. Dawn posed with the strangers, still wondering if this was some kind of joke.

But it wasn't. After Mona snapped the shot a middle-aged couple came forward with the same request.

"Can we get a picture with you, too?" They grinned wildly, like kids at Christmas.

"I didn't do nothing but sing a song," Dawn protested.

"And you were great!" the man said.

"You're gonna be famous one day," his wife predicted. "When you get big, I'm gonna tell everyone I was on a cruise with you!"

Mona was already in position for the shot, so the woman handed her a digital Sony. "Can you take a picture of us?"

"Anything for *Dawn*," Mona said, with just a little sarcasm.

Dawn's smile was as big as Mona's ego in the second picture. She hoped everyone would leave her alone after that, but someone else shouted "Miss Minnie!" when she tried to walk away.

Dawn turned and was surprised to see a man making his way through the crowd. He was tall, about six-two, and stout, around two hundred and twenty pounds. He didn't have a woman with him. Dawn couldn't believe he wanted to take a picture as well.

"Hey, how are you?" he asked when he got closer. "My name is Calvin." He stuck out a hand, and Dawn shook it. Calvin's grip was strong, but not too tight. He wore wire-rimmed glasses and a full moustache. "I didn't mean to call you Miss Minnie," he said with a smile. "But I wouldn't be surprised if that was your real name. You killed that song tonight. I never heard anyone do it better."

"Thanks," Dawn said. "My name is Dawn."

"*Right*. I remember now, from when the DJ announced you. It's nice to meet you." Calvin smiled and Dawn smiled, too.

She wasn't sure what his intentions were, but she thought he was handsome. He was older than her, maybe up to ten years, and he was a nice dresser. He wore white slacks with a black button-down tucked in neatly. His shoes had a crisp shine, and he didn't have a gut hanging over his belt. His hair was short. His skin was dark like brown M&Ms.

"My wife sang that song at our wedding," Calvin said, and Dawn's heart sank. "I mean my *ex-wife*," he said, and Dawn's chest felt warm again.

"You don't know if you have a wife or not?"

The stranger laughed. "Of course I know if I have a wife or not. I'm just not used to referring to her as my *ex*. We were physically separated for more than five years, but our divorce just got finalized four months ago."

"I'm sorry to hear that."

"It's okay," Calvin said.

"Why were y'all separated for so long?" Dawn asked, and she immediately thought better of it. "I'm sorry. I didn't mean to get all up in your business."

"It's okay," Calvin said, still smiling. "I'm the one who approached you. My ex-wife, Karen, she was a good woman, but she made a lot of mistakes. She was an investment broker. She made good money, but it was never enough. The woman had very expensive tastes."

Before Dawn could ask how one loses their expensive tastes, Calvin said, "She's in prison. Big time embezzlement scheme. And it wasn't her first offense. They gave her fifteen years."

"Wow," Dawn said. "That's messed up."

"That wasn't even the worst of it," Calvin said. "I stayed with her for five years after she got locked up, until I found out she was planning to run away with her co-defendant. They bought plane tickets and everything, a lover's nest in Florida…" He looked around and noticed Rene and Mona were watching them. "It's a long story. She played me like a fool, but I got over it."

"Glad to hear it," Dawn said.

"Anyway, Karen sang that song for me at our wedding," Calvin recalled. "I used to hate to hear it after everything that happened, but tonight you made me fall in love with Minnie Riperton all over again."

Dawn grinned and looked away in embarrassment. "That's sweet."

"Would you like to go somewhere to talk?" he asked. "I can't stay out too late 'cause I got my kids with me."

By then Dawn was pretty sure he was hitting on her, but she wasn't positive. No one had done that in so long, she forgot what it felt like. "You got children?" she asked as a distraction.

"Yeah," Calvin said. "My boys are twelve and thirteen. They're good kids, but they've been acting out on this boat."

"Um, how old are you?" Dawn asked. Her face burned as soon as the question came out, but Calvin's smile intensified.

"I'm thirty-six," he said. "Sorry, am I too old for you?"

Dawn's eyes widened and her jaw went slack. *He is hitting on me!* But that proposition was as frightening as it was exhilarating. Her heart thumped like she saw a ghost.

"No," she said. "I'm twenty-eight. But I was, um, I was going to kick it with my friends tonight."

"Oh, that's okay. Maybe I'll find you again tomorrow."

"Okay," Dawn said. "That would be cool."

Calvin nodded, and then he turned and walked away. Dawn turned back to her girlfriends and they were watching her with much interest.

"Mmm-hmm," Rene said. "What was that all about?"

"I think he likes me," Dawn whispered.

"Why you say that?" Rene asked. Her smile was ear-to-ear.

"He wanted me to go with him to talk," Dawn hissed.

"Why are you whispering?" Mona wondered.

"I don't know," Dawn said.

"Why didn't you go?" Rene wanted to know.

"I don't know," Dawn said. "I was kinda scared."

"Scared?" Rene frowned. "Dawn, what the hell are you afraid of? You need to get–"

"Hello, Mona?"

The ladies looked up and saw one of the hottest men on the ship standing before them. Bartolo Romero wore a black silk shirt with black slacks. His shirt wasn't tucked in, and it was unbuttoned far enough to reveal a nice crease between his bronze pectorals.

"*Hey,*" Mona purred. She threw her arms around his neck and gave him a nice, slow hug.

When they separated, Bartolo looked her up and down and put a hand to his chest.

"Wow. Your dress. You look amazing."

"Thanks," Mona said. "Where's your friend?"

"Xavier, he wanted to swim—at the pool," Bart explained. "Me, I wanted to look for you."

"Well, you found me," Mona said. She snaked an arm around his waist and led him away from her friends. "Now, what are you going to do with me?"

∽✧∾

Bart tried to play the slow game again that night, but Mona wasn't having it. They had a few drinks at the Society Bar, and the chemistry between them was nearly at a boiling point.

"You are such beautiful," Bartolo told her. He leaned with one elbow on the bar, staring deeply into her eyes, as if in a daze. His curly hair glistened under the lamplight. His unbuttoned shirt was like a tease. Each time he moved his arm, Mona thought she would get a glimpse of his nipples, but they were always barely out of sight.

"You make me very happy," Bart said, "to be here with you."

"You make me happy too," Mona replied. She leaned close and kissed him on the lips. His mouth was warm, and she could taste the cognac he'd been drinking. Up close Bart smelled like Paul Sebastian cologne, with an underlying scent Mona could not place. It wasn't a body wash or shampoo or anything artificial. Rather, it was an aroma that Bart emitted from his very pores. It was a primal scent. Animalistic.

The bartender approached and asked if they wanted another round.

"No," Bartolo told him. "We are going to leave." He looked at Mona. "Would you like to go dancing?"

"We can dance in my room," Mona said. "*In my bed.*"

Bart's eyes widened and then narrowed. "I would like that, Mona. I would like that very a lot."

❧

In her cabin, Mona felt confident and powerful. Bart was all over her as soon as she closed the door behind them, but he wasn't as rough as Mona would've liked it. He kissed her delicately and kept his hands glued to her waist. Mona wanted him to yank her skirt up to her belly button. His tenderness was driving her crazy.

She grabbed his arms and turned him abruptly. Before Bart could react, Mona pushed his back against the wall and clawed at his shirt buttons. They were still lip-locked, but Bart said something and then pushed her away when she ignored him. He restrained her with more force than Mona would've tolerated with anyone else, but she wanted to get a rise out of him, so she didn't complain.

"Stop," Bartolo said.

"What do you mean?"

"You are too fast," he said. "You're too, eh…" He couldn't come up with the word. "You're too much like a, like a man."

Mona frowned. "You think I act like a man?"

Bartolo's smile was disarming. "You're, too much rush. Do not push me. I don't like it. That's not, eh, like a lady…"

Mona's frown intensified. If she didn't know any better, she would've swore Bart just told her what *not* to do.

He kissed her forehead and softly kneaded the knot of flesh between her eyebrows with his thumb.

"Are you upset with me?"

"No," Mona said. She smiled and kissed him back. Bart's lips parted and his tongue cautiously slipped into her mouth. Mona closed her eyes and returned the favor. Their tongues met like thieves in the night and wrestled like mating serpents.

Mona pulled away first this time. She went to the bed and crawled across the mattress to reach the remote control on the nightstand. She turned the television on and found a station that played R&B videos. Musiq Soulchild was singing his fan favorite *Half Crazy*. Mona looked back and saw that Bart couldn't take his eyes off her legs and ass. She narrowed her eyes and grinned at him.

"What are you looking at?"

"I believe it is heaven," Bart said.

Mona crawled back to him and sat with her legs dangling over the side of the bed. Bart took a deep breath and stepped slowly in her direction. He flipped the light switch when he passed it.

"Turn that back on," Mona said.

"Why?"

"I like to keep the lights on."

"I do not like the lights on," Bart countered. "The TV, it gives enough light."

"I still want the lights on," Mona insisted.

Bart shook his head. "No. I'm sorry, Mona. The light will stay off. It is more romantic. Too much light is like, dirty movie."

Mona frowned again. She started to get up and flip the switch herself, but her butt remained glued to the bed. She knew Bart wasn't going to give in, and although it went against every fiber in her being, she didn't fight to get her way.

Bart came and sat next to her, and he kissed her again. Mona's frown went away instantly, and she reached tentatively to undo his shirt buttons again. This time Bart allowed her to undress him. He sucked her tongue playfully and fondled her breasts.

Mona pulled away and watched his eyes when she pulled his shirt off his shoulders. Bart slid his arms through the sleeves, and Mona admired his upper body. She shook her head and sighed. Bart was young and fit; the model of anatomic perfection. His muscles weren't excessive. They were just right, well-defined and perfect for his frame. Even with the limited light from the television, Mona could see a field of goose bumps on his arms and chest.

She kissed his neck, and Bart tilted his head to give her better access. His skin was warm, and his primal scent was stronger now. Mona licked his flesh and started to suck as she worked her way towards his collar bone. Bart worked on her blouse in the meantime. He removed it and tossed it carelessly to the other side of the bed.

His breaths started to quicken. Mona sucked her way back to his mouth and fondled an already rigid bulge in his pants while he undid her bra. When her breasts were exposed, Bart tore away from her mouth and latched on to one of her nipples. Mona threw her head back and moaned in appreciation. She cradled the back of his head and ran her fingers through his hair. Bart jumped from one nipple to the other, licking her areolas while his free hand crept between her legs. He ran his fingers across her damp panties, and Mona gasped. Her grip on his hair tightened. She thrusts her hips forward and stroked his manhood through his pants.

"Do you have a condom?" Bart asked.

"Yes," Mona breathed. She let go of him and stretched towards the nightstand on the other side of the bed. Bart bent to take his shoes off while she retrieved the Trojan. He removed his pants and underwear as well and was completely nude when Mona turned back around.

She inhaled deeply when she saw how big he was. She reached for his manhood and a delighted smile parted her lips.

"Damn, Bart."

He leaned back on his elbows and watched while she fondled him. "You like?"

She nodded. "Mmm-hmm." She wrapped her fist around the shaft and stroked slowly while she tore the condom open with her teeth. Bart grew steadily beneath her hand, and he was throbbing by the time she had the contraceptive ready. Mona applied the condom herself. She stared into his eyes, and Bart lay very still, except for the rise and fall of his simmering pectorals. But he resisted when Mona tried to climb on top of him.

"No, Mona. *You* lay down."

"I want to get on top," she said.

"Maybe later. You lay down first."

By then Mona's brain was racing. She didn't like the lights being off, and she didn't like the pace or the control she was relinquishing. Not only was she more experienced than Bart, but she was older. She was used to men yielding to her in all aspects of life — especially the bedroom. It didn't make sense that she should let some *boy* dictate how she got her rocks off. Even more peculiar was how Mona complied with his orders.

She lay on her back, and Bart stood and positioned himself between her legs. He pulled her skirt and panties off in one smooth motion and eased down on top of her. Mona raised her knees, but Bart didn't go immediate for the jackpot. Instead he kissed her again. Mona kissed him back, and their tongues were soon intertwined.

Mona could feel his manhood pressing against her pubic hair, and the lack of penetration was driving her crazy. Her clitoris throbbed and ached. She sensed he was teasing her on purpose, so she tried to play it cool. But it was hard, mentally and physically.

Bart sucked her bottom lip and then kissed her neck, under her ear, and between her breasts. Mona turned and exhaled into the pillow. Her fingers were already leaving faint scratches on his back, but Bart was patient like a surgeon. He fondled her breasts and sucked her nipples again. He licked down her stomach and twirled his hot tongue in her belly button.

Mona's hips squirmed on the mattress. She grabbed hold of his head and tried to push him further, but Bart wouldn't budge. He looked up at her and frowned.

"What is this?"

"Kiss it," Mona pleaded. Her labia gleamed in the darkness. She knew he wanted a taste.

Bart shook his head. "I'm sorry, Mona. But I cannot."

"Why?"

"Do you have, eh, *dental dam*?" he asked. "Plastic wrap?"

Mona's head spun, and she knew she had entered a warped parallel universe. She was being punished for all of the mean things she did to her lovers over the years. This wasn't lovemaking, it was her reckoning.

But Bart got settled between her legs, and his offering was anything but punishment. Mona was so wet he didn't have to reach down to guide himself in. His head was big like a plum, and the pressure made Mona inhale sharply. She gripped the sheets like she was wringing a dishtowel.

Bart pushed in slowly, stretching her walls with his considerable width. Mona threw her head back and cried out in pleasure, but also pain. He paused, and she thought he was all in, but Bart still had a few inches to go. He pushed deeper, and when he finally hit the back end, Mona thought she might pass out. Her throat caught, and she couldn't even scream this time.

Bart looked down at her and stopped moving altogether. "Are you all right?"

Mona's mouth hung open. Her tongue moved, but she couldn't articulate her pleasure. She nodded.

Bart smiled and began to work his hips. "I can't believe you finally have nothing to say," he said with a smile.

There was so much blood rushing past her ears, Mona barely heard him.

"It is good," Bartolo said. "I like it, like this."

He kissed her again, and Mona's eyes rolled to the back of her head. She came within twenty seconds of the initial penetration.

This had to be a new record.

∽౫఼

Mona's orgasm did not stop or slow Bart down. He pretended not to notice, but Mona knew he felt it. Her vagina contracted and squeezed him mercilessly, and things became fifty percent more slick down there. Bart used the extra lubrication to see how deep he could really go before the neighbors in the adjacent cabins thought someone was being murdered in there.

The Brazilian explored depths that had been neglected for years, and Mona couldn't help from howling like a cat in heat. When she came a second time, Bart hiked her knees over his shoulders and pounded so hard Mona could feel him in her chest. Her eyes widened and she stared into his dark orbs with an almost horrified expression; wondering if he was man or machine.

When her climax subsided, Bart wiped the sweat from his face and rolled Mona onto her stomach. This was absolutely taboo. Mona hardly ever allowed a man to take her in the doggy style position because she felt that was domination at its purest.

Yet Bart put her in this position with no resistance at all, partly because Mona was too exhausted to fight against him, and also because at that point Mona knew resistance was futile. And strangely enough, Mona *liked* to give up control to Bart. She didn't have to think about anything. She didn't have to plan, and she didn't have to manipulate. All she had to do was lay there and take the dick, and she was rewarded was the best sex imaginable. Maybe the best sex—dare she say—*ever*?

Bart slipped in from behind and Mona caught a second wind and threw it back at him as best she could. Bart squeezed her ass with a lot less gentleness than he exhibited twenty minutes ago, and after two more R&B videos Mona felt a third eruption bubbling within her. She held off for as long as she could, but Bart's sex game was masterful. He timed each thrust perfectly and hit her clitoris whenever he pleased. Mona buried her face in the pillow and shrieked like a wild woman, and *finally* she felt Bart pulsating inside her. He grunted uncontrollably, and Mona's legs gave in to exhaustion.

She slid to her stomach, and Bart followed her down, pushing harder the whole time. They climaxed together. And even though this was Mona's third, it felt like her first. Bart hovered over her, supporting himself with his sinewy arms. He breathed into the back of her neck, and he clawed the mattress with his toes, trying to dig deeper still. Mona almost screamed for him to *Stop! There's no more! That's it!* But even if she had the strength to speak, she wouldn't have said a word to dissuade him.

Mona may have been a fierce lioness, but on that night Bartolo was her lion king, and he had only to growl at her to get her to obey.

They fell asleep in each other's arms and went at it again when they woke up at three in the morning. Bart said she could get on top that time if she wanted, but Mona declined. She sensed she would never meet another man who had mastered missionary like Bart. And submitting to his doggy style was utterly delightful, taboo or not.

CHAPTER 16
FORGET ME NOT

The next morning Dawn got up the earliest, and she went to the upper deck before checking on her friends. The weather was already nice that morning, and the ocean always looked beautiful. Dawn thought about all the places she and her friends had gone and all of the wonderful sights they'd seen.

It was sad to know this was their last day on the boat, but a part of her was eager to get back to Overbrook Meadows. Dawn missed her mama and her boys something fierce. A sharp pain twisted her gut when she thought about how things would play out with Henry, but she didn't dwell on that. She didn't have to think about him for at least one more day, and she preferred to do just that.

Dawn re-entered the ship at eight-thirty. Mona's room was the closest, but Dawn didn't see her friend for the rest of the night after she took off with Bart. There was a good chance Mona was still curled up in the sheets with her Latin lover. Dawn headed to Rene's room instead, and she ran into her friend in the hallway.

"Hey," Dawn said. "I didn't know you was up."

"I didn't want to sleep late," Rene said. She pulled her door closed and grinned at her friend. "Have you been to Mona's room yet?"

Dawn shook her head and giggled. "I started to. Do you think we should check on her?"

"Uh-uhn," Rene said. "Mona always gets up early. If she's still in there, I guarantee you she's not sleeping. You hungry?"

"Like a runaway slave," Dawn said, and then caught herself. "Dang, that was wrong."

"You think?" Rene said. She shook her head and laughed.

The ladies headed for the cafeteria in good spirits. Dawn loaded her plate with bacon and fried potatoes, but she looked down at the meal with disgust when they sat down to eat.

"*Blech*! Look at this mess. This is why I'm fat now."

"It's all right," Rene said. "I told you not to worry about your weight while you're on this cruise."

"No, I got to start somewhere," Dawn said. She went and got a grapefruit and yogurt instead.

"That's all you're eating?" Rene asked when she got back.

"I want to be skinny again," Dawn confided. "Or at least *thick*. I've been thinking about what it will be like when I'm single again." She shook her head. "I'm not…I know it sounds like I'm weak, but I don't like to be alone. That's why I stayed with Henry for so long. I don't feel right if I don't got a man."

"There's nothing wrong with that," Rene said, "so long as you find the *right* man. When you get skinny, it'll make it that much harder."

"How come?"

" 'Cause *everybody* will want you. And seventy percent of them will want you for the wrong reason. The best guy for you won't care how big you are. He'll like you for you."

"I haven't had too much luck finding somebody like that," Dawn said.

"They're all around," Rene assured. "You just give them the wrong signals. Like that man who tried to talk to you last night. You shot him down cold."

"No, I didn't."

"Men are big and strong, and they act tough," Rene informed her, "but deep down, they're all a bunch of babies. It took a lot of nerve for him to come and talk to you. And you told him 'no' when he asked if you wanted to go somewhere with him."

Dawn thought about it and realized that was a rejection. "I didn't...*dang*. I didn't mean to."

"So you liked him?" Rene asked.

Dawn smiled. "He looked good. And he had a deep voice. And he got some kids, like me. He's divorced."

"He's still on this boat *somewhere*," Rene said.

"I guess if it's meant to be, he'll find me again," Dawn replied.

Rene started to tell her that sometimes you've got to make things happen for yourself rather than rely on fate, but Mona appeared out of nowhere, and she didn't look like herself at all. She plopped down next to Dawn wearing dark sunglasses and baggy shorts. She didn't have on any makeup, and her hair was a little unkempt.

"Well, look who decided to step away from the dick," Rene teased.

Mona propped her elbows on the table and cradled her chin on her fists. She sighed.

"Did you have a good time?" Dawn asked, and a satisfied smile stretched her friend's lips.

"It was *magical*," Mona said. Her voice was gruff. She looked parched.

"Magical?" Dawn said.

"Did you get any sleep?" Rene asked.

"I got a few hours," Mona said. "And yes, *magical*. That boy, hmmmm. He was, he was something else."

Rene laughed. "So, did you make him beg? Did you break out the whips and chains?"

"*Oh, noooo*," Mona said with a chuckle. "I wasn't the dominatrix last night. Bart was like, a grown-ass man. He wouldn't let me do anything I wanted."

"What?" Rene couldn't believe it.

"It was crazy," Mona said. "Everything I tried, he was like, '*No, Mona. I do not want to do that.*' "

Her friends laughed because she tried to match Bart's accent.

"He was teasing," Mona said. "And I was fiending. And when he finally gave it up, I almost *cried*." She shook her head. "He's big, y'all. But he's good, too. I know he's young, but he had me howling like a dog. When he got through, he said I could do it how I wanted now, but I couldn't even move. I must've came about five times last night."

Dawn's eyes widened. "*Five times?*"

"No shit," Mona said. She removed her sunglasses and rubbed her eyes. Rene gasped when she saw how baggy they were.

"Girl, you look tired as hell! Why didn't you stay in bed?"

"I'll be all right," Mona said. "I just need some coffee. Will you go get it for me?"

"I'm not getting your coffee." Rene frowned. "You just passed four coffee machines on your way to this table."

"I tried to get it," Mona said. "But I dropped my cup. I think I broke it."

Dawn got up with a chuckle. "I'll get it for you. You want some cream?"

"No, I want it black," Mona said. "Thanks."

"So, what's going to happen with you and Bart?" Rene asked when Dawn was gone. "Sounds like you really like him. Are you going to try to work out a relationship or something?"

Mona shook her head and yawned. "He lives in another freaking country, girl. I told you, this is just a fling. When we get off the boat, that's it. We'll go our separate ways."

"But if he's laying pipe like that, how can you let him go so easily?"

"I didn't say it would be easy," Mona said. "I said that's the way it's going to be. I talked to Bart, and he understands. If I ever take a trip to Brazil, I might look him up, but I'm not trying to get sprung on some long-distance shit. Plus he plays ball *and* he's fine. Shit, I'd drive myself crazy worrying about who's throwing their panties at him.

"I just wanted to have some fun, and I did. But I didn't expect him to work it like he did. Last night was an eye-opener for me, Rene. I'm a different person now. I feel it."

Rene was skeptical. "I never thought dick would change you."

"It wasn't just the dick," Mona said. "The dick was the bomb—don't get it twisted—but what Bart did for me was mostly mental. He made me respect him as a man and take my place as a woman."

Rene shook her head. "This is weird."

"How do you think I feel?" Mona said. "I'm telling you, you'd better jump on Xavier and see what he got to offer. Maybe it's a cultural thing. He might could do the same for you."

Dawn returned to the table with Mona's coffee.

"Thanks, Dawn. You're a *real* friend—unlike this heifer over here." Mona glared at Rene.

Dawn took her seat and pealed the lid off her yogurt. "What y'all talking about?"

"I'm trying to get Rene to give Xavier some booty," Mona said. "She knows she likes him."

"Everybody knows that," Dawn said.

"What do you mean *everybody* knows?" Rene asked. Mona laughed.

"Last night he came and talked to Rene while we was at the disco club," Dawn told Mona. "They was dancing and looking all in each other's eyes. You don't have to know nothing about nothing to know they like each other."

Mona shook her head. "I don't know why you trying to hide it," she told Rene.

"I'm not trying to hide it," Rene said. "I'm just not going to sleep with some boy I don't even know."

"He's not a boy," Mona said. "He's a grown man, with grown man parts."

Rene chuckled. "I'm still not doing it."

"To each his own," Mona said and took a sip of her coffee. "All I know is, my toes are *still* curled up." She shivered. "Ooh! Aftershock!"

⤙✦⤚

Mona was back to her old self after breakfast. The Finley Sisters left the cafeteria hoping to squeeze in as much fun as possible before the *Ecstasy* docked in Galveston tomorrow morning.

For the next few hours they ran from one event to the next, partaking in all kinds of activities from an ice carving demonstration to tea time at the Neon Bar. Dawn got a black panther painted on her arm, and Mona bought a beautiful print at an art auction in the Starlight Lounge.

After lunch the friends happened upon an impromptu volleyball tournament on the Sun Deck, and they were surprised to see Xavier and Bartolo waiting to take the court. Bart's eyes lit up when he spotted Mona. He called her over with plenty of enthusiasm.

"Hey, Mona!"

She went and gave him a more-than-friendly hug. Xavier and Rene exchanged a much more subdued, "Hi."

"You girls should come play with us," Bart suggested. "We need more players for our team."

"I'm no good at volleyball," Mona admitted.

"I am," Rene said. "I wanna play."

"Me, too," Dawn said. She actually played a little in high school, and she was pretty sure she still had a decent serve.

"All right," Mona said. "We'll play with y'all. Give us a minute to go change."

The girls went to put on bikini tops with shorts, and when they returned, they were the hottest thing on the sandy court. Dawn was the only one with a one-piece bathing suit, but she didn't feel self-conscious anymore. Her temporary tattoo was beautiful, and her big boobs were absolutely succulent, with nary a stretch mark.

"I'ma be wearing a two-piece by this time next year," she told Mona.

"I believe it," Mona said. "You can do anything you set your mind to."

The volleyball game with the Brazilians was ridiculous. Neither team had a good player on their side, and there was more laughing going on than scoring. And Rene and Xavier's flirting was at an all-time high. They let half a dozen balls sail into the sand right in front of them because they were too busy giggling at something the other had said or staring at the curves on their mutually gorgeous physiques.

Xavier didn't have a shirt on, and his chest and arms were cut like a middle-weight boxer's. Rene had a slim waist and flat stomach like a dancer. Xavier couldn't take his eyes off her jiggling breasts when she occasionally did make a play on the ball.

The couple virtually separated themselves from the group by the end of the game, and when it was over, no one was surprised that they had disappeared altogether.

∼✖∽

Rene and Xavier went to their cabins to shower. They changed into shorts and tank tops and attended a yoga class in the spa. Rene couldn't believe how limber Xavier was. She tried to keep her mind out of the gutter, but it was hard—especially when the Brazilian offered to help guide her body into some of the more difficult stretches she wasn't accustomed to.

They followed that up with a couples' massage session and a leisurely stroll through some of the gift shops on the Atlantic Deck. Later the couple found an empty lounge, and they talked for more than an hour. Rene was impressed by Xavier's intelligence, and it was hard not to be blown away by his otherworldly charm.

At six-thirty Rene had to return to her room so she could change once more for supper. Tonight the ship was hosting a special event called the Captain's Dinner, and everyone in the dining room was required to dress formally.

Xavier had to go to his own cabin to change into a tuxedo, but he was polite enough to walk Rene to her room first.

"I wish today was not our last day," he said as they strolled past a beautiful Rolls Royce on the Lido Deck. "You are a very special woman, Rene. I would like to get to know more about you."

"I want to know more about you, too," Rene said. "I think what you've accomplished is awesome."

"I have not accomplished anything important," Xavier said. "I am a poor boy, from a poor city. I play sports for the university, but it is very hard to make it as a professional soccer player. That is why my major is engineering."

"That's what I'm talking about," Rene said. "You're athletic, but you know an education is more important. You're smart and handsome. I think you're going to do something great one day."

Xavier laughed. "That, that is nice of you to say, Rene."

"I'm not just saying it. I mean it."

"Well, that is even better," Xavier said. He opened his mouth to say something else, but thought better of it.

"What?" Rene asked.

He shook his head. "No. It is not always good to say what's on your mind."

"Why not?"

"It could, at times, be very awkward."

"Sometimes," Rene agreed. "But other times it's good to follow your heart. Like me, for instance; I didn't think I should tell you how I feel, but I may never see you again, and I'm not going to leave here with regrets."

"But you have not told me how you feel," Xavier said.

"I know," Rene said. She grinned and looked away coyly.

"Maybe what you have to say is the same as what I have to say," Xavier guessed.

"I get the feeling it is," Rene said.

They were at her room by then. Rene leaned with her back against the door. Xavier stood before her with his hands in his pockets. He looked like he wanted to kiss her good night but was too nervous to do so.

"Maybe you could invite me inside," Xavier said, *"for coffee.* And we could talk more about our feelings."

Rene smiled and looked into his eyes. She shook her head. "I don't have any coffee in my room, Xavier."

"That is okay," he said. "I do not drink coffee."

Rene watched his eyes for a moment longer, and then she turned and opened her door. She stepped inside her cabin without looking back. Xavier followed her in and closed the door softly behind them.

Mona and Dawn arrived at the captain's dinner at the same time, both looking as stunning as Angela Bassett on the red carpet. Mona's dress was yellow and strapless, with an empire waist and a full, silk skirt. Dawn's gown was metallic gray with spaghetti straps and a long-sleeved bolero jacket.

All of the other guests were dressed to the nines as well, and the atmosphere was quite regal. Dawn felt like she was at her senior prom—except there were no dumb jocks there with their shirts un-tucked and their bowties stuffed in their pockets.

For dinner the guests had a choice of roasted veal with mushroom cream sauce, seared pike perch with mixed vegetables or durum wheat pasta tossed with eggplant, zucchini, and plum tomato sauce. Before Dawn and Mona contemplated ordering without their friend, Rene entered the dining hall wearing a strapless chiffon gown. It was grapefruit pink with a sweetheart neckline and sequin bodice.

"Hey, y'all," Rene said. She took a seat with her friends and casually lifted her menu from the table. Dawn and Mona stared at her until she looked up and noticed their expressions.

"What's up?"

"What's up with *you*?" Dawn asked.

"Nothing," Rene said. "Why y'all looking at me like that?"

"Cut the shit," Mona said. "Tell us where you been."

Rene laughed. "Damn. Quit being nosey."

"Girl, you'd better quit playing and tell us what happened," Dawn said.

"You slept with Xavier, didn't you?" Mona wanted to know.

"No, I did not," Rene said, but her smile was much too sneaky.

Dawn put a hand to her mouth. "You did!"

"No, I didn't," Rene promised, still beaming.

"Yes, you did," Mona said.

"I think I would know," Rene said.

"You been with him for four hours," Mona calculated.

"Yeah, and?" Rene returned her attention to her menu, but Dawn snatched it from her.

"Tell us what happened."

"Y'all are really tripping," Rene said.

"You slept with him," Mona said. "Admit it."

"I promise you I did not sleep with Xavier," Rene said. "We just kicked it."

"Where'd you go?" Dawn asked.

Rene chuckled and shook her head. "We went a lot of places. We went to one of those yoga classes."

"Yoga?"

"Yes, yoga," Rene told Dawn. "It was fun."

"All that stretching and bending…" Mona said. "I know it got a little heated."

"It was nice," Rene said. "We went shopping after that, and we talked for awhile. And then he walked me to my cabin, and I changed and got ready for dinner. That was it."

"He walked you *to* your cabin, or he walked *in* your cabin?" Mona asked.

"What do you want, a play-by-play?" Rene asked.

"Yeah," Dawn said.

"I want the truth," Mona said.

"All right, he did come inside," Rene said, "but *we just talked.*"

"Yeah, right," Mona said.

"What'd y'all talk about?" Dawn asked.

"Y'all know I like him," Rene said. "He likes me, too. We talked about what it would be like if we tried to date or whatever. I was trying to figure out if a relationship was even possible, and we decided it wasn't."

"Why not?" Dawn asked.

"He lives in *Brazil*," Rene reminded her.

"But he comes to Dallas every summer," Dawn said.

"No." Rene shook her head. "I'm with you on this one, Mona; I can't do the long-distance thing. But it's okay. I had a nice time with Xavier. We're good friends, and we'll always have our memories."

"That's it?" Mona asked. "You're not going to keep in touch at all?"

"I'll probably say hi to him every now and then on Facebook," Rene said, "but as far as a relationship, no. We're not going to try that."

"Did y'all kiss when he was in your room?" Dawn asked with a grin.

"A little," Rene said.

Mona's eyes widened.

"Did he touch on you?" Dawn asked.

"Not that much," Rene said.

"You slept with him," Mona said.

"I told you I didn't," Rene said. "But he did leave me a nice video message to remember him by."

"I wanna see," Dawn said.

"All right," Rene said. "But you'd better not start tripping. I'm telling you I didn't sleep with the boy. I don't know why y'all don't believe me."

"I believe you," Dawn said.

"Thanks," Rene said. She had her camcorder strapped to her wrist. She opened it and played the last file. Mona and Dawn leaned over her shoulders and watched the brief message.

"Hello, Rene. It is me, Xavier. I wanted to record this video so you would remember me after the cruise and maybe watch it sometimes, if you think of me."

Xavier was wearing a blue tank top, and he spoke directly to the camera. Rene wasn't in the shot, and it was clear she was holding the camcorder.

"I enjoyed the time I spent with you on this ship," Xavier went on. He smiled. It was a bright, beautiful smile. "I wish our circumstances were different," he said. "I believe you and I could have had something special. But life is not perfect, and these are the cards we were dealt.

"Maybe our decision is right. Maybe we are wrong. I suppose we may never know. What I can say for sure is you are a smart and beautiful woman, Rene, and I will not soon forget you. I wish for you all of the blessings under the sun. Hopefully we will meet again, one day…"

Xavier smiled, and then he walked towards the camera. The scene went out of focus as his chest filled the

291

screen. The camera jostled, went out of focus again, and then recorded the ceiling. Next there was a sound that was immediately recognizable as smooching.

"Are you still recording?" Xavier asked.

"No," Rene said off screen, and the video ended abruptly.

"*Mmm,*" Mona said and settled back in her chair.

"That was *beautiful,*" Dawn said. She sat back in her seat with a wistful grin.

"What'd y'all do *after* you recorded that?" Mona asked. "It looked like he was getting closer—and *closer...*"

"I already told you we kissed," Rene said. She returned her camera to its pouch and took her menu from Dawn.

"If y'all did something, you need to tell it."

Rene knew Mona wasn't going to believe the truth, so she toyed with her friend's head. "What happened between me and Xavier is *our* business. I'll never tell you what really went on."

Dawn's jaw dropped. Rene turned and gave her a conspiratorial wink. Dawn giggled like she understood.

"I knew it!" Mona said. "You need to tell it, Rene!"

"You will *never know what happened,*" Rene repeated and stared down at her menu. "Ooh, I think I'm having the veal."

CHAPTER 17
THE LAST DAY

After dinner the girls went to the bar and sipped appletinis while they contemplated what sort of mischief they could get into on their last night on the boat. Dawn wanted to check out one of the Vegas-style shows in the Blue Sapphire. Rene and Mona wanted to go to the karaoke club again. They hoped to get a repeat of last night's performance, but Dawn told them sequels always fall short, and they should leave well enough alone.

"Sequels don't always fall short," Mona said.

"Yeah they do," Dawn said. "Think about it: *Carrie II* was dumb. *Jaws II*, *City Slickers II*, *Basic Instinct II*, *Gremlins II*—all a bunch of crap. You know the first *Superman* was the best one."

"You been watching too much TV," Mona said.

Dawn laughed. "I be wanting to escape," she admitted. "Sometimes it's better to think about other people's problems for awhile."

Mona nodded, and the mood at the bar became somewhat somber. "Have you been thinking about how it's gonna go down with Henry when you get home?"

Dawn shrugged, staring down at her drink. "It's scary. I try not to think about it too much because my heart starts beating fast, and I start shaking. I know y'all think it's easy; all I have to do is get my stuff and leave…"

"I don't think it's easy," Rene said.

"When we had cable," Dawn said, "I used to watch a bunch of them true crime shows. I liked *Cold Case Files* and *The First 48*, you know, stuff like that. A lot of times, when a lady gets killed, it be by some man she was going with, somebody who used to beat on her." She looked away, and her eyes went out of focus.

Mona cleared her throat. "You shouldn't be thinking like that."

"No, she's right," Rene said. She looked worried, too. "One of my friend's sister got killed by her boyfriend a couple of years ago. You never know what can happen when you try to leave them."

Dawn shook her head. "Naw. Henry's not like that. I just be thinking about everything that *can* go wrong."

"Me and Rene, we're gonna go home with you," Mona said. "We need to be there when you get your stuff out of Henry's house. We can have the police there, too."

"That's a good idea," Rene said. "That's not a problem for me at all."

"Y'all tripping." Dawn chuckled nervously. "It don't make no sense for y'all to do all that."

"Yes, it does," Mona said.

"I don't think you know how serious this is," Rene said.

"I do," Dawn said. She looked her friends in the eyes one at a time. "And I appreciate y'all trying to help me. But I don't need you following me home for this. I got a sister and a mama, and my uncle stays close by. I got some more family in Dallas."

"But–"

Dawn cut Rene off. "And even if y'all came with me to get my stuff, what would that help? If Henry really wants to do something bad to me, he don't have to do it that same day. He know where my mama stay. He know where I work. He got all the time in the world to think about what he gon' do to me. This one lady I saw on TV, her boyfriend didn't get her for a whole year."

That freaked Mona out even more. "Then you need to come to Austin with me. I can give you a job in my office. You can start a whole new life. You can stay with me 'til you get on your feet."

Dawn smiled. "I appreciate that, Mona, I really do, but I'm not going to Austin. I'm not going to Houston, either," she said before Rene could suggest it.

"Why not?" Rene asked.

"Because I'm not running from everything and everybody I know just to get away from *one person*," Dawn said. "I been scared of Henry for two years already. I don't wanna be scared no more. I don't wanna run. I want to look him in the eyes and let him know I'm not scared no more. I want him to be scared of me for a change. I got to convince him that if he ever even *think* about coming after me, he's gonna have something worse than the police to worry about."

"How are you going to do that?" Rene wondered.

Dawn chuckled. "That's the part I ain't figured out yet. But I'll have it figured out by tomorrow. Don't worry."

"I am worried," Mona said. "I'll probably follow you home anyway."

"Don't do that," Dawn said with a chuckle. "You gotta trust me. I got all the help I need at home. But when it comes down to it, *I'm* the one who has to leave Henry. I'm going to take care of it, and nobody's gonna get hurt. You'll see. We'll all be on three-way tomorrow night laughing about all of this."

Rene wiped her eyes and sniffled. She reached and gave Dawn's hand a comforting squeeze. "We'd better be."

"Now I done ruined the whole mood," Dawn said. "Let's get away from here before we all crying." She hopped off of her stool and straightened her dress. "For real, y'all. This is our last night on the boat. We need to forget about this mess and have some fun."

Mona sighed, not sure if she could get Henry off her mind, but willing to try.

"Do y'all want to go change?" Rene asked.

"Naw, I never get to wear a dress this pretty," Dawn said. "I'ma keep it on all night."

"So are we going back to karaoke?" Mona asked. "I wanna laugh at some of them fools who get up there even though they can't sing."

"Like you?" Dawn said, and then slapped a hand over her mouth.

Mona cocked her head. "I thought you said I sounded good…"

296

"Uh, yeah. You did," Dawn said.

"Tell the truth," Mona said. "Did I sound bad or what?"

"Girl, you *know* you sounded bad," Rene said. "Why you wanna make Dawn tell you? You know it's hard for her to be mean to people."

Mona downed the rest of her drink and slid off her barstool. "Y'all lying heifers ain't finna have me feeling bad. I *know* I sounded good. I heard the way those men were screaming, and all of the women were *hating*. They wouldn't have been hating like that if I didn't sound good."

"Yeah, that must be it," Rene said. She shot Dawn a look and rolled her eyes.

The girls headed for the karaoke lounge, but Dawn didn't get a chance to flex her vocal pipes again that night. When they passed the grand piano in the main atrium, a familiar gent approached the trio.

"Dawn?"

She looked back and saw the good-looking fellow from last night, the one who was so enamored with her Minnie Riperton impression. Today he wore a black suit with a black tie. He had two young boys standing on either side of him. Dawn guessed these were the sons he told her about.

"Hi," she said. "Calvin, right?"

"Yes, I'm Calvin." He smiled warmly. "I'm glad you remembered me."

Dawn smiled, too, but she didn't know how to respond to that.

"Are you headed for karaoke again?" Calvin asked.

"Um, I think so…" Dawn looked back to her friends, and to her surprise both Mona and Rene pushed Dawn in the stranger's direction.

"No, we're not doing anything," Rene said.

"You can take her with you," Mona said.

Dawn's face reddened. She couldn't believe they would pull such a stunt.

Calvin chuckled heartily. "Actually, I'd like that very much. These are my boys," he told Dawn, "Devin and CJ. They were on their way to the arcade, weren't you?"

"Yes," the older one said. He eyed Dawn curiously with a slick grin pasted on his face. His brother was more of a conniver.

"I don't have any more money." He looked up at his dad and stuck a hand out like a begging wife.

"Heh heh, kids…" Calvin said. He stuffed a hand in his pocket and came out with a crisp twenty.

The younger boy snatched the bill and said, "Thank you."

He and his brother told Dawn "Nice to meet you!" before they took off towards the video games.

"Nice to meet you, too," Dawn said. She turned and saw that Mona and Rene had already disappeared. She looked back at Calvin and giggled.

"I guess it's just me and you," he said.

"I guess so," Dawn said. "Do you, um, do you wanna go to the upper deck? I try to watch the sun set every night I'm here."

"That sounds great," Calvin said. "I would love to."

❧

Dawn told Calvin a little about her life and about her boys while they leaned on the boat's railing and watched the fire fade from the sky, leaving a purple luminescence in its wake. Dawn was so nervous her hands were sweating, but Calvin was very friendly and disarming. He didn't make Dawn feel like she had to talk a certain way or behave in a particular manner to keep his attention.

It was hard to believe this fine man was really interested in her. Calvin was smart and handsome. He could've had his pick of any single woman on the boat, but he fell in love with Dawn's song and stepped to her. He thought she was pretty, and Dawn could tell he liked her figure, too. She was so shy should could barely keep her thoughts straight, but Calvin thought even her meekness was adorable.

"I can tell you're not a grandstanding type of person," he told her. "That's why that song was perfect for you. Minnie wasn't a diva, either. She was talented, but she didn't have huge shows with lasers and cannons and a hundred and fifty backup dancers. She didn't shoot her videos half naked. She didn't throw her greatness in your face, but you couldn't help but notice."

"I'm not really talented," Dawn said.

"You know, there's a fine line between being subtle and not believing in yourself," Calvin warned. "I think you're a lot more special than you give yourself credit for, Dawn."

His words made her swoon. Dawn couldn't remember the last time a man complimented her so often. She thought Henry might have said kind things in the beginning, but that was so long ago she wasn't sure anymore. Calvin made Dawn feel like she was in a fairy tale, like all of her dreams might come true. She tried to relax so she could enjoy this night to the fullest.

"Do you want to go to the Blue Sapphire?" Calvin asked. "Have you checked out any of the shows?"

Dawn's eyes lit up. "I was just telling my friends I wanted to do that."

"You have a beautiful smile," Calvin said.

Dawn blushed and looked away slightly. "Thank you."

"So, it's a date?"

Dawn thought about that and decided she liked the way it sounded. This would be her first official step away from Henry. She could already feel a slight pulse of power growing in her bosom. "Okay," she said. "It's a date."

❧

The couple watched an hour and a half *Show Girls* performance. The auditorium was packed, and the seats were very close together. Dawn's body grew warm whenever she and Calvin bumped elbows as they went for the same arm rest. Each time he leaned close to whisper something in her ear, Dawn felt a tingle down her spine. She inhaled deeply to savor his cologne. Her heart knocked so loudly, she was sure he would hear it over the music and singing on stage.

Afterwards Calvin took her to the Society Bar, and they had just one drink a piece. They talked for over an hour, and Dawn felt like they were totally compatible. She didn't want to get too far ahead of herself, but it was hard not to see the magic and feel God in their presence. Calvin made her laugh, and he stared into her eyes sometimes like she was the most beautiful woman in the world.

The dread of what she had to do tomorrow gradually melted away, and Dawn gave in to the promise of their encounter. She wouldn't dare consider that maybe she was fulfilling her oath of romance, but at the same time, she couldn't get the thought out of her head.

"I don't think I've ever connected with someone this easily," Calvin told her.

"I've been thinking the same thing," Dawn said. "Maybe it's the boat."

Calvin chuckled. "Are you saying things would've been different if I met you at, I don't know, the mall or something?"

Dawn nodded. "Yeah. I think so. A lot of things have happened since I've been on this ship. It's been… really special."

Calvin smiled. "I think I know what you mean."

Dawn's mouth went dry, and her heart started to thump again. She lifted her glass, but there was nothing left but a few small ice cubes. She sucked on one of them and met her date's eyes again.

"Do you want another?" Calvin asked.

Dawn shook her head. "No. I'm fine."

"Do you want to go on *another* date?"

Dawn grinned. "Definitely."

❧

They left the bar heading for a comedy show. The comedian wasn't all that funny, but the lounge was nice and cozy, and Dawn felt she was growing closer to Calvin by the second. They held hands for the first time when they left the club at eleven-thirty. They enjoyed their first hug a few minutes later when they returned to the upper deck for more stargazing.

"I had a real good time tonight," Dawn said. She looked up at the constellations and silently thanked God for bringing her so much happiness on this trip. "Thank you for taking me out tonight. I never spent this much time with somebody I just met."

"I hope it doesn't end when we get off the boat tomorrow," Calvin said.

"It doesn't have to," Dawn replied and a crowd of goose bumps sprouted on her arms. Calvin already told her he lived in Mesquite, which was only forty-five miles from Overbrook Meadows. The proposition of starting a new relationship was scary, but it wasn't as scary as other things on Dawn's to-do list.

"I never thought I'd meet someone like you," Calvin said, "after what happened with my ex." He led her to the side railing with a hand around her waist. His touch still made Dawn tense, but she was starting to look forward to his closeness rather than fear it.

"The person I am on this cruise," Dawn mused, "isn't the same as the person I am at home. I don't have a lot of money. I work for a dry cleaners. I never wear dresses like this. I just go to work and go home. I don't have a life."

"Maybe I could help with that," Calvin offered.

Dawn sighed. This man was too good to be true. Dawn didn't want to, but she knew she had to divulge her one last secret: "I, um, I got one more thing to tell you…"

Calvin stared into her dark eyes and his smile went away. "I don't like the sound of that."

"It's, um… It's something I should've told you already. I don't know why I didn't."

Calvin sighed and shook his head in disappointment. "Are you married?"

Dawn shook her head. "No. But I do have a boyfriend. I mean, not really—not anymore. I broke up with him while I was on this cruise. I just haven't told him yet."

Calvin frowned and didn't say anything for a few heartbeats. "How do you break up with someone without telling them?"

"I'm going to tell him as soon as I get home," Dawn promised.

Calvin put a hand to his face and rubbed his forehead. "I…" He sighed. "I gotta admit, that does sound pretty fishy, Dawn. Why would you break up with your boyfriend while you're on vacation? What could he have done wrong if you haven't talked to him in a week?"

"He did plenty," Dawn assured. "And I didn't mean to lie to you. I feel like I'm single — even if he doesn't know it yet. If you knew him, you would understand. I know it sounds like I'm doing him dirty, but I'm not."

Calvin watched her eyes for what felt like a long time. He took hold of both of Dawn's hands and smiled. "Dawn, I don't know what's going on with you and that fool waiting for you in Overbrook Meadows. But I'm usually good at reading people, and I don't think you're playing games with me."

"I'm not," Dawn said. She looked up at him. Her eyes glistened in the moonlight. Her heart did not beat at all until he spoke again.

"I think that whatever he did must've been really bad," Calvin said. "And you probably should've left him a long time ago."

Dawn nodded.

"But if you want to reassure me," Calvin said with a grin, "I think this would be the perfect time for a friendly kiss…"

Dawn put a hand to her mouth and giggled. She took a deep breath, and shook her head. "I'm sorry, Calvin. I can't give you a friendly kiss because I don't want to be your friend. But if you want a *real* kiss, I can give you one of those…"

Calvin chuckled. "I thought you were going to say something else."

"I know," Dawn said. "I can't believe I'm trying to be funny. You have no idea how nervous I am."

"Probably not as nervous as me," Calvin said. "I haven't kissed a woman other than my ex-wife in over six years." He leaned down for the smooch, but Dawn giggled again.

"We're gonna bump noses," she predicted.

"Why do you say that?"

"We've been talking about it for too long now. Something's gonna go wrong."

"You might be right," Calvin said. "Let's plan this out. How about I go right, and you go left."

"My right or your right?"

He laughed. "You go to your right, and I'll go to my right."

Dawn pictured it in her head. "I think that will work."

"Okay," Calvin said. "Let's do this." His hands moved to the small of her back, and he pulled her closer.

Dawn looked up at him, and then she saw the stars, and then she closed her eyes and concentrated on her directions. She figured she was too nervous to pull it off, and she was not mistaken. She thought RIGHT but tilted her head LEFT at the last second. She and Calvin bumped noses and brushed lips only slightly. They backed away laughing.

"That's another thing," Dawn said. "I'm not too smart."

"Stop it," Calvin said. "You're perfect in every way." He leaned in again, and Dawn closed her eyes again, and their kiss was as smooth as silk this time. Dawn felt an unexpected tingle in her chest and stomach. She saw stars that were much brighter than the ones hovering above them.

"That was nice," Calvin said.

"I think we need to try one more time," Dawn whispered.

"Of course," Calvin said. "That's what I meant."

∽✕∾

Calvin escorted Dawn to her cabin at midnight, but she was too excited to stay there when he took off. She ran up to the Verandah Deck and was happy to find both of her friends in Mona's room. Mona was just getting started on her packing, and Rene was helping her. They took a break to listen to Dawn's animated story about what had to be her best date *ever*.

Rene and Mona were genuinely happy for her. Mona said that if only one of them sparked a relationship they could continue when they got home, she was glad it was Dawn. Rene felt the same way, and she wanted to celebrate—not just for Dawn's good fortunes, but for everything they'd been through and all of the good times they shared on the boat.

The Finley Sisters drank more on that night than any previous time, and they were all fully wasted by two o'clock in the morning. They went to Rene's room and laughed and talked until their words were no longer coherent and their eyelids forcibly closed themselves.

❧

The next morning Dawn awakened to her very first hangover, but it wasn't as bad as she expected. Her tongue felt like carpet, and her intestines were tied in knots. But her headache wasn't too severe. She was sleepy, more than anything else, but she was also excited and worried, and her brain started racing as soon as she opened her eyes.

Henry.

Yes, it was time to think about him now, but Dawn still didn't want to. She didn't have a solution yet; only bits and pieces of a plan that seemed stupid every time she gave it some real thought. So she forced Henry from her mind for the time being and concentrated on more pressing needs, like the fact that it was seven in the morning, and they had to be off the boat by ten. Dawn still had some packing to do, and she promised to help Mona collect the rest of her things. And, if possible, Dawn wanted to squeeze in one last breakfast with her sisters.

Dawn woke Rene up, and they worked on her room first. Rene was the most organized of the three, and she had most of her things packed already. They just had to get her toiletries from the bathroom and pull her wrinkle-free dresses from the hangers in the closet. Dawn's cabin was equally neat. It took only twenty minutes to get the last of her things zipped up in her suitcases.

Rene and Dawn didn't wonder where Mona went last night until they were on their way to the Verandah Deck.

"She was there when I fell asleep," Dawn said. "I remember; she was laying at the head of the bed."

"That's what I thought, too," Rene said. "Wasn't she too drunk to leave?"

The girls didn't have to contemplate the mystery for very long. When they got to Mona's hallway, they saw a very tired Bartolo slipping out of their friend's room. Bart was barefoot, wearing pajama bottoms and no shirt. Even in his fatigued state, he was ruggedly handsome. And he was happy. He smiled affectionately and nodded at Rene and Dawn when they passed him.

"Good morning, my friends."

Dawn laughed and Rene rapped lightly on Mona's door when they reached it. Mona answered wearing only a bathrobe. She didn't look tired at all. It was clear she'd been up for a while.

"I thought it was just a one time thing," Rene said with a smirk.

"You talking about Bart?" Mona replied. "No, I said it was a one time *fling*. And now it's over."

"Was he just as good the second time around?" Rene wondered.

Mona sighed and stepped aside to allow her friends entry. "All I know is, I'm taking a trip to Brazil next summer. Y'all wanna go?"

∞

Mona's packing took the longest, but with three people helping, they managed to get done by eight-thirty. The *Ecstasy* was docked in Galveston by then, but the best friends wanted to enjoy their last free meal before they were kicked off the ship and their pampered life came to an abrupt end.

At the breakfast table, the main thing on everyone's mind was what Dawn was going to do when she got home. But Dawn didn't want to spend their last moments on the ship talking about an asshole like Henry. She wanted to remember the good times; like the hours they spent watching the stars and the beauty of Cozumel. They talked about the men who stole their hearts and the one crazy guy who faked his suicide to hurt Mona's feelings.

They talked about the dance clubs and delightful dinners and elegant dining rooms. The remembered the funny-looking people they made fun of at the karaoke club, and they would never forget the night Dawn took the stage and blew everyone away with her incredible high notes.

When they were called to disembark, the Finley Sisters got porters to tote their luggage outside and load them into three separate vehicles that would take them to three different cities. Rene and Mona pleaded again for Dawn to let them go with her to help get things settled with Henry, but Dawn assured them she had plenty of support at home.

"I'm not as weak as I was when I first got on this boat," she said. "And Henry's not as bad as he thinks he is. Me and my peoples, we're gonna take care of the problem. You gotta trust me."

"I do trust you," Mona said, but it was clear she still had doubts.

Rene and Mona planned to break up with their boyfriends that day, too, and the friends made plans for a three-way call that night so they could discuss the results.

"We're gonna be friends forever," Mona said. *"For real this time."*

Everyone agreed they would be, but that didn't stop the tears from filling their eyes. For each of them knew they made this same vow ten years ago. And the scars from that broken promise were still visible on all of their faces.

CHAPTER 18
THE BREAKUPS

Mona drove a rental car back to the airport. It was a lovely Saturday morning, but she didn't take a moment to admire the beautiful Galveston scenery. Mona had her Bluetooth on and her radio off, and she was all about business as soon as she got on the freeway.

Mona's real estate agency was open six days a week, and Saturdays were always busy. Mona gave her employees every Sunday off plus another random day throughout the week, but everyone was required to be there on Saturday.

Mona's right hand in her office was a petite Asian woman named Sue. Sue briefed Mona on the highlights of the week she missed, and everything seemed to have gone well—with one exception. One of their clients backed out of a two-million-dollar property deal entrusted to Theresa Hester.

Theresa was one of the newer realtors at the agency, and she was already on Mona's bad side because of an account she nearly lost three weeks ago. Mona had to step in and personally save that deal, and she was sure she could've salvaged this last one if she wasn't on vacation.

But it wasn't Mona's job to look over her employees' shoulders 24/7. If she couldn't depend on them while she was away, what did she need them for?

"Where is she?" Mona barked into her earpiece. "Is she at her desk?"

"Yes," Sue said. "She's real sorry, Mona. She was crying yesterday. She thinks you're going to fire her."

"I am going to fire her," Mona confirmed.

"I, I really don't think it was her fault," Sue protested. "That client was skittish from the start. He was giving her problems the whole time."

"I don't care about that," Mona said. "When I started this company, it was just *me*. Every one of my clients gave me problems, but I didn't lose *one single deal*. Theresa doesn't know how to talk to people. That's the bottom line."

"But it's a recession," Sue said. "Theresa was unemployed for five months before she found this job. She doesn't have anywhere else to go."

"She can sell Avon for all I care," Mona growled. "Why are you sticking up for her?"

"I don't know," Sue said. "She tries hard. And yesterday was her birthday."

"What?" Mona shook her head in exasperation. "I don't give a damn about her birthday! You can buy her ass a cake on her way out the door. Put her on the phone."

"You're going to fire her *now*?"

"Yes. I want her gone by the time I get there. If I see her, it's just gonna piss me off again."

"So you're coming in today?"

"I'll be there by lunchtime," Mona confirmed.

"Did you have a good vacation?" Sue asked. "It doesn't sound like you relaxed at all."

"I had a great time," Mona said, "until you told me that woman lost another commission. Transfer me to her office, Sue. *Now*."

Sue sighed, and then she placed Mona on hold. Twelve seconds later an older woman's voice was on the line.

"Hello, Ms. Pratt?"

"Hello, Theresa."

"How, how's it going? Welcome back from your trip. Did you have fun?"

"I don't want to talk about my trip," Mona said. "I want to talk about some money you lost while I was gone."

"I'm so sorry, Ms. Pratt. I did all I could, but they were being unreasonable. I, I told Mr. Swanson he was asking for too much from the beginning. He had me running around in circles, going back and forth between these buyers when he knew they weren't going to pay that much. I did everything I could, but he was being a jerk. And then he blamed *me* when I couldn't sell it."

"If I hired you to sell something for me, and you couldn't do it, I'd blame you, too," Mona informed her.

"But it wasn't my fault," Theresa pleaded. "I did everything I could for him! I called everybody–"

"Do you remember that Pennington file we had problems with before I left?" Mona asked.

"Pen-Pennington?"

"You came in my office crying, saying *it was all over*. You said you did everything you could, and the seller was going to back out. And all of the time and hard work you invested was about to be lost. Do you remember that?"

"Yes," Theresa said. "But that was–"

"And then I met with Mr. Pennington, and we had that contract signed in five minutes," Mona said. "Do you remember that?"

"Ms. Pratt, this was different. I swear I did everything I could with Mr. Swanson's property. *I swear to God!*"

She was on the verge of tears, but that only reminded Mona of how weak she was.

"I'm sorry, Theresa, but your services will no longer be needed. I'm gonna need you to clean out your desk. If you need a couple of weeks–"

"What? No, Ms. Pratt. *Please don't fire me*! I need this job. I'll do better. I promise I'll do better!"

"Theresa, I've already made my–"

"Ms. Pratt, I'm begging you. *Please let me stay*! I got three kids at the house. I don't have no money saved, and I can't find another job. I need this, Ms. Pratt. I'll do better. I promise!"

"How do you have *kids* at your house?" Mona wondered. She knew Theresa was in her late forties. If she just had a birthday, she might have hit the big 5-0.

"They my, they my daughter's kids," Theresa explained. She sniffled loudly, breathing hard into the phone. "My baby on that *crack*," she confided. "I took her babies so CPS wouldn't get 'em. You know once they get in that system, they life won't never go back to normal. I'm doing the best I can to feed these kids, Ms. Pratt. Please give me another chance. I know I'm not as smart as you, but I can learn, if you help me…"

Mona wasn't in the mood to help anyone—especially some uneducated grandma who had been trying to find something she was good at for the last four decades with no success. But there was something about Theresa that was uncomfortably familiar. Mona didn't want to see the parallels between her incompetent employee and her best friend Dawn, but the similarities were glaring.

Mona learned a lot about her friend during the cruise, and she now understood how Dawn's life turned out the way it did. With no intervention, Dawn might end up like Theresa one day. That was no reason to keep the middle-aged woman on her payroll, but something in Mona's heart wanted to at least try to help.

She sighed. "All right, Theresa, I'm going to put you through training again. Starting Monday you're going to be shadowing Sue. We'll see how things are going at the end of the week, and maybe we'll let you try another client by yourself."

"Oh, thank you!" Theresa said. "Thank you, Ms. Pratt. Thank you—thank you—thank you! I won't let you down again. You'll see! I'm gonna get it right this time. I promise."

"That's fine," Mona said. "You can go ahead and take the rest of the day off. Come back Monday, and we'll get you started with Sue."

"Yes, ma'am," Theresa said. "Thank you, Ms. Pratt. You won't be sorry."

"All right," Mona said. "Talk to you later."

She disconnected and watched the freeway for a while, wondering what the hell just happened. It wasn't like her to be sucked into someone's misfortunes like that. She knew her time on the cruise had something to do with it, and she hoped this was just a one time thing. The last thing Mona wanted was to find herself giving money to every sorry sap with a sad enough story to tell.

Mona's flight back to Austin took only thirty minutes, and it was rather boring after all the time she spent on the *Ecstasy*. Her equilibrium was used to the strange gravitation shifts her body was enduring. Mona didn't even have to chew gum to keep her ears from popping.

When she landed at Bergstrom International, Dennis was already there, waiting to give his girlfriend a ride back to her condo. Mona barely thought about the pharmacist while she was away, but Dennis missed his woman terribly. He rattled on and on about how much he loved her and how lonely he was without her.

Mona knew it was over between them. She came close to breaking up with him during the ride home, but she didn't want him to start crying on the freeway. Plus she still needed Dennis to carry her bags up when they got to her building.

But when they pulled to a stop in front of her condo, something shifted in Mona's heart, and she didn't feel right about using him one last time. Dennis put his car in park, and Mona stopped him before he got out to unload her suitcases.

"Hey," she said, "how come you haven't asked me about marrying you again? You said you would ask me when I got back."

Dennis stared into her eyes and sighed. "I don't know, Mona. I wasn't really getting the right vibes, you know? I told you I missed you, and you didn't say you missed me back. I'm happy to see you, but you don't look excited about seeing me. I, I guess I figured you still needed more time to think about it—before you gave me an answer. I don't mind waiting."

Mona shook her head. "How can that be, Dennis? Why are you willing to give me so much time?"

"I don't want to rush you," Dennis explained. "I want to be with you, Mona, and if it takes you a little longer to decide you want to be with me, too, that's fine. I think you're worth it."

Mona smiled. She reached and gently touched his cheek. "You're sweet, Dennis. That's really nice of you."

He nodded, but he was guarded.

"I think you might be too nice for me," Mona said.

He shook his head. "Don't say that. Don't even start."

"Dennis, I–"

"I don't want to hear it," he said. "Do you think you're the first woman to tell me that? If I'm such a nice guy, if I'm so freaking sweet, then how come you don't want to marry me? Why won't you take my ring? Do you want some asshole who's gonna choke you and slap you around?"

"No," Mona said. "Nobody's ever going to treat me like that."

"Then what do you want?" Dennis whined.

"I want a *man*," Mona said. "I want someone who respects me *only* if I respect them back. I want someone who can tell me I'm full of shit when I am. Someone who can put their foot down and not let me have my way all the time. But still they have to be gentle when I need it. They have to be passionate and loving, but still hard and rugged. I want a *man*, Dennis. Not somebody I can manipulate."

"You manipulate *everybody*," Dennis said knowingly. "And the person you're looking for doesn't exist! As soon as a man puts his foot down, you're gonna run the other way."

"That's not true."

"There's no such thing as somebody who's *hard and rugged* and *passionate and loving* at the same time. You can't have 'em both."

Mona thought about her Brazilian friend and said, "Yes, I can."

Dennis' eyes widened and then narrowed. He nodded. "Okay. That's the way you want it? Cool. I can do that." His face hardened. "Mona, I want you to shut up and stop complaining. I, I, I want you to get up to your room and take your clothes off, and, and I'm gonna come up there and screw your brains out. And I want you to wash my drawers by hand when we're done. And, and, and fix me a sandwich."

Mona was stunned silent for a second, but then she burst into laughter. "You're funny."

But Dennis wasn't laughing at all. In fact he lowered his head and started crying.

"You're not, not going to marry me, are you?"

"No," Mona said. "And it's not because you're too nice a guy. You're a great guy, Dennis. Just not the man for me."

"Are, are you still gonna be my girlfriend?"

Mona shook her head. "No, Dennis. I'm not going to do that anymore. I shouldn't have done it for this long. It's not fair if I stay with you knowing I don't love you. I'm blocking your blessing. I want you to find a girl who will treat you right."

"Whatever," Dennis said. He wiped his eyes and squeezed the steering wheel so hard his fingers trembled.

"Don't be mad," Mona said.

He didn't say anything.

"Do you still want to help me with my bags?" she kidded.

"Get 'em yourself, bitch."

Mona chuckled. "All right, Dennis. That's enough role-playing. I told you; you don't have to change for me."

"Just, just get out." Dennis reached down and pulled the trunk release without taking his eyes off the dashboard.

Mona saw that he was fighting to maintain composure. This sort of sensitivity usually irritated her, but Mona felt bad about what she did to him for the past eight months. Rene said it was wrong to go through life without a care about whose heart she broke, and Mona knew her friend was right.

It was too late to repair the damage she caused Dennis, but at least she was up front with him. He was young enough to recover and fall in love again, and if Mona was lucky, maybe she could find true love as well.

She got out of the car without another word and hefted her luggage from the trunk all by herself. Dennis took off before she got her things inside the building, but that was okay. Mona knew she had to learn a lesson about using people, and this was as good a time as any.

When a handsome and muscular gentleman approached and ask if she needed help, Mona offered him ten dollars to haul her things to the elevator. She didn't smile or bat her eyes at the stranger, and she definitely didn't give him a hug afterwards. It was just honest pay for honest work.

Mona didn't feel an overwhelming sense of *sexiness* at the end, but no one was crying or threatening to drown themselves, either, and that was just as good.

∞

Rene didn't have to go to work that Saturday, so her drive home was much more relaxing than Mona's. And Houston was a lot closer than Overbrook Meadows, so it only took Rene an hour and a half to get back to her River Oaks neighborhood, compared to Dawn's five-hour trip.

Rene took a rental car from the Carnival docks rather than request a ride from her soon to be ex-boyfriend

Blake, and she didn't attempt to contact him right away. When she got home, Rene dragged her luggage inside and did a quick inspection to make sure no burglars had violated her space while she was away.

She spent the next hour checking and responding to her emails, and then Rene made a cup of noodles to nibble on while she watched a couple of programs her TiVo recorded during her vacation. It was almost two o'clock when she got done. Blake still hadn't called to see if she made it back okay. Rene grumbled as she sent him a text message:

I'm back.

Blake responded a few minutes later:

Cool. In meeting. Call you later.

Rene tried to keep her frustration to a minimum, but it was hard. Her "boyfriend" hadn't seen or heard from her in an entire week, and all he had to say upon her return was "Cool." Rene wanted to call him and curse him out, but she went back to the computer and pulled up her Facebook account instead.

She looked through her friends until she found Blake's profile, and then she scanned Blake's friends until she found his other woman. Rosalyn Lynch was twenty-five years old with brown hair and fair skin. She had small eyes, a small nose, and full lips. She was attractive.

Rene met her a few times at various functions at Blake's place of business. Rosalyn was Blake's secretary when he first started at the Provincial Investment Firm. Blake got promoted a couple of times since then, and he left Rosalyn behind—professionally, but not sensually.

Rene had suspicions that Blake and Rosalyn were having naughty interactions the first time she met her. Blake denied this wholeheartedly, but a woman knows when she's in the presence of her man's mistress. Rene could feel Rosalyn's eyes on her from across the room, and every time she looked in the secretary's direction, Rosalyn rolled her eyes and looked away quickly.

Rene ignored these signs because she knew she wasn't living up to her responsibilities as Blake's girlfriend. She cooked for him, cleaned for him, and got freaky with him whenever Blake was in the mood. But Rene couldn't force herself to fall in love with Blake. It wasn't hard for him to find someone who would.

But that was then.

Rene now knew that it was okay to fall in love. Her heart might get broken a few times, but that was okay, too. You have to take the bitter with the sweet. Before she could start on her new path, however, Rene had to put an end to the counterfeit relationship she'd been nursing for the past two years.

She sent Rosalyn a friend request. Rene looked through Rosalyn's photos while she waited, but she was only allowed to see three of them until her friend request was accepted.

Rene went back to the sofa and tried to watch another one of her favorite programs, but she couldn't follow the plot. Her mind was too preoccupied. Forty minutes later her iPhone beeped to inform her of a new email.

Rene opened the message and chuckled. She couldn't believe it: Rosalyn accepted her friend request. Her heart knocking, Rene went back to the computer and sent Rosalyn a message:

Are you sleeping with Blake?

She looked through the rest of Rosalyn's photos while she waited for a response, and Rene learned that Rosalyn liked to party. She had whole photo albums filled with pictures from one nightclub after another. Rosalyn posed with drinks in hand, a group of her girl-friends surrounding her with wild, inebriated smiles.

In some of her pictures, Rosalyn got a little risqué and grabbed her friend's ass or boob. In other photos, she turned and stuck her booty out for the camera. Rosalyn wasn't prettier or finer than Rene, but she looked like she might be down for more slutty activities, like sex in the corner of a crowded club or a three-way with one of her friends after a long night of partying.

Rene went back to Rosalyn's profile to see what schools she listed in her bio, but then she got a message from the tramp:

Who are you?

Rene responded right away:

I'm Blake's girlfriend. I met you at some of the office parties.

Rene didn't think Rosalyn would respond after that, and she was right. But she got a response nonetheless. Rene's cellphone rang three minutes later, and she saw Blake's number on the caller ID. That was all the con-firmation she needed.

"Hello?"

"Hey, what are you doing?"

"I thought you were in a meeting."

"It's over now."

"Really?" Rene said. "When did it end, when I sent Rosalyn that message? Or was your *meeting* between Rosalyn's legs?" She chuckled at her own wit.

"What are you talking about?" Blake said.

"Cut the crap," Rene said. "I know Rosalyn told you I sent her a message on Facebook."

Blake weighed his options and decided to be honest for now. "Uh, yeah, she did. What's going on? Why would you ask her that?"

"I wanted to see if either one of you would tell the truth."

"The truth about what, Rene? There's nothing going on with me and Rosalyn. You know that."

She sighed. "Blake, how the hell am I supposed to know anything about what you're doing? You work seven days a week. Do you think I'm stupid? You think I don't know who you're screwing?"

"Listen, Rene, I don't know what happened on your cruise, but–"

"I found myself," Rene said. "That's what happened. And I don't need this shit anymore. You can go ahead and be with your little freak full-time now."

"Rene, you need to calm down."

"I am calm, Blake. I'm not mad at you. I just don't want you no more."

"I'm coming over there."

"Why? You didn't want to come when I told you I was back. Why do you want to come now?"

"You, listen, Rene. Don't go anywhere. I'm on my way."

"Fine. You can come get your shit," she said and disconnected.

∞⚬∞

Blake's office was thirty minutes away, so Rene figured she had at least that much time before he showed up. He might be there sooner if he was coming from Rosalyn's house, depending on where the whore lived. Either way, Rene was sure she could pack up all of Blake's things in just a few minutes.

What she forgot to take into account was the twenty-five months she and Blake had been together. Her ex-boyfriend had a little bit of everything at Rene's home, from shoes and socks to his Xbox 360. Rene was only able to get Blake's clothes out of the closet before he walked into her bedroom—exactly seventeen minutes after she hung up on him.

Blake wore blue jeans, sneakers, and a Houston Rockets tee shirt. His typical work attire? Rene thought not.

"All right, what's this all about?"

"Those bags are for you," Rene said, pointing to two stuffed Heftys on the bed. "I'll get the rest of it together tonight. You can come get it in the morning. And gimme my key."

Blake frowned and stuffed his keychain in his pocket. "Rene, we need to talk. I don't know where you're coming from with this."

"You don't know where I'm coming from?" She put her hands on her hips and stared at him in amazement. "You don't even have the decency to tell me the truth, Blake? It's over! I know you're sleeping with her, and I don't want to be with you anymore. Now gimme my key."

"Rene, listen—"

"I don't wanna listen anymore, Blake. I've been listening to your same tired lies for two years. Why can't you tell me the truth? Huh? God! I can't stand you!"

"All right. All right, Rene. Calm down." He held his hands out to her, but didn't dare touch her. "All right… Okay." He wiped his forehead and rubbed his hands on his pants.

Rene waited.

"Rosalyn, she, she means nothing to me," Blake said. "We hung out a few times, but I don't love her. I love you, Rene."

"You didn't hang out with her, Blake. You *screwed* her. You've *been* screwing her. There's a difference."

"What do you want from me? What are you, why are you doing this?"

"I want you to tell the truth!"

"All right! I did it, okay?" Blake's face was red and glistening. He ran a hand through his curly hair and sighed loudly. "I did cheat on you, Rene. But she means nothing to me. I love *you*. I want to be with you."

"It's too late for that."

"Why is it too late? I'm telling you, you're the one I want to be with. I love you."

"You wouldn't have had sex with her if you loved me."

"What do you know about love?" Blake demanded. "You're the most frigid woman I know. Do you remember what happened the first time I told you I loved you? Do you remember that?"

Rene didn't.

"*Nothing*," Blake recalled. "*Nothing* happened, Rene. You just gave me a kiss and rolled over and went to sleep. Do you know how that made me feel? Do you have any idea?"

"That's no reason—"

"You don't know what you're talking about, because you don't know what I've been through! Have you ever been with the perfect person, but they won't return any of the love you give them? Do you know what that's like?"

Rene shook her head and softened visibly. "Blake, I understand what you're saying. I know I didn't return the love you showed me. I had a wall up, and even you couldn't get to my heart. I know that. It was my fault, and I accept responsibility."

Blake took a deep breath, and a glint of hope twinkled in his eyes.

"But that doesn't give you the right to cheat on me," Rene said. "If you didn't like what I had to offer, you should've left me, Blake. That's the bottom line."

"But I do want what you have to offer, Rene. I love everything about you."

"Except the fact that I couldn't love you back," Rene said. "And that's a big deal, Blake. You should've

327

manned up and made a better decision. But you tried to have your cake and eat it, too, and that's where you messed up."

"But, but we're talking about things now. We can work through this."

"*Blake!*" Rene folded her arms over her chest and spoke slowly. "*It's over. We're through.* Give me my key and leave."

Blake's eyes grew large, and his jaw became unhinged. Rene was sure he'd make one last ditch effort, but Blake snorted and dug his keychain from his pocket. He removed her one house key from the ring and placed it on the dresser. He looked into Rene's eyes with an expression that was easily recognizable as *Your loss*, and then he turned to leave.

Rene followed him to the living room and locked the door behind him. She didn't feel nervous, but her fingers were shaking. She knew she made the right decision, but this was still a two-year relationship down the drain. Things were going to be different now, maybe even a little scary for a while.

Rene wondered if Mona and Dawn followed through with their breakups, and if either one of them felt the same apprehension she was feeling.

CHAPTER 19
REGARDING HENRY

Dawn's sister Denisha picked her up from Galveston as they planned one week ago. The first thing Dawn inquired about was how her sons and her mother were doing, but Denisha wanted to fill her in on Henry's bizarre behavior.

"I don't care about him," Dawn told her. The Ecstasy was still visible in the rear view mirror, and Dawn was getting adjusted to being on solid ground again. "Tell me about my boys. How's Tim and Luther?"

"They're fine," Denisha said, a little perturbed by her sister's prioritizing.

"They didn't give Mama no trouble?"

Denisha shook her head. "No, they been good. They wanted to come with me to pick you up, but I told them 'No.'"

"How come?"

"Cause it takes *five hours* to get down here," Denisha said. "And another five on the way back. I can barely take them across town before they start whining about being in the car too long."

Dawn grinned. "I miss 'em so much. I can't wait to see them."

"They can't wait, either," Denisha assured.

"How's Mama?" Dawn asked. "She been feeling better?"

"She had a couple of bad days," Denisha said. "I had to come over to cook for everybody. But she's been okay, mostly."

Dawn nodded. Their mother had a bad case of sugar diabetes, but everyone believed she would conquer the disorder. Dawn prayed for healing so much, she was sure there was a whole slew of angels working overtime to keep her mother healthy.

"What about them knuckleheads up the street?" Dawn asked. "Tim didn't get into it with them while I was gone?"

"Who you talking about?"

"I don't know they names," Dawn said. "I know their mama works at the post office. They was messing with Tim and Luther a while back, throwing rocks and stuff. Tim got in a fight with one of them."

"Oh, that's Rodney," Denisha said. "I didn't know they was fighting. I guess they made up. Him and his brother was at Mama's house yesterday."

"For real?" Dawn chuckled. She always taught her boys to turn the other cheek, but she was never sure any of it got through.

"You shoulda seen the inside of that boat," Dawn said with a smile. "It was like four mansions stacked on top of each other."

"Yeah?" Denisha said.

"They had a casino," Dawn recalled. "A bunch of swimming pools, a spa… The dining rooms looked like something out of a movie." Her eyes twinkled. "The waiters all had tuxedos, and they had all of these forks and spoons spread out on the table. I didn't know what to do with any of them, but I learned a little bit. The waiter helped, 'cause he would take away a couple of forks and spoons after every plate, so I knew those were the ones I was supposed to use with the appetizer. Can you believe it, D? We had *three course meals*. Lobsters, and veal... All kinds of desserts."

"That's tight."

"Mexico was a trip," Dawn went on. "We went to two different cities. I didn't get a chance to see the first one that good 'cause we had an emergency, but I spent a lot of time in Cozumel. I finally went horseback riding! My friend Mona had this crazy stalker following her around. He tried to drown hisself in the ocean, and they made him stay in Mexico. It was crazy."

Denisha nodded. "Sounds like it."

"We met these Brazil—"

"I want to hear about your trip," Denisha interrupted, "but why won't you let me tell you about Henry? You acting like you trying to ignore me on purpose."

"I am," Dawn said, and the smile slipped from her face. "I know whatever he did was *ignorant*. And it don't even matter—long as he ain't messing with Mama or the boys."

"He did come and talk to Mama," Denisha said. "That's what I'm trying to tell you. He came by the house twice, and he called a bunch of times."

Dawn sighed, and a lump of dread got stuck in her throat. She looked out of the window and then gradually back at her sister. "All right. Tell me."

"The first time was on Monday," Denisha reported, "the day after you left. I think he woulda came that same Sunday, but he knew I was gonna be there. He came early in the morning when I was at work, and he asked Mama if it was true you was gon' be gone for a whole week."

Dawn shook her head. In her mind's eye she could see Henry stepping cautiously up her mother's porch. Henry was intimidated by her mother, and he avoided her at all costs. If he bit the bullet and paid her visit, then he must have been seriously troubled by Dawn going on the cruise without him.

"What she tell him?"

"She told him it was true," Denisha said. "And she told him she knew about how he grabbed your hair and pushed you down when you went to get your curling iron and stuff."

Dawn's eyes widened. "How she know that?"

"I told her," Denisha said. She knew Dawn wouldn't approve, but she was defiant. "It's all out in the open now, Dawn. We not gon' keep it a secret, hoping it'll go away on its own. Everything that happens in the dark eventually comes to the light."

Dawn knew that was true, but she didn't like the idea of her mother knowing about the abuse. Mama had too much to worry about already with the bills and her diabetes.

"What Henry say?" Dawn asked.

"He said he was sorry," Denisha reported. "He told her he never put his hands on you before, he was just mad 'cause you didn't tell him until the last minute."

"He said that?"

Denisha nodded. "He said it was just, like a reflex. He said he didn't know why you was treating him like that. If you woulda told him you wanted to go, he wouldn't have said nothing."

Dawn's nostrils flared. They were on the freeway now. The sun was still bright in the sky, but there were dark clouds on the horizon. Dawn knew they were heading into a storm.

"Mama told him he was wrong for handling you like that," Denisha said. "She told him it ain't never a good reason to put his hands on a woman. And Henry started crying, saying he was sorry."

Dawn's mouth fell open. "He cried?"

"Mama said he did," Denisha said. "But he coulda been faking. You know Mama don't never want to think somebody's lying to her."

Either way, Dawn couldn't believe it. She never once saw Henry cry. Even when his father died from a stroke a year ago, Henry never shed a tear. He just looked mad, like he wanted to whoop the Grim Reaper's ass or something.

"Anyway, Mama told him you *was* gone out of town, and y'all would have to talk about it when you got back. But I guess that fool didn't believe her, 'cause he came back Tuesday night."

Dawn frowned. "You was there?"

"No," Denisha said. "Mama told me the next day. She said Henry was looking real sad—even worse than he did on Monday. Mama told him you wasn't back yet,

333

and you wouldn't be back for a whole week, so it wasn't no need for him to keep coming back every day."

Dawn's stomach cramped. "He didn't come back no more."

"No, but he called a couple of times," Denisha said. "I talked to him Thursday, and I'm the one who told him to stop calling."

Dawn swallowed hard. "What all did you say to him?"

"I told him it wasn't no need in him calling no more because you was on vacation, and you wasn't coming back until Saturday. I told him if he doesn't believe you, that's his problem, but he didn't have no business stressing our mama, 'cause she already sick."

Dawn's tongue was bone dry. She put a hand to her mouth and chewed on her thumbnail.

"I told him he'd be *lucky* if you went back to him," Denisha went on, "after the way he attacked you while I was standing *right there*."

Dawn stared through the front windshield, watching the black clouds up ahead. They were heading into a storm, all right. From the looks of it, it was going to be a real nasty one.

"What, what he say?"

"He said he was sorry for grabbing you and for cussing at me like he did. He said he was gonna make everything better when you get back—but you bet not believe that shit. It don't never get better with niggas like him. He scared now, so he'll probably act good for a week. But after that it's, like, *Ding-Ding*." She motioned like she was ringing a bell. "Get ready to put your boxing gloves back on."

"I know," Dawn said. "You right."

"Did you know Tim and Luther don't like him?"

Denisha was just stating the facts, but with each word Dawn felt like she was being stabbed in the chest, intentionally and painstakingly, with rusty bayonets. "They told you that?"

"Tim did," Denisha informed her. "He said Henry makes you cry, and he wants to beat Henry up, but he's too little."

Dawn's eyes filled with tears. She sniffled and wiped them away before they could fall. "I didn't, I didn't know he felt like that."

"You shouldn't put them through that," Denisha lectured, "living with some man they're scared of. It ain't right. You never know what could happen."

Dawn nodded even though her sister was wrong; Dawn knew perfectly well what could happen. Tim may not have been big enough to fight Henry, but one day he would learn that weapons evened up the playing field. There was an assortment of butcher and steak knives in their kitchen at home. Tim was already tall enough to reach any one of them.

"It's okay," Dawn said. "I'm not going back home with Henry."

"Really?" Denisha smiled for the first time since Dawn got in the car. "When you decide that?"

"On the cruise," Dawn said. "Me and my friends were talking about stuff. They wanted to come with me to make sure Henry don't try nothing stupid when I go get my stuff, but I told them I already had some people at home who can help me."

"You do," Denisha agreed. "You know I'll go with you. We can take my boyfriend with us, and you know Byron don't never get into nothing without his home-boys. We can take Uncle Elvin and pick up Kevin and them from the projects, too." Denisha laughed. "Girl, we can go *beat his ass*! He gon' wish he never put his hands on you."

Dawn shook her head. "No. Not like that."

"What you mean?"

"I'm not gonna take all those people over there," Dawn said. "And I don't want nobody beating on Henry."

"Why not? He beat on you."

"But I'm not him," Dawn said. "I'm not like him. A fight ain't gon' do nothing but start more trouble. You know how niggas is. If they whoop him, Henry gon' wanna get his revenge. And it's gon' keep going until somebody ends up in the hospital."

"So what you wanna do then?" Denisha asked.

"I'm just gonna tell him I'm leaving," Dawn said. "And we'll see what happens after that."

"You already know what'll happen after that," Denisha said. "He gon' go upside yo head."

"That would be the worst mistake he could make," Dawn said. Her face was hard. Her eyes were cold like steel. "Henry stupid, but he ain't that stupid."

"What if he is?" Denisha ventured. "You got something ready if he do hit you?"

Dawn told her she did have something planned for that scenario, but she wouldn't go into detail, no matter how hard Denisha pressed. They eventually dropped the subject altogether and discussed the adventures Dawn had on the cruise. Dawn was still excited about her trip, but she was a lot less animated now that Henry was on her mind.

Rain started to tap the roof of the car when they passed through Huntsville, and they were in the midst of an all-out thunderstorm by the time they reached Overbrook Meadows.

❧

Dawn was physically and mentally exhausted when she pulled into her mother's driveway and threw Denisha's car into park. She and her sister switched seats midway through the drive home, but Dawn thought she got the worst end of the deal because of the rain. Denisha's windshield wipers only worked half as good as they should, and one of her front tires had virtually no tread left on it.

But they made it safe and sound, so Dawn gave Jesus a big *Thank you!* as she ran from the car, shielding her head from the rain with a stack of newspapers Denisha had in the back seat.

Inside, Dawn's mother was in the kitchen whipping up a batch of her world-famous butter rolls to go with her equally awesome tuna casserole. The house smelled like home and good home-style cooking, and that was better than any aroma Dawn encountered on the cruise.

Virginia's face lit up when she saw Dawn, but there was also a stitch of pain in her eyes. Dawn couldn't tell if her mother was feeling ill, or if there was something else weighing heavy on her soul.

"Hey, baby!" The older woman dropped her spatula and threw her arms out.

Dawn stepped into the embrace and clung to her mother. "Mama, I missed you!"

"How was your trip? Did you have a good time?"

"I did. I never had so much fun in my whole life."

"That's good, baby."

The women backed away and watched each other at arms' length. Dawn's mother had a radiant smile, but it waned as she wiped her hands on her apron. She looked around indecisively.

"You know, Henry been by here looking for you."

"I know," Dawn said.

"How come you didn't tell me he was putting his hands on you?" Virginia wanted to know.

"I'm sorry, Mama. I was…" Dawn trailed off because she heard loud footsteps running in their direction. Tim and Luther rushed in from the living room.

"Mama!"

They ran and threw their arms around her waist.

"We missed you!" Luther's face was buried in Dawn's side, and his words were muffled.

"I thought you wasn't *never* coming back!" Tim said.

"I missed y'all, too," Dawn said. She rubbed the top of Luther's head and caressed the back of Tim's neck. She kissed them both and squeezed them tighter. "I thought about y'all *every day*. Y'all been good for Grandma?"

"Yes," Tim said.

"Are we gonna go home?" Luther asked. "I wanna stay here."

His words were like a slap in the face, and the whole house fell silent. Dawn looked from her sister's eyes to her mother's. Neither of them spoke, but Dawn knew they felt her pain, and she had their unwavering support.

"I have to talk to your grandma about that," Dawn told her son. "But first, why don't y'all go get some of my bags out of Aunt Denisha's car, and I'll show you some pictures of my boat. Don't try to get those big suitcases; they too heavy."

The boys ran off obediently, and Dawn caught a shiver when they were gone, like someone walked on her grave. She looked at her mother, who had the same look in her eyes.

"Henry been calling, too," Virginia said.

"I know," Dawn said. "Denisha told me."

"You going back to him?" her mother asked.

"Not if you let me stay here."

"You don't even have to ask that," Virginia said. "This is one place you always welcome, baby. You'll be safe here."

Dawn smiled, but she knew her mother was only half right. She might be welcome in her childhood home, but safety was a bit more elusive. That was something Dawn had to attain on her own.

⤜⤛

After they got all of her luggage in the house, Dawn went to the living room with her family and told them about her time on the *Ecstasy*. She left out all of the *spicy* stories about the men they grew fond of and the one *crazy* story about Mona's stalker, but even without those juicy tidbits, her trip sounded like the best vacation ever. Everyone wanted to go on a cruise like hers, and Dawn was sure they could pull it off if they put back a few dollars a week for the next year or so.

When she was done reminiscing, dinner was ready. Dawn fixed plates for Tim and Luther, and then she slipped away to have a talk with their grandmother. They went to Virginia's room, which hadn't changed much since Dawn was a little girl.

The only thing missing was Dawn's father, who spent most of his time on the king-size bed during the last few months of his life. Elijah Wright surrendered to emphysema two years after Dawn graduated from high school, and his absence was still felt in nearly every aspect of their family.

Virginia said she had no problem with Dawn moving back in. The new arrangement would put the boys in a different school zone, but it was summertime; they wouldn't have to make the transition in the middle of a semester. And there were two unused bedrooms in Virginia's house, so the move wouldn't cause any cramped conditions for anyone.

Another plus was Dawn could spend more time with her mother. She'd be there to help out when Virginia had a bad health day or needed extra finances for the bills. Also the boys would be in an environment that was emotionally and physically safe. They wouldn't have to witness their mother's abuse anymore, and any mental scars they currently had could hopefully be healed.

The only drawback was the blow Dawn's independence would take when she moved back in with her mama. Birds don't come back to the nest after they've learned to fly and care for themselves in the real world. Dawn didn't make enough money to buy or even rent her own home, and she couldn't help but feel like a failure.

"Child, don't even think like that," Virginia told her. "This is just a hump you gotta get over. Just a little speed bump in your life. You don't never fail until you stop trying."

"I'm gonna do better," Dawn promised. "I'm gonna get a good job and move into my own place."

"You ain't gotta convince me," Virginia said, cradling her daughter's hands comfortly. "I ain't never stopped believing in you, Dawn."

The women sat on the side of the bed together. Dawn leaned over and gave her mom a hug. A knock at the door interrupted their tender moment.

"Come in," Dawn said.

Denisha opened the door and peered in with a worried expression. "Henry on the phone," she announced. "He wanna know if you made it back yet."

Dawn felt a stab of tension in her chest, but she wasn't as fretful as she was on the boat. She looked into her mother's eyes and Virginia patted her knee and nodded.

"Tell him I'm on my way," Dawn told her sister.

"You going over there?" Denisha asked.

"Yeah. In a minute," Dawn said. "I wanna pray first."

Denisha looked from Dawn to their mother. "Oh. Okay," she said and slipped quietly out of the room.

Virginia got to her feet and left the bedroom also, so Dawn could have some private time with the Lord.

❦

Thirty minutes later Dawn and her sister were in the car again, heading for a south side neighborhood known as Berry Hill. The rain was still coming down hard, and the thunder claps were like shotgun blasts in the sky.

Denisha was upset because she and Dawn were the only two people in her car. But Dawn was calm, filled with a peace that only the Holy Spirit can provide.

"This don't make no sense," Denisha complained. "You know he gon' start some mess. He don't care about me being with you. Look what he did last time I went with you; he didn't give a damn."

"It'll be all right," Dawn promised. She stared straight ahead, wondering how her life could go from two extremes so quickly: Just yesterday she was on the upper deck of a beautiful cruise ship, watching the sun fade into a pure blue ocean. Today she was in a raggedy car, avoiding potholes in the middle of a thunderstorm in Overbrook Meadows' poorest neighborhood.

"No, it ain't all right," Denisha said. "What am I supposed to do if he starts hitting you? We need to go get my boyfriend. You said we was gon' take Uncle Elvin and them with us."

"We will," Dawn said, "when we go get my stuff. But we don't need them right now. I'm just going to talk. As a matter of fact, I don't even want you to come in with me. I'm going in by myself."

That was even more shocking. Denisha almost slammed her foot on the brake.

"*What?*"

"Calm down," Dawn told her. "I prayed about it. It's gonna be all right."

"Look, I ain't saying I don't believe in God," Denisha said, "but you tripping. You can't run up in there hoping Jesus is gonna have your back. I'm finna go get Byron."

Denisha tried to turn at the next intersection, but Dawn reached and put a hand on the steering wheel. Her face was the picture of serenity. Denisha didn't understand how she could be so composed.

"Dawn, I'm not going along with this! This is…"

Denisha trailed off because Dawn pulled something out of her purse that made their uncle Elvin look like an invalid. The gun was black with a dark brown, wood grain handle. It was a revolver with a huge six-inch barrel. It was almost too big to fit in Dawn's knockoff Coach bag. It looked powerful enough to stop a bull in full charge.

Thankfully Denisha was at a red light; she couldn't move for a full five seconds.

"Where, where'd you get that?"

"Mama's room." Dawn spoke softly. She was still strangely serene, like they were discussing a nail file she found on the floor.

"Is that, is that Daddy's?"

"He left it for Mama," Dawn confirmed. "But she hates it. You know she wouldn't never use it, even if a thief was kicking her door down."

"She gave it to you?"

Dawn shook her head. "I was in there praying next to the bed, and God told me to look under the mattress. Mama don't know I got it."

"Guh-God told you?" Denisha wasn't an all-out heathen, but she was an admitted skeptic.

"I don't know how to describe it," Dawn said. "I didn't know what to do, but when I started praying, something told me to look under the mattress. As soon as I saw the gun, I knew it was Daddy's. When I picked it up, a huge feeling of peace came over me, and I knew God wanted me to take it with me."

"Are you, you gonna kill him?"

Dawn casually placed the gun back in her purse. "I'm gonna tell him I'm leaving, Denisha. Whatever happens after that is up to Henry. I don't wanna hurt nobody. But I'm not gon' let him hurt me, either."

Denisha's eyes were still wide, but a slight smile crept to her lips.

"You *could* kill him," she said. "Everybody know he been hitting on you. If you say he attacked you again, everybody will believe you."

"Are you talking about *murder*?" Dawn couldn't believe she would suggest such a thing.

"Naw, I'm just saying…" Denisha backpedalled. "If you *did* have to shoot him, everybody would believe you. Won't nothing happen to you."

"I know that," Dawn said. She folded her arms over her chest and took a deep breath. "I'm not worried about me. I hope it don't come to that, but if he raise his hand to me again, that will be his last time. That's why I want you to wait outside. I don't want nothing provoking him."

Denisha nodded, finally seeing things as her sister did. "All right, Dawn. If you going in there with that thang, I'll wait outside. But if I hear some shooting, I'm running up in here."

"If you hear some shooting," Dawn said, "you ain't got to worry about running. I promise, his soul will already be in the air by the time you get out the car."

Denisha was stunned by her sister's fierceness. Her smile quivered and then disappeared entirely.

Someone behind them honked their horn, and the girls looked up and saw that the light had turned green. It was only six o'clock, but the storm clouds blocked the sun completely, ushering in a premature darkness.

"Come on," Dawn said. "Let's get this over with."

CHAPTER 20
HENRY'S LAST STAND

Henry's truck was parked in its usual spot in the driveway. Denisha pulled in next to it and kept the car running.

"Why you leaving it on?" Dawn wondered. "You gon' leave me here?" She chuckled nervously.

Denisha shrugged. The interior of her car was dark, which made the whites of her eyes seem extra white. "We might have to book it out of here."

"We're not doing a *driveby*," Dawn said. "You need to stop thinking the worst. Everything's gon' be just fine. I'm gon' walk out of there in about two minutes with no troubles."

"What if you have to shoot him?"

The question hung in the air like the stench of death.

"If I shoot him, it'll be self-defense," Dawn said. "I'm not gonna take off running like I committed some crime. I'm gonna call 911 and sit in the living room and wait for them to get here."

Denisha thought about that, and she reluctantly turned the ignition off. "I don't get you," she said. "How you go from being scared all these years, and now you gon' walk in there like it ain't nothing?"

"I did a lot of soul searching," Dawn said, "when I was on that cruise. I'm not weak. Henry made me feel like I was. A lot of people did. But that's not who I am, not deep inside. I think I had to get away from everything to see that, to see who I really am."

Denisha stared in silence, and Dawn opened the door and stepped out into the rain.

"Don't kill him," Denisha said finally. "It ain't worth it, Dawn."

Dawn closed the door without responding because she was done taking advice from people on the outside looking in. Unless you've been berated in front of your children or slapped for not making enough food for your boyfriend to have seconds…

Unless you've been punched in the stomach for not waking your man up in time for work or put in a choke hold because you didn't want to have sex on your period—and then forced to take the sex anyway…

Unless you've walked in Dawn's shoes for the last two years and felt your heart freeze up every time you heard your boyfriend's truck pull into the driveway, you couldn't say what constituted sufficient cause to kill a man.

The only people who could make that decision was Dawn, the man upstairs, and the long-barrel Smith & Wesson she had in her purse. Everybody else could take their opinion to Montel or Maury Povich or someone else who liked to talk a good game but didn't have the balls to put predators like Henry in their place.

Dawn stepped slowly through the downpour with little regards for her perm or her clothes, which were completely soaked by the time reached the porch. The front door of the two-bedroom home was unlocked. Dawn walked inside and was immediately struck with a sense that something was not quite right.

The living room was filthy, but that was to be expected. Dawn was the only one who cleaned the house regularly. She'd been gone for a full week, and Henry did a lot of drinking during that time. Most of the debris was scattered around the coffee table, but there were a dozen or more empty beer cans strewn about the hallway leading towards the bathroom. Dawn didn't want to think about how bad the bedroom looked.

The television in the main room was on and tuned in to a ballgame. Again, this wasn't out of the norm. It was a Saturday evening, and Henry liked nothing more than to watch millionaires shoot hoops or tackle each other, only occasionally getting up to void his bowels.

Dawn looked around, and it struck her that the thing that was out of place was not something she could *see*. Rather it was her nose that registered something strange. If she didn't know any better, Dawn would have sworn she smelled *cooked food* mingled with the stench of stale beer and body odor. She looked towards the kitchen just in time to see her ex-boyfriend appear in the entrance.

Henry wore baggy black jeans with a grimy white tee shirt. His hair was unkempt and oily, like he thought about combing it, but decided to just grease it down instead. Henry's face and neck was slick with sweat. His skin was black like oil. His eyes were nearly bloodshot with dark lines underneath. He smiled hesitantly when he saw Dawn. He wiped his grubby hands on his pants.

"Hey, baby. You, you just got back?"

Dawn nodded. She didn't move from her doorway, and Henry didn't move from his. They were nearly twenty feet apart, but this was too close for Dawn. She held her purse with her left hand. Her right hand was at her side. She thought she could retrieve her daddy's gun in no more than two seconds, but Henry could close the distance between them in the same two seconds.

"I, I made dinner," Henry said. "For you and the boys. So you don't have to cook tonight. I made some fried chicken and some corn. I made some biscuits, too, but they didn't come out right." He chuckled. "The outside was good, but the inside was still sticky. I tried to put em back in, but they ended up getting burnt. We got some bread, though. I'll, I can go back to the store and get some more biscuits, if you want."

Dawn's curiosity intensified. Not only did Henry *never* cook a meal, but he definitely wouldn't run to the store for last-minute biscuits.

"I got you some flowers," Henry said. He pointed towards the dining table, and Dawn saw that there was a bouquet of roses in a clear vase set up as the center piece. Furthermore, the dining table was already set for dinner with four plates in front of each chair, a fork and spoon next to each plate.

Dawn was stunned silent. Henry abused her plenty of times, but he never tried to make up for it with kindness of this magnitude. Dawn guessed the extra special groveling was because Henry knew the gig was up. Dawn's sister and her mother knew about the abuse now, and Henry would have to turn over a new leaf if he wanted to keep his punching bag around.

What Henry didn't know was Dawn was fully prepared for these tactics. Denisha didn't have all of the answers, but one thing she said kept playing over and over in Dawn's head like a mantra: *He'll probably act good for a week. But after that it's like, Ding-Ding. Get ready to put your boxing gloves back on.*

"You, uh, where the boys at?" Henry asked. He took a step in her direction, and Dawn inched her right hand towards her purse. Henry stopped, and Dawn did the same.

"The boys ain't coming," she said. Dawn was accustomed to being meek when she had to give Henry a bit of bad news, but not this time. She spoke with volume and confidence, and the bass in her voice struck Henry like a punch in the nose. "I'm not coming back, either," Dawn said. "That's what I came to tell you, Henry. We moving out."

It felt like a full hour passed while Henry processed this information and Dawn waited to see if she would have to shoot him or not. When Henry finally responded, it was first with a flare of his nostrils and then with a slow shake of his head.

"You, you leaving me?"

"I can't take it no more," Dawn confirmed. "I'm sick of you hitting on me, Henry. I'm sick of being scared. But I ain't scared of you no more."

Dawn spoke with a defiance Henry didn't recognize, and his innate reaction was anger. Dawn saw a knot of flesh bunch up between his eyebrows, but in the next second it was gone. He sighed and looked remorseful again.

"Look, Dawn, I'm sorry, all right? I'm sorry for grabbing on your hair like that. I didn't mean to. You just, you caught me off guard when you said you was leaving."

"Hmph. I must've caught you off guard damned near every day since we been together."

Henry shook his head. "Why you, why you wanna say something like that? I don't be messing with you like that, Dawn. You know I don't."

"Yeah, you right," Dawn conceded. "You only hit me about once a month, yell at me three, four times a week. But you right; it ain't every day."

Henry frowned and took another step towards her. Dawn inched her right hand towards her purse again. Her breaths were slow and hot. Henry stopped, and she stopped.

"Why you, why you acting like that?" Henry asked. "It's them bitches you been with? You let them hos mess with your head, girl? What they tell you, they was gon' be there for you now? They gon' be your friend, so you don't need me no more? That's what you been listening to? You letting them bitches gas you up? You just gon' forget about the last ten years when they didn't give a damn about you, when I was there taking care of you and them hos didn't even remember your name?"

Dawn smiled. This was the Henry she knew. This was the one she was comfortable with.

"What the hell is so funny?"

"You," Dawn said and chuckled. "You got yo head so far up your ass, you want to blame *my* friends 'cause *you* can't keep your hands to yourself. You need help, man. You need to talk to somebody. Better yet, you need to go put your hands on a grown man and get *your* ass kicked for a change. See how you like it."

"What the hell?"

"It's over, Henry. I ain't living here no more. I wanna get my stuff out of here."

Henry's blood boiled, and Dawn watched him turn into the monster that tormented her dreams for the last two years. The only difference was she wasn't frightened this time. And that was something Henry absolutely could not stomach.

"I don't care what them hos done told you, you ain't finna talk to me like that."

He took four quick steps, and Dawn's hand disappeared inside her purse. Henry stopped, and so did she.

"*What the hell you got in yo purse?*" he barked. His hands were down at his sides, and they were balled into those all-too-familiar fists.

Dawn's surprise wasn't a surprise anymore, so she wrapped her hand around the butt of the pistol and pulled it slowly from her Coach bag. The .38 didn't come out as easily as she expected. The barrel was too long, and the butt snagged twice before she finally twisted it free. If Henry rushed her, he could've easily knocked the purse from her hands and overpowered her.

But he didn't move. He just stood there like an idiot until Dawn had the barrel of her father's gun pointed squarely at his nose. Henry was as angry as a caged tiger, but he didn't like having a gun pointed at him, and it showed. His eyes grew big like half dollars, and he threw up his hands in a futile attempt to block any bullets coming his way.

Dawn didn't want to take pleasure in this, but she couldn't help but feel like this was justice at its finest. She couldn't count how many times she wore the same look of terror on her face. She couldn't count the times she screamed and begged him to stop, but Henry laid into her anyway.

A satisfied grin curled her lips, and Henry took her smile as a sign of weakness. He lowered his hands and narrowed his eyes. His chest rose and fell slowly. He even had the gall to take another step towards her.

"Get that thang out my face!"

"Or what?" Dawn's smile twisted into a sneer, and there was something awful in her eyes that Henry had never seen before. Dawn pulled the hammer back on the .38 just like her daddy taught her, and she took two bold steps forward. If they were playing a game of chicken, she was in an eighteen-wheeler. Henry was on a motor scooter.

There were only ten feet between them now. Dawn's outstretched arm took up two of those. The barrel of the gun took away another six inches. Henry threw up his hands again and took four quick steps back.

"*Dawn, get that thing out my face!*"

"*Or what?*" She continued to advance on him. "*Or what, Henry? What you gon' do? Huh? Tell me what you gon' do?*"

Henry retreated further, but the house was small. Soon the dining table blocked his escape. He yelped like a dog when he backed into it, and then he fell to his knees. Dawn's new roses fell over, and the water from the vase spilled over the table. It splashed on Henry's neck, and he flinched and screamed, thinking it was his blood dripping down his back.

A huge boom of thunder ripped through the house accompanied by a bright flash of lightening that illuminated the whole dining room. The **CRACKLE** was so loud Dawn thought the gun went off. Henry did, too. He yelled and jerked away from her, slamming the back of his head into the corner of the table.

"*Stop, Dawn! Please!*"

He held his hands over his head. Dawn saw that every finger was trembling.

"*Don't kill me!*"

Henry's face was turned away from her, and his eyes were clinched closed. Even so, thick tears escaped and rolled down his cheeks. Snot leaked from his nose. A dark stain appeared between his legs and quickly blossomed.

This was the most disgusting yet wonderful thing Dawn had ever seen. She might have laughed if not for a sudden boost of adrenaline that made her whole body feel like she was on fire. Every hair stood on her head and arms. Her teeth were bared and her trigger finger twitched, and her hotwired brain screamed for her to **DO IT! SHOOT HIM! THIS IS YOUR CHANCE TO END IT ALL! SPLATTER HIS BRAINS ON THE TABLE! KILL HIM! DO IT NOW!**

"Please, Dawn! No!"

Henry cowered so much he nearly squeezed under the table.

Blood rushed past Dawn's ears. Hot, white fury burned behind her pupils. Her finger jumped on the trigger. She knew it would be so easy. It wouldn't take much, about the same amount of force she used to button her jeans and *POP!*

Henry's face would disintegrate right before her eyes.

But that wasn't what Dawn came for, and she knew it. She also knew it wasn't God telling her to pull the trigger. That voice in her head wasn't her daddy, either. It was the one who came to steal and to kill and to destroy, and if Dawn let the devil guide her, her life wouldn't be worth any more than the piss staining Henry's stanky drawers.

She wouldn't pull the trigger unless she absolutely had to, and the trembling piece of shit in front of her posed no threat whatsoever. Dawn kept the gun pointed at him, though, because after all the hell Henry put her and her family though, he deserved to squirm just a little while longer.

"I'll be back in *one hour*," Dawn said.

Henry peeked up at her through his shaky fingers. *"Take that, take the gun off my face,"* he begged.

Dawn ignored him. "I'll be back in one hour, Henry. I'm coming to get my stuff and my boys' stuff."

"All right! Okay!"

"If I see you here," Dawn continued, "I ain't got no choice but to shoot you. If I see you at my mama's house, I'm gon' shoot you, Henry. If I see you at my job—"

"Fine! Just leave!"

"No, you listen to me!"

Henry piped down and sniffled. "Okay, Dawn, just, just stop pointing that gun at me! It might go off."

"If it do, you deserve it," Dawn said. "If I ever see you at my job, I swear to God I'll shoot you, Henry. If I *ever* see you again, I'ma think you coming for me, and I'ma get you first."

"You ain't gon see me, Dawn! I swear to God! Just leave! Get that gun out my face! I done pissed my pants!"

Dawn paused. She couldn't believe how easy this was. She thought Henry would put up more of a fight, but the proof was trembling right before her eyes. This bastard really was terrified of guns. Dawn wished she had thought of this sooner. She could've saved herself countless nights of heartache.

She finally lowered the weapon and took a few steps back. Henry didn't take the opportunity to lunge or make any other moves in her direction. He lowered his hands and watched her like he no longer had any idea who she was.

"I'll be back in an hour," Dawn said. "Henry, if you got any sense in yo head *at all*, you bet not be here. If I see you, I'm not gon' ask no questions. I'm just gon' start shooting, and I ain't gon' stop until you good and *dead*."

Henry didn't respond, but there was no doubt he would heed her warning. Dawn gave him one last look of disdain before she turned and walked out of the house. She was poised to spin around with her gun blazing if she heard the slightest creak on the floor behind her, but that sound never came.

Dawn stepped out into the rain and casually got in the car with her sister.

Denisha watched her for a few heartbeats and then asked, "Did you shoot him?"

Dawn shook her head. "Didn't have to."

Denisha started the car. "He gon', he gon let you go?"

Dawn nodded and wiped the rain from her face.

"You look like you almost did it," Denisha said as they backed out of the driveway. "It's good you didn't, though. You don't want that on your conscience."

Dawn felt the same way. She zipped her purse closed and thanked God for giving her the strength to fight against her flesh. She also thanked her earthly father for always being there for her, just as he promised he would.

She and Denisha returned to the house an hour later with a car full of hooligans and two more relatives following in an Astrovan. Everyone was prepared for the worst, but Henry's truck wasn't in the driveway, and he was nowhere in sight. All of the extra muscle was used to transport belongings only.

Dawn purchased a lot of the furniture in the house, but she was mostly interested in taking clothes. She did make sure to get everything out of her sons' room, plus the flat-screen TV she bought for her bedroom.

Everything else was part of her past, and Dawn was eager to turn her back on it.

At eight o'clock that night, the Finley Sisters got together for their three-way telephone call. Tim and Luther were running around so much, Dawn had to go to her new bedroom (which was her old bedroom) and close the door so she could hear what her friends were saying.

Dawn knew her sons were excited about her being back from vacation, and the idea of never seeing Henry again had them even more giddy, so she didn't chastise them about the racket they were putting up. This was just day one. Tomorrow she would teach them that just because they were at Grandma's house didn't mean it was going to be all fun and games.

All three ladies on the phone were proud that they kept their word and broke up with the men in their lives, but it was Dawn's story that garnered the most attention. Rene couldn't get over how God led Dawn to her father's pistol, and Mona couldn't believe Dawn had the balls to cock it and point it at her abusive ex. Both of them thought Henry sniveling and snotting and peeing on himself was the funniest thing ever.

"You a bad bitch," Rene told Dawn.

"For real," Mona agreed. "Why didn't you shoot him?"

"I almost did," Dawn said. "That was the scariest part. I felt like I had all the power. His life was in my hands. I kept remembering all those times when he kicked me and choked me. I wanted to pull the trigger so bad. Y'all just don't know."

"You could've done it," Mona said. "Everybody would've told the police how he's been beating on you. You would've got away scot-free."

"I know," Dawn said. "My sister told me that, too. But when I was standing over him with the gun, I knew it wasn't right. It woulda been like shooting a stray dog; that's how pathetic he was."

"Aren't you worried about him coming back?" Rene wondered.

"No, that's one thing I *don't* have to worry about," Dawn said. "I'm not gon' see him no more."

"How do you know?" Rene asked.

"It's a feeling," Dawn said. "It's hard to describe. It's something I feel in my stomach. Like, you know when you done crossed the line with somebody. You know when you reached a point of no return. Henry was scared to death. He wasn't faking. He knew I was an inch away from taking his life, and he don't want no more of that. I told him if I ever see him again, I'm not gon' ask no questions, I'm just gon' start shooting. He knows I wasn't lying."

"So you gotta keep carrying that gun?" Mona asked.

"No, I don't think so," Dawn said. "I might keep it in the trunk of my car for the next month, but–"

"You won't be able to get to it fast enough," Mona interrupted.

"That's what I'm trying to tell you," Dawn said, "I'm not gon' need that gun again. It's over. I know y'all don't understand, but I know Henry's not coming around no more. He's not gonna show up at my job or anywhere else he think I might be. If you woulda saw the fear in his eyes like I did… It was sick. I mean, he actually peed on hisself."

Mona laughed. "That's what I wanna talk about. Did his eyes get *real* big like he might have shit hisself, too?"

Rene laughed. "That's nasty."

But Dawn wasn't amused. "It's not even funny, y'all. Seeing a man cry like that… It was probably the worst thing I ever saw. It's like seeing somebody you looked up to in the worst condition they could possibly be in. Like, y'all remember when we found out Mrs. Mitchell was on crack?"

All three girls remembered that. Mrs. Mitchell was their favorite teacher at Finley High from their freshman year all the way through the eleventh grade. Mrs. Mitchell was beautiful, and she always dressed nice, but her students later learned she'd been an undercover drug addict the whole time. Her life started to unravel in 1998, and when the crack fully took over, it hit her hard and fast.

Mrs. Mitchell started missing days, at least two a week. And when she did show up, she was disheveled and stinky, a mere shadow of her former self. She eventually quit coming to work altogether in 1999. Her former students later heard she was whoring herself on the streets, living in motel rooms every night, skinny as a toothpick and cracked out beyond recognition.

"It can't be that bad," Rene said. "You didn't even like Henry."

"It don't matter if I liked him or not," Dawn said. "It's just the point of seeing somebody at their lowest. I mean, he deserved it, but it ain't nothing to laugh about."

Rene and Mona were surprised by Dawn's empathy.

"Damn, she *told* you," Mona said to Rene.

"Please, she was talking to *you*," Rene said, and they both laughed.

"Well, anyway, Dawn," Mona said. "I'm glad it's over. You got your life back."

"I got rid of Henry," Dawn said. "But I don't know about having my life back. I gotta live with my mama. I don't have nothing. I didn't even get my furniture from over there."

"You can still go get it," Mona said. "Just go back with your .38 and tell Henry, '*Move around, clown!*'" She and Rene laughed, but Dawn sighed.

"Girl, quit tripping," Rene told her. "This is exactly what you needed, Dawn. You may be back at square one, but you get a fresh start."

"That's right," Mona said. "You got time to reevaluate your life and get your priorities straight again. The first thing you need to do is go back to school."

"That's *number one*," Rene agreed. "You shouldn't even think about moving out until you get some education under your belt."

"I don't have time for school," Dawn griped.

"All right, we need to change your number one goal," Mona said. "*First* you need to readjust your attitude, Dawn. You bad enough to make Henry pee on himself…" She giggled. "But you ain't bad enough to go back to school?"

"I work a lot," Dawn said. "I don't see when I would have the time."

"Then you have to cut your hours," Rene said. "You're back at home with your mom, so you shouldn't have as many bills."

"Yeah, that's true," Dawn said.

"And me and Rene are adopting Tim and Luther as our godsons," Mona said. "We're going to get them new shoes and school supplies and winter coats and stuff whenever they need it."

"Yeah," Rene said. "And we got their birthdays covered. And we're going to visit more so we can really be a part of their lives."

"At least once a month," Mona agreed.

Dawn was taken aback. "You, you what?"

"We already told you," Mona said, "things are going to be different now. You're our sister, Dawn. We got your back."

"And if you ever need help with your school work," Rene said, "you can call us. If I can't help you, I can at least point you in the right direction."

"Naw, you better call *me* if you need help with your homework," Mona said. "Rene wasn't the best student in the world…"

"Please, I was better than you," Rene said.

"My GPA was 3.89," Mona reminded them.

"That's because you took Art and P.E. as much as you could," Rene said.

"I did that because I'm smarter than you," Mona said. "What I need advanced calculus for? Me and you got the *exact same* diploma—except your GPA wasn't as good as mine. And you forgot all of that calculus by now."

Rene couldn't argue with that. She never used calculus outside of high school and college. "Well, you can call me if you want to actually learn something," she told Dawn. "I guess you can call Mona if you want to cruise through."

"Ain't nothing wrong with cruising," Mona said, but then she noticed Dawn hadn't said anything about their grand plans for her. "Dawn? You still there?"

She sniffled. "Yeah."

"Girl, what's wrong with you?" Mona asked.

"You're not, are you crying?" Rene asked.

"A little," Dawn admitted.

"Why?" Mona asked. "You don't want to go back to school?"

"No, I mean, yeah. It's not that," Dawn said. "I was still thinking about what y'all said about Tim and Luther. I can't believe y'all would do that for them."

"I don't know why you can't believe it," Rene said.

"Dawn, this is the last time I'm gonna say this," Mona said. "*We got your back.* So get used to it. I know it might seem strange, but we're not gonna hurt you."

"We come in peace," Rene said, and they all laughed.

"Hey, have you called that man yet?" Mona asked.

"What man?" Rene said.

"Not you," Mona said. "I'm talking to Dawn."

"What man?" Dawn said.

"Don't play," Mona said. "You know who I'm talking about; the one you met on the boat."

"Oh," Dawn said. She smiled. "You're talking about Calvin."

"Yeah, *Calvin*," Mona said. "Have you talked to him yet?"

Dawn shook her head, and then she remembered they couldn't see her. "No."

"Why not?" Rene asked.

"You should call to make sure he made it back home safely," Mona suggested.

"I'm scared to call him," Dawn said.

"Why?" Rene asked.

"I don't know," Dawn said. "I feel weird, like I went back in time or something. I'm already living in my old bedroom. I get butterflies in my stomach when I think about Calvin."

"You know he likes you," Mona said. "Why you scared?"

"I didn't say I was scared," Dawn said.

"Yes, you did!" Rene said and laughed.

"Stop procrastinating," Mona said. "Call him right now."

"Now?" Dawn's heart quivered. "We're on, we're on the phone now."

"Did you call her?" Mona asked.

"I sure did," Rene said.

"Could you kindly hang up on her?" Mona asked.

"All right. We'll talk to you later," Rene told Dawn. "Call us back after you talk to him, if you want."

"But I–"

"Call your man," Mona said.

"Wait, I–" The phone abruptly went dead in Dawn's ear. She shook her head and burst into laughter.

Dawn hung up the phone, and suddenly she could hear her boys again. She didn't know what they were playing, but there was too much footwork involved for Dawn's tastes. She went and opened her door just as Luther was running by. She grabbed hold of his arm and brought his forward progress to a halt.

"Boy, what in God's name are y'all doing in here?"

"Playing checkers," Luther said and laughed. He was nearly out of breath. His eyes were wide and wild.

"What checkers got to do what running around the house?" Dawn wondered.

365

"It's a new rule," Luther explained. "Every time one of your men gets jumped, you have to do a lap around the house."

"Where'd you get that rule?" Dawn asked.

"Grandma taught us," Luther said. "She's playing, too—except she don't do the running."

"It's all right!" Dawn's mother called from the living room. "This is our last game, and they gon' sleep good tonight!"

Dawn grinned. Every time she thought her boys were taking advantage of their dear old granny, Virginia was always one step ahead of them.

"Are you still on the phone?" Luther asked.

"Yeah, I gotta make one more call," Dawn said. "It won't take long."

"All right," Luther said, and he took off again.

Dawn closed the door and found Calvin's number on her dresser. She took the phone to the bed and punched the numbers carefully, ignoring her moist fingers and the gradual rise in temperature.

Someone answered after two rings. "Hello?"

"Hello?" Dawn said. "May I speak to Calvin?"

"This is he. Is this Dawn?"

She smiled. That was a nice touch, but also a little risky. Either Calvin already knew her voice well enough to make the guess, or he didn't have enough women calling to get her confused with someone else. Either way, Dawn liked it.

"Yes. It's me."

"I'm glad you called," Calvin said. His voice was still smooth and deep. It gave Dawn goose bumps despite her sudden hot flash. "So how'd it go with your boyfriend? Did you break up with him today?"

"Yes," Dawn said. "We're definitely broke up."

"How'd he take it," Calvin inquired, "if you don't mind me asking?"

"He, um, it didn't go that good," Dawn confided. "There was some yelling and screaming. But it's all over now. I moved back in with my mama."

"That's great," Calvin said and then chuckled. "Did he cry?"

"There was, um, there was some waterworks," Dawn said. She giggled, totally forgetting that this was the same kind of joking she cautioned her friends against. "But I think he got hisself cleaned up by now. He'll be all right…"

CHAPTER 21
THE FINAL CHAPTER
RESURRECTION

The next day was Sunday, and Dawn couldn't wait to get to her house of worship. She didn't feel like she went against God's teachings when she pulled a gun on her no-good ex-boyfriend, but she knew it was wrong to delight in Henry's suffering and savor his terror the way she did.

On bended knees, Dawn asked for forgiveness, and she felt it was granted. A voice in her heart told her she wouldn't have to be afraid anymore, and there would be peace in her life. Dawn gratefully accepted the blessing, and a huge burden lifted from her shoulders. When she rose to her feet, there were tears of joy in her eyes, and no one could doubt the Holy Spirit was upon her.

Before she left church, Dawn asked the choir director if she could try out.

"There are no try outs," Sister Maples said. "We'll take anyone who's called to serve. We may have some people sing softer than others," she said with a wink, "depending on their skill level, but everyone's welcome. Do you have any singing experience, Sister Wright?"

"A little," Dawn said. "I was in my high school choir, but now I mostly just sing around the house. My friends think I'm pretty good."

"I'm sure you are," Sister Maples said. "Rehearsals are Saturday night at seven."

"I'll be at work," Dawn said. "But I think my schedule's changing in a couple of months."

"We'll still be here waiting on you," Sister Maples said, "but don't take too long. If God's calling you to service, you *must* be obedient."

"I will," Dawn promised. "I'll see you next Sunday."

❧

Dawn returned to work the following Monday. She realized, for the first time, really, how much she truly hated her job. Her boss, Mr. Le, was relentlessly ornery, and Dawn was sick of working like a dog for very little pay. She complained to her friends when she talked to them later that night.

"Have you looked for another job?" Rene asked.

"I got a paper right here," Dawn said. "I want to work in an office, but I never did nothing like that before. Everything else, I either have to have experience for, or it's some fast food place. I guess I could flip burgers."

"Uh-uhn!" Mona said. "You're not flipping no burgers, Dawn."

"That wouldn't be any better than what you already have," Rene agreed.

"Have you thought about what classes you want to take when you go back to school?" Mona asked.

"I wanna be a nurse," Dawn said. "I was talking to my friend at work, and she said her sister went to school for three years and now she's an LVN. That's something I've always thought about doing."

"That's a good idea," Mona said. "Where do you want to go?"

"The community college," Dawn said. "I can get a full degree from there; I won't have to transfer to a big, four-year school."

"You need to get your application in this week," Rene suggested. "Classes start in a couple of months."

"I don't have time to go down there tomorrow," Dawn said. "I can probably get off early Thursday if I—"

"Oh, I forgot you don't have a computer," Rene said.

"I can send you one," Mona offered. "I replaced all of the Compaqs in my office with Dells last summer. I still got a couple of the old ones in the back somewhere. They're a little outdated, but it's better than nothing. You'll be able to get on the internet and do your application at home."

Dawn marveled at the idea of having her own computer. "Thank you. I really appreciate that."

"How'd it go with Calvin last night?" Rene asked.

Even over the phone, they could hear Dawn smile. "It was cool. We talked for a whole hour."

"What does he do for a living?" Rene asked.

"He has an awning company," Dawn reported.

"Really?" Mona said. "His own company?"

"It's not that big," Dawn said. "But he has two shops and about twenty people working for him."

"I love me some black entrepreneurs," Mona said. "You'd better hold on to that one."

Dawn had no intentions of doing otherwise. "What about y'all? Did Blake call you back yet?" she asked Rene. "I know Dennis came crawling back to you, Mona."

"Blake called a couple of times today," Rene confirmed. "But I didn't call him back."

"Dennis hasn't called me," Mona said. "I think I hurt his feelings. Maybe I should call to see if he's all right."

"To see if he's all right, or to invite him over for one last lay?" Rene wondered.

"Damn, you know me so well," Mona said with a sigh. "Y'all just don't know how good he licks the kitty. He'll have you ready to pass out."

"But you're not using men anymore, remember?" Rene said.

"I know," Mona said. "But it ain't nothing wrong with reminiscing."

"No," Rene said, thinking about Xavier's hot lips on her neck and chest. "Ain't nothing wrong with that."

∽✞∾

Dawn received a huge package in the mail a few days later. Inside it was her very first computer. Mona said it was a little outdated, but Dawn couldn't tell. It

371

didn't even look like it had been stored away for any lengthy period of time.

Her sons knew more about technology than Dawn did, so she enlisted Tim and Luther's help in setting it up in the living room. The next day she called AT&T, and a technician came to the house to set up her internet services. Dawn called Calvin later that night to express her excitement and fear of the World Wide Web.

"I heard there's a lot of porn on the internet," Dawn said with a shudder. "I don't want my boys getting into that mess."

"You can change your preferences," Calvin said. "I'll show you how, if you want."

"Yeah, I'll go to the computer now," Dawn said.

"Let me know when you're ready," Calvin said, then, "Oh, I've been meaning to tell you, I've got some worked lined up in Overbrook Meadows next week. I was wondering if you'd like to have lunch with me, maybe Monday or Tuesday."

Dawn blushed. "I would love to see you again. But I work those days. I only get forty-five minutes for lunch."

"That's fine," Calvin said. "I'll pick you up from your job, if that's okay…"

"I wanna get pretty for you," Dawn said. "But I won't be able to if you pick me up from work. I have to wear an ugly uniform. I don't wear makeup because it gets hot in there sometimes."

"That's okay," Calvin said. "I'll be installing awnings all morning, so I won't look my best, either."

"You install awnings yourself? I thought you had a crew working for you."

"I do," Calvin said, "but I need an excuse to come to Overbrook Meadows, so I'm going to drive one of the trucks and work alongside my men."

"Oh." Beads of sweat formed on Dawn's forehead as she took a seat behind her computer. She couldn't believe he would go through all of that just to see her.

"You ready?" Calvin asked. "I'll take it slow, but you have to trust me; I've got a lot of experience with this. If you want me to go faster, let me know. We can do it however you like."

"You, uh… Huh?"

"Your computer," Calvin said. "Didn't you say you wanted me to help you with your security preferences?"

"Oh, uh, yeah," Dawn said. "I'm, um, I'm sorry. I'm at my computer now."

"Uh, what did you think I was talking about?" Calvin asked.

Dawn giggled. "You don't even want to know."

"All right," Calvin said. "Now the first thing I need you to do is carefully place your hand on the mouse and caress it gently, until it becomes warm and hard to the touch."

Dawn smacked her lips. "All right, now I know you're messing with me!"

"Yeah, I am," Calvin said. "I'm sorry."

"It's okay," Dawn said. "You're funny. You make me laugh."

"You make me laugh, too," Calvin said. "Among other things…"

Dawn dared not ask what those other things were. "Is it, is it hot in your house?" she asked instead.

"Very," Calvin said.

Dawn took a deep breath and let it out slowly. "I can't wait to see you next week."

"Do you promise to give me at least one kiss?"

"At least one," Dawn assured.

"A hug, too?" Calvin asked.

"If you want," Dawn said.

"Is it hot in your house?" Calvin asked.

"It wasn't till I got on the phone with you," Dawn said. "But it's okay. I like it…"

∽×∾

On Monday Dawn found out she qualified for *a lot* of student aid and grant money because of her low monthly income and the two kids she was raising without a father in the home. Her out-of-pocket costs for her first semester of college was a nifty *zero dollars and zero cents*. According to her registration form, she could put that on a payment plan if she couldn't come up with it all at once.

The next day Calvin picked her up at lunchtime for what was to be their first official date outside of the cruise ship. Calvin wore black Dickeys workpants with his company tee shirt and tennis shoes, but his hands and nails were perfectly clean. He didn't look like he'd done any hard work that day.

And even without her makeup, Calvin told Dawn she looked as beautiful as she did when he met her on the *Ecstasy*. Dawn knew he meant it because he couldn't take his eyes off of her the whole time they were together.

They had a quick meal at Chili's and then had to hurry back to the cleaners so Dawn could clock in on time. When Calvin dropped her off, Dawn gave him the hug and kiss she promised, as well as a few extra kisses that weren't on the agenda.

When she got home that night, Dawn couldn't wait to call her friends and express her elation. She couldn't get ahold of Rene, but Mona answered her cellphone right away.

Dawn told her about her special day and then dropped a bombshell: "I think I love him! He treats me so good. He makes me so happy."

"What? W*hoa*. Slow it down, missy. I know you didn't say *love*."

"Yes, I did. I know you don't believe me, but–"

"I believe you *think* you're in love," Mona said. "But you can't give up your heart that easily, Dawn."

"Why not?"

"Because you barely know him. You might get hurt."

"I don't think he's gonna hurt me."

"That's the thing," Mona said. "You never know. That's why you have to be careful."

"I am careful."

"No, you're not. Not if you're falling in love with him so soon."

"But I can't help it," Dawn said. "What am I supposed to do, put a lock on my heart? I thought we said we weren't going to do that."

"Well you gotta do *something*," Mona warned.

"No. I like the way I feel," Dawn said. "I haven't been happy like this in a long time. If it doesn't work out, I guess I'll get my heart broke. But I'm not going to stop feeling like I do."

"All right, go for it then," Mona said with an exasperated sigh. "I wish you the best."

"Thanks," Dawn said. "And thanks again for the computer. Every day I fall more and more in love with that thing."

"That's all right," Mona said. "Did you apply for all of your classes yet?"

"Yeah, I'm all done," Dawn said. "School starts August 27."

"How do your boys feel about you going back to school?" Mona wondered.

"They think it's great," Dawn said. "Tim said he was proud of me. I never thought I'd hear something like that from my son."

"I'm proud of you, too," Mona said. "Don't forget to call me anytime you need help with your homework. And I wanna see that first progress report."

Dawn laughed. "You sound like my mama."

"How's Miss Virginia doing, by the way?"

"She's doing great," Dawn said. "She's glad to have me home, and I'm glad to be here."

In July the Finley Sisters met up for the first time since the Carnival cruise. Rene and Mona came to Overbrook Meadows, and they stayed all day Saturday and most of Sunday before returning to their own lives and obligations back home.

While they were there, Mona and Rene took Dawn's boys to the museum and later out for ice cream and shoe shopping so they could get new sneakers for the upcoming school year. Dawn was not pleased when she got off work and saw that Tim and Luther both had a new pair of seventy-dollar tennis shoes. Rene and Mona took her complaints with a grain of salt.

"This is the first thing we ever bought them," Mona said. "We had to get something nice."

"You could've got something nice for twenty dollars," Dawn griped.

"My godsons are not wearing *twenty-dollar tennis shoes*," Mona said. She gave Tim a sideways hug and palmed the top of Luther's head.

"Mama, Aunt Rene said we can go visit her in Houston sometimes," Tim reported. "Can we go?"

"Sure," Dawn said. "Maybe during winter break. Did y'all have a good time today?"

"Yes," they both said.

"Mama, did you know a girl won't go out with me if she don't like my shoes?" Luther asked.

Dawn sighed. She didn't even have to ask where he got that dating tip.

"That stuff only matters when you get older," she said.

"It's never too soon to teach them how to be proper gentlemen," Mona countered.

Dawn shook her head and looked over at Rene. "Has she been like this all day?"

"Yeah, but she's not *totally* shallow," Rene said. "I think Mona's gonna make a great mother one day."

"Oh, no I'm *not*," Mona said. "I'm not gonna get fat and sick for nine months—*on purpose*. Uh-uhn. I'm just fine with these two boys right here."

She hugged Tim and Luther, and they hugged her back, and Dawn knew her sons were truly blessed to have Rene and Mona in their lives. Dawn still wasn't sure she deserved such good friends, but she wouldn't give them back for anything in the world.

❧

In the last week of August, Dawn started her freshman year at Tarrant County College. Being in school again was exciting and scary, and Dawn had plenty to discuss with her friends on the phone that night. Unfortunately, this was also the day Rene experienced her first heartbreak since her ex-husband over a decade ago. Dawn's story took a backseat to her sister's suffering.

"I didn't know you liked him like that," Mona said. "Didn't you just meet him in June?"

"Yeah, it's only been three months," Rene said and blew her nose. "But he was smart and sweet. We went out five times. I wasn't head-over-heels, but I did give

378

him my heart. I trusted him. I thought he might be the one, you know?"

"That's why I keep telling Dawn she needs to slow down," Mona said. "You can't trust nobody these days. You never know what's really going on with these sorry-ass niggas."

"No," Rene said. "I'm not going back to the way I was, Mona. Just because Robert's an asshole doesn't mean they all are. I'm still gonna find the right one for me."

"I don't like it when you're upset like this," Mona said. "It pisses me off."

"What'd he do?" Dawn asked. She felt like she was coming in on the back end of the conversation.

"He wanted me to get on the pill so he wouldn't have to use a rubber," Rene explained. "I told him I would do it, but he still had to use a condom 'cause, you know, babies aren't the only thing I'm worried about."

"Ain't that the truth," Mona said.

"He told me if I wasn't going to sleep with him without a rubber, he'd find somebody who would," Rene went on. "I thought he was playing, but he called me the next day and said, '*Are you ready to get down like I want now, or do I have to sleep with somebody else again tonight?*'"

Dawn was shocked. "He told you that?"

"Like it wasn't nothing," Rene said.

Dawn shook her head. "You're better off without him, girl. If he's slinging his stuff around like that, he probably got something."

"If he do, he ain't giving it to me," Rene said. She sniffled.

"I'm trying to tell y'all to watch out for that love *crap*," Mona advised. "It ain't nothing but trouble."

"Don't listen to her," Rene told Dawn. "You can't let one person mess up your head. You do need to be careful, but I think Calvin's a good man."

"I think so, too," Dawn said.

"Y'all better watch it," Mona said.

"You made the same promise as us," Dawn reminded.

"Yeah, but it's going to take someone *really special* to make me give up my heart," Mona said. "I haven't seen nobody lately who even comes close. I miss Bart."

Dawn's eyes widened. Rene was equally surprised.

"You *miss* him?" Dawn asked.

"You must've had some pretty strong feelings for him," Rene said.

"I did," Mona admitted. "But it wasn't love—if that's what y'all thinking."

"How do you know?" Dawn asked. "If you're still thinking about him three months later, and nobody else can compare to the way he made you feel, isn't that love?"

Mona thought about it and said, "No. I don't think so."

"Why not?" Rene asked.

"Because he's *gone*," Mona snapped. "Why would I be in love with somebody who lives in a whole 'nother country?"

Rene and Dawn didn't have an answer to that question, but it was probably for the best because Mona was no longer in the mood to talk about her Brazilian heartthrob.

"Rene, I hope you find somebody else," Dawn said.

"No, they're gonna have to find *me*," Rene said. "I think I'm done looking for a while."

⁜

The next few months were hectic for Dawn as she adjusted to college life, but the transition wasn't as hard as she envisioned.

"I should've moved back in with my mama and did this ten years ago," she told Mona one day. "The only bad thing about it is being in class with all of those little kids. But so far the school work's not that hard."

"That's good," Mona said. "Oh, and I was meaning to tell you; you're right about why I'm still thinking about Bartolo."

"What, you lov–"

"*Shhht!*" Mona said. "Don't even say that word."

Dawn laughed. "But you do?"

"I think I *did*," Mona said. "Or I *was*. But don't tell Rene I told you. I'll never hear the end of it."

"There's nothing wrong with the L-word," Dawn said. "It's a good thing. It feels good to be in love."

"So you're officially in love with Calvin?"

"Yes," Dawn said with a bright smile.

"You told him, I mean, y'all tell each other?"

"Yeah," Dawn said. "We say it all the time."

"That's cool," Mona said. "I might start looking for somebody for me."

"You should," Dawn said. "It'll be fun."

"I wanna go to *Brazil*," Mona moaned.

Dawn laughed. "You can do that, too."

"No," Mona said. "I'm going to find me a good old American boy. But if he breaks my heart, I'll cut his balls off."

"I'll pray it doesn't come to that," Dawn said, " 'cause I think you might actually do it."

"I will," Mona said. "No doubt about it."

EPILOGUE

By June the following year, Dawn had a full year of college under her belt, and her dream of being an LVN was already yesterday's news. Dawn found out that with just one additional year of training she could become a full-fledged *RN*, and that was her new career goal. Her mother always taught her to never settle for second best, and Dawn was finally at a point in her life where she could spread her wings and reach her full potential.

It had been a year since the Finley Sisters went on a cruise together, and they were still the best of friends, despite the hundreds of miles that separated them physically, and the vast ideologies that separated them mentally.

Rene got over her heartbreak with Robert fairly quickly, but she experienced the same heartache with her very next relationship. And she broke up with the next two losers before they had a chance to show their true colors.

She eventually met a biology professor named Reginald who seemed to be a good match for her. They started dating in February. Four months later Rene was still happy with the way he treated her. She wouldn't say she was *in love* with Reginald, but she conceded that they were "getting there" whenever Dawn asked for a progress report.

Mona continued to be Mona for the most part, but after her confession to Dawn that she might have been in love with Bartolo, she did change, just a little. The main problem with her was Mona needed sexual gratification more often than Rene and Dawn, and she couldn't wait until she had a "steady relationship" going before she jumped in the sack with someone. But thankfully she altered the way she secured her one night stands.

"I don't have to lie to them," Mona explained, "because niggas think the same way I do. When I tell them to come over, they know it's on. When I tell them to leave, they know the deal. I don't break nobody's heart."

"But you don't love any of them," Dawn told her a few times. "You said you were going to give love a try."

"I'm open for whatever," Mona said. "I just haven't felt that way about anybody. But if it happens, it happens. Like with Bart; I didn't try to fall in love with him. He just swooped in and stole my heart. If somebody else can do that, I'm ready for 'em. Until then, I gotta be me."

Dawn accepted that because she loved her friend, even though Mona lived (what some might call) a rather promiscuous lifestyle. Dawn knew Mona would settle down when she was good and ready. Until that day came, she would always have the wildest and juiciest men stories to tell.

෧ඎ

On the first official weekend of summer, Dawn invited her friends to Overbrook Meadows for a special dinner on Saturday night, an invitation to her church on Sunday, and a church picnic right after the morning service.

Rene brought her new beau with her from Houston, and Dawn was happy to meet him for the first time. Reginald was tall, at least six feet, three inches, with rich, dark skin that was as smooth as butter. His lips were full and pink, and he wore no hair on his head other than his slightly arched eyebrows.

Mona's new boy toy was a high-yellow brother with a cropped afro and a neatly trimmed moustache and goatee. His physique was cut like a ball player's. Even with a long-sleeved Polo on, you couldn't miss his well-toned shoulders and his protruding pectorals. Mona said his name was *Junior*, and she made it clear he was more of a plaything than a possible soul mate or even a proper boyfriend.

"Don't ask him too many questions at the same time, or he'll get confused," she told Rene and Dawn before they left for the restaurant.

"I just have one question," Rene said. "Has he been to prison?"

"What brother *hasn't* been to prison these days?" Mona said, and Rene burst into laughter.

Dawn still hadn't said what occasion they were celebrating that night, but her friends assumed it was her miraculous weight loss. Dawn wore a black, form-fitting dress that evening, and her waist and hips were noticeably smaller. She was still a plus size, but her weight distribution was a lot more pleasing to the eye now. Dawn had serious curves. Mona guessed she was missing thirty pounds or more.

"I lost thirty-two pounds," Dawn confirmed. "But I lost it slow. I don't know why y'all just now noticing."

"I knew you were losing weight," Rene said. "I told you that last month. But I've never seen you with anything like *this* on. Dawn, you *fine!*"

"Thanks," Dawn said, and blushed. "But no, this is not the surprise. Calvin's meeting us at the restaurant. Let's go."

For dinner they went to Mille Fleurs, arguably the classiest French restaurant in the city. Dawn and Calvin were inseparable from the moment they met up in the lobby, but Rene and Mona still had no idea what the surprise was until they took a seat at a large table and ordered drinks.

"Okay," Dawn said with a big sigh. "I know y'all been wondering what I had to tell you that was *so* important…" Her smile was ear to ear. Her eyes literally twinkled under the soft lighting. "*I'm getting married, y'all!*"

Dawn thrust her left hand forward so everyone could see the big rock on her ring finger. Rene and Mona leaned over the table with their mouths ajar.

Calvin leaned back in his chair with a proud grin, fully aware that he'd claimed a very valuable prize indeed.

"*Oh, my God!*"

Dawn's friends jumped to their feet and rushed to hug and congratulate her. Nearly everyone in the restaurant turned to see what all of the squealing was about.

∾

The next morning Mona and Rene brought their dates to Dawn's church to see what the Good Lord had cooking. Mona hoped to sit with her friend so she could check out Dawn's engagement ring again in the brighter lights, but Dawn was nowhere to be found as the service started.

"You seen Dawn?" Mona whispered to Rene as they took their seats.

"Nuh-uhn," Rene said, "but there's Calvin, and Tim and Luther, and Calvin's boys..."

Mona followed Rene's gaze and saw the new family all sitting together in a pew to their left.

"I know she didn't tell all of us to come, and she isn't even coming," Mona told Rene.

Rene shook her head. "She wouldn't do that." But she couldn't come up with a better explanation.

The mystery was solved a few minutes later when the choir took the stage to begin praise and worship. Dawn walked in with them, wearing the same white and purple gown as everyone else. But she stood out because of her radiant beauty, and also because she took the center microphone at the front of the group.

After a quick prayer, the choir broke into a soulful rendition of "Awesome God" that had the church rocking from the first note. Dawn sang the lead, and she was no longer the timid crooner her friends saw on the *Ecstasy*. Dawn had power in her eyes, her voice, and in her movements. She whipped her hair like Whitney Houston and clapped louder than anyone in the sanctuary. And when she pumped her fists, even the ushers standing outside the main entrance felt it.

Mona and Rene stared in awe at first, and then they joined the crowd in cheering and yelling, occasionally singing the parts they knew.

The choir sang three songs in all, and Rene and Mona were tired and sweating and nearly hoarse when the pastor took the stage. Dawn re-entered the sanctuary a little while later, but she went and sat with her family. Mona and Rene had to wait until after the service to congratulate her.

∽⚬

The church picnic was a festive celebration, and everyone thought it was right on time. Mona wasn't used to sitting through such long sermons. Her stomach was growling before the pastor called for an altar call, and it was roaring by the time he ordered everyone to "go have fun, and *eat*!"

Their heavenly meal consisted of barbecued leg quarters, potato salad, baked beans, corn on the cob, and more homemade pies than you could shake a stick at. The Finley Sisters ate together, and then they lounged on a park bench beneath a cool pecan tree while their men tossed Frisbees and footballs to the many children who were eager to play.

"That was some good food," Mona said. She leaned back and sucked her fingers.

"Yeah, Dawn," Rene said. "This was a great weekend. I'm so proud of you. *You getting married!*"

"*I'se gettin' married!*" Dawn agreed. Her smile was priceless.

"So I guess you're the first one to fulfill your oath," Rene said.

Dawn sighed. "I told y'all it would be worth it. I never been this happy in my whole life."

"I'm happy, too," Mona said with a sinister smirk.

Her friends followed her eyes and saw what she was so happy about. Her "friend" Junior had taken his shirt off. His arms and torso were beautifully sculpted. Every muscle stood out hard and strong, glistening with sweat.

"You're still at church," Rene scolded. "You'd better watch those nasty thoughts."

"What about you?" Dawn asked Rene. "I seen the way you and Reginald be all hugged up. Are y'all in love?"

Rene smiled and looked down at her hands. "I don't want to call it that right now, but we're doing good, so far. He makes me happy."

"It's gonna work," Dawn said. "I can feel it."

Rene nodded and looked up at her. "Yeah. I feel it, too."

"I was thinking it's about time for us to go on another cruise," Mona said. "I know y'all miss that awesome boat, drinking mojitos on the upper deck, the stars, those beautiful blue waters…"

Rene and Dawn's eyes glossed over as they reminisced.

"Yeah, I think it is time for another trip," Rene said.

"I know y'all got good relationships now," Mona said. "But your men shouldn't mind if we go on vacation together, just us girls."

"That's cool with me," Rene said. "Reginald won't mind. He trusts me."

"What about you?" Mona asked Dawn. She and Rene watched her expectantly.

Dawn looked across the field at her fiancé, and then she met her friends' eyes.

"I'm down with whatever my girls are down with," she said and they all laughed, with the same knowing grins spread across their faces.

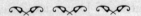

About the Author

Keith Thomas Walker is a graduate of Texas Wesleyan University where he earned a bachelor's degree in English. He enjoys reading, poetry, and music of all genres. Keith currently works in administration at one of the city's largest hospitals. He lives in Fort Worth, Texas with his wife and two children. Keith is the author of *Fixin' Tyrone*, *How to Kill Your Husband*, *A Good Dude* and *Riding the Corporate Ladder*. Visit him at **www.keithwalkerbooks.com**.

2011 Mass Market Titles

January

From This Moment
Sean Young
ISBN-13: 978-1-58571-383-7
ISBN-10: 1-58571-383-X
$6.99

Nihon Nights
Trisha/Monica Haddad
ISBN-13: 978-1-58571-382-0
ISBN-10: 1-58571-382-1
$6.99

February

The Davis Years
Nicole Green
ISBN-13: 978-1-58571-390-5
ISBN-10: 1-58571-390-2
$6.99

Allegro
Adora Bennett
ISBN-13: 978-158571-391-2
ISBN-10: 1-58571-391-0
$6.99

March

Lies in Disguise
Bernice Layton
ISBN-13: 978-1-58571-392-9
ISBN-10: 1-58571-392-9
$6.99

Steady
Ruthie Robinson
ISBN-13: 978-1-58571-393-6
ISBN-10: 1-58571-393-7
$6.99

April

The Right Maneuver
LaShell Stratton-Childers
ISBN-13: 978-1-58571-394-3
ISBN-10: 1-58571-394-5
$6.99

Riding the Corporate Ladder
Keith Walker
ISBN-13: 978-1-58571-395-0
ISBN-10: 1-58571-395-3
$6.99

May

Separate Dreams
Joan Early
ISBN-13: 978-1-58571-434-6
ISBN-10: 1-58571-434-8
$6.99

I Take This Woman
Chamein Canton
ISBN-13: 978-1-58571-435-3
ISBN-10: 1-58571-435-6
$6.99

June

Inside Out
Grayson Cole
ISBN-13: 978-1-58571-437-7
ISBN-10: 1-58571-437-2
$6.99

2011 Mass Market Titles (continued)

July

The Other Side of the
  Mountain
Janice Angelique
ISBN-13: 978-1-58571-442-1
ISBN-10: 1-58571-442-9
$6.99

Holding Her Breath
Nicole Green
ISBN-13: 978-1-58571-439-1
ISBN-10: 1-58571-439-9
$6.99

August

The Sea of Aaron
Kymberly Hunt
ISBN-13: 978-1-58571-440-7
ISBN-10: 1-58571-440-2
$6.99

The Finley Sisters' Oath of
  Romance
Keith Thomas Walker
ISBN-13: 978-1-58571-441-4
ISBN-10: 1-58571-441-0
$6.99

September

Except on Sunday
Regena Bryant
ISBN-13: 978-1-58571-443-8
ISBN-10: 1-58571-443-7
$6.99

Light's Out
Ruthie Robinson
ISBN-13: 978-1-58571-445-2
ISBN-10: 1-58571-445-3
$6.99

October

The Heart Knows
Renee Wynn
ISBN-13: 978-1-58571-444-5
ISBN-10: 1-58571-444-5
$6.99

Best Friends; Better Lovers
Celya Bowers
ISBN-13: 978-1-58571-455-1
ISBN-10: 1-58571-455-0
$6.99

November

Caress
Grayson Cole
ISBN-13: 978-1-58571-454-4
ISBN-10: 1-58571-454-2
$6.99

A Love Built to Last
L. S. Childers
ISBN-13: 978-1-58571-448-3
ISBN-10: 1-58571-448-8
$6.99

December

Fractured
Wendy Byrne
ISBN-13: 978-1-58571-449-0
ISBN-10: 1-58571-449-6
$6.99

Everything in Between
Crystal Hubbard
ISBN-13: 978-1-58571-396-7
ISBN-10: 1-58571-396-1
$6.99

Other Genesis Press, Inc. Titles

2 Good	Celya Bowers	$6.99
A Dangerous Deception	J.M. Jeffries	$8.95
A Dangerous Love	J.M. Jeffries	$8.95
A Dangerous Obsession	J.M. Jeffries	$8.95
A Drummer's Beat to Mend	Kei Swanson	$9.95
A Good Dude	Keith Walker	$6.99
A Happy Life	Charlotte Harris	$9.95
A Heart's Awakening	Veronica Parker	$9.95
A Lark on the Wing	Phyliss Hamilton	$9.95
A Love of Her Own	Cheris F. Hodges	$9.95
A Love to Cherish	Beverly Clark	$8.95
A Place Like Home	Alicia Wiggins	$6.99
A Risk of Rain	Dar Tomlinson	$8.95
A Taste of Temptation	Reneé Alexis	$9.95
A Twist of Fate	Beverly Clark	$8.95
A Voice Behind Thunder	Carrie Elizabeth Greene	$6.99
A Will to Love	Angie Daniels	$9.95
Acquisitions	Kimberley White	$8.95
Across	Carol Payne	$12.95
After the Vows	Leslie Esdaile	$10.95
(Summer Anthology)	T.T. Henderson	
	Jacqueline Thomas	
Again, My Love	Kayla Perrin	$10.95
Against the Wind	Gwynne Forster	$8.95
All I Ask	Barbara Keaton	$8.95
All I'll Ever Need	Mildred Riley	$6.99
Always You	Crystal Hubbard	$6.99
Ambrosia	T.T. Henderson	$8.95
An Unfinished Love Affair	Barbara Keaton	$8.95
And Then Came You	Dorothy Elizabeth Love	$8.95
Angel's Paradise	Janice Angelique	$9.95
Another Memory	Pamela Ridley	$6.99
Anything But Love	Celya Bowers	$6.99
At Last	Lisa G. Riley	$8.95
Best Foot Forward	Michele Sudler	$6.99
Best of Friends	Natalie Dunbar	$8.95
Best of Luck Elsewhere	Trisha Haddad	$6.99
Beyond the Rapture	Beverly Clark	$9.95
Blame It on Paradise	Crystal Hubbard	$6.99
Blaze	Barbara Keaton	$9.95

Other Genesis Press, Inc. Titles (continued)

Other Genesis Press, Inc. Titles (continued)

Do Over	Celya Bowers	$9.95
Dream Keeper	Gail McFarland	$6.99
Dream Runner	Gail McFarland	$6.99
Dreamtective	Liz Swados	$5.95
Ebony Angel	Deatri King-Bey	$9.95
Ebony Butterfly II	Delilah Dawson	$14.95
Echoes of Yesterday	Beverly Clark	$9.95
Eden's Garden	Elizabeth Rose	$8.95
Eve's Prescription	Edwina Martin Arnold	$8.95
Everlastin' Love	Gay G. Gunn	$8.95
Everlasting Moments	Dorothy Elizabeth Love	$8.95
Everything and More	Sinclair Lebeau	$8.95
Everything but Love	Natalie Dunbar	$8.95
Falling	Natalie Dunbar	$9.95
Fate	Pamela Leigh Starr	$8.95
Finding Isabella	A.J. Garrotto	$8.95
Fireflies	Joan Early	$6.99
Fixin' Tyrone	Keith Walker	$6.99
Forbidden Quest	Dar Tomlinson	$10.95
Forever Love	Wanda Y. Thomas	$8.95
Friends in Need	Joan Early	$6.99
From the Ashes	Kathleen Suzanne	$8.95
	Jeanne Sumerix	
Frost on My Window	Angela Weaver	$6.99
Gentle Yearning	Rochelle Alers	$10.95
Glory of Love	Sinclair LeBeau	$10.95
Go Gentle Into That Good Night	Malcom Boyd	$12.95
Goldengroove	Mary Beth Craft	$16.95
Groove, Bang, and Jive	Steve Cannon	$8.99
Hand in Glove	Andrea Jackson	$9.95
Hard to Love	Kimberley White	$9.95
Hart & Soul	Angie Daniels	$8.95
Heart of the Phoenix	A.C. Arthur	$9.95
Heartbeat	Stephanie Bedwell-Grime	$8.95
Hearts Remember	M. Loui Quezada	$8.95
Hidden Memories	Robin Allen	$10.95
Higher Ground	Leah Latimer	$19.95
Hitler, the War, and the Pope	Ronald Rychiak	$26.95
How to Kill Your Husband	Keith Walker	$6.99

Other Genesis Press, Inc. Titles (continued)

Other Genesis Press, Inc. Titles (continued)

Other Genesis Press, Inc. Titles (continued)

Other Genesis Press, Inc. Titles (continued)

Soul to Soul	Donna Hill	$8.95
Southern Comfort	J.M. Jeffries	$8.95
Southern Fried Standards	S.R. Maddox	$6.99
Still the Storm	Sharon Robinson	$8.95
Still Waters Run Deep	Leslie Esdaile	$8.95
Still Waters…	Crystal V. Rhodes	$6.99
Stolen Jewels	Michele Sudler	$6.99
Stolen Memories	Michele Sudler	$6.99
Stories to Excite You	Anna Forrest/Divine	$14.95
Storm	Pamela Leigh Starr	$6.99
Subtle Secrets	Wanda Y. Thomas	$8.95
Suddenly You	Crystal Hubbard	$9.95
Swan	Africa Fine	$6.99
Sweet Repercussions	Kimberley White	$9.95
Sweet Sensations	Gwyneth Bolton	$9.95
Sweet Tomorrows	Kimberly White	$8.95
Taken by You	Dorothy Elizabeth Love	$9.95
Tattooed Tears	T. T. Henderson	$8.95
Tempting Faith	Crystal Hubbard	$6.99
That Which Has Horns	Miriam Shumba	$6.99
The Business of Love	Cheris F. Hodges	$6.99
The Color Line	Lizzette Grayson Carter	$9.95
The Color of Trouble	Dyanne Davis	$8.95
The Disappearance of Allison Jones	Kayla Perrin	$5.95
The Doctor's Wife	Mildred Riley	$6.99
The Fires Within	Beverly Clark	$9.95
The Foursome	Celya Bowers	$6.99
The Honey Dipper's Legacy	Myra Pannell-Allen	$14.95
The Joker's Love Tune	Sidney Rickman	$15.95
The Little Pretender	Barbara Cartland	$10.95
The Love We Had	Natalie Dunbar	$8.95
The Man Who Could Fly	Bob & Milana Beamon	$18.95
The Missing Link	Charlyne Dickerson	$8.95
The Mission	Pamela Leigh Starr	$6.99
The More Things Change	Chamein Canton	$6.99
The Perfect Frame	Beverly Clark	$9.95
The Price of Love	Sinclair LeBeau	$8.95
The Smoking Life	Ilene Barth	$29.95
The Words of the Pitcher	Kei Swanson	$8.95

Other Genesis Press, Inc. Titles (continued)

ESCAPE WITH INDIGO !!!!

Join Indigo Book Club©
It's simple, easy and secure.

Sign up and receive the new
releases
every month + Free shipping
and
20% off the cover price.

Visit us online at
www.genesis-press.com or
call 1-888-INDIGO-1

Order Form

Mail to: Genesis Press, Inc.
P.O. Box 101
Columbus, MS 39703

Name _____
Address _____
City/State _____ Zip _____
Telephone _____

Ship to (if different from above)
Name _____
Address _____
City/State _____ Zip _____
Telephone _____

Credit Card Information
Credit Card # _____ ☐ Visa   ☐ Mastercard
Expiration Date (mm/yy) _____ ☐ AmEx   ☐ Discover

Qty.	Author	Title	Price	Total

Use this order form, or call **1-888-INDIGO-1**

Total for books	_____
Shipping and handling: $5 first two books, $1 each additional book	_____
Total S & H	_____
Total amount enclosed	_____

Mississippi residents add 7% sales tax

Visit www.genesis-press.com for latest releases and excerpts.